Books by

STAR FORCE SERIES
Swarm
Extinction
Rebellion
Conquest
Battle Station
Empire
Annihilation

IMPERIUM SERIES
Mech Zero: The Dominant
Mech 1: The Parent
Mech 2: The Savant
Mech 3: The Empress
Five By Five (Mech Novella)

OTHER SF BOOKS
Technomancer
The Bone Triangle
Z-World
Velocity

Visit BVLarson.com for more information.

Annihilation
(Star Force Series #7)
by
B. V. Larson

STAR FORCE SERIES
Swarm
Extinction
Rebellion
Conquest
Battle Station
Empire
Annihilation

ISBN-13: 978-1482653458
ISBN-10: 1482653451
BISAC: Fiction / Science Fiction / Military

-1-

The day the Macros came back into our tiny slice of the universe I wasn't ready for them. I thought I'd prepared for everything they could do—for any contingency, but I was wrong.

By Earthly calendars it was a Thursday night, the end of the first day of May. That was a detail which shouldn't have mattered at all, since I now lived in the Eden star system. But it *did* matter to me. I missed May, and springtime, and all the lost traditions from my old life.

I stood on a high battlement atop a spire of rock on Eden-8. It was one of the highest peaks on the planet. I'd built an impressive fortress up here, which clutched the granite pinnacle of the mountain and wrapped around it like a coiled snake. I'd named the fortress "Shadowguard".

Of the three worlds the Centaurs had ceded to humanity, Eden-8 was the farthest from the central star. Compared to the hotter worlds of Eden-6 and Eden-7, the planet was relatively cool. In comparison to Earth it was a warm world, ranging from steaming jungles at the equator to balmy temperate zones around the poles.

Eden-8 orbited its yellowy star very evenly. The planet had less than a one-degree tilt to its axis and it didn't wobble much. Earth's six degree tilt gave her four seasons, but here on Eden-8, there were only two and they were practically indistinguishable from one another. As a result, there wasn't really a summer or a winter. It rained a little more one half of the year than it did during the other, but a newcomer would barely notice the difference.

1

Besides the lack of seasons, the most noticeable thing about the terrain was the vast carpet of forestlands. We had *real* trees here. They were over a thousand feet tall in places. Even Earth's great redwoods didn't compare.

On the biggest continent in the southern hemisphere, I'd built my fortress in the middle of a forest of the largest trees. Shadowguard perched on a pinnacle of rock overlooking a sea of trees. It served as a communications relay station and garrison headquarters for the inner habitable worlds, but that was only part of the reason I'd placed it here.

I'd chosen my new headquarters because I liked it up here on top of this pleasant world. The view was spectacular, even at night. More importantly, at this altitude, it was always cool and often cold. There were very few spots on the three planets owned by humanity in this system that could make that claim.

Building on this site had been expensive in terms of resource allocation—we no longer thought in terms of dollars when constructing things. With the amazing factories we'd captured from the Nanos and their lumbering cousins the Macros, we were able to produce anything we wished given enough time and materials. Thus, when I calculated expenses, I did so by tallying the number of hours a given factory had to work to churn out whatever it was I needed. Combined with the number of human and robotic subsystems that had to be committed to do the assembly and the gathering of the necessary raw components, I arrived at the final cost.

Building Shadowguard had required a staggering number of hours of effort, numbering in the thousands. To lower the production burden on systems that could be better used building ships, I'd employed my idle crews. I'd ordered them to participate in lengthy exercises that amounted to fetch-and-carry missions. Every garrison ship equipped with a segmented arm had flown countless missions, ferrying modular structures up to the mountaintop one at a time. This effort had reduced the strain on the worker machines, but the project had still taken more production than it was really worth.

When it was finished, however, I found myself pleased with the results. I'd built a retreat that pierced the clouds and enclosed some thirty thousand square feet of space—not including the exposed ramparts that served as balconies around most of the chambers.

It was on those lofty turrets that I found myself pacing tonight. Darkness shrouded Eden-8, and at this altitude, the nights frosted everything with a glaze of ice. Fortunately, my various physical alterations made the environment comfortable for me.

"Why did you build this place, Kyle?" Sandra asked.

I glanced around, but didn't see her. After a moment, I stopped trying. She was somewhere nearby, that was nothing unusual. She almost always was. She was my guardian angel—or perhaps I should say, my guardian *creature*. She wasn't entirely human, and she wasn't exactly an angel.

"Don't you like it here?" I asked.

"I love it," she said.

"That's why then. I built it for you, out of love."

"Bullshit."

I smiled. "Where the hell are you, anyway?"

There was a swirl of movement. I flinched as she jumped down beside me from the conical, snow-crusted roof of a nearby tower. It must have been a thirty foot leap down, and Eden-8 had a goodly twenty-one percent higher gravity than Earth, but she landed neatly. I only heard a tiny, audible grunt out of her.

She smiled at me in triumph, but her face fell as I skipped back in alarm. A shower of snow had followed her down from the roof. It splashed on her back and hair a moment later. She sputtered and brushed at the snow.

I stepped forward and helped her remove fine, white granules of ice from her suit and hair. We kissed and smiled at each other. Then we both laughed.

"This is a romantic place," Sandra admitted.

I turned away and walked to the crenulated walls. The parapets circling Shadowguard's battlements had a very medieval look to them, which was by design. The walls resembled the jaws of a predator with lines of big, square teeth. I leaned on one of these granite teeth, gazing down at the night world below.

It was twenty-one thousand feet to the bottom, and it looked twice that far. The forests were shrouded in darkness at the base of the cliffs. The sky was a span of velvet blue above, dotted with diamond-white stars. The starlight wasn't enough for my eyes to see much detail in the lands spread out below me. The planet had no moons, and that made the nights darker than they were on most worlds.

Eden-8 was the most heavily inhabited of the star system's worlds—at least the most thickly inhabited by humans. But by Earth standards it was practically empty. There were a few pinpoints of white light down there, dotting the landscape. The lights marked small farms and colonial ranches, places where we'd managed to clear glades from the giant forests. Lands had been granted by Star Force to enterprising families who'd sworn to build their homes and have their children here. As of our last monthly online census, there were over twelve thousand registered humans on the planet.

I scooped up some snow and crushed it into a ball in my hand. I looked at Sandra. She eyed me warily. We'd had plenty of snowball fights in the past. When you have bodies full of nanites, upgraded by biochemical edits, hurling snowballs could be serious business.

I held up the snowball. "This is why I built up here. I wanted something humanity will be forever denied in the Eden system. A truly *cold* place to live."

She nodded. "That's a good reason," she said. "I believe that one. You've always liked the winter."

I hurled the snowball over the walls. After years of enhancements, I've got a good arm on me and I doubt any baseball player in all history could have pitched it farther. The snowball flew away into the night like a streak of white. Finally, gravity took hold and it began a long slow lob that turned into a hurtling drop. Seconds later it was sucked down in the darkness below us and vanished from sight. Sandra leapt up onto one of the square merlons and perched there on the edge, watching it fall.

"I can still see it," she said. "It might make it all the way to the trees."

I stared, but my eyes weren't much better than the ones I'd been born with. For me, the darkness had swallowed up the falling ball of whipped ice.

"It's May back on Earth, you know," I said. "I miss having seasons. Now I can experience winter any time I want, just by coming up here."

She still crouched on the wall, staring down into the darkness intently.

"Don't tell me you can still see that ice-ball," I said.

4

She put up a flat hand to shush me. She shook her head. "Didn't make it," she said. "It hit a spur of rock about two thirds of the way down."

"Too bad."

She looked at me. "It's not the seasons you miss, Kyle. It's Earth itself. I doubt we'll ever be completely at ease here. I mean, it's a lovely world and all, but it will never be home."

"I don't know... People have migrated before. We've done it for a thousand generations."

"Yes, but never to a brand new planet. There are things in our genes, in our instincts, that can't be adjusted. The length of our days and nights, for example. I'm finding these fourteen hour cycles to be annoyingly short."

I had to agree with her there. Seven hours of daylight were always followed by seven hours of night. Many of us were having trouble adjusting our sleep patterns. I frowned suddenly, disliking the melancholy turn of the conversation.

"Listen to us!" I shouted. "Such defeatism. We'll see home again."

Sandra's face tightened. She nodded her head, but looked away.

"What?" I demanded.

"I don't know. If we do go back—we'll bring war. I can't imagine any other way it will happen now. I don't want to burn down half of Earth just for our comfort."

"Doesn't have to go that way. There are always factions when someone makes a power grab. Maybe they'll rise up and kick Crow off the throne. Maybe he'll have a heart attack, or choke on a barbecued shrimp."

This last comment finally made her laugh and broke her somber mood.

"Okay," she said. "What are we going to call this palace of yours?"

"It's not exactly a palace..."

"Oh, come on. Of course it is. I bet Crow has seven of them by now. Don't be shy! What do you want to call your first one?"

I felt uncomfortable with the subject, but forced a smile. "I've already decided," I said. "I'm going to call it Shadowguard."

"Why?"

5

"Because it will help prevent our enemies from sneaking up on us, hopefully."

She blinked at me.

I shrugged. "It's not just a vacation spot, you know. It serves a military purpose. There's a lot of equipment on this rock, including the best sensor array in all six of the known star systems."

"Show me," she said.

Smiling, I offered her my arm. She clasped it formally and we walked together down the icy granite steps to a portal. Like all the doors in the fortress, this one was made of smart metal. It sensed us, identified us and dissolved to let us in. The opening yawned and warmth gusted up into our faces.

A single operator was on duty. The operator was a young lieutenant who looked up shyly as we approached. Almost apologetically, she lifted a tablet and waved it slightly, trying to gain my attention.

"What's this?" I asked, taking it from her.

"Something relayed from Welter Station, sir," she said.

I frowned. "This isn't the standard daily report. Any hostile activity should have been reported to me immediately."

The young woman's face registered alarm. "I'm sorry, Colonel. But it isn't about *hostile* action. It's labeled as a diplomatic message."

My frown deepened. I swiped a finger over the screen, passing the opening bullshit on the first pages. How was it that bureaucracy always snuck into any organization? Already, there were three pages of dates and details on every report and document that came to me. The reports seemed to grow fatter and less informative by the month.

The first useful section dealt with unusual readings—mostly from Eden-12, the homeworld of the Blues. That was nothing new. There had always been unusual readings coming from that gas giant, which was inhabited by enigmatic beings. Today there had been large energy releases of unknown origin. I rolled my eyes. After all, it was a *gas giant*. Huge storms rolled across it every day. Some of my people needed to take a course in basic astronomy.

Finally, on page twenty-seven, I reached the heart of the matter. I read it quickly, then gave the device back to the lieutenant.

"Well?" asked Sandra. "Who's it from?"

"The Crustaceans," I said.

6

Sandra gave a callous bark of laughter. "Oh, those lovable bastards? What kind of love-note did they send you? Are they sending us a big wooden horse this time?"

I shook my head. "No. They're asking for help. They say they're under attack, and are requesting any aid we can spare."

Sandra looked at me, and her smile faded. I knew in an instant what was going on in her mind. It was the same dilemma that raged in mine: should we help our enemies? They'd sided with the Macros in the last conflict, and done us grievous harm. But I had to admit, I still held out some sympathy for the arrogant shellfish. After all, hadn't I committed Earth troops to serving under the Macros when we'd faced extinction? I'd attacked the Worms, exactly as they'd attacked us. We'd fought with the Worms, but in the end they were alive and the machines that had attacked Helios weren't.

"They are biotics," I said. "Maybe this is a chance to mend fences with them. Maybe they've finally realized the machines will never let them coexist in peace. We can always use another ally."

"But we can't trust them," Sandra said. "It could all be a trick. Another ruse like the last one. Designed to get us to lower our guard and help the machines destroy us."

"I know," I said, "and I agree that we'll have to proceed cautiously."

Sandra turned her attention to the star map in the holotank in the center of the room. She reached out her hand and tapped the controls. The holotank shimmered in response and brought up a detailed three dimensional image depicting the Crustacean home system, which was one jump from Eden. We'd named the F-class star "Thor".

All told, we'd discovered six connected systems. Thor was at our end of the chain of star systems, the last system we'd discovered beyond Eden.

The Thor system consisted of three gas giants and a load of other airless rocky worlds. The central binary stars were tight tag-team, an F class white star and a tiny red dwarf. I'd named the big one Thor and the smaller sun Loki.

We called our closest hostile neighbors Crustaceans, but really they were alien beings that resembled giant, man-sized lobsters. They came from three water-moons that orbited the innermost gas giant.

"What else does the report say?" Sandra asked. "Are there Macro ships orbiting their worlds?"

7

"No."

"No signs of conflict? What kind of trouble can they be in?"

"Nothing that we can see from space," I said, working the tablet. "But there are strange sensor readings from their moons, particularly Yale. Seismic spikes—explosions, possibly. And the oceans…the temperature of the water is rising. They've risen one-point-one degrees over the last few days."

"One degree?" Sandra asked. "Big deal."

I began to pace.

"I've learned a little about planetary climates and geology over the last few years," I said. "A one degree change in a volume of water that great is very significant over such a short period of time. It means a huge amount of energy has been released."

Sandra zoomed in on the gas giant that dominated the sky for every Crustacean. It was bluish in color, like the Solar System's Neptune. The gas giant itself wasn't inhabited as far as we could tell, but it was in the zone that supported liquid water. Circling that world were several water-moons, the homeworlds of the Crustaceans. Each of these moons was comparable in size to Earth and covered by oceans.

Sandra and I both stared at the planetary system in the holotank. I knew she was thinking the same thing I was: *What the hell was going on out there?*

"You're going to fly us out there," Sandra said to me. "You're going to risk Star Force lives to save Lobsters, aren't you?"

"Yes," I said. "I think I am."

"They don't deserve it, Kyle."

"You're probably right. But I have to try to make peace with them."

Sandra muttered something else, but I didn't hear her. I'd already left the warmth of the command center and walked out onto the battlements again. The frosty winds were stronger now, as it was nearing midnight. The wind felt good against my skin.

Rather than gazing down onto the night-shrouded treetops below me, I turned my eyes upward into the sky. Above me hung the droplets of fire we call stars. They appeared ice-cold to me tonight, and I saw them as my ancestors must have. They were like the staring eyes of a thousand gods.

I knew something was happening up there, but I had no idea what those heartless, glittering gods had in store for me.

-2-

Just before dawn, we left Eden-8. Sandra and I boarded a destroyer and were taken swiftly up into the sky. The ship whisked us away toward the outer rim where Welter Station circled the coldest rock in the star system.

On the way, I kept checking every few hours for changes in the situation—any kind of update from Thor would be nice. But there was nothing. No new information from our sensors, scout ships, spy-probes or the Crustaceans themselves. The only measurable data that came in was an ominous detail: the temperature of the oceans on Yale had risen another tenth of a degree. This was neither encouraging nor enlightening.

We didn't get a proper night's sleep on the long haul out to the battle station. My mind and my command staff couldn't help playing out grim scenarios. Could it be a natural disaster? Volcanic action? Some kind of civil war? We just didn't know.

During the final hours of the journey we drew closer to the station and began decelerating hard. For several long hours, the destroyer shuddered and maintained a steady, teeth-throbbing four Gs of braking thrust. That's what space flight consisted of for Star Force veterans: endless sessions of pulling hard G-forces as we accelerated up to cruising speed then turned around and decelerated just as powerfully so we could dock rather than smashing into the landing bays.

I'd had plenty of time to review what little we knew, but not enough input to decide on a course of action. Since I didn't have much to go on, I focused on what I could do with clarity of purpose: shore up our own defensive posture.

I was feeling paranoid, and I had very good reasons for it. The last time the Crustaceans had sent us a cryptic message they'd sent an emissary ship along with it. The ambassador inside had blown herself up and the EMP blast had disrupted my battle station, nearly crippling it. If the Crustaceans were involved in some kind of new conflict, my first concern had to be the security of my own backyard.

I began reviewing our defenses for the tenth time since I'd left Shadowguard. Fortunately, the Eden system only had two points of entry—at least that we knew of. There were two rings that connected this star system to others. Each allowed instantaneous interstellar travel to another system.

One path led to the Helios system, which was occupied and patrolled by our allies the Worms. Beyond Helios and farther down the chain of rings was the Solar System. Unfortunately, Earth could not be considered friendly at this time.

Still, with the Worms and several systems serving as a buffer, I didn't fear a sneak attack from that direction. In the other direction was a single known system: the Thor System. In my view, it was more dangerous than Earth. If the enemy came at us from that flank we would have only a day or two of warning at best.

We knew there was at least one other ring that connected Thor to some unknown location owned by the Macros. The machines had launched attacks on us via that ring several times.

Judging the Thor system and the unknown numbers of Macro fleets beyond it to be the greater threat, I'd built a battle station on the border, right next to the ring that connected Eden to Thor. Known as Welter Station, the structure had survived its first battles, but only barely.

Things had changed a lot since I'd first built the battle station. She was monstrous now, and instead of being nearly deserted, the fortress teemed with Star Force personnel. The refugees from Earth had stepped up and manned the station with a crew of over a thousand, which was what it had been originally designed for.

"This thing is huge, Colonel," Commodore Miklos said when the station came into visual range. His tone indicated he believed the battle station was too big.

The Commodore had joined us on this trip out to the border. He was my exec, and overall second in command.

I nodded, but avoided Miklos' eye. "I'm sure you've seen it before."

"Of course I have. But it's bigger—the volume is three times greater than what was proposed in the original design documents."

I nodded again, but said nothing. Miklos was one of my best. I'd come to trust and rely on his judgment and loyalty over the last few years, but that didn't mean I always listened to his frequently-offered advice. He was Fleet and therefore wanted every hour of production to go into building more ships. It was only natural for him to view any other expenditure as counterproductive.

He looked at me, frowning. "Why did you put so much effort into rebuilding it—into making it bigger? I thought it was a failure."

"A failure? Hardly."

"The first battles this monstrosity was involved in were not promising. It was pushed over like a tin can. A *giant* tin can."

I felt a sensation of growing annoyance with him, but I tried to keep my reaction off my face.

"I was alarmed by how easily our enemies circumvented this behemoth station during her last action," I said. "I freely admit that the station did not perform optimally in combat."

"If the station can't defend itself, it is useless, Colonel."

"It *can* defend itself," I snapped back at him, my voice rising in volume. "It took out a great number of ships in its first engagement."

Miklos fell to brooding quietly. After a minute or two, I heaved a sigh.

"All right," I said. "I admit, I took a gamble by putting so much of our resources out here at this outpost. After its relative failure in previous engagements, I felt I had a decision to make: either to put the station on the back-burner and build fleets instead, or to expand its capabilities."

Miklos nodded slowly. "I understand completely, sir. You doubled your bet."

"Yes. I chose to double-down."

Miklos didn't appear surprised. He did look concerned, however. He began to list reasons why ships were superior to fixed fortifications even though fortresses were more cost-effective.

12

"Mobility is a force-multiplier," he lectured me. "Big guns do no one any good if they aren't able to reach the critical battle. Historically, fortresses have always fallen to mobile forces. The Maginot Line, for instance…"

I rolled my eyes. I'd taken his lecture as good-naturedly as I could up until this point, but now he'd annoyed me enough to shut him down.

"The Maginot Line?" I demanded incredulously. "Let me assure you, Commodore, this station won't go down in the history books as 'Rigg's Greatest Folly'. Over recent months, while Crow has been licking his wounds back on Earth, I've assumed the Macros have been building another invasion fleet. To meet that inevitable threat, I shored up this battered station. That's all there is to the story."

Miklos fell quiet again. He wasn't pouting, however. I knew him too well to believe his feelings could be hurt by a scoffing tone in my voice. Unfortunately, I also knew his opinions hadn't been swayed by my little speech. Not in the slightest. He was simply being polite and biding his time to make his case again. The man could be relentless.

We went back to watching the station swell as we rapidly drew closer. The last time I'd been out here the station's primary characteristic had been the asteroid rock that armored the central torus. That had drastically changed. I'd captured and added a new asteroid to the station to create more mass. This new section was hollowed-out; we'd leached the metals from it and left the stone as armor. The surface of the entire thing was dotted by equipment embedded into the natural rock. Instead of occasional battlements and sensor arrays that resembled outcroppings of metal, I'd added an entirely new superstructure that formed a thick band around the center of the station. The structure was vaguely disk-shaped, and the crewmen had come to call it "the saucer".

The new battlements were anything but fragile, however. They were built with heavy structural components, mostly steel and yard-thick polymers.

Inside the saucer, clusters of weaponry were closely massed and capable of incredible firepower. The saucer was encrusted with missile batteries, beam turrets, railgun emplacements and more.

I broke the silence with Miklos first. "You should learn more about what this station can do, Commodore, before you scoff at it."

"I do not recall making any scoffing sounds."

"No, but your tone makes your opinions self-evident. Please turn your attention to the most innovative of the additions: the new fighter bays. From each of seven bays, a wing of fighters can be launched within minutes of identifying a threat."

Miklos nodded thoughtfully, arching his eyebrows. "I've read the reports on the fighter bays, but the technology is unproven."

"We've seen them in action, on the side of the Empire," I said, struggling to keep my voice even. "My fighters are based on their designs."

"What is the strategic advantage of these fighters?"

"After the Lobsters disabled this base with a single well-place bomb, I decided that a localized mobile defense was a good idea. The fighter wings are under orders to scramble with paranoid regularity. A squadron or two is always on orbital patrol. Even if we do get sucker-punched again, all our eggs won't be in a single basket. The fighters are there to harass any approaching enemy. If the station is disabled again, they will provide some defensive capability."

Miklos looked interested, but far from pleased. I knew he considered a fighter to be a type of ship, even if they had a limited range. To Miklos, any ship was a good ship. But he would rather have a more mobile force.

"May I suggest something, Colonel?"

I nodded, knowing I was going to hear his ideas eventually, whether I wanted to or not.

"I'm thinking about the current situation," he said. "In the coming days, we might want to move to the Crustacean homeworlds to help them. We have a lot of new armament here at the battle station, but the water-moons are out of range. Perhaps we could produce carrier vessels to transport the new fighter wings."

"You're proposing that we strip the fighter wings from the station and use them as a mobile force assigned to these carriers?" I asked.

"Temporarily, yes. We could put the carriers into production immediately. We would not have to build the fighters, only the carriers. We could do that fairly quickly, as they would only have to have a large structure and engines."

"What about armament?" I asked.

"No weapons would be required on a carrier. The fighters would be their weapons."

14

I considered his idea. I glared at the growing image of the battle station. It bristled with weaponry and appeared invincible from space. Despite its strength, I wasn't excited about the idea of weakening this monster I'd built. As it was, it was an absolute barrier to entry into the Eden system. With it standing here on watch, I felt one of my flanks was secure. On the other hand, if I was going to have to send my ships out into a hostile system, I would want those fighters to cover my fleet.

Miklos seemed to sense my indecision. He sidled closer to me and continued with his arguments.

"We could use standard cruiser engines and structure. No redesign necessary. They would probably be slower-moving, but they could serve as strategic platforms. Think of them as flying bases, able to move in and provide an anchor for the fleet wherever you wish. In this situation, they could orbit the Thor gas giant and cover all three inhabited moons."

I thought about it. Really, it did make sense.

"All right," I said at last. "I'll go talk to Marvin and discuss a design and how long it would take to assemble such a vessel. I'm not sure we'll have time to pull it off, however. If we're going to save these Lobsters from whatever is killing them, we'll have to move fast."

Miklos handed me a computer tablet. I glanced down at it.

"What's this?" I asked.

"I took the liberty of running some numbers. Also, key components are already in preproduction. As we've moved some of the duplicators to the battle station, I thought we might as well get a head start."

I glared at the tablet. I was angry, but at the same time I didn't want to quell initiative taken by my staff. I reminded myself that delegation of authority was part of successful leadership. That part had never come easily for me.

I calmed down with an act of will and looked at what he'd given me. The numbers were not too presumptive. He'd changed standing production orders, but only directed the duplicators to construct components that were useful as spare parts or for any fleet-support ship we might care to build. Even if I'd shot down his ideas, the production wouldn't be wasted.

I nodded and handed the tablet back. "I'm surprised you put this into motion so quickly. And without full approval. But, I can see that you've done it in a way that does not disrupt standing orders. I approve of the action. Continue."

Miklos beamed. It was rare his bearded face smiled, and I was glad to see the expression. I realized he'd been sweating my decision and fearing a possible reprimand. I was glad I didn't have to chew him out. As a top leader, I had to be careful. A few words from me could crush a spirit. I wasn't really worried about having that effect on Miklos, but I knew I'd done it to others in the past.

I left the bridge and went to my private quarters. Sandra was there, already strapped onto an acceleration couch. I grunted and strained as I got into place beside her. In order to maximize our speed we'd applied most of the ship's power to the engines, rather than niceties such as the gravity stabilizers. I was really feeling the Gs today.

Sandra worked her tablet controls as I got into place for the final burn. The ship had to go to full thrust to slow us down enough for docking. There were always jarring, last second adjustments.

Sandra caused the forward screens over our acceleration couches to light up. The battle station loomed. It was a dark hulk in space, sprinkled with gleaming lights. It resembled a bristling sea anemone as much as anything else I could think of. Batteries of railguns, beam turrets and missile silos dotted the uneven surface.

"Why did you rebuild this thing, Kyle?" Sandra asked me.

I made a sound that was somewhere between a sigh and a grunt. I felt I'd answered this sort of question enough today already.

"I'm a sucker for big, cheap defenses," I said. "I looked at it, and I just couldn't come up with a better way to expend our resources and get more firepower out of each nut and bolt."

She nodded, unsurprised. "It failed the first time, but you still believe in it?"

"Absolutely."

"But what if the enemy comes from the other direction next time—from Earth?"

"Earth was trashed less than a year ago. So was every player in this game. But I know one thing about the Macros: they can rebuild amazingly fast. I decided to put most of our resources into stopping them first."

16

"Are you sure they're the greater threat?"

I nodded. "Those alien machines would exterminate us all if they could. Crow would only enslave us."

Sandra gave me a flickering smile. "Encouraging," she said.

I guess she didn't like the fact that we were surrounded by enemies. We held Eden, and had a foothold in the Helios system. But that was the extent of our influence. I'd stopped patrolling the Lobster system and Alpha Centauri long ago due to lack of resources.

"I hope you've done it right this time," she said sincerely.

"So do I."

After this short conversation, I went back to rechecking data I'd already rechecked, scanning for new details that I might have missed, and which I pretty much knew weren't there. It was agonizing going into a conflict without intel. I'd done it before, but I hated it just as much today as I had the first time. How do you plan and prepare for the unknown?

I guessed that recent military leaders back on Earth over the last century had had it pretty good. Back in the days of planet-wide satellite coverage and Cold War intel, there were years of research and planning to back up anything you encountered. When the Soviets made a move, NATO was rarely surprised. They'd gamed out everything. Orders were already in a vault, ready to be distributed within hours.

Those days were gone. Out here on the frontier of space, meeting new species and new threats every few months, I had to fly by the seat of my pants most of the time. My military decisions were based on guesswork as much as anything else. I'd never even seen the next system in the chain of rings, the one the Macros appeared to be coming from. We'd sent in probes of course, stealthy robotic things that we'd been sure would evade detection long enough to employ passive sensors and scan the environment.

None of these probes had ever returned. The Macro system beyond the ring in the Thor system remained to this day a mysterious black hole in our knowledge. Because of this, we had to operate as if an attack was coming from that sector at any moment. We had to assume the worst, because we had no idea what the truth was.

I was reminded historically of the colonial period in Earth's history. I felt akin to the explorers and colonial governors of centuries past. They had small garrisons on wild coastlands. All

17

around them local native populations simmered with resentment. Worse, other colonial powers or out-and-out pirates might arrive on any given day to raid their settlements or even conquer them. Back then, there weren't any satellites or instantaneous transmissions, and the distances were comparably huge. It took months to voyage home, possibly a year between requesting assistance and getting it from your home country. I was in a similar situation. Effectively, we were on our own, and we had no idea what was going to come over the horizon.

By the time we docked, I was ready for action. I jumped off the couch and suited up. Sandra was right behind me when I hit the airlock. I was unsurprised to find Miklos already there, waiting for us.

The door swished open, and another familiar sight met my eyes. It was Marvin in all his unholy, metallic glory.

-3-

Marvin was my science officer. He was also a robot. He'd built himself, and he liked to fiddle with things—including his own structure. Sometimes, he could fly. On other occasions, he slithered and dragged himself with whipping nanite arms. Usually, whatever form he took, he was large and had a dozen or so tentacles. Some of them held cameras at various angles, sending input into his amazing nanite-chain brain. Others propelled him by dragging his body around. A few were reserved for directly manipulating his surroundings, like human hands.

Today, he was in a floating configuration, gliding around on gravity repellers. I paused in concern to inspect his propulsion systems, making sure they weren't powerful enough for full flight. He'd been forbidden to outfit himself as a ship. He'd gotten into serious trouble every time I'd allowed him that luxury. Flitting around the station was one thing, but having full run of the star system was quite another. I'd made the mistake of giving him flight permission in the past and he'd provided me a large number of sleepless nights in return.

The trouble with Marvin wasn't that he was an enemy. He was definitely on our side—but he got *ideas*. These ideas were things that no human could ever come up with, much less put into action. He was brilliant and useful, but also easily fascinated and obsessed. When I assigned him a critical task, often something no one else could do, it would get done eventually. But along the way he might become distracted by some idea of his own. He might want to grow a

19

culture of intelligent microbes, for example, or explore a neighboring star system without permission.

"Marvin!" I said, stepping forward and saluting him.

He returned the gesture by slapping a tentacle to his brainbox. It wasn't even close to a real salute, but it was the best I was going to get, so I didn't complain.

"Greetings, Colonel Riggs."

I did a quick count on the number of cameras he had following me. Often, Marvin gave away his true intentions by focusing more or fewer cameras on a subject. Things that bored him were covered by one drifting electronic eye. Things that fascinated him received the attention of multiple panning, zooming cameras.

This time, to my surprise, Marvin had several eyes on Sandra. I frowned, not understanding what he had in mind. Deciding I didn't have time to try to figure it out, I shrugged and pressed ahead.

"I've got a new project for you, Marvin. I want a carrier ship produced quickly, with minimum downtime. Here are Miklos' initial plans. Go over those, make adjustments for performance and faster production times. When you're done, oversee the production."

By the end of this little speech, I'd gained the attention of four more of his cameras.

"I'm surprised by these instructions, Colonel," he said. "I've been working on the sensory data incoming from the Thor system. I've—"

"Yes, I know that was your prior assignment. Do you have any new datum to report?"

"No, Colonel. I—"

"Then perhaps you've come up with a hypothesis to explain the situation?"

"No, sir. However, I haven't been allowed to make direct contact with the Crustaceans. If I were allowed to converse with them myself, I'm sure—"

"Not going to happen, Marvin," I said. "But I'm here now, and if it makes you any happier, you'll be the first to know what is discussed between Star Force and the Crustaceans."

"Ah," Marvin said. "I see. I'm to serve as a translator-bot again?"

"You're still better at it than the other brainboxes. So, yes."

I could tell Marvin was miffed. He wanted to be given diplomatic tasks to complete. I'd long since decided that was never going to happen. The mere suggestion gave my command staff fits. But I hardly needed their cautioning. Marvin could do the job, certainly. He understood the languages of the various races in our local space better than any being in existence. He was also very good at manipulation and getting what he wanted out of a conversation. Unfortunately, I couldn't trust him to take such a conversation in the direction I wanted it to go. If he came up with any idea of his own, which he no doubt would consider extremely interesting, the entire diplomatic exchange might well transform into one of Marvin's crusades to gain some tidbit of information the rest of us found useless.

The group proceeded up to the center of the station, into the primary control center. Marvin was watching all of us, but mostly me and Sandra. I knew he was thinking about something, but I simply didn't have time to play games with him.

When we reached the center and began going over reports, Miklos got my attention.

"Yes, what is it, Commodore?" I asked.

"Sir, I could not help but notice you've already altered my blueprints."

He thrust a tablet at me. I glanced at the tablet in his hands, but didn't take it.

"The design is essentially unchanged," I said.

"I know that, sir, but I'm talking about the number of carriers to be produced. I see only one listed here. The *Defiant*. You've typed in that name at the top."

"You don't approve of the name? Don't worry, it's only a placeholder. The new captain will rename her as per our traditions. Maybe you want me to call it *Barbarossa* again?"

Twice in the recent past, we'd built ships named *Barbarossa*, the first of which had been Miklos' command. Both ships had been destroyed within months of their construction. It had become something of a joke among the enlisted men. They often told one another they'd just been assigned to the third version of *Barbarossa*, and were therefore certain to die soon.

Miklos looked pained for a moment. "*Defiant* is a fine name, sir. But my original plans called for three carriers, not one."

"Ah, I see," I said, nodding my head. I'd known what he was getting at all along, but I hadn't felt like making this easy for him. "It is quite possible the second and third ships will be constructed. We'll

21

do them one at a time. If the first one proves itself, there will be more."

Miklos thought about that. I could tell he didn't like it. "Building components for all three, then assembling all three, would be faster, sir."

"Only by a few hours. I checked. Also, if we do it my way, we'll have a working ship up in a few days. That gives us something to deploy right away if needed."

Miklos nodded in defeat. "Yes sir. I understand your logic."

He turned away and began a surprise inspection of the gunnery crews. I could tell he was in a bad mood. The crews were going to have a long day.

Sandra stepped close to me and spoke quietly. "He really want's those ships."

"He's Fleet," I said. "He can't get enough ships. Never."

"What kind of hardware do you like best, Kyle?"

I looked at her, bemused by the question. "I like whatever destroys the enemy most effectively. Watching them blow up gives me a surge of joy. It really does."

"I believe you."

I began going over the latest reports while Miklos eyed his tablet in frustration.

There was no intel coming in from the Thor system. Nothing. We'd sent a number of requests to the Crustaceans and they'd all been ignored. I was increasingly curious and annoyed at the same time. Somehow, the Crustaceans always managed to irritate me. They just had that kind of personality. Every interaction we'd had with them had resulted in us being surprised at the result—and not in good way.

My staff transferred themselves to the battle station, merging with the regular crew on the command deck. It was an impressive affair. When building a station the size of a small moon with nearly limitless supplies of materials, you can afford to go big.

After having the station nearly knocked out due to losing the bridge area in previous engagements, I'd overhauled the design and drilled deep into the bedrock of the asteroid the station encompassed. The command deck could no longer be easily taken out, not without destroying the entire structure. It was at the very center of the asteroid itself.

The primary chamber of the command deck was a good ten thousand square feet in size and enclosed by four foot-thick walls of steel laced with self-repairing smart metals. Beyond those walls was a belt-like corridor that connected staff living chambers and specialized command equipment rooms. A spray of corridors radiated out from the beltway corridor like spokes on a wheel. Under the command deck was the cavernous main hold, full of ordnance and supplies. Above us was the troop barracks and armory. Beyond all of these was a wall of dense rock about two hundred feet thick. Outside the rock wall was the saucer-shaped superstructure, encrusted with weaponry. The new fighter bays were located in the superstructure.

I reviewed our state of readiness carefully. We were tight and ready for action.

It was galling. I'd built this entire monstrosity to face the last threat—an attack by the Macros via the Thor system. Once again, I'd failed to anticipate our next need, which now appeared to be providing support for the inhabitants of the Thor system.

"Colonel?" asked Miklos.

I turned to him, almost startled.

"You're back?" I asked. "Are you sneaking up on me?"

Miklos smiled faintly. "I've been standing right here looking at your screen. Am I right in assuming the station is in an excellent state of readiness?"

"You are absolutely right on that point. Where's Major Sloan? I want to congratulate him on his accomplishments here. He's gone beyond what I thought was possible in six months."

"He's inspecting the fighter bays," Miklos said.

I looked at him questioningly.

Miklos cleared his throat. "I took the liberty of telling him about the carriers we're building. He's deciding which wings to send, which pilots are best suited to the task."

I laughed. "*One* carrier, Miklos! Just one for now. If it proves itself, we'll talk about building more."

"Of course, sir."

I shook my head and turned my attention back to my screens. Miklos was my executive officer, and we had made a decision together. But somehow I'd expected to bring it up at a general staff meeting. Apparently, things weren't happening fast enough for Miklos' taste.

Miklos didn't wander off. He lingered at my side.

"What's on your mind, Commodore?"

"May I show you something, sir?"

I frowned at him, then I caught on. "You've got another design, don't you?"

"Just a few ideas. You can pull up the file there."

He pointed to a blinking icon on my desktop. It hadn't been there a moment ago. I tapped on it and frowned as a schematic unfolded. There were layers and decks and details—my frown deepened.

"You've been working on this for months. No one could come up with it so fast."

"My staff is very efficient, sir," he murmured.

"Don't bullshit me. I've got a lot of experience designing ships—and with bullshitting."

"Just so, sir."

I heaved a breath and began going over the plans. They were very detailed. I liked them immediately, except for one thing: they weren't simple. There was no way this ship could be slapped together with existing parts.

"Hold on," I said, interrupting Miklos' pitch. "This isn't what we agreed to."

"Are the designs flawed?"

"No, of course not. This ship will be a magnificent addition to the fleet when we build it. But I'm not ready to commit so much material and specialized components. I want something we can slap together like a Macro cruiser. These point-defense systems, for example—elaborate and expensive."

"The mothership must be protected from missiles."

"Right, well, you told me the ship would be protected by its fighters. You said it would operate as a simple garage for a mass of smaller ships. This is much more than that. This is a miniature version of this battle station."

"A *mobile* version, sir."

"And the primary guns? What the hell were you thinking? I don't want this ship anywhere near a battle that requires heavy railguns."

24

Miklos' expression was a combination of chagrin and stubbornness. "The fighters aren't able to bombard a world themselves, sir. They lack heavy weapons."

"Yeah, I know. That's the whole bloody point of a fighter."

We both stared at the designs for another minute in silence. I knew I had some hard decisions to make, and Miklos wasn't going to like them. I figured that was just too bad.

"All right," I said. "We'll keep your designs—for later. When we have the time and resources to build a showboat. But for now, I'm going to make a copy of this whole thing and do some serious editing for the first prototype ship."

I closed the project file and tapped at the screen. I copied the entire folder of data and renamed the new copy: "Showboat". Then I brought up the original file and began deleting things.

The first thing I did was tear out generators. Big ships the size of a Macro cruiser normally had three generators, two to run the engines and one to run the weapons batteries. Miklos had no less than six power systems in his design, overkill in my opinion. I deleted all but two.

Miklos looked physically ill. "Colonel," he protested, "the vessel can't possibly—"

"Hold on, I'm not done," I said. I brought up the forward batteries and removed all the heavy railguns and laser turrets. I left only six small point-defense lasers. At each of these scattered emplacements, I added a garbage-can sized generator. I did this by dragging and dropping components with my fingers.

"See?" I said. "Those power-consumption meters are already out of the red and into the yellow."

"The ship won't have the capacity for most mission assignments with these changes. And the power usage is still overloaded."

"That's because I'm not done editing yet," I said.

He looked horrified.

"Look," I said, "I've taken into consideration your concern about missiles. These little turrets are the only armament this ship is going to have, but they'll stop a mild missile assault. With independent power for all the PD turrets, they can't be knocked out at once. Even if the ship's main power is gone, they'll still function."

"But the engines, sir. Two primary generators won't carry the load."

I swiped the screen rapidly, paging through the decks until I had the engine rooms displayed. There were three primary engines. I removed one.

"That'll fix it."

"She'll be slow. She won't be able to keep up with the rest of the fleet."

"Yes," I agreed. "She'll be slow. Remember the design goals: this vessel is a strategic platform. We'll only move it into regions we consider to be safe. Once it gets into position, it will set up camp. It's not designed to fly into battle as a front line ship. And I know how I can speed it up even more."

I brought up the hull specifications next, and began thinning down the outer shielding. Miklos tugged at his beard in distress, but said nothing. By the time I was done, the ship looked something like what I'd envisioned when Miklos had originally sold me on this idea.

I saved the design and mailed him a copy. Then I turned to him.

"Two days," I told him.

"What, sir?"

"To build this thing from scratch would take six days," I said, tapping the indicated estimate at the upper left corner of the design screen. "But you don't have six days. You've got two. That's all."

Miklos looked at me in bewilderment. I turned to face him and straightened my spine. He did the same. All my people understood the body language and the look I gave him next. They knew when they saw that stare, I meant business. In this case, Miklos knew he was about to get an order he didn't like. He wasn't wrong about that.

"You have two days to build this thing, Commodore," I said, jabbing my finger at the image on the screen. "After that, I'm flying out to see what's heating up Yale's oceans. I don't care if the Lobsters answer us or not in the meantime. I don't care if your ship, fighters and pilots aren't ready yet. We're leaving in two days."

"But we don't have the production capacity..." Miklos began, then trailed off. "Most of the factories and materials are back on Eden-8, sir. We can't even fly them out here that soon."

I could tell that my pronouncement had shocked him. He was a hard man to rattle, but I think I'd managed it this time.

"We have many of these components in storage," I said. "You'll use the stores aboard the battle station first, then build new elements second. If you have to strip a few pieces out of this station, I'll

26

approve it. The only thing you have to build fresh is the bones of the ship, and then do the assembly. I'll talk to Sloan about that, don't worry about him giving you the run-around. You'll have his entire crew to help out. A thousand of them, suited up and ready to do the assembly by hand."

Miklos raised his eyebrows at this offer of support and nodded. "May I ask a question, Colonel?"

"Certainly."

"Why two days?"

"Number one, because I've calculated it can be done in that amount of time, if you work around the clock. Number two, because I already ordered a complement of ships to meet us here from the Helios ring garrison. We'll form up a fleet and fly when they get here."

"And the need for speed is...?"

"Because I don't like what I'm seeing in the Thor system. I don't like watching something strange happening just beyond our borders. I'm going to go out there and find out what it's all about. And I'm flying two days from now."

"Two days," said Miklos, his eyes looking unfocussed. He nodded a moment later, then turned around and ran out of the command center.

Everyone on duty swiveled their heads in surprise. When a nanotized member of Star Force decides to really kick it into gear, it's a startling thing to watch. One second he was standing and calmly deliberating over plans with me, and the next second he bounded over tables, pushed off from the ceiling twelve feet over our heads, then slammed down on his feet and sprinted to the doors. He surprised the doors themselves, even though they were made of fresh smart metal. He slipped through them the moment they flashed open widely enough to allow him to pass, folding his body and causing a spray of droplets like mercury to shower the beltway corridor beyond.

After that, he vanished from sight. The staff looked at me, but I turned back to the designs and ignored them. On the floor, droplets of silvery metal chased one another. They would eventually form veins of shimmering liquid then coalesce into a door again.

I smiled contentedly. I didn't know where Miklos was going, or what he planned to do first. But I always like to see my people hustle.

27

-4-

Two days later, the fleet arrived. It amounted to half my complement of ships from the Helios ring garrison. No one really liked the idea of stripping ships from that border, as Earth had attacked us with a serious armada not long ago through that very ring. But that was the only ready supply of ships I had, so I had no choice.

The fleet was a small one. All told, there were less than a hundred vessels. Two thirds of them were smaller ships: ugly, stubby gunboats. Each of these were armed with a single heavy railgun that was the equivalent of a Macro cruiser's belly turret. They had little armament other than that one heavy gun. The rest of the ships were Nano-type cruisers and destroyers.

Absent from the roster was one carrier. Miklos had not quite managed to pull it off yet.

"Sir, give me one more day," he said.

I shook my head.

"No."

I thought I'd said gently, but I could see he wasn't happy. He was red-eyed and squinting from lack of sleep. He fought visibly not to have a public outburst, which would no doubt turn into a gush of curse-words thrown in my direction.

I watched him with interest. Miklos had never quite been in such a state of frustration, at least not that I'd seen. I chalked it up to the lack of sleep.

"You've done very well, but your best was not quite good enough," I said. "Also, you need to get some rest, man. Part of an

28

officer's responsibility in my fleet is to maintain his readiness. All things in moderation, as they say."

Miklos glowered at the screen, unable to lift his burning eyes up to me. I walked away to the big viewscreens on the walls. They were so high-resolution they looked like windows.

Outside the station sat a hulking shadow. It looked quite a bit like the carrier I'd designed in a ten minute stretch a few days earlier. But there were holes in it—in the hull. Not all the smart metal had been troweled over the exterior.

"Shame about the holes," I said.

For some reason, this put Miklos over the edge. "For your information, Colonel," he snapped, "those holes are *your* doing."

I glanced back at him in surprise. "Really? How did I manage that?"

"By redesigning the ship with too thin of an exterior layer of smart metal. The ship was designed to use the thick hull as part of its structural integrity. We haven't been able to compensate."

I nodded and made a clucking sound. "Well, my design was only a starting point, really. You can adjust it."

"We will," Miklos said, "but there just wasn't any time in the schedule for a redesign and correction."

I frowned at the ship. Really, it was an impressive effort.

I felt myself bending. I didn't like it, as bending wasn't my way. To get things done, a leader had to establish the rules and stick to them. If people started getting the idea your deadlines were only *guidelines*—they would relax and nothing would get done. It was only human nature.

Still, I liked the idea of having this ship on the expedition into the Thor system. It would transform a thin force into a much stronger one. I'd begun to think of the carrier as a small mobile battle station, and the idea of having such a flying fortress to back me up was seductive.

"I'll tell you what, Commodore. The task force will get underway now, but I'll leave behind ten small ships. They will form your carrier's escort. When your carrier is ready, send it out the Crustacean worlds after me."

Miklos looked startled. "You want the ship to come in later? As a relief force?"

"Yes. In some ways this improves the plan. We can head out with the vanguard at top speed and render any assistance we can. Then your carrier group will follow to a safely established position. This way, the ship won't slow down the entire fleet. If you finish tomorrow, it will come in two days behind us. That's not too long to wait for the support."

I glanced at him again. The transformation in his mood was obvious and dramatic. The light of hope had returned to his dark eyes.

"You will get that support, sir," he said. "But did you say *carriers*, as in the plural form…?"

"Yes," I said. "I'm impressed by the design, and the versatility is there, at least on the planning boards. I want two of them. Stay here after the first one is done and finish a second. Don't let anyone sit on their hands here at the station. Double-shifts for everyone."

I heard a few groans from the staffers, but pretended I hadn't noticed.

"You'll stay here," I continued, "When you finish the second ship, send it with another fighter wing stripped from the battle station to the Helios ring garrison. That will make up for having their strength reduced so significantly. You'll stay in-system even after the ships are built. In my absence, you'll be in charge of defending our colonies."

Miklos nodded rapidly. "I can do that, sir."

I almost laughed. Given the chance to build a second of his beloved carriers, all his plans to rave at me had instantly faded. I had to admire his dedication to Fleet. He was passionate about his forces.

"Uh, who should command the first carrier, sir?" he asked a moment later.

"Give it to Captain Sarin. She's a senior officer, and she's in line for a new ship."

Captain Jasmine Sarin had an interesting history, which was intertwined with my own. She and I had worked together from the very start of Star Force, and we'd become—close. Too close for my girlfriend Sandra's comfort.

Sarin had left my service and joined Crow last year, thereby gaining a promotion to the rank of Admiral. But she'd soon seen the error of her ways and returned to my banner with the reduced rank of Captain. As of today, I had her captaining a destroyer with a crew of only six. I knew she'd see the new captaincy as a promotion, one which I thought she'd earned.

Captain Sarin was informed of the change in plans and requested a private channel with me. I took the call in my stateroom aboard the cruiser *Lazaro*, which was to serve as my command ship for this mission. The small fleet was just getting underway. Sending through a few ships at a time, we wriggled through the ring and glided into the Thor system.

"Colonel Riggs?"

"Hello Jasmine."

"I just got the news from Miklos. Thank you very much! I won't disappoint you, sir."

Her pretty face appeared on my screen, her image updating a few seconds behind her voice due to transmission relays and other propagation delays. My cruiser was in the Thor system now, accelerating away from the ring toward the gas giant the Crustacean moons circled. Jasmine was still back on Welter Station.

"I know you won't, Captain," I said. "That ship is ugly and slow, but she's powerful."

Jasmine was as pretty as ever. Dark hair, dark eyes, perfect nose and lips. I'd been taken with her since the first time I'd met her. She was slight and quiet, but tougher than she looked. And she was always, always competent.

"Any special orders for me, Colonel?"

"Yes," I said, "get that ship finished and get out to Thor as soon as you can. If possible, take over the task of playing assembly-boss from Miklos. He's not taking proper care of himself."

"Uh, isn't he just doing what you asked him to do, Colonel?"

"A man's got to learn to pace himself."

"But, Colonel, if you order a man to do something and give him an impossible schedule, he's going to overwork himself. Surely you can see that."

I frowned at the screen. "You want me to take responsibility for the man's condition? I guess I may have accidentally over-motivated him—if such a thing is possible. But in any case, he needs a few hours off."

"I'll see what I can do, sir," she said. I thought I heard a small sigh escape her.

"Very good. Riggs out."

31

* * *

A day later, we were half-way to the Crustacean homeworlds. Happy news came in from Welter Station: the carrier was finished. Miklos reported this to me with obvious pride. I thanked him, praised his efforts, then ordered him to build the second one immediately.

"And get some sleep, man. You look like hell."

"Yes, sir."

When I broke the connection, I found Sandra standing behind me with her arms crossed. My immediate thought was: she's found out about my giving the carrier to Jasmine, and knew I was bringing her along on this mission.

She did looked annoyed, but not openly pissed. This was a fine line in her expressions. I decided to play it cool.

"Hey honey, how about we get some chow down at the wardroom? This cruiser has the best food in the fleet. I ordered up a supply of frozen air-swimmers from Eden-8 just for you."

Her expression softened, but her arms stayed crossed. "Dinner now?" she asked. "We're only hours away from planetfall."

I shook my head. "Plenty of time. Nothing's shooting at us yet."

"I wanted to talk to you about something first."

There it was, I thought. It was the Jasmine-thing. It had to be. Jealousy was a prime-motivator on Sandra's hierarchy of emotions. It outweighed hunger every time.

"I want to ask you about Miklos," she said. "I think you've been working him too hard."

I blinked. This was an unexpected but welcome turn of conversation. I began to smile. "He's been driving himself too hard lately, I agree with that. I just told Jasmine—ah, Captain Sarin—to take over the construction effort from him."

"He's been driving himself because you ordered him to do it, Kyle," Sandra admonished me. "You can't tell people to work harder and at the same time tell them to take breaks."

"I just want people to do their best," I said. "They often don't take into account the need for balance in order to achieve that."

"What it sounds like to them is a set of contradictory orders."

32

I shrugged. "How about those air-swimmers? They're great when broiled. I'll have the cook dip them in butter and garlic."

"Okay," she said, weakening.

I stood up and took her arm. We headed toward the exit when I got an idea. I bent and kissed her. She kissed me back. We stopped and didn't take another step toward the door for a while. Somehow, we'd begun making out.

"What happened to dinner?" she asked.

"I'm not that hungry."

She laughed, then pulled away a fraction. Her eyebrows knit together. "You gave a new ship to Jasmine, I heard."

Damn, I thought. Talk about a mood-deflator.

I tried to smile. "Yeah. She's senior, and her talents were wasted on a destroyer."

"What ship did you give her?"

I hesitated. I could tell she already knew the answer. How could she have heard the rumor without knowing what it was about? She just wanted to see a full confession.

"The new carrier," I admitted.

"You know what she's going to call it?"

"No, not yet."

One of Star Force's oldest traditions dictated that new ships were named by the Captain. It dated back to the early days, when Nano ships plucked their captains out of their beds. After passing the deadly tests and taking command, the new people had been given the honor of naming the ship that had tormented them.

"She's going to call it *Gatre*," Sandra said.

"You seem to know more about current events than I do."

"That's part of my job."

I moved in for another kiss, but she dodged me.

"Don't you want to know what *Gatre* means?"

"Um…no, not really."

"It means something like 'calloused' or 'stubborn' in Hindi."

I frowned. "Did she tell you that?"

"No. I looked it up."

I nodded, but had no idea why we were having this conversation. I reached out a hand toward her shapely hip, but she pushed it away automatically. I could see the look on her face was one of concentration. She really was interested in this carrier.

33

Her eyes studied mine with sudden intensity. "Why did you give that ship to her, Kyle?" she asked.

My face went blank in surprise. When it comes to women, I'm a bumbling idiot, but I've learned to sense traps when they're laid at my feet. I was on guard immediately. I knew I had to step very carefully.

"Uh..." I began, my mind churning, "because she deserved a serious command?"

"Yes, I know that," she said, her eyes searching my face. "But I don't think you made the right decision. People have feelings you know."

I heaved a sigh. I didn't like where this might be going. Was she going to have another jealous fit?

"I'm sorry," I said. "I didn't mean to upset you."

"Me? I'm not talking about *me*."

"Then what are you talking about?"

"Miklos, of course. He wanted that command. He built the ship, he has dreamt of it for months. He hardly talks about anything else, you know."

"No, I didn't realize that. But don't worry. I'll give him the second ship."

"The second one?"

I filled her in on Miklos' new orders. By the end, she was satisfied, and a few minutes later we were back to kissing. Soon I was as satisfied as she was.

By the time we made it down to get our platter of broiled air-swimmers, the kitchen had run out for the night. But after a disappointed look from me, they headed back to the freezers and thawed another batch. Rank does have its privileges.

34

-5-

The first day's voyage into the Thor system was tense, but uneventful. We were expecting something to happen at any moment. Every hour we stared at the screens, made countless attempts to open channels and continuously scanned the moons ahead.

"What if we're too late?" Sandra asked me.

I glanced at her, then went back to staring at the screens. The same thought had occurred to me. What if the Crustaceans had been too proud to ask their enemies for help? What if they'd waited until the last and what we'd heard had been the last gasp of a civilization? Now that we'd finally responded, there might not be anyone home to answer our call.

"Nonsense," I said. "They're just stuffy and prideful. They're probably too embarrassed to tell us they have problems."

"You think they regret calling on us? That they're too proud to admit they need help?"

"Exactly," I said. "But we won't know the truth until they talk to us or we get more solid data."

More long hours passed. During this time, the carrier *Gatre* was crewed and launched back in the Eden system. It came into the Thor system behind us, trailing its tiny flotilla of support ships. When a call finally did come into my command center, it was from Captain Sarin, rather than the Crustaceans.

"Where are their ships, Colonel?" Jasmine asked me when I opened the private line to her carrier.

"I don't know," I admitted. "We haven't seen them fly above their atmosphere on any of the three worlds since we entered the Thor system."

"I don't like it," she said, "it looks like a trap."

"That, or the aftermath of a tremendous catastrophe."

Jasmine didn't answer me for a while. When she finally did, her voice was hushed, almost as if the things we were discussing were too terrible to be spoken aloud. Perhaps we were.

"You think they're *all* dead?" she asked. "That's why they aren't talking?"

"We'll find out when we reach orbit."

"But it might be too late by then. If there is something so powerful it could erase a species from three worlds that quickly— your fleet may not stand a chance."

I chuckled. "If this entire fleet turns into vapor, your orders are to do a U-turn with that carrier and get back to Welter Station. Then close all the shutters and hide in the cellar."

She didn't seem amused. "Don't you at least have a theory, Colonel?"

"Of course I do," I said. "But I've got nothing to go on. Guesses aren't helpful, so I'm going to wait until we have some hard evidence."

Privately, I felt certain the prideful Crustaceans would never have called me for help unless they were desperate. Whatever was going on out here, it was serious.

The second day went on as had the first. We sailed through space, coming closer and closer to the gas giant in the habitable zone. More than a day's flight behind us was Captain Sarin's carrier group. I monitored the new ship's vitals from the beginning. There were a few glitches, and she was slow. I calculated that it would take *Gatre* more than two days to reach the home planets of the Crustaceans—it would be closer to three days.

The moons, Yale, Harvard and Princeton, now were visible using our long-range optics. They were strange worlds, beautiful in their own way. I reflected that calling them moons was really only a technical description. They were planets, just like any other. They did happen to be locked in orbit around a larger planetary body, but isn't every planet is locked around its star? They were nothing like the sterile rocks we called moons back in the Solar System.

Two of the worlds had so much water on them there was virtually no land to be found on the surface. The depths of these oceans were tremendous. As we drew closer, our readings indicated that the third moon—Yale—had the deepest oceans of the three, and that it was even more alien than we'd thought. Yale had no land at all.

Submarines can't normally go deeper than a few thousand feet due to the tremendous pressure. The requirement for breathable gas inside creates such a difference in pressure that the hulls of most subs will collapse if they continue to sink.

On Earth, our oceans are about thirty thousand feet at their deepest. But the oceans of Yale were deeper still. Our instruments measured the rocky bottom, and detected it at some two hundred thousand feet down in places.

At that depth, there is so much pressure that water transforms into alternate states. Back on Earth I'd been accustomed to ice, steam and liquid water. But when you stack up water deeply enough, with enough crushing weight, it takes on new physical properties. It becomes solid, and hotter. A type of "hot ice" develops. Our Fleet eggheads told me about it with a strange light in their eyes.

The pleading transmissions had come from Yale, as well as the strange readings we were getting now. The oceans there were a full six degrees hotter than they'd been a week ago. And still, there was no discernible reason for any of these changes.

When we were only nine hours out from orbit, Marvin came to consult with me. He seemed to be in a state of agitation. He couldn't stand still. His metal tentacles slapped at the deck like fish in the bottom of boat. It was very distracting, but I'd seen this behavior before. Marvin was excited about something.

"What is it, Marvin?" I asked him. "You look like you're about to pee your pants."

"Reference unclear. I do not urinate. In fact, I have few liquids in my structure, with the possible exception of lubrication reservoirs. Are you suggesting I've sprung a leak, Colonel? Or is this somehow an apt reference to my findings?"

I chuckled. "It's an idiom. I'm suggesting you're excited and agitated."

Cameras studied me. "You can infer that from my behavior?"

"Yes. Now, tell me what you want. I've got a lot of data to go over."

"That's exactly it, sir. I think there's something in the data we've missed."

He finally had my full attention. "Tell me about it."

"It all came from my previous geological studies concerning the smaller celestial bodies in this system. Remember when we flew into the system and scanned it? I've been comparing that data to the current scans we've been reading since our arrival in the Thor system."

"What have you found?"

"It's very interesting. There's a discrepancy on my readings of the third moon, Yale. A variation in measurable mass."

I frowned. "In *mass*?" I asked. Suddenly, I understood his earlier remark about me making an apt comment. He meant the world had really sprung a leak. "So...the planet is smaller than it was before?"

"Yes," he said.

"What could be causing such a change?"

"A leak, of course."

I stared at him for a moment, finally catching on. I turned to the screens and flipped through maps and models.

"You're telling me their oceans are draining away," I said. "How long has this been going on?"

A camera snaked over my left shoulder and gazed down at the table with me. I knew it was only Marvin's way of seeing something from my perspective. He did this from time to time, peeking over people's shoulders with one of his many eyes. It helped him to understand what we were talking about when discussing visual input, because he could study what we were seeing. Most found it disconcerting, but I understood why he did it and it didn't bother me. Marvin's visual input was different from the human norm. He had many more eyes—variable numbers of them, actually. And he could be looking at several things at once. Unlike humans, who were built to visually study one part of their environment at a time, Marvin could see many at once. His cameras weren't as good as our eyes, but he made up for that by having a lot of them.

Due to this major variation in visual input and processing, his perspective on the visual environment around us was quite different. Rather than looking only at the item we were discussing, he liked to use his mobile visual sensory systems to try to see my point of view.

He wasn't very good at indirect empathy, but he excelled at direct mimicry of behavior.

Finally, I had the data he was referring to. It had been in an old file saved months ago. "According to this, the planetary mass of Yale is about one percent lower than it was when you made your original readings. That's incredible. Have you got anything else, Marvin?"

He slid up beside me at the table. "Possibly," he said.

I looked at him expectantly. He studied me with many cameras at once. I knew he wanted me to ask him more about it, and to praise him for his accomplishments. He was odd that way—he liked it when people begged him for facts. He also liked to keep secrets. Sometimes he used critical details of information as bargaining chips to gain privileges. Usually these privileges came in the form of an approval to perform some kind of nasty experiment.

I'd played his little game many times. Over the years, I'd worked up a counter to his manipulations. I decided to employ it now.

My first move was to nod and tap the screen, closing the file.

"Very good, Marvin," I said. "I think I have enough for now. You've done an excellent job. Once again, you've proven to me that my decision to make you my Science Officer was the correct one."

Marvin's cameras flicked from the blank screen to my blank face and back again.

"Don't you wish to study the matter further, Colonel Riggs?" he asked.

I shrugged and reached for a cup of algae-based coffee. "You're the Science Officer. You've made the call. Your commander has been briefed, and you've decided he's heard all there is of value to know. I trust your judgment on this one."

"That's very gratifying, Colonel Riggs."

"Good. Now if you don't mind, I have a number of issues to attend to before we reach orbit. We're only a few hours from planetfall."

"But I think there might be something else to discuss."

"Oh yeah?" I asked, trying to look bored. I fooled with my coffee mug, adding cream and sugar. I hated cream and sugar.

Marvin appeared disappointed. His tentacles drooped and stopped thrashing. "Yes, there's a localized point where the leak is occurring."

"You know where the leak is?" I asked.

"Yes—at least I have it down to a one hundred square mile region of the southern oceans."

I nodded. With languid slowness, I reached out and tapped at the screen. I knew I couldn't afford to appear eager. I opened the file but didn't bother to flip to the appropriate screen. Instead, I paused to sip my coffee.

Algae-based coffee tastes pretty bad to begin with. But with sugar in it, the flavor had moved from sewery to sugary-sewery. I winced, but tried to hide my disgust.

Marvin studied me and finally couldn't handle it anymore. He reached up with two tentacles and touched the screen, making spreading motions and spinning the globe of Yale to the correct angle. I smiled slightly. It was kind of fun to make him impatient for once.

His tentacles rattled and scratched on the touchscreen until he had the correct view displayed. By this time, several staffers had taken note of our conversation and stepped up to watch. I ignored them and pretended to be enjoying my coffee. It was a good thing, I figured, that Marvin had no sense of smell. If he had, he'd have known right away I was faking.

On the screen, he'd displayed a region known as "Light Blue" on the moon's surface. For the most part, Yale had no real features. It had clouds and a little scrim of polar ice at the top and bottom of the world, but no land. With only an endless ocean encircling the core of the world, there wasn't much to see.

But, in spots like Light Blue, the ocean floor had heaved up closer to the surface. In this region the color of the surface changed. Most of the world was so thickly covered in deep water it was almost black, even when the bright light of Thor shined down directly upon it. But Light Blue was different, it looked like one of Earth's oceans.

"The shallow area?" I said. "Isn't that the highest underwater mountain range on Yale?"

"Yes, it's also one of the most thickly inhabited regions. The Crustaceans can't survive in the deepest oceans, which have an estimated depth of two hundred thousand feet."

I studied the imagery. It didn't look right to me. "Is that a whirlpool?" I asked incredulously.

"Yes," Marvin said. "It's so large, I believed it to be a storm at first. But now I know the truth. The water is circling, draining away."

40

"What could be down there?" I asked. "What could possibly swallow such a fantastic volume of liquid?"

Marvin was perking up. He sensed my interest, and I'd given him urgent questions which could be evaded. I knew instantly what he was thinking: soon, he might manage to gain a hold over me.

I smiled, because I knew his game. And for once I was one jump ahead of the sneaky robot. I'd figured out the answer to my own question before I'd asked it.

I snapped my fingers as if getting a sudden flash of insight. "I know!" I said. "It's a ring! It's got to be. A ring at the bottom of the sea, draining the water away to nowhere. What else could it be?"

Marvin looked stunned. For a full second, none of his numerous limbs or input devices moved. When they moved again, they were deflated, like a dozen wilting flowers on a hot August day.

"That matches my assessment," he said.

"Somehow," I said, "a ring has opened up at the bottom of their ocean. What an ingenious form of attack."

"You think this is an attack?"

I nodded. "Either that, or the Crustaceans were experimenting. Maybe they tried to open up a pathway from their homeworld to another star system. Maybe the attempt backfired horribly."

I proceeded to disseminate Marvin's data to the command staff and the entire fleet. I made sure it was transmitted back to Eden as well. While this went on, Marvin studied me and the data. I knew he was horribly disappointed. He'd given up his data without getting anything for it.

When I managed to slip out of his sight, I dumped the ghastly coffee on the deck of the conference chamber and watched the ship's nanite hull absorb it. Moments later it was released outside the hull as the waste it truly was. The ship knew garbage when it encountered it.

But Marvin wasn't quite done yet. He came to me less than an hour later. "I have a new theory, Colonel. Would you like to hear it?"

"If you think it's absolutely necessary," I said. "I'm very busy."

"It concerns Yale's ocean—I believe I know the cause for the rise in temperature."

"Oh, that. Never mind then."

Marvin appeared to be stunned again.

"You don't have any interest in this critical detail?" he asked.

41

"I'm interested all right. But I've already figured it out. As the oceans recede, the deep, deep hot-ice is being exposed. The rapid lowering of the sea is causing the hot ice to break down and heat up the water. Does that match your theories, Marvin?"

"Yes," he said. Crushed again, he wandered away a few minutes later.

Since my conversation with Marvin, I'd been poring over science texts. I'd learned about the changed state of water at great depths, and the hot-ice phenomenon. It had been difficult, but the look on Marvin's structure was worth it all now.

I grinned after him and whispered to myself: "We'll chalk that one up for the dumbass human."

-6-

When we were about half an hour out from Yale, all hell broke loose. At the time, I was in the ship's head relieving myself. The ship was under heavy deceleration—but when you have to go, you have to go.

Operating a ship's elimination system when under several Gs of force can be a difficult operation by itself, as anyone who's done it can tell you. Things went from bad to worse, however, when the ship's klaxons went off and the vessel heeled-over, engaging its automatic evasion routines. I cursed and found myself sliding on my back across the chamber. Fortunately, spilled wastes were quickly removed by the smart metal floor.

When I managed to get out of the head, I struggled up the corridor to the bridge. I was slammed from one side to the other as the ship rocked and lurched. The inertial stabilizers were off-line due to power requirements. The engines were burning at full throttle to keep us from crashing into those deep, blue oceans, and the rest of the power went to the weapons systems.

I crawled into the command center and found a crash seat to strap into. It wasn't the one I was assigned to, but that was just too bad for whatever staffer I'd displaced. I managed to connect to the Fleet command channel and listened to the chatter long enough to figure out what was going on. We were under attack.

"This is Riggs," I said, trying to sound calm. "Give me counts and ranges. What have we got incoming right now?"

"Missiles sir. No ships, just missiles. About two thousand of them."

My mind glazed over. I didn't have to do the math. We were at close range, and we didn't have enough time to lock-on and shoot down that many missiles—not if Crustacean missiles were as good as Macro missiles at finding their targets. They were going to hurt us, and hurt us badly.

"It was all a trick, Kyle," Sandra said on a private line to my helmet. "Those bastards. We'll lose half the fleet. Fire everything we have back at them. We can at least hurt them this time."

My mind had come out of shock and was now racing. I couldn't believe it. These vicious Lobsters had done it twice in a row. I'd not underestimate them again—if I ever got another opportunity.

"Stop decelerating!" I roared. "I want every pilot to plot an individual course. Bring your noses around and accelerate toward Yale, but do it at an angle. I want you all to miss the moon, naturally. But slowing down will just make us easier targets. We need to do a fly-by as fast as we can, giving them as little opportunity to shoot us down as possible."

Within twenty seconds, the pilot of *Lazaro* had followed my orders. The results were gut-wrenching. A normal human without nanite-hardened organs would have passed out, or quite possibly died. For us marines, however, there was no such simple relief. We lived, remained conscious, and suffered. It felt as if someone had a firm grip on my intestines and was hell-bent on unraveling them.

The point-defense systems were firing now, on full automatic.

"Vacc-suits, everyone!" I shouted over the command channel. "Assume your vessel will lose pressure before this is over. I want zero casualties from decompression."

It was all up to a few thousand brainboxes now. The missiles would be hitting their first targets within eight minutes. I'd been watching the counters displayed on the big wall-screens. I'd learned to count again by this time. We weren't going to get them all. Some of my ships were about to be destroyed. The only question was whether or not any of us would make it home.

As I got over my initial shock, the emotion that followed wasn't fear, it was rage. None of this made any sense. Why would the Crustaceans do something like this? Sure, they didn't like us. But going to the trouble of draining their own world, of damaging their own habitat, just to make this ruse convincing? I couldn't fathom that kind of dedication to deceit.

44

I tried to think, but it was difficult to do anything other than keep my guts in place and watch the ticking numbers on the displays.

Red slivers were arcing closer every second. Occasionally, one of them blinked out. But the rate of defensive hits was far too slow. My hopes that the majority of their missiles would be shot down faded. They were quality weapons. Probably, they were spinning and coated with reflective polymers to deflect our lasers. Maybe they even had aerogel mists enveloping them, technology we'd only recently mastered ourselves.

I slammed my fist down on the arm of my stolen chair. Even as I did so, a confused looking lieutenant came into view. She was crawling toward me. I frowned at her, then saw her look up at me in shock. I realized then she must be trying to make it to the chair I was in—her chair.

I waved her away. She turned and crawled out of my sight. My mind wanted to feel bad for her, wanted to wonder if she would survive the next...*six minutes*, the displays reported...but I didn't feel bad for her. I didn't have time.

I had to think. I sucked in a breath and contacted Marvin.

"Marvin!" I shouted.

"Yes, Colonel?"

"Are you aboard this ship?" I demanded.

"What ship, sir?"

"No games, Marvin. Are you on the same ship I am right now?"

"Yes sir, at the moment."

I felt relief. In general, when Marvin knew or even suspected an attack was coming, he tended to bug out early. Sometimes, *very* early, before anyone else even knew what was going to happen. The fact that he was still aboard was encouraging. It meant he was just as surprised as I was.

"Marvin, I need you to translate for me. Open a channel to these treacherous Lobsters."

"They've never responded, sir."

"I don't care! I know they've been listening. Probably, whatever I say will amuse them greatly. But I don't care about that, either. Open the channel and translate."

"Channel open."

I paused to suck in some air, and then I let loose: "To the people of the water-moon under the shadows of my ships, you're the least honorable of any species I've ever encountered. You are cheaters. You are ignorant, and savage. I am a professor among my people. I hereby give you all a failing grade!"

There was no response for several seconds. I'd hoped to elicit some kind of defensive response out of them with my verbal attack. After all, they had no reason to stay quiet now. Their trap had been sprung, and staying quiet no longer benefited them. I also knew they were an arrogant, talkative race that valued academic achievement. Talk of failing grades should sting.

But they didn't respond. I narrowed my eyes, squinting at the readouts. Less than four minutes left now until their missiles were among us. Four minutes from now, crews would die because I'd screwed up and believed these Lobsters again.

My anger deepened. My next thought was a dark one: I considered bombing their cities. They hadn't given us any ships to shoot at, but their civilian populations were vulnerable. We knew where they lived in their shallow reefs and deep grottoes. We knew some of them were still alive.

I lifted a fateful hand to press the transmission button again. The crews were waiting for my order to fire. I could feel it in my bones.

But about a second before I gave the order to commit a billion intelligent beings to death, I had another thought.

"Scan those missiles!" I roared. "Has anyone done that? Are there Macros flying those things?"

My thought was simple and horrible. What if the Lobsters themselves, god love the son-a-bitches, weren't actually attacking us? What if the Macros were behind it all?

I knew the Lobsters weren't easy to get along with, but I also knew they weren't suicidal. They must know what we could do to their populations. They would have done the math long ago. I could understand an ambush, but why would they let us get in so close before launching their surprise attack?

Perhaps they hadn't. If Macros held their underwater cities, and were the ones firing the missiles, perhaps it was their math I was witnessing in its perfection.

The Macros had a treaty with the Crustaceans, we knew that. Just as they'd had a treaty with several other races. Of course, the first thing these machines always did when they signed a new treaty was try to find a way to break it. It was like making a deal with the

46

proverbial wolf at the doorstep: it never stopped seeking a way in, a way to devour those it has bargained with.

The Macros might have suckered us in, then launched this late attack to provoke our response. That way, the Lobsters would suffer mass casualties, we would lose a fleet, and the machines would be smiling as they presided over our collective funerals. They'd achieved the deaths of millions of fools at the cost of a few missiles and transmissions.

"Answer me!" I roared. "Are those missiles piloted by Macros or not?"

"No, sir," Marvin said. He sounded as calm and unruffled as he always did.

"No? Confirm that. The missiles are from Crustacean bases?"

"Yes, Colonel," he said. "Every indication is that the Crustaceans have launched this attack."

"I have no choice then. Commanders, target their civilian populations. Input special order Z."

"Do we have to, Kyle?" Sandra asked me on a private channel.

I ignored her. I stared at the blue, blue world below me. I wondered what it would be like to sail a ship on that glass-like sea. The water was warm—hot now, even. The skies would be cloudy. But on a clear day, the world would be an endless perfect expanse of blue. The tides were very large due to the gravitational tug of the gas giant in the sky, but I knew that even tidal waves back on Earth were small bumps in the road when out in the open ocean. They only became deadly when they washed up on shores. Those seas had to be idyllic. And I was about to turn them into radioactive soup.

Two minutes left. Everyone was waiting for my final order to fire.

"Is that channel to the Crustaceans still open, Marvin?" I asked.

"Yes, Colonel."

"Okay, transmit this: we do not understand your actions. Possibly, we never will. We are different from you, but not without compassion. It is very possible the make-up of your brain structure does not allow for compassion. In that case, there can probably never be peace between our two peoples—not until one of us is wiped out."

I paused, then continued on. "We came here to help you. We came here because you called us. We know your oceans are draining. We know they're heating up. We suspect that the machines have

47

opened a ring under the sea and the water is escaping from your world. Worse, this is causing the temperature to heat up, due to the hot-ice in the deepest—"

"Where did you come by this information?" a voice asked.

I blinked in surprise. I'd been in the middle of a death speech, a haiku that was to lead to the annihilation of a world at the end—and quite possibly my own death. It took me a precious second to realize the enemy had at last responded.

"Where did we get this information?" I repeated. "We figured it out on our own! You said you needed help, and we came to give it. Along the way out here, we deduced what your problem was. We aren't stupid."

"Congratulations. You've achieved civilization. Please stop firing at our missiles. They have been deactivated. We have lost a fair number, and we need the rest."

"Marvin, mute the channel for a second."

"Done."

"Are they telling the truth? Are the missiles deactivated?"

"Yes—apparently. They are no longer powered. Many have deviated course."

"Don't trust them Kyle!" Sandra said with vehemence. "They are just playing yet another trick. Melt their cities! It's all we have left."

I was surprised she'd been listening in. I shouldn't have been, but I was. I didn't have time to try to kick her off the line now, so I tried to ignore her words.

But I found that I couldn't. She could be right. This could be one last trick, designed to cause us to absorb the blow of a thousand missiles, letting them get in even closer before igniting the sky with the light of a million suns.

"Divert your missiles and they won't be destroyed," I told the Crustaceans.

I switched to the command override channel a second later:

"Commanders, gunners, this is Colonel Riggs. Cease firing on any missile that is not directly targeting your vessel. That is an order. I'm attempting to negotiate a cease-fire."

The point-defense lasers that had been chattering steadily for several minutes slowed, then came to stop. The sound reminded me of the final beats of a dying drum.

48

Next, I opened the channel to both my people and the Crustaceans. "This is Colonel Kyle Riggs. If one of those missiles gets through, just one, and destroys a Star Force ship, I want every ship in the fleet to bomb your preassigned civilian targets. That is an order."

There were thirty-one seconds left. No one said anything to me as the clock ticked down. I had time to wonder how many Star Force personnel I'd just gotten killed by trusting the Crustaceans one last time.

-7-

For the most part, the crews obeyed my orders. They stopped firing on missiles that weren't a direct threat to their own ships. This was possibly the biggest risk I'd taken. Not all my ships were able to defend themselves against incoming missiles. The gunboats in particular were vulnerable to this type of weapon. The cruisers and destroyers had numerous point-defense systems, which were essentially automated laser turrets controlled by brainboxes with their own sensors. Normally, these larger ships had the job of screening the smaller ones. But today, I'd ordered them to turn off that screen to comply with the deal I'd made with the Crustaceans.

I couldn't even watch as the two lines converged on my screen. A shower of red splinters met with my ragged row of ships.

But there were no hits, no explosions. The missiles diverted themselves or simply sputtered out and drifted. They sailed away from our fleet, falling into a broad orbit over Yale.

Within a few minutes everyone on my staff was sighing with relief and a few were high-fiving one another. I guess they felt happy just to be alive. My own mood was much darker. I was angry with these aliens who'd tricked us and then turned the trick into some kind of test. I felt I'd been toyed with, and that the Crustaceans were playing a deadly game with countless lives for their own strange amusement.

My ships flew past the moon and scattered. When I was sure none of the missiles were following us, I ordered Marvin to reopen the channel. I wanted to talk to these crazy shellfish personally. I wanted to know what the hell they thought they were doing.

50

"Channel open," Marvin said.

"Hello, are you listening, Crustaceans? This is Colonel Kyle Riggs, commander of all Star Force and Earth's representative in this system."

"We're listening. We've always been listening. Your every statement and action since our first encounter has been weighed and judged."

"That's great. Who am I talking to? Please identify yourself."

"This is Professor Hoon."

"Professor?" I asked. I'd been expecting something more like a governor or an admiral. But I had to remind myself that these people valued an academic structure more than anything else.

"Yes. In addition to teaching at the highest levels, I've been a Principle Investigator in many ontological—"

"Yeah, that's great," I said. "No need to give me your full resume, Hoon. Let's talk seriously for a moment. Did you realize as our ships approached Yale that we were coming on a mission to render aid to your people?"

"Of course. I'm afraid I'm going to have to lower your cognitive score by an additional 1.5 points. Your question was poorly worded and worse, it demonstrates a clear lack of understanding of the situation."

I stared at the walls for a second, my eyes unfocussed. I was beginning to get a black, sick headache. When my eyes came back together, I spent a few seconds gazing at the deep blue of Yale's oceans, covered by swirls of white clouds. My expression shifted into a mask of rage.

"What the hell is wrong with you?" I demanded. "Do you think this is some kind of game? Why did you fire on my ships when you knew we were on a rescue mission?"

"Because by our estimations, you could not help us. A hostile barbaric fleet in orbit over our dying world represented nothing other than an additional threat."

"But you called us out here!"

"Immaterial. I must warn you, Riggs, you're dangerously close to losing another half-point."

I muted my mic and cursed for a while. Around me, the staff looked nervous. The battle was on hold, but clearly the situation could go bad again at any moment.

51

"All right," I said when I'd calmed down. "You called us out here, but figured we couldn't really do anything to help you. So, you decided to blow us out of the sky with an ambush at the last moment so we couldn't cause any harm, either. But it is your logic that I find greatly flawed. Your test results are coming back in, and the tally is woefully low."

"Absurd. Our actions were impeccably logical."

"I will give you this single opportunity to improve your score," I said as officiously as I could.

There was a brief hesitation while they mulled this over.

"What form will this opportunity take?" Hoon asked finally.

I smiled. They'd taken the bait.

"The assessment will take the form of a series of questions," I said. "Remember, your responses are being carefully judged. Every word is recorded and weighed by our academic panel."

"We are prepared. Ask your questions."

"Why did you nearly cause me to attack and kill millions of your own population?"

"Because the population of World Three is doomed."

I frowned. "You mean that if they were going to die anyway, you figured it didn't matter if we killed them all right now?"

"A follow-up query was not specified, and breaks the format agreed to. Worse, the answer to your follow-up is self-evident and thus unnecessary. I'm afraid there's nothing I can do. You're cognitive score has been lowered by a half-point."

I felt like having another round of cursing. I passed on that, but raised my arm to hammer on the chair armrest. I stopped myself with difficulty. Somehow, their nonsense about tests and constant insinuation that we were uneducated rubes—barbarians, really—was getting to me. I didn't want to prove them right, no matter how irritating they were, so I held back my fist pounding display with difficulty.

"Fine," I said. "You're saying that you decided we couldn't help, and since we were a possible threat, you ambushed us. You didn't care if we killed the population of Yale—um, World Three, because they were as good as dead already. I have to ask, however, did you ever consider the possibility that you were *wrong?* That your actions might have needlessly killed my people and yours?"

"Certainly not."

52

I thumped my helmeted head back against the headrest. Around the command center the staffers were listening in, and they murmured to one another. No one could believe it. Compared to the risk I'd taken, these people were insane. They were so arrogant, they never seemed to question their own conclusions.

My anger had faded somewhat during this interchange. After all, they'd been at greater risk than I had from the start. I'd nearly lost a fleet, but they'd nearly lost a world. What mattered most was the fact the disaster had been averted. I told myself I needed to focus on that. Then a new question sprang into my mind.

"What was it that caused you to change your judgment concerning our capacities to help you?" I asked.

"Your last transmission stated that you knew about the lowering sea levels, and the physics behind the rising temperatures."

"That was it?" I asked incredulously. "You were waiting to hear that we understood your problem?"

"If you'd been unable to discern the nature of the emergency on your own, you certainly could not be capable of rendering significant aid."

I thought about it, and there was a certain twisted logic this. After all, their engineers were probably working on the problem desperately. If they hadn't been able to stop the draining of the oceans, then it must be a difficult trick to pull off. Anyone capable of solving this problem probably *would* have quickly figured out what the problem was based on the data presented. They'd given us a couple of days in-system, then judged us morons when we didn't seem to figure it out. The penalty for academic failure among the Crustaceans was a harsh one: death.

"All right," I said finally. "We're here, and we're at peace. Now let's discuss the political state between our two species. Let's agree to a peace treaty."

"Is that absolutely necessary?"

I rolled my eyes. "Yes, I think it is. Before we agree to work with you, we have to be at peace. Can't you see the logic of that? Or do I need to lower your scores yet again?"

"You're confusing your own cultural norms with logic, but the error is excusable in this case. We find this sort of confusion is common in alien species, and does not represent a lack of mental capacity."

53

By this time I was rubbing my temples and wondering what had possessed me to fly out here and help these people. It was going to be a long mission.

Professor Hoon wasn't done yet: "Another significant failure in your response is represented by the nature of your fleet: it is essentially made up of warships. These are not the best vehicles to render the aid we require."

"That's because you didn't tell us what kind of help you needed. We assumed you were under some kind of attack."

"We are, but we still feel the nature of the attack is, and always was, self-evident. Before you even launched your fleet, many on the committee had lowered your percentile chance of rendering significant aid to the single digits. I would point out that I did not go with the prevailing trend of my colleagues on this matter. I estimated, and still do, a fourteen percent chance you will manage to provide us some type of meaningful assistance."

"Well," I said, "at least I've got that going for me."

"I request that you do not embarrass me by failing too grossly at the task."

"We wouldn't want that, would we? By the way, where are you located personally? I mean, are you on Yale, or one of the other moons?"

"What is the significance of using the term 'Yale' to describe our stricken world?"

"It's a famous university back home, on our homeworld."

"Indeed? Then it is a complimentary term, and I will adopt its use during our discussions. In response to your original query, yes, I'm on Yale."

I smiled slightly. We'd named their worlds after famous colleges back home precisely because the Crustaceans reminded me of snooty academics. I decided not to enlighten Hoon, as I doubted he would get the joke. If he thought it was a compliment, maybe that would help us all get along.

As a secondary thought, I was impressed that this Lobster had the gonads to still be sitting on Yale. He'd pretty much ordered his own death by firing on us. That took a serious belief in oneself, not to mention a willingness to self-sacrifice, which was rare in my experience. Perhaps for the Crustaceans self-sacrifice wasn't an unusual trait. I reminded myself that the "ambassador" that had

54

flown out to my battle station months earlier had done so knowing she was going to die. She'd killed herself and my electronics in an EMP blast, arrogantly insulting me with her last breath.

"Have you tried plugging the hole?" I asked.

"Of course. Unfortunately, the hole is large and the pressure difference between our ocean depths and open space is too great to withstand for any material we've put in place."

I questioned him then on the precise depth and size of the hole in their ocean. From those numbers, I knew our people could calculate the amount of pressure that was involved. Without getting into the math, I was able to estimate that it would be tremendous, more than enough to fold foot-thick steel like tinfoil.

Really, they were talking about *suction*. On one side of the ring in question there was open space. On the other side was a deep, dark ocean. The water at that depth was crushing in the extreme. When faced with a hole, very little friction, and a vast pressure difference, the water must have been gushing through with fantastic force. Probably, wherever it was coming out, it was a spectacular sight. It would turn instantly into ice and form a long, frozen stream like a glittering comet's tail that grew steadily in space.

"How did the hole in your oceans come to exist?" I asked.

"The Macros opened it. Is this not obvious?"

"Yes," I said thoughtfully. "I suppose it is. But I thought your people and the Macros had a treaty and were cooperating."

"During our last battle, we took certain tactical steps that the Macros found unacceptable. They are still technically allies, but they are actively seeking ways around their agreements."

I thought about it. The Crustaceans had operated as marines in our recent battles. They'd played the role my own troops had when we'd been working for the Macros. As I went over their actions in my mind, I figured out what he was talking about.

"You mean they are upset with the way you handled yourself in the Eden system? I recall you attempted to retreat, and then finally surrendered your forces to us. The Macros don't like allies that surrender, right?"

"Correct. The Macros found these actions unacceptable and contrary to our prior agreements. If you ever find yourself serving the machines, know that you have been forewarned."

I snorted. I probably knew more the topic that Hoon did. Star Force had begun its forays into deep space in the belly of a Macro transport. I'd been a mercenary leader then, nothing else.

"I know all about the ruthless nature of the machines," I said. "We served them in the past, before we threw off our slave yokes and rebelled. They used my men like machines, ordering us to attack world after world. They'd planned from the start to grind us down until we were all dead."

"In this rare instance, our experiences have been similar."

"Let's get back to our problem and what we can do to help. Possibly, I can use my ships to evacuate your population. How many individuals do you have on Yale?"

"Approximately one trillion."

My mouth dropped open, and it was a second or two before it closed again. "A *trillion*?" I asked.

"Approximately. Our young are numerous, and quite small. Unfortunately, they are more vulnerable to changes in heat in pressure than are our adults."

"I see," I said. I envisioned clouds of young the size of brine shrimp. "Tell me Hoon, how long do we have? How long until these environmental changes become intolerable to your species and your young begin to succumb?"

"The process you describe has been on-going for many days. Our population was nearly two trillion a few weeks ago."

I was staggered. They'd lost hundreds of billions of lives already? The evil of the Macros was overwhelming.

At the same time, I felt guilty. They'd suffered so much already, and I'd been about to bomb them myself. In a moment of emotion, I'd ordered my ships to unload on their dying civilian populations. Were a few insults and a hundred lost human ships worth that kind of slaughter?

It was a troubling question. But I felt I knew the answer: I'd been in the wrong to give that order.

No matter how irritating our intended victims were, genocide was the business of the machines, not Star Force. I urged myself to remember that in the future.

-8-

We spent another fruitless day watching their oceans drain away while the water that was left heated up steadily. It was dismal and sad.

On the morning of the second day, I ordered Marvin to board a Nano ship and fly down to the surface. I wanted him to observe the phenomenon from within the atmosphere of the planet itself.

We could measure the phenomenon with radar and sonar, but the surface was now obscured. The entire world was wrapped in thick clouds. Really, this was steam, rising up from the warming oceans.

I didn't need to ask Hoon how things were going for his civilian population. The young must have all perished by now. Only the thicker-shelled adults could survive the warm waters and migrate to areas that were cooler. They were clustering around the poles at both ends of the moon, grimly clinging to life.

There wasn't much we could do for them. With hundreds of billions of individuals, any evacuation effort would only save a handful. Probably, the panic created by our efforts would kill more than it would save. If I lowered a ship into the atmosphere with an open hold, thousands would try to board. The results might even capsize the ship. Worse, the aliens were aquatic and would require water aboard the rescue ships in order to breathe for an extended period of time. The weight would be tremendous.

No, rescue and evacuation was out of the question. We had to use what we had to save them in another way.

When he returned from the surface, I summoned Marvin. He was in a state of agitation when we met in the conference room. His tentacles were slashing the chairs and cracking like whips on the walls. Fortunately, smart metal furnishings were self-repairing.

"What have you got for me, Marvin?" I asked.

"I've completed my preliminary study on the situation. The ocean is draining at a slightly decelerating rate as the pressure drops, but the rate of change is not significant."

"How long until the oceans drain all the way down to where this spot is exposed and the process stops?"

"Approximately thirteen days."

"Hmm," I said. "That gives us a little time, then. And it's good to know the oceans won't go all the way down."

"No, they won't."

"So, the situation isn't entirely dire."

"That depends upon our goals."

I frowned at him. "What do you mean?"

"If Star Force wants to colonize this world one day, then the situation is beneficial. If our real mission is as stated, however, this is very bad news."

I stared at him. "Our mission is clear. We're here to help out the Crustaceans. We're here to turn them into allies, one more powerful biotic species to stand shoulder-to-shoulder against the machines."

"Then my report is very dire. The population of this world will be completely annihilated before the thirteen days are up, or shortly thereafter."

I thought about it. "The heat. You're saying it's going to get worse."

"Yes. Every day the hot ice at the bottom of the oceans is further exposed. This world has very deep oceans, but it would be primarily coated in surface ice if it weren't for internal heat from geological sources and the compressed hot ice. Now that the oceans are receding, the cool water in the middle depths of the ocean is being drained away. It is true that the ocean will eventually cool again, but it will take some time. Thirteen days is not long enough."

"Exactly what temperature will the oceans reach by the thirteenth day?"

"The oceans will be near the boiling point by then."

"Two hundred degrees Fahrenheit?" I asked, incredulous.

"Higher than that. This is saltwater, after all. The boiling point is slightly higher."

I massaged my temples. I realized dully that a thousand billion sentient beings were going to be boiled alive over the next two weeks if I didn't get cracking.

"What can we do to stop this?"

"Unknown."

"That's not good enough, Marvin. What have you tried? Have you sent in a probe?"

"I've sent in many submersibles of various makeshift designs. Few of them were able to survive the turbulence on the way down to the aperture. Most stopped transmitting telemetry and readings even before they reached the event-horizon and vanished. The few that did make it all the way down never came back."

"Not surprising, really," I said. "They were programmed to attempt to come back to this side after scanning whatever was on the far side, I assume?"

"Naturally. But there was little hope they would succeed. The gushing pressure on the far side is almost insurmountable. Even if one of the probes did get up enough velocity to punch into the water and reach our side of the ring, they would not survive the impact with high-pressure water."

"Right," I said, thinking of the time I'd come back into the atmosphere of Venus from the blue giant system. "Even hitting gas is like hitting a solid object when you're moving at thousands of miles an hour. Hitting liquid—it would be like smashing into a brick wall. The probes would be obliterated."

Marvin was watching me carefully from multiple angles. This made me nervous. He wasn't asking for anything, and I was the only thing in the room for him to study, but I was still wary.

"You've got something else in your brainbox," I said. "Talk to me."

"I have another possible approach to the situation, Colonel."

"Yeah. Of course you do. Just tell me."

"Would I be held responsible for the possible side-effects of experimentation?"

I laughed. "You want me to sign a prenuptial agreement? I'm sorry Marvin, I'm not going to absolve you of responsibilities for some idea I haven't even heard about yet."

He scrutinized me for another full second before continuing. "The rings have capacities other than the transmission of physical matter between two locations."

"You're talking about relaying transmissions, right? The vibration thing?"

"Not just that. They can be switched on and off. The flow of material can also be reversed. In a sense, they can be opened and closed like doors."

I nodded, seeing what he was getting at. "That's self-evident in this case. The ring was always there, the Crustaceans have told us. But it was inactive. Now, someone has figured out how to turn it on and use it to drain their oceans away. My money is on the Macros of course. They're always looking for a quiet way to kill off their biotic allies that doesn't violate their existing agreements."

Marvin's cameras drew closer to me. "I believe I can gain at least partial control of the ring."

"What? That's great!"

The cameras rose up a little higher, showing he appreciated the praise. I had to wonder why he hadn't brought this up in the first place.

"Yes," he said. "It's something I've been pondering for a long time. It's closely related to the process of using the rings to relay vibrations from on system to another. You see, the rings are really in two places at the same time. That is their secret. There aren't really two rings, there's only one."

I nodded impatiently. "Yeah, that makes sense. This is a wonderful development, Marvin. I want you to grab control of that ring and turn it off."

"Naturally, that would be the happiest outcome."

I paused and my eyes narrowed. "What do you mean, 'would be'? I thought you said you could control it."

"I said I could take control of it. I can put it into program-mode, so to speak. But I have no real idea of what commands to send it. I don't know its protocols or packet control structures. I would have to experiment once I opened a session."

I nodded slowly and my face fell. I was beginning to understand his hesitation. I also understood now why he'd asked for absolution before making an attempt to do this.

"Marvin," I said. "I get it. You're talking about hacking this thing. About attempting to get it to do what you want. But you know you don't understand the interface. You'd be making guesses, and bad things might happen as a result."

"Exactly."

I thought about it. What if Marvin reversed the ring's direction of flow and put the other end of it into the flaming surface of an unknown star? Anything was possible. He might destroy Yale, or save it.

I knew a little about hacking. It was a hit-or-miss thing. Usually, there were a lot of misses before hits were registered. It would take time, and it would be dangerous. But really, what other choice did we have?

"You know Marvin, this interchange represents a shift in your behavior. I think you might be maturing. Instead of hiding the possible disasters that may occur, you brought them up ahead of time. I'm proud of you, Marvin. You're learning about responsibility and honestly, I think you're growing up."

"That's an unexpected compliment, Colonel Riggs."

"Keep it in your RAM," I told him. "I don't give a lot of those."

"Audio saved."

I smiled and summoned Captain Jasmine Sarin and the rest of my command staff. We had a decision to make.

"I think the Crustaceans have to decide, Colonel," was Jasmine's opinion. I wasn't surprised. Everyone felt that way. We'd discussed it for nearly an hour, and the prevailing decision was clear.

I nodded and contacted Professor Hoon. They all listened intently. No one seemed more interested than Marvin himself. He desperately wanted to make the attempt, of course. His main interest in this meeting was spreading the blame for it afterward, in case it turned into a royal shit-bomb. No one could blame the crazy robot if he'd gotten us all to agree it was risky.

Professor Hoon's answer was quick and decisive.

"Yes, by all means. Make the attempt. But be warned: there will be an investigation afterward. If this is an elaborate ruse to increase the speed of our world's demise, there will be a censure forthcoming."

I tried not to smile. After all, we were talking about billions of possible deaths. The fact they were all doomed in the near future seemed almost immaterial to them. What mattered more was the correctness of the procedure. I thought about asking Hoon who he thought was going to perform this investigation and censure, but held back.

"Understood, Professor Hoon. We'll take every precaution."

"We also request dissemination of the results," Hoon continued.

I hesitated. This was a sore point among my staff. If we did gain some level of control over the ring, they didn't want to give that powerful technological advantage away to the Crustaceans. They'd been hostile just a month ago. They were cooperating now, but were not really our allies.

"We will consider it after the successful conclusion of the operation. Possibly, we will utterly fail, in which case there's nothing to disseminate. If it does work out and relations between our governments are normalized we can consider sharing technologies. We have a lot of things to share, far more than just this little trick."

"We accept your conditions, because we have no choice."

I turned to Marvin and the rest of them. Marvin was barely able to crouch at the conference table, he was so excited. No one else was sitting within a chair or two of him for fear they'd get slapped by a tentacle or knocked in the head by a drifting camera.

"Can I proceed, Colonel?" he asked.

"Yes," I said, "there's no time to waste. See if you can turn off that damned ring, Marvin."

"Channel open," he said.

Suddenly, Marvin froze up. Every tentacle stopped moving, and he resembled a still-motion photograph. The effect was uncanny. No human could have gone from such a state of agitation to a completely motionless state. It was as if someone had switched off his primary generators, but he still had enough residual power to maintain rigidity.

"What's wrong with him, Kyle?" Sandra asked.

"I think he's okay," I said, standing up and walking close. "I think he's switched over all his computing power to this hacking effort."

"I think he's locked up," Kwon said, poking at a camera near his elbow.

Marvin made no response, so Kwon prodded him more vigorously. "I see this all the time. He crashed. He needs to reboot, or something."

I waved Kwon back. "Just give him some air," I said, getting nervous. I was as worried as the rest of them, but tried not to show it.

About a minute after he'd frozen in place, Marvin finally came back to life. We all began breathing again in relief.

"Transmission sent," he said.

"Well? How did it go? Give me a full report, Marvin."

"Impossible," he said, "to verbalize a full report of my transmissions would require a period of time longer than your projected lifespan, Colonel Riggs."

"Yeah, okay. Give me the condensed version. What did you do?"

"I sent a sequence of likely codes to the ring."

"How many of them did you send?"

"Just over six billion."

"Did you try everything then? What are the results?"

"Unknown."

I brought up the display of Yale on the conference table. The world looked pretty much the same. But I knew the currents of a worldwide ocean would take longer than a minute to reshape themselves.

"What do you mean, 'unknown'? Did you get through to the ring or not? Did it accept any of those six billion commands?"

"Yes. It accepted one. The last one I sent."

"Okay... So you sent a barrage of spam at the ring, and apparently it finally took one command and executed it. That sounds like blind hacking, Marvin. I was under the impression you had some idea of what you were doing."

"It was not a sophisticated algorithm," he admitted.

"What command did it finally take?" Sandra demanded suddenly. "What did you tell the ring to do?"

"I have no idea. That's why I stopped when it accepted a command. In order to learn how to control an unknown device, experimentation is required. The next step is to observe its behavior, and thereby update my knowledge base."

"I don't like the sound of this," Sandra said. "I thought you knew what you were doing. It sounds like you just pushed every button on the remote control until something happened to the TV."

63

"An accurate analogy," Marvin said.

"But what if you found the self-destruct button?" she demanded.

"I doubt that function exists. But if it did, and I had managed to trigger it, we would have seen dramatic results by now."

All of us stared down at the conference table. Yale was depicted there, blue-white and lovely, filling the screen under our collective elbows.

Everyone was squinting. Several gritted their teeth, as if wincing in pain or worry. What had we done to this beautiful, stricken world? Had we made things even worse somehow for the hapless inhabitants?

Like Marvin, I figured we would find out soon enough.

-9-

"Professor Hoon is attempting to contact us, Colonel Riggs," Marvin said. "He seems agitated."

"Probably because you did something horrible," Sandra said.

I hesitated before I told Marvin to open the channel. Hoon was in a much better position than we were to know what had happened down there. Very possibly, Marvin had turned the suction effect up a notch, shifting the controls to *high*.

"Aren't you going to talk to him, Kyle?" Sandra asked.

"Yeah, sure. Open the channel and start translating, Marvin."

"Channel open."

"Professor Hoon," I said, doing my best to sound upbeat. "We've made some preliminary tests, and—"

"I'm astounded," said Hoon, interrupting me. "All of my academic staff have been forced to reevaluate your ratings. It's obvious to me that our screening systems are inadequate. We've misjudged you by a startling margin."

"Well," I began, uncertain where he was going with this, "I can safely tell you I've been misjudged more than once."

"Yes. Your seemingly simplistic, emotional responses to stimuli had us fooled. Despite measuring at a nearly bestial level of reasoning, your species has performed a miraculous feat of engineering. We're trying to explain it, and would like your help in investigating the matter."

"Um, okay. We can do that. But first let me ask: the results are positive?"

There was a hesitation on the channel of several seconds.

65

"You're response casts suspicion on your accomplishments, Colonel Riggs. It indicates a lack of confidence in the results, which in turn indicates a lack of competency in the instigator."

"Look," I said, becoming annoyed again despite my intentions. "We've performed an experimental attempt to improve your conditions. We don't have the same level of equipment at the scene to measure the results. I'm just asking you for confirmation."

"But you omitted a key element of the confirmation query. You have not asked us to confirm a specific change in the situation. I'm afraid this is a familiar pattern. When an apprentice queries his master in this fashion, it often indicates one of two possibilities: either he cheated, or he got lucky."

I looked at Marvin. The Lobsters had nailed it this time. If we had solved their problem, we'd both cheated and gotten lucky. I didn't want to tell them that, however. For one thing, this race bugged the hell out of me. But also, they might be less grateful and willing to work with us if they knew the truth.

"Professor Hoon," I said sternly, "we in Star Force are unaccustomed to accusations of incompetence. Let's review the facts: you've been dealing with a catastrophic technical problem for an extended period of time. You failed to solve the problem or to mitigate it in any significant way. You called us for help, we arrived to render assistance, and you attacked us."

"We've explained our reasoning. Repetition of points previously made is not customary for our species."

"I'm not asking you to repeat anything. I'm making a point. Despite your failures and your thoughtless attack, we've managed to fix your technical problems within hours. After all this, your prejudice against Star Force has led you to yet another folly: Rather than graciously assuming the role of the student at his master's feet, you've persisted in coming up with fantasies. Here at Star Force, we deal in measurable facts. Now, as the Principal Investigator in this experiment, I've requested twice for confirmation of critical data."

"You've not specified what data you are looking for."

"I want a raw report. Specifying what we expect to see will bias your input."

"Ah," said Professor Hoon, as if in sudden understanding. "I apologize. We've misconstrued your intentions. I apologize again for our suspicious line of questioning. You are correct. In this situation we must assume the lowly role of apprentice, despite the fact we're unaccustomed to it. Perhaps there is bias in our system. Interesting. I will demand a full analysis of our entire interchange later today—but never mind that now. The key fact is that the ring in the bottom of our sea is no longer transferring liquid mass off-planet."

I smiled, and everyone around me smiled. Only Kwon leaned back in his chair, bored. The rest of them were breathing sighs of relief.

Sandra got up out of her chair, walked to Marvin and hugged his chassis.

"You pulled it off, you crazy robot," she said.

Surprised, Marvin lofted his cameras and viewed her from every angle, but he didn't flinch away. I chuckled. It was probably his first hug from a real, live girl.

"You really do like nerds, don't you?" Kwon asked her.

"Yes," she admitted.

I wasn't quite sure how to take that, so I ignored it. I considered the situation with Hoon. It was time to press for concessions from him, I decided. When would it be a better time? We'd just saved a third of their population.

"Professor Hoon," I said officiously. "Now that the current crisis has been averted, I would ask you to consider another matter."

"I'm very busy, but I'll allow the interruption on this occasion."

"You'll be glad you took time from your busy schedule to listen to this, Hoon. I'm offering you a golden opportunity, right here, right now. Switch allegiances. Leave the service of the Macros and join our federation of worlds. Star Force will be officially obliged to protect you once you do so. Cast off your people's chains. Be a free biotic species. What do you say?"

"An odd appeal," Hoon said. "We are currently at peace with the machines. Why would we declare war on them by allying with your organization?"

"Because the machines are traitors. They turned on that ring and drained your oceans, you realize that, don't you?"

"Obviously. Star Force lacks the intellectual and technical capacity to have managed this achievement."

I almost pointed out to him that if we'd just turned it off, we might have been the ones to turn it on, but stopped myself. I decided that wouldn't help my argument.

"The machines aren't at peace with you, not really. They have an agreement with you, and will stick to the letter of it, but not the spirit. They will try with regularity to circumvent it and destroy your population, even while demanding you fight their wars for them. We've beaten the machines time and again, including doing great harm to your forces. If you're in this war anyway, why not join the winning side?"

"There are compelling points to your arguments, Colonel. But I'm afraid we must deny your request."

"Just like that? Don't you have a committee to report to, or something? Shouldn't the others be consulted? I'm surprised you have the unilateral power to make such a high level policy decision."

"I don't. Not as an individual. But it was previously determined you were likely to make this type of request at some point, as you've made it before. At our committee hearings days ago, before we summoned you to aid us, it was decided to refuse your offer. The vote was unanimous, by the way."

I rested my chin on my hands. These people were tiring to deal with. "Can I at least hear your reasoning for the decision?"

"Certainly, although be forewarned, we aren't interested in pleas. The decision is final. We've carefully examined the size of your fleet, and judged it to be inadequate to stop the next Macro wave of ships."

"What about our battle station?" I asked. "We've built it up and the fortification can withstand an assault even bigger than the last one."

"Agreed," Hoon said. "Unfortunately, that does not help us or alter our calculus. The battle station protects the Eden system, but does nothing to stop a Macro invasion of the Thor system."

He was right, I knew. He was making the same argument Miklos had made to me days ago. We'd built a tremendous bulwark at a critical bottleneck, but it didn't solve all our problems. The fortress couldn't move. If a fight occurred somewhere else, it would be useless.

"All right," I said. "I understand your reasoning. But if matters should change, if there should be a clear change in the balance of power, I would strongly suggest you reconsider. Star Force doesn't want to go to war with your people again. That's why we're out here saving your bacon today."

68

"'Saving our bacon' is an odd and potentially offensive reference. That portion of your comments has been deleted from your statement to make it more comprehensible."

"It's an idiom," I explained. "If you witness shifts in the balance of power in the near future, I want to you to reconsider our offer. Make your decisions very carefully."

"We always do."

The conversation went on for a minute or two, but the critical elements had been covered. We'd saved their world, but they weren't ready to join us despite the fact their current allies were trying to kill them.

I understood their reasoning, to a degree. They knew they were weak militarily and what they really wanted was some kind of neutrality. Unfortunately for them, neither Star Force nor the Macros were in a peace-loving mood.

As the crisis seemed at least temporarily averted, I headed for the mess hall to eat the first real meal I'd had in days. Then I had a shower and flopped onto my bunk.

Sandra joined me a while later and we had celebratory sex. Today hadn't gone the way I'd thought it might, and I was happy about that. So was she. Somehow, she figured I was a hero now, and Marvin was an even bigger hero.

"That robot is the strangest thing," she said. "He's a traitor one minute and a savior of billions the next. I really don't know what to think of him."

"Well, you're probably trying to understand him as a human personality. He really isn't one of us. That's not entirely a bad thing, but you can never forget it while dealing with him. His motivations are his alone. He's effectively a species of one."

"When you talk like that, it makes me think we should quietly turn him off."

I looked at her in surprise. Her head was resting on my chest, and her eyes looked up at me seriously. I could tell she meant it.

"Why?" I asked. "You just got done telling me he was a big hero."

"Sometimes he is, but sometimes he's evil. Remember what he did when experimenting on the Centaurs? On their young ones?"

"I try not to think about that."

"Yeah, me too. But something you said forced me to start thinking: You said he was as species of one. But it doesn't have to stay that way. What if he decides to reproduce? To copy himself? What if there were a thousand Marvins—or even a million? He's much smarter than the Nanos or the Macros. An army of Marvins might kill us all, if they decided it was for the best. Maybe they'd do it just for curiosity's sake, for the fun of cutting us up and poking around in our guts."

We both fell silent after that. A few minutes later, Sandra fell asleep with her head still resting on my chest. It was a nice feeling, and I was very tired, but I found I couldn't let go and relax.

I laid there for the next hour, listening to her soft, rhythmic breathing. My thoughts didn't let sleep come. Her words had disturbed me.

-10-

Our ships spent two more full days hanging over Yale. Captain Sarin had joined us with her carrier, and the fighters patrolled constantly. I was impressed by her carefully maintained vigilance.

We watched the ring in the seabed that Marvin had somehow switched off. For the first day or so, we were nervous, waiting for something bad to happen. But nothing did and by the end of the second day, I began to feel confident that we'd solved the problem.

Below us, the oceans settled and the storm clouds dissipated. It was going to take years for the climate to reorganize itself. The planet had lost about three percent of its mass, and that translated into about four miles of ocean depth gone down the drain. There were spots of land now on a world that had previously been covered by seamless ocean.

The new lands were alien-looking. The freshly revealed sea floor was white and rocky. The newly revealed lands formed islands which dotted the surface of Yale. These islands steamed and were covered in rotting seaweeds and dead fish. Seen from above, they reminded me of the jagged teeth of an ancient leviathan, revealed for the first time in a billion years.

We sent down probes to the ring when the currents and storms had subsided. But when the probes went through the ring, which was still under a thousand feet of water, they simply found the seabed on the far side. They weren't transported anywhere. As far as we could tell, the ring had truly been switched off.

I was about to give orders for Star Force personnel to land and investigate the region on foot, when a message came in from Miklos,

71

who I'd left in charge of the Eden system. A communique from Earth had been received at Shadowguard.

The rings allowed for more or less instantaneous communication between star systems, but we rarely heard from Earth these days and when we did I had left explicit instructions: I was to be immediately alerted. I took the hardcopy to my office and read it over twice.

The message was from General Kerr, who had commanded the last fleet from Earth and who had personally led the attack against Eden. Despite a long history of conflict, Kerr and I had always been able to talk man-to-man. Essentially, the message said he was coming out for a visit, and that he wanted to discuss normalizing relations between Crow's Empire and Star Force.

I was elated, but the rest of my staff was hostile.

"He's coming out here to spy!" declared Kwon with absolute certitude. "Trust me, Colonel Riggs. I've known my share of dictators. Crow is just like the rest. Dictators only send out ambassadors to do two things: to spy, or to get free stuff. Don't let General Kerr anywhere near Eden."

I opened my mouth to respond, but didn't get the words out before the next objection came out of Sandra.

"Kwon's right," she said. "But I would handle it differently. When he gets here, let's capture him and make him a prisoner. That will give them one less good commander for their side. We can tell them he had an accident aboard his ship, and his people were all lost."

I looked at her in surprise. "Remind me never to put you in charge of diplomacy," I told her.

She crossed her arms, sat back in her chair and glared at me.

"Possibly," Captain Sarin said, "we could be more diplomatic. But I don't trust Kerr any more than the rest of this group. It's my suggestion we meet with him in the Helios system on a neutral ship in neutral space. That way, he can't learn anything of our operational strength."

"Well, I'm glad no one here feels restrained when airing their opinions," I said. "But I'm going to let them in."

There was a chorus of complaints and warnings. I lifted my hands and waved for quiet.

72

"Don't freak out," I said. "I'm not a fool. I'm not going to give them the ten-dollar tour. They will see exactly what I want them to see."

"May I speak?" Sandra asked angrily.

"Be my guest."

"The moment their ship crosses into our space it will be cataloguing and counting every gun we have. That has got to be at least part of the purpose of this effort."

"Of course it is," I said. "But their ship won't be coming into our space. We'll meet them at the doorstep, in the Helios system on the far side of the ring from the Eden system. We'll take their committee off their ship and transport them into our space under our control."

"I like that idea," Kwon said. "They can't see much from the window of a spaceship. When I look out these windows, all I see is the sun, maybe not even that. Not even the planets are big enough to see without instruments."

"Exactly," I said nodding to Kwon. I could always count on him to see logic. He almost always took my side.

"I still don't like it," Sandra said. "He's up to something. They'll bring something in. Something in their personal baggage. A spying tool or a bomb, maybe."

"I have to agree," Captain Sarin said. "We can't trust them. Remember Marvelena."

I winced at the mentioning of that name. Marvelena had been a lovely, voluptuous spy who had attempted to assassinate me. She'd done rather poorly, and had paid for her failure with her life.

"I understand your concerns and I share them," I said. "But they can't have a scanner small enough to fit on their person which would be capable of reading much about our fleets."

"What about weapons, Kyle?" Sandra asked. "What about assassination?"

I shrugged. "The moment they cross into our space, we'll do a body scan and make sure they're clean. Remember, they aren't nanotized. They won't be much of a match for our people, even if they're armed. But don't worry, I'll keep them under guard anyway."

I could tell none of them were really happy about it, but the decision had been made, and they all knew it. I wasn't known for changing my mind when it was made up, so they quickly gave up

73

trying. Still, I could tell they were unconvinced, except possibly for Kwon.

"All right," I said. I was annoyed with them, but I managed to keep my irritation out of my voice. "I know you all think I'm making a rash move. But the stakes are very high. Let me explain my own thinking: We need to reconnect with Earth. The possible benefits for Star Force and all humanity are immeasurable. We could become trading partners, and inevitably there would be immigration. We need people out here. There are barely forty thousand humans in the Eden System, not enough to fill these lovely worlds for a thousand years. Most importantly, this is a chance to ally with Earth for the next round with the Macros. Every member of our species must come together to stand against the machines. Divided, we'll fall eventually."

Jasmine leaned forward, frowning. "I think our primary worry is Crow himself," she said. "We all know him. We know what he's capable of. I think he's grown worse and worse as time has passed. He's become a megalomaniac. I was there, Kyle. I've seen him as Emperor Crow."

"I know Jack Crow very well. I agree, he's not the man I flew with in the beginning—or maybe he is, but he has changed for the worse. Still, we've always been able to come to some kind of arrangement in the past. I'm willing to give him another chance."

No one met my eye.

"So," I said, clapping my hands together loudly. "Let's get to the details. How are we going to pull this off?"

Slowly, they came around to helping me solve this part of the problem. Involving them in the minutiae and taking their suggestions on details helped massage damaged egos. I'd overruled them all, and I knew that could cause sour feelings. I had to give them something to fuss about.

In the end, the plan they came up with was simple and clever. I contacted Miklos to set things up.

Boarding the cruiser *Lazaro*, Sandra, Kwon and I flew back to the battle station. I'd left Captain Sarin behind in the Thor system with her carrier and most of the fleet. When we reached the battle station, I transferred over to the new carrier ship, the *Defiant*. It was the third ship to bear that name in Star Force. Miklos had named it himself, as was customary.

74

Miklos stood on the massive hangar deck when I came out to meet him. It was amazing. There were rows of fighters and cylindrical launch tubes through which they could be deployed. When the fighters launched, they didn't use their primary engines. Instead, they were propelled out using gravity repellers in the tubes. The technology was impressive, because the hangar deck itself was pressurized. The tubes also acted as air locks, and the released gas helped launch the tiny ships that much faster.

"Spacious!" I said while touring the hangar. "This is the first time I've boarded one of these motherships. I never got the chance to inspect Captain Sarin's *Gatre*."

"The ships are essentially identical," Miklos said, "but I have made minor improvements in the design of *Defiant*."

"I'm impressed," I said as we traveled down a long echoing passage that traveled along the spine of the ship.

We soon reached the officer's quarters. These chambers were simple steel cubes with nanite-laden smart doors. I was stunned by their starkness, but I tried not to let on. Even the bunks were flat planes of shiny steel.

"The accommodations are bare-bones..." I said, "but I guess that's to be expected."

"Exactly sir," Miklos said. "We have very few amenities for such a large vessel. I had a very tight schedule to meet to get her up into space on time. But the ship is effective. She is a beast of war, not a luxury liner."

Miklos proudly walked at my side down another echoing corridor to the ship's bridge. Here, he had not spared any expense. He had installed our best sensory systems, shock-absorbers and consoles. Even the brainboxes were veterans, I could tell by their serial numbers.

"Did you take some of these gunnery control systems from Welter Station, Commodore?"

Miklos cleared his throat. "I thought it might be for the best, sir. These ships were built to fly directly into a war situation. I didn't want baby brainboxes in place, cutting their teeth in battle, so to speak. The boxes come from the battle station, while new ones have been installed there. I felt it was better to have the fresh, inexperienced components placed on the battle station where they would have time to learn. Eventually, they will operate at top efficiency.

I nodded, thinking it over. I decided it had been a wise decision to outfit the two carriers with the veteran boxes rather than having the ships' AI be hopelessly green.

"Well done," I said. "We'll fly *Defiant* out into the Helios system with a full complement of fighters and crews. We'll meet the Earth ship and make no mention of this design being new. We'll just act natural about it, like it's no big deal. When they ask about it, we'll tell them it's one of our carrier ships, without an explanation. If we don't tell them we only have two of these monsters, they'll naturally assume we have several of them."

Miklos liked the plan, and the voyage began. At first, the plan went without a hitch. We flew to the Helios system and sat there at the ring in our carrier. A single ship approached us.

I knew right away when I saw it that Crow was trying to impress us just as hard as we were trying to impress him. The ship was a monster. About the size of two Macro cruisers sandwiched together, the vessel was an oblong rectangle that bristled with equipment, sensors and gun tubes. It probably displaced more mass than our carrier.

"That, gentlemen, is a battleship," I told my staff as they eyed the ship in concern.

We gave them docking instructions and waited tensely. I'd have been nervous if I hadn't been surrounded by twenty gunboats and several destroyers. Altogether, I was certain we outgunned the battleship.

When channel request came in hailing us, I nodded to Miklos to answer.

"This is Commodore Nicolai Miklos," he said. "Please dispatch a pinnace to transfer your committee to our ship."

The other ship slowed and stopped only fifty thousand miles from our bow. She was huge. I tried to look like I didn't care, and that seemed to calm my crew. They stopped murmuring and staring.

"This is General Kerr of Earth's Imperial forces," said a very familiar voice. It had a southern twang and a Texas swagger to it. "I don't want to talk to any underlings," Kerr said. "Get Kyle Riggs on the horn, pronto...please."

76

Miklos looked at me again. I nodded to him curtly. We had a plan, and I wanted to stick to it. I knew it was possible this monstrous ship had come out here for the express purpose of giving us a sucker-punch. If Kerr thought I wasn't aboard, he was much less likely to take a shot and unload at close range.

"I'm sorry sir," Miklos said. "I'm in command of this ship. You will be transferred aboard and transported to Shadowguard. There, you'll meet with Colonel Riggs."

"Shadowguard? What the hell is that? Some kind of penal colony?"

"No sir, it is a fortress. A command center on Eden-8."

"Hmm, so Riggs is dodging me, is that it? Too scared to come out and talk like men? Why should I put myself at risk? Why should I trust you lot when you won't return the favor?"

"General, may I remind you that you requested this meeting. Our last encounter with Imperial forces was less than cordial. If you are as you claim to be—an ambassador—then transporting yourself and your staff to our ship should not be a hardship."

"Cagey Riggs...making me come to him. Well, tell him for me I won't be on my knees. Not unless he chops off my legs at the shinbone!"

"We have no such intentions, sir," Miklos said patiently. "Will you be coming aboard?"

I had to smile. The General had always been demanding and flamboyant. He was, however, a very sharp man. Sometimes I thought his entire act was designed to throw off casual observers. He came off as an arrogant blowhard, but he was dangerous.

Kerr grumbled some more, but eventually he boarded a small ship and floated across the last few intervening miles and docked with my new carrier. I headed down to the hangar deck to meet him.

I surprised myself as I walked the long passages. I was actually looking forward to seeing the General again. I didn't trust him, however. Not even as far as I could throw him—which was a considerable distance.

-11-

Kerr was naturally annoyed to meet me on the hangar deck.
"I thought you weren't here!" he roared, not even bothering to extend his hand.

I let my hand drop slowly. "I didn't know you cared so much about my whereabouts, General."

He eyed me suspiciously for a few seconds. "I don't like starting off talks like this—with lies and tricks. What's going on here, Riggs? What are you trying to pull? Am I under arrest or what?"

As he spoke, a number of my stern-face marines approached the General and his party. They had guns—but they had instruments in their hands as well. They ran the scanners over every member of the General's staff, all six of them.

"They're only here to make sure you are unarmed and not carrying any kind of contraband."

"What? You think I smoke weed, boy?"

I chuckled. "No sir, I was thinking more along the lines of bombs, or transmission devices."

"Found it!" shouted one marine. He tugged at the waistband of a major in General Kerr's group. A device with dangling wires popped out.

"That's nothing but a music player!" Kerr complained.

"We'll check it out and return it if—"

"She's wearing one too," said another marine. He pointed to a small young lady wearing a lieutenant's bars. He was pointing to her chest.

"Harassment, pure and simple!" Kerr declared.

The woman looked at Kerr, and he nodded slightly. She reached up under her shirt and removed a device. I was under the impression she'd pulled it out of her bra.

I had to smile. It was a game, but quite possibly a deadly one. When we finally had all the devices on a table, they were analyzed and identified. Scanners, recorders and compact radios designed to transmit coded data that resembled static or background radiation. There was nothing deadly, other than their sidearms.

I picked up the General's revolver and returned it to him. He looked at it in surprise.

"I can wear this?"

I nodded. "Yes sir. But I don't suggest you shoot any of my marines with it, not even as a joke. You'll seriously piss them off and I can't be held responsible for their natural reaction."

General Kerr snorted, but he strapped his gun into place. He looked pleased to have it back on his hip.

Kerr then proceeded to introduce his staff to me. I was immediately bored. I disliked shaking hands and mumbling greetings, but I guess it's all part of the job. When I came to the woman who'd had a scanner in her bra, however, I perked up. She was quite attractive, almost innocent-looking. She appeared to be of mixed heritage, part Asian and part Caucasian. It was an entrancing combination.

"This is Alexa. She's the daughter of a friend of mine, Field Marshal Brighton."

"Lieutenant," I said, taking her hand gently and nodding to her.

"The famous Colonel Riggs," she said. "You seem less dangerous in person."

I smiled. "The news vids lie."

"Not always!" Kerr said, stepping closer.

I let Alexa's hand drop reluctantly.

"Let me give you a tour of the ship," I said.

The party followed me out of the hangar. As we left it, a shadow dropped down from the steel trusses in ceiling. No one else noticed, I don't think, other than me. It was Sandra of course, stalking the group like a hunting panther. I went back over the greetings in my mind. I bit my lip briefly as I thought of how I'd greeted Alexa differently and personally. I hoped Sandra hadn't witnessed that and taken it the wrong way. It was a faint hope.

Partway through the tour, Kerr stopped and interrupted me. He stared at me in sudden concern.

"We're moving, aren't we?" he asked.

"Why, yes General. Of course we are. As I said before, we're on our way to Shadowguard."

"And my crew back on the *Carrington* just let you slip away with me aboard? Without any kind of communication authorizing it?"

I smiled at him. I'd had Marvin compile the General's voice from a large variety of recordings in order to imitate him. Marvin had done such a good job, the battleship had just stood there and watched as we slipped away.

"I'm surprised that you're surprised, sir," I said. "This ship does have good stabilizers, but any Fleet midshipman would have known we were underway."

"You're avoiding the question, Riggs. This is typical of you. Bait and switch. The old shell game. I've been conned again."

"Nonsense, General," I said. "I told you upfront what the invitation entailed and you accepted."

Breathing hard, the General waved me forward. I had no idea what he had intended to happen, but apparently this sequence of events was not to his liking. I wasn't sure if this indicated hostile intent or not, but I was glad things weren't going his way. I'd once read a quote that went like this: "When holding a snake, it's best not to let go." That summed up my theory on interaction with Kerr and Crow. They were both snakes, in their own individual ways. I had to keep them off their game, surprising them, never letting them make a move on their own. Otherwise, one of these snakes was going to bite me in the ass eventually.

After the tour was over, I showed them their stainless steel cubicles. They weren't impressed. We'd dolled them up a bit with blankets and pillows, but there was no hiding the fact their quarters made prison cells look luxurious.

"Riggs, I have to say I'm not surprised. You people have so much iron in your butts you don't even need a mattress. That's what this is meant to convey, isn't it? That you're tougher than we are?"

"Not really, General," I said. "Honestly, we didn't even think about it."

"You've still got nerve endings, don't you boy?"

"Yes sir. They just don't get as much use as yours do."

80

He glared at me and huffed. I left him there and walked away. I was headed up to the bridge when I heard soft footsteps behind me. I turned, expecting to see Sandra.

I was surprised that it was the lovely Lieutenant Alexa Brighton instead. I smiled at her immediately.

"You should go back to your quarters now, Lieutenant," I said.

"Why? Are we under arrest?"

"Not exactly, but I've got a lot to do and I'm sure you're tired after your long journey out from Earth. If you sleep now, you'll arrive at Shadowguard well-rested. There's more to see there."

"I'm looking forward to it. But I'm not tired at the moment."

We stared at one another for several awkward seconds. She took two steps closer and smiled up at me. I like the shape of her eyes and mouth. She was quite young, no more than twenty-five.

"Call me Alexa," she said.

"Okay."

"Could you show me around a little more, Colonel?" she asked. "I have some things I'd like to discuss."

"Uh..." I said, looking at her.

She took a few more steps closer until she was within arm's reach. Her hand lifted slowly toward me, as if to touch my shoulder.

I barely saw it coming, but Alexa was taken completely by surprise. A shadow dashed up behind her, grabbed her rising hand and twisted it around behind her back. Her gentle, peaceful expression changed into one of shock and agony.

"Sandra, let her go. Don't you dare break her arm."

"She's trouble, Kyle. I've been watching her almost as much as you have."

"I'm sure you have. Now let her go. She's unarmed."

Reluctantly, Sandra let Alexa go. The young woman whirled around angrily, but with one look at Sandra's murderous eyes, her protests died in her throat. She pushed past and ran down the corridor holding her shoulder which was probably numb and throbbing.

"Cry-baby," Sandra said. "I didn't even break it."

"Are you sure?"

"I would have felt the bones crack."

"Sandra, may I remind you I'm trying to make peace with Earth? That this is a diplomatic meeting between the Empire and Star Force?"

81

"That's how you see it. I see it as a security risk."

I sighed and headed back up to the bridge. I knew there was no point in arguing with Sandra. Quite possibly, she was right anyway. This girl might be star-struck by me, or she might be putting on an act. Either way, it was probably for the best that I kept my distance.

"Do you think she's pretty, Kyle?" Sandra asked me as she stalked along at my side.

"I guess so... In a childish way."

"That's bullshit."

I tried to keep my face neutral. I knew she was watching me closely. I'd found Lieutenant Brighton very attractive, but I wasn't going to let Sandra know that. The lieutenant would live longer if I pretended I didn't care about her.

"Look, she's just somebody's kid who got assigned to coming out here to further her career. You need to control that jealous streak of yours."

"She'd better not be planning to further her career with your help," Sandra said dangerously.

"If advancing her career is the plan, she should be running from me," I said with a laugh. "I'm not exactly on Emperor Crow's A-list—more like his 'most wanted' list."

Sandra fell silent, but I could tell she was pissed off about Alexa. I knew enough about women to take the "silent treatment" for the gift it was. I kept my mouth shut all the way up to the bridge.

I checked every report in my queue and read about a thousand emails. When I finally retired to my quarters, Sandra shadowed me. She still wasn't talking, and that was just fine with me. There were less than nine hours left before we arrived at Eden-8 and slid into orbit. I was tired and didn't want to waste them.

I flopped out on my bunk, arms over my head. I didn't even bother with a shower. About ninety seconds after my head hit the pillow, I fell into a light dream. It was a good dream, something about hunting crows in cornfields and orchards with an old .22 rifle I had as a kid.

I had a thin smile on my lips when I was rudely awakened. I grunted in surprise as a weight thumped down on my chest. My arms snapped up and gripped my assailant. I squeezed—it was reflexive to do so.

"Ow," Sandra said. "I can't believe this, but you're actually hurting me. You can't do that to a normal person, Kyle. You'd break their bones."

My eyes fluttered open. Sandra was sitting on my chest like an insolent housecat. I had her wrists clamped firmly in my hands. She struggled, but couldn't free herself.

Like all Star Force marines, we had both been nanotized. That meant our bloodstreams were teeming with millions of tiny robots. These robots had the job of healing our bodies, but more importantly, they had already altered them. During an excruciating multi-hour ordeal, they changed the internal structures of any human they were injected into. The Nano technology was beyond our own, but we used it wherever we could. Our bones were harder, our muscles more dense. We moved faster and hit harder than any other humans in history.

Even with all those physical improvements, Sandra and I stood out as unique. Like very few others, we'd gone through additional treatments. We'd been improved by taking microbial baths administered by Marvin. The Microbes in question were a sentient species, capable of collective thought and action. They'd worked on our bodies at a biochemical level, altering them. As a result, Sandra was one of the fastest beings I'd ever encountered, and I was one of the strongest.

She writhed in my grip as I came fully awake.

"Let me go, or I'm going to kick you," she said.

I kept my grip and smiled. "When you jump on a sleeping marine's chest, you've got some explaining to do."

"I'll kick you."

"I don't think so."

She glared at me darkly, and I let her go a moment later. I was having fun, but I also wanted to have sex again at some point in this relationship.

Sandra jerked her arms away from my hands and crossed them under her breasts. She stayed sitting on my chest, however. I didn't complain about that. She had been a fit, shapely young woman when I first met her. After undergoing physical transformations, she was as cut and sculpted as an Olympic gymnast. Due to my own physical alterations, her weight didn't bother me at all. To me, she felt as if she weighed ten pounds or so.

"Clearly, you want to tell me something," I said.

"I'm feeling jealous."

"You don't say? Never would have suspected it."

"You liked that girl. She was normal, soft, young. You *liked* her."

"She seemed friendly. But she's only a kid to me."

She slapped me across the face. She moved so fast, I couldn't react quickly enough to grab her wrist. A trickle of blood ran from my cheeks where they'd been smashed into my teeth. A normal man would have been seriously injured. In my case, it didn't really hurt, but it did sting a bit.

"What was that for?"

"For lying. I was a young girl when we first met. You went for me quickly enough. Don't forget I can read your physical responses, Kyle. I could hear your blood pound in your veins. I could hear your breathing accelerate."

"Yeah? Did Alexa get turned on too?"

I shouldn't have said that. I *knew* I shouldn't have said that. But I was stinging a bit from the bash in the mouth. I was tired, and sometimes when I'm tired my mouth gets one second ahead of my brain. This was one of those times.

Her hand flashed out of the dark again. This time, I knew it was coming. I had my own hand up to block hers.

Unfortunately, I'd guessed wrong. I'd expected her to go for a right-cross again. But she surprised me, using her left. She was ambidextrous, and I should have anticipated the move, but I didn't. She caught me a good one, slamming me in the right ear. This hurt even more than my cheek did. Something about getting hit in the ear—even after all my treatments, it hurt.

I grunted and grabbed her. We grappled for a second, and I flipped her over on the bed and landed on top of her. A normal woman would have been crushed down by my weight and pinned, helpless.

But Sandra was no normal woman. My weight meant nothing to her. She kneed me, twisted and I was flying across the room. She was so fast!

I bounced off the lockers and came up in a crouch. We faced one another, breathing hard.

We'd fought before, but this was more serious than usual. The whole thing surprised me.

"What's wrong?" I asked.

She heaved a huge sigh and stretched out on the bed. "I'm sorry," she said.

I stood straight, but I didn't step closer to her. Sandra was moody, but this was unusual, even for her. I didn't say anything. Blood dribbled from my chin, but I ignored it.

"I don't know," she said. "I suppose it's because she's a normal human girl. Younger, prettier, but most of all...normal. I know you miss that. I hate that she's something you want. I hate that she's something I can't be."

I opened the lockers and rummaged out a bottle of vodka. Usually, I was a beer man. But tonight I felt the need for something stronger. I poured and she appeared at my side.

"I don't like it straight," she said.

Funny comments swam in my head, but this time I managed to stop them before they came out of my mouth. Instead, I got out a mixer and gave her a drink. Our glasses clinked and ice cubes tinkled inside.

We drank our beverages in relative silence. I didn't bother to make up lies, telling her I wasn't attracted to Alexa, and that she was prettier than that Earth-girl tramp. I didn't even bother to apologize for the changes in my heart rate when the girl came near. She was too smart for that kind of talk. More importantly, I knew that if I made any more false moves, she might go off again. I did my damnedest to say nothing at all.

So we drank, and afterward we made love. She'd always been a demanding, strenuous lover, but this time our activities were more intense than usual.

It was good, and when I finally did get some sleep, it was the sleep of exhaustion.

-12-

We made planetfall precisely on time over Eden-8. I sipped coffee and blinked my red eyes. The nanites cleared the toxins left over from alcohol faster than normal human livers could ever manage, but somehow I still felt hard liquor in my brain the next day.

"There's a report from the task force in the Thor system, sir," Miklos said.

I glanced at him. "Anything serious?"

"If it was I would have awakened you."

I nodded, and flicked my finger over the screen of a tablet. It was from Captain Sarin. I'd left her in charge out there. She said there were some odd readings from the bottom of the seabed on Yale. I frowned.

"Nothing's changed? Just these vibrations?"

"Right sir, looks as if someone is trying to use the ring to communicate."

When the rings were used to relay transmissions from one star system to another, they did so through a process of sympathetic resonance. Since the rings were essentially in two places at one time, if you could cause one to vibrate slightly, you were logically vibrating the one on the far side at the same time. Using this system and applying a code to the vibrations allowed for the instantaneous transmission of message over countless lightyears.

"Jasmine is blocking this, right?"

"Of course, sir," Miklos said. "The instant the signal was detected, the fleet began jamming it."

"But we still don't know who is trying to send what message through, do we?"

"No sir. We do know the message is not intended for us. It could be the Macros trying to talk to the Crustaceans, or the other way around."

I frowned. "What possible motivation could the Crustaceans have for communicating with their masters now? Don't they know the machines are trying to kill them all?"

Miklos shrugged. "Anything is possible, sir. We just don't know. I feel forced to remind you that the Crustaceans did not agree to ally with us. For whatever reason, they are still technically allied with the Macros."

"I don't like it. But I do understand it. The Crustaceans are coldly logical when it comes to their own survival. They don't fear us as much as they do the machines."

Miklos made a vague gesture that seemed to indicate I could be right, but he wasn't agreeing fully. I ordered some coffee and headed for the docking ports. The carrier wasn't built to land in an atmosphere, so we boarded smaller ships to take us down to Shadowguard.

When I finally stood on the battlements of my castle in the sky, I felt better. I liked it here. There were good memories already building, and somehow the place made me relax. I paced the walls for an hour, watching the sun drop over the horizon. The nights fell quickly here, and dawn was never far away.

Tonight we were having a formal state dinner. This was the perfect place for it, and it would be our first. General Kerr had told us he'd make a formal announcement concerning Earth's diplomatic intentions at the dinner. I wasn't sure how I felt about that, but I was looking forward to the meal. The kitchens and chefs on staff at Shadowguard were the best in the Eden system.

I started off the evening by showing General Kerr and his entourage around. Alexa was noticeably present, but subdued.

Sandra was noticeably absent. But I knew she was lurking around somewhere nearby. She might be on the battlements or on the central mountain crag that anchored the fortress. My relationship with her was an odd one. She was part bodyguard, part lover—and part something else. We'd been through so much together I couldn't imagine life without her shadow casting itself over mine.

I knew that wherever she was, she was watching me, but I tried not to think about her. I knew I needed to clear my mind.

I showed them most of the rooms, but not the command-and-control center, of course. We passed a number of dungeon-like doors which hid sensitive equipment, leaving them unopened. I knew that just looking at our hardware wouldn't be enough for them to gather much intel about it, but decided to err on the side of caution.

Instead, I showed them the battlements, the views and the ballroom where we would shortly have dinner.

"This is it, huh?" Kerr asked me. "Let me tell you something, Riggs. This is a fine medieval castle. The trouble is I've seen them before, plenty of them. We've got them all over Europe clutching the top of one Alp or another. I'm not terribly impressed by anything other than the view."

"I'm sorry you feel that way, General," I said evenly.

"I know you're hiding your real tech somewhere. I'm surprised you aren't proud enough to show off what it can do. Have you figured out how to spy on Earth through the rings, yet?"

I blinked, startled. I'd never even thought of the idea. It was alarming, but I guessed immediately that it might be possible. Even if you just hooked up a remote control camera to the rings and used the vibration system to transmit back the images…

"You know as well as I do that we're both jamming the rings, sir," I told him evenly.

"Yeah, right."

General Kerr was watching me closely, and I knew I'd probably revealed too much with my face. Damn the man, he was cagey.

"Are you ready yet to make your formal proposal," I asked, deciding it was a good time to switch the topic. "I've yet to learn exactly why you're here."

"Let's start with the salad. I'm starved."

"All right," I said, and led them to the dinner table. I wasn't quite sure why Kerr was stalling about delivering his message, but maybe it was his natural flair for the dramatic.

Sandra appeared when the dinner bell rang as if she'd been waiting for it. I knew that she had. One second there was a shadow in a doorway, the next she was seating herself at the table.

I had the kitchens lay out our finest fare. It was different from an Earth meal, naturally. We'd had some livestock and edible plants transported from Earth and grown here. Most of these had come with the refugee fleet I'd rescued last year, along with the majority of our civilian population.

I'd avoided eating the few goats, chickens and cattle we had. Instead, I wanted to use them as breeding stock and build up to a nice harvest next year. I explained this to Kerr and his people as we sat down to our first course.

"At the moment, we'd even made it illegal to eat most of our earthly foodstuffs," I said. "Anything that can be used to grow more food—especially animal herds—has been protected. We've got a few things that are ready to harvest like coffee and beans, but most of our food comes from local alien crops. Eating unknown digestible has given us a few thousand tummy-aches, but we've sorted out what can be eaten and how to prepare it."

"I can't wait," Kerr mumbled doubtfully.

We started with six platters of seafood.

"Most of these mollusks were flown in from Eden-6," I explained. "Our hottest tropical world. Over ninety-five percent of Eden-6 is covered by seawater. The fishing is excellent in the shallower regions."

"Mollusks?" Kerr asked doubtfully. "Forgive me for the 'C' I got in biology thirty years ago, but are you talking about *snails*, Riggs?"

I cleared my throat in annoyance. "Just try one, General. They're toasted to perfection. Dip them in that garlic-butter sauce, you won't be disappointed."

Making a face, Kerr tried it and chewed doubtfully. After a few seconds, his face softened. "Weird-tasting."

"Well, I quite like it," said Alexa.

I glanced at her and smiled, but quickly took my eyes off her. Sandra was sitting at my side, and she watched me with careful interest.

The table was long and rectangular. Some of my staff had pushed for a circular table, saying it went with the knights-and-castle theme, but I'd refused. I wasn't King Arthur, and this wasn't some kind of egalitarian round table. I sat at the end of the big table with Kerr on my left and Sandra on my right. Most of Kerr's staff members were placed close to us at the head of the table, with Miklos mixed in on the left side. Alexa was three seats down on my right, across from

Kerr and Miklos, but on the same side as Sandra. I didn't want to give Sandra any excuses to stare at the girl.

Sandra had been irritated when I'd allowed them to bring sidearms to the dinner table. I assured her it wasn't a problem. A low caliber bullet was unlikely to bring down any marine, and we were armed too, with much more sophisticated weaponry. Our needlers could burn a hole through inch-thick steel—most likely before the Imperials could get a weapon out and aimed properly.

Real military people on the frontier felt naked without a weapon near at hand, and I understood that natural desire. We didn't have many traditions in the Eden System yet, but we knew instinctively that a table full of armed men usually guaranteed a polite dinner would be had by all. Accordingly, I'd ordered all of my people to be armed at all times while in the presence of our visitors.

The salads came next, excellent bowls of green and blue vegetation. These were local to Eden-8, as was the main course. When the roasted air-swimmers were brought out, everyone sighed in anticipation. The smell alone was intoxicating. Even Kerr's eyes lit up. I felt a surge of pride. If we had a single meat that could challenge anything from Earth, I was our fresh-killed and roasted air-swimmers.

We were talking in a lively fashion and just starting to dig in when I noticed Lieutenant Alexa Brighton. She was standing at attention. Her plate of air-swimmers lay before her, untouched.

Everyone quieted and stared. I felt Sandra tense. Most of us wore an expression of surprise. Sandra's was one of dark suspicion. I knew she was ready to spring at the girl if she presented any kind of threat.

For once, I made no attempt to restrain Sandra. I didn't like this either, and I decided Sandra's natural paranoia might prove correct today.

General Kerr spoke first. "Yes, Lieutenant?" he asked formally. "Did you want to be excused?"

"No sir," she said. She bit her lip. Her eyes didn't meet any of ours. They stared off over our heads. She was standing at full attention, as one might do when on a parade ground. "I wanted to make a statement."

The crowd had been murmuring, but now they fell quiet as a group. The clicking of forks and knives died with the whispers and speculations.

"There's no need to be formal," Kerr said softly. "We are all engaging in polite conversation."

"No sir," she said. "You don't understand. This isn't conversation."

Kerr narrowed his eyes at her. His fork was poised in mid-air. He'd been devouring his air-swimmers with gusto, despite himself. Now, he placed the fork neatly beside his plate. He dabbed his lips with his linen napkin and sat back in his chair.

"Let's hear it then. And I'm hoping it's something that will make your father proud back home."

Alexa glanced at him for a moment, then looked dead ahead again. "I don't know about that, sir. But General Kerr, Colonel Riggs—I wish to defect. I'm formally resigning my commission from the Imperial forces. I would like to simultaneously submit my application for any role available in Star Force."

The room fell into a deadly silence. Miklos and I exchanged glances. Miklos seemed as surprised as I was. I looked at Sandra and Kerr, but neither of them met my eyes. They were both staring at Alexa. Neither of them wore happy expressions.

"Now?" Kerr demanded. "*Now* you choose to announce you're a traitor? This is a state dinner. You've embarrassed everyone here, most significantly your father back home. I formally reject your request to resign. I doubt Riggs would want you in any case."

Alexa looked at me then, for the first time. There was a desperate look in her eyes.

"I—I await Colonel Riggs' decision," she said. "This is his territory. It's his choice."

There were a lot of eyes on me now. Everyone was in shock. I wasn't quite sure what to do. I was certain the girl had caused herself a great deal of trouble back on Earth if she was to be dragged home. Kerr would have her arrested and who knew what else. The Imperial government was not a soft one, by all accounts. It was an iron-fisted dictatorship.

My mind swam, trying to foresee the possibilities. If I accepted her plea, gave her my protection and granted her asylum, she might be able to give me invaluable intel on the Empire's military. On the other hand, it would be a diplomatic nightmare. It was just the sort of incident that had occurred with regularity during the Cold War between the dictatorial East and the free West. I now understood

91

what those leaders must have been thinking when these things had occurred on their watch.

"I'm surprised by your request," I said at last. "I'm sure you can understand that. If I were to accept your application—and I'm only thinking about it now, mind you—I wouldn't want that to sour the improving relationship between the Empire and Star Force."

It was at that moment I heard a click. It was a quiet sound, almost inaudible under the boom of my own voice. But it was there, and it was unmistakable. Having been in military action for years now, the sound was very familiar to me.

Someone had drawn their weapon and readied it to fire.

-13-

Kerr was quiet and quick, but not smooth enough. Sitting on my left side, he had drawn his weapon under the table and aimed it carefully.

I didn't have any time to think, or I might have pulled the blow. He was only a normal human, and one in his fifties at that. He'd been nanotized, but it looked to me as if he needed a fresh dose.

I knew I didn't have much time. A single second, possibly less. I had to move now.

Sandra had heard the sound as well. Her senses were enhanced and so was her speed of movement. But she was across the table from Kerr, a good six feet away. She couldn't get there before I did.

But she did act. I could feel her rise up behind me, looming and blocking the light. I didn't know exactly what she was doing, and I didn't have a split second to turn and look. Instead, I lifted my arm and brought it down on Kerr's wrist. I brought it down hard—too hard.

There was a snapping sound and a sharp intake of breath. The gun clattered to the floor, dropped by numb fingers.

Kerr lifted his arm into view in shock. It had snapped down at a right angle. Both the bones in his forearm, the ulna and the radius, had been broken. The arm hung limply, his hand twitching feebly in an unnatural position.

With Kerr disabled, I had time to turn my attention to Sandra and the rest of them. There she stood, my crazy woman, right on the dinner table. She loomed over Kerr and had a pistol in her hand, trained with unwavering precision on his left eye socket.

Alexa, for her part, still stood at attention. Kerr had been aiming his gun at her, planning to shoot up through the table to kill the defector. I realized with sudden clarity that I'd doomed her in his mind. When I'd said I had not yet accepted her application for asylum, that meant she was still under his command and still his to execute if he wished to. The situation had unfolded so fast that I'd been taken by surprise.

"You've assaulted an Imperial officer on a diplomatic mission," Kerr said through gritted teeth.

"I'm sorry," I said. "But I'm not accustomed to having dinner guests shoot one another at my table—not unless I ordered the action myself."

"Dinner is canceled," Kerr said, hissing out the words in agony.

I looked at him and nodded. I couldn't argue with that.

"Maybe we should adjourn for now," I suggested. "We can pick up in a few days when you've recovered from this unfortunate accident."

Kerr stood up, swaying slightly. Chairs rasped on flagstones. All his staff members stood up with him. The Imperials wore white faces that matched their uniforms.

"There might not be any further discussion," Kerr said. "It's up to you, Riggs. Do you want a deal, or do you want to abuse your guests and interfere with their internal politics? This is a serious diplomatic breach, and I can't do anything more until I contact the Emperor and make a full report. I'm not sure how he will react."

I looked glum. I knew exactly how Crow would react: with rage.

I stood up too, and now all the Star Force people stood with me. They were all as stiff and uncomfortable looking as the Imperials.

"I can understand that," I said. "I don't have a policy in this situation yet. I'll arrest Lieutenant Brighton and place her in a holding cell."

"Colonel Riggs?" called Alexa. "May I speak?"

"What is it?"

"I'm sorry to have caused you this difficulty. But may I point out you offered amnesty and protection to thousands of refugees from the Empire before this. They came out to you and found new homes. They're all around us."

I realized she was right, of course. But this situation was different. "Those people left with Earth's blessing," I said. "Once

94

they entered our space I was obliged to protect them as civilians. You're part of a military organization. You've sworn an oath to them."

"Exactly," interjected Kerr. "I demand that you remand the Lieutenant into my custody."

I shook my head. "Given tonight's incident, I can't do that."

"Then I must retire and seek medical aid."

I watched him go and then turned back to Alexa with a grim expression. "That could have been handled better," I said. "Couldn't you at least have waited until after he made his proposals?"

"I'm sorry sir," she said. "I was only thinking of myself. I've been building up my courage to make this move for months. I just had to try it tonight. I was afraid I'd lose heart and let the moment slide if I passed this by."

I understood her, even if I was annoyed. It was a very human, emotional thing. I thought of her as a young woman in an abusive relationship. She had to move when she had the courage to do so.

But oh, how I wished now she had waited. I was in a dilemma now. The easy thing to do would be to quietly ship her back to the Empire. Perhaps to transfer her back to the battleship she'd come from bound and gagged. That way, very few would know what had transpired.

But the story would get out if I did that. I had to think about the future. This girl wouldn't be the last of her kind. She wouldn't be the only one to defect. We had a Cold War of our own going between Earth and Eden, and I couldn't afford to frighten every future defector and refugee. If they knew I would turn them away and toss them back to Crow's tender mercies, they would fear to even try it.

And then there was the lovely innocent girl herself. She'd come here to get this chance. She was the daughter of a high-ranking officer, a man who would be lucky to come out of this without being retired or even imprisoned. I doubted she realized what she'd done to her family back home. Crow had a jealousy of me that had grown over the years. He was also afraid of me. He wouldn't go easy on her or her family if he got his hands on them.

I thought of sending her back to the Empire, handcuffed and terrified. What would they do to her? Torture? Mutilation? Quiet murder?

How could I order her away, knowing what her fate would be?

95

I couldn't. I knew that with a sudden, crushing certainty. Like it or not, I was stuck with this young woman and I'd lost an opportunity to seal a new deal with the Empire. How could I claim to be the voice of freedom and justice in the universe if I crushed someone like this?

I knew I'd met my match. In battles, I felt at home. I understood how to face an enemy and destroy him. But this was different. This was a choice with no right answer and with bad consequences no matter what decision I made. There was no neat way to win—or at least, none that came easily to my mind.

Everyone was looking at me, I realized. They weren't able to hear my thoughts, so I appeared to be dithering and indecisive. I didn't want to look weak, so it was time to take action.

I flopped down in my chair and began eating roasted air-swimmer again. The dish didn't taste quite as hot and good as it did a few minutes ago, but I wasn't going to let anyone throw them away.

Around me, my staff sat and ate too. All except Alexa.

"Am I under arrest, Colonel?" she asked when I looked up at her.

"Yeah, I guess," I said. "Now sit down and eat. Let's not let all this good food go to waste."

Alexa trembled slightly as she sat down and took up her fork for the first time. She took small bites and chewed each one for a long time. I could tell her heart wasn't into the meal after her near-death experience. It was a shame, really. The air-swimmers were superb tonight.

My staff was subdued. Conversation was light and was kept to a minimum. To make matters less comfortable, Sandra leaned forward to glare at Alexa every few seconds for the rest of the meal. Both Alexa and I pretended not to notice this.

When I finally sighed and pushed back from the table, I felt relaxed for the first time this evening.

"Now *that* was some good food," I said. "I'm going to go down to the kitchens and tell the cooks they outdid themselves."

"Don't you think there's something more important to worry about right now?" Sandra asked in an acid voice. She nodded her head toward Alexa, who sat very still with big eyes.

I looked at Alexa and noticed her plate was only half-empty.

"You going to finish those?" I asked.

"Kyle, are you going to send her to the brig or not?" Sandra demanded.

I gave her a surprised look. "Why no, I'm not."

"You said she was under arrest."

"Yeah, she is. So what? She's in the middle of Shadowguard, one of the highest security structures in the star system. She's not going anywhere."

Sandra looked pissed. I wasn't quite sure why.

"So, by *prisoner*, you meant she's a guest that can't leave."

I nodded. "Yeah, that pretty much sums it up. We have to decide how to handle this situation with Kerr. I'm hoping he'll cool off by morning and we can get back to business." I turned my attention back to Alexa. "You're going to have to stay out of sight for now. We'll give you new quarters, somewhere down with the enlisted people under the castle. Might as well let Kerr think you're sitting in chains someplace. Could you take care of that, Miklos?"

"Of course, Colonel," he said. He got up and left the chamber.

I could tell Sandra wanted to see real chains on the girl, but she was going to be disappointed. I didn't want to mistreat her. She could be a valuable source of information. If we treated her like a guest under restriction, she would stay friendly. I didn't know much about what was happening back on Earth, and she was connected to the people who did. I couldn't explain all this to Sandra with Alexa sitting right there, so I took Alexa's plate and finished it.

Somehow, this made Sandra more irritated. She watched me eat, wearing an expression that reminded me of an angry housecat.

I did my best to ignore her and enjoy the dish. Really, it was too much good food even for my gut to handle. I felt a bit uncomfortable when I'd finished.

Miklos came back as they rolled in the dessert trays. I waved them off. I was too full to enjoy something sugary now.

Miklos whispered at my shoulder. "There's a problem, sir."

When Miklos worried, I worried too. I didn't ask him what the problem was. I got up, excused myself and followed him to the main gallery.

As we exited the room, Miklos paused. "Lieutenant Brighton? There is a new room for you on level seven. Please ask the stewards for directions."

"Uh...okay," she said.

Sandra stood up in our wake. She looked after me and then after Alexa. I could tell she was undecided who she should shadow. Finally, she followed me.

She walked a good thirty paces behind us, and Miklos was whispering, but I knew she could hear every word.

"Tell me what's going on, Commodore," I said.

"I apologize for further interrupting the dinner."

"Never mind about that. It was a total disaster before you arrived. Just make your report."

"We've received a message from Captain Sarin. She says there are strange signals emanating from the ring on the surface of Yale."

"What kind of funny signals?"

"They're communication signals, origin and destination unknown."

"Any clue what they're saying?"

"No, sir. No known code is being used. I've given all the data to Marvin, but he's come up with nothing as well."

We'd dealt with unknown signals being relayed by the rings before. The rings were communication devices after all, if used appropriately. Unlike radio signals however, they operated on a principle of entanglement, which was kind of like the way Voodoo dolls were supposed to work. If you jabbed one, the other felt it. Unlike radio, there was no way to detect the transmission's source. You couldn't easily figure out who was jabbing a needle into whose doll.

"Let's go over the list of suspects," I said. "Are either of the other rings in the system vibrating?"

"No sir. Just the seabed ring on Yale."

"Okay then, that eliminates Earth and the Blues—unless they've figured out some new way to bypass our jamming and detection systems. Assuming they haven't, we're down to two known participants in this conversation: the Crustaceans and the Macros."

Miklos nodded slowly, frowning. "We went in there to help them, and they talk to the very monsters that are seeking to destroy them all. Why would they do that, Colonel? Why wouldn't they side with us?"

"I can understand their reasoning. Look at it from their perspective. They just suffered hundreds of billions of civilian casualties. They aren't interested in right or wrong or honor. They're

98

interested in survival. If they have to kiss up to their conquerors, they're going to do it."

"But they've seen us defeat the machines more than once…"

"Yes, but much of our military strength is based on our battle station. That doesn't help them, because their three worlds are on the wrong side of it. The fleet we sent out there didn't impress anyone. The Macros display ten times our fleet strength when they send out a wave of ships—no offense meant to Fleet, Commodore."

"None taken," he said stiffly. "I've tried relentlessly to convince you of our need for more ships."

"Relentlessly, indeed. But that's got to be it, then. The Crustaceans fear the Macros more than they do us. It's as simple as that."

"What do we do next, Colonel?"

"I'm not going to accuse them of anything or give them any ultimatums. If the Macros have given the Crustaceans new marching orders, I don't want to be caught by surprise. Transfer all production to Fleet. Postpone all civilian and ground-force orders at the factories."

Miklos' eyes were shining as he took in these happy orders. I could tell he was excited to have his beloved Fleet back at the center of our strategy.

"I'll make the preparations, sir!" he shouted, saluting.

He turned as if to trot away, but I called him back.

"There's more," I said. "We need a show of force. We'll fly out there with every ship we can spare from the home front and prepare to do battle."

"If you will excuse me, Colonel?"

I nodded. "Move fast. We fly out of here in three hours."

He ran off like a kid that had to pee. The second he was gone, Sandra came out of the shadows. She'd been standing closer than I'd realized. This castle was lit in the old-fashioned way, with fewer, dimmer sources of illumination.

"We're leaving so soon?" she asked.

"Did you hear everything?"

"Yes."

"Well then you know the score. We have to get out there and find out what's going on."

I left the chamber and went downstairs to my quarters. Sandra followed me on silent feet.

Our quarters were sumptuously appointed. We had velvet draperies and thick soft carpets. The bed itself was a four-poster carved from local hardwoods. I'd looked forward to spending the night here again.

"This has become home, this castle of cool stone and cold winds," I said, looking around. "Now it seems I'm not going to get to spend any time here."

"I know. I'll miss it too. But there's something you'll have to decide about before we go: Kerr and his entourage."

I looked at her suddenly. "Right—the negotiations. Well, Kerr himself said that was on hold now until he could get new instructions from Crow. Since Earth is still jamming the ring to Sol, transmitting back and forth will take nearly two weeks. We might be back by then if we're lucky. He'll just have to sit here and eat our stocks of air-swimmers until we return."

When the rings were jammed, we could still communicate using radio signals to relay a message across the systems themselves. Each message had to crawl across each system to a ship waiting at each ring. The ship then crossed to the other side and relayed the message. This way, the transmission followed the chain until it reached its final destination. As radio signals traveled at the entirely inadequate speed of light, it took a long time for a message to reach across the stars. By the time Kerr did talk to Earth and get back a reply, the transmission would have crossed Alpha Centauri, Helios, Eden and the Solar System twice. The roundtrip time was about two weeks.

Sandra walked to the bed and swung herself around the nearest bedpost like a dancer. She paused, hanging upside down at an angle that would be impossible for nearly any normal human. I watched her with a mixture of amazement and alarm. My girlfriend was part pole-dancer and part bat.

"What about the girl?" she asked me suddenly. "Will you leave her here as well?"

"Oh, Alexa…right," I said thoughtfully. "I'm not sure that would be a good idea with Kerr so near. There might be an incident. He nearly murdered her at dinner, after all."

"What are you going to do with her then?"

"I guess we'll have to take her with us. We can interrogate her on the flight out. She's sure to have good intel on the Empire. This could be a boon for us. We've had very little information on the political and military situation of Earth since Captain Sarin defected. We've got to make the most of these opportunities."

"Will you conduct these interrogations personally?" she purred.

My next breath froze in my lungs. I realized in that instant that I'd stepped out onto thin ice. Her questions had been calmly delivered, but I could see where they were going. She was feeling jealous again. I knew I needed to defuse her before Alexa and I both suffered.

"You know," I began, thinking fast, "I think I'm going to be too busy for that. In fact, I'd like you to take over the task, if you could."

"Me?" she asked. She looked at me, hanging upside down by one foot. Her hair nearly touched the flagstones.

"Yes. Don't sweat her, just be her friend. Do the girl-talk thing. She'll probably tell you all about her family and what's going on back on Earth."

"That's a very sexist thing to say, Kyle."

"It is? Um...sorry."

"But I'll do it anyway."

"Good!" I said, riding a wave of relief. I felt as if I'd just taken two flying bullets and slammed them into one another, canceling the momentum of both. It was the perfect judo-move, a deft stroke of the sort I'd rarely managed when dealing with women.

Naturally, I had no idea at the time what the repercussions would be.

-14-

The flight out to the Thor system quickly became more urgent. Just as we left Eden-8, we got a new communique from Captain Sarin, who was still at her post in the Thor system.

The ring on the seabed had become active again, but this time, instead of sucking out the moon's vast oceans, it was allowing things to crawl through onto the ocean floor. These things were unmistakable, as we'd seen them time and again: they were Macros—the big models.

Also, unlike most of the Macros we'd seen recently, these units had shields. I recalled that back on Earth, when we'd first battled them, the biggest machines had been large enough and had generators powerful enough to project their own bubble-like domes of force. That had been the reason for the development of my marines in the first place. We'd needed to get under those shields and shoot up into the bellies of these hundred-foot tall metal monsters.

Now, it was happening all over again, to another unsuspecting world. The machines were marching, masses of them. Like a long line of army ants they came up from the seafloor and strode out onto the newly revealed, salt-crusted lands.

"We're going to have to gather the fleet again," I told Sandra as I dressed and prepared to go to the bridge. "We'll pull everything together into one single fist this time. With Miklos' new carriers, we'll have a stronger force than we've ever had."

"Why go out there at all?" Sandra asked me. "Why not retreat to hide behind our battle station? If the Macros come, let them. The Crustaceans don't want to join us anyway. Let them deal with it."

"You're a cold woman, Sandra."

"That's not what you said last night."

I chuckled and shook my head. "They've just lost hundreds of billions of lives. That represents a vast loss of sentient biotic beings. Whether these Crustaceans agree to cooperate or not, I consider them to be my natural allies. Every one of them that dies weakens our side."

"So we're going to protect them?"

"We're going to try."

When we arrived on the bridge, my command staff was already in emergency mode. Marvin had remained out at Thor with Jasmine's fleet. I summoned him online to grill him. I wanted to know how the Yale ring had been reactivated.

"Marvin, you told me you'd shut off the ring," I said.

"Not exactly, sir. I said that it *appeared* I had shut off the ring. The truth is not yet known."

I rolled my eyes. Marvin never took the blame for anything. Somehow, when the crap really hit the fan, it was always some other guy's fault.

"If you didn't really shut it off, why did it stop sucking out the ocean?" I asked. "And more importantly, why is it allowing troops through into Yale's ocean now?"

"There are two possibilities that have risen to the top of my stack of logical deductions."

"Name one."

"Possibly, I did shut down the ring. However, the Macros have turned it back on again and purposefully reversed the flow of the ring. In this hypothetical scenario, they are now using it to transport their ground troops directly to the planet."

"What's the other?"

"When I turned off the ring, it is possible I didn't actually turn it off. Recall that the command I sent was a random hit. It is well within the domain of probability that what I actually did was reverse the direction of the ring's flow. In this scenario, the ring was never actually disabled."

I nodded slowly. He was right. One of those two possibilities had to be it. Really, it didn't matter much which one had occurred. What mattered now was that Yale was under attack. They had a full-scale ground invasion going on down there.

I frowned at the onscreen maps. "We'll have to deal with the machines directly. We can bombard them from orbit, but they're notoriously hard to kill. Those shielded behemoths are only going to die one way. We've got to get down there, land ground forces and get in close."

"That's very hazardous duty, sir," Marvin pointed out.

"Don't you think I know that?" I snapped. I knew I was being irritable, but I felt I had a right to be. This wasn't going as planned. Nothing was.

I contacted Miklos and gave him grim orders: "Call up the transports," I said. "I want an emergency muster. I want ten thousand marines in space within twenty-four hours."

"Yes sir—I'll try, sir."

Over the next day, Miklos came pretty close. I had my ten thousand troops thirty hours later. That man knew how to get people moving. About half of the marines were human while the rest were Centaur volunteers.

Instead of assembling an organized fleet at Welter Station and sailing out as a tight group as I'd planned, we scrambled and put up everything we could. I left only Miklos' carrier and two dozen gunboats behind to defend Eden in case Earth attacked us.

I didn't like leaving Eden relatively undefended, but I figured the odds of a sucker-punch coming from Earth were low right now. Emperor Crow had just sent us an envoy, after all, and technically we were still in the midst of peace negotiations. As far as I could tell, Earth had no way of knowing what our fleet movements were, and they didn't have much of a fleet of their own left to hit us with after the Macros had plowed into the Solar System last year.

Most importantly, it just wouldn't be like Crow to risk losing his last ships in a bid to knock me out. He'd always been the type to build up quietly; massing forces until he felt victory was assured before he moved. In a way, he reminded me of the Macros, but with less guts even than they had. At least when they made a play, they didn't try to beg and plead their way out of it when things went badly. They just lost their fleets and built new ones.

Crow was more like a Mongol leader in that he stayed well behind the front lines and would run if it looked like he was going to lose. Unfortunately, his tactics were as effective as they were dishonorable.

My ships reached and passed Welter Station on the dawn of the third day. It took two more long days to reach Yale. By that time, Captain Sarin had managed to knock out about a dozen of the big machines, mostly by continuously bombarding them from space. Our gunboats had a long range and powerful punch. She'd kept them firing down into Yale's atmosphere, sending a steady stream of blue balls of light from orbit to the surface. Single railgun salvos weren't enough to break the machines directly, especially not the ones that stayed under the cover of the ocean. But once they dared to march up on the land and establish a beachhead, they were pounded with withering fire. The gunboats, all concentrating on a single target, could bring a machine down after an hour or so of steady fire. The trick was to hit a given machine several times within the span of a few seconds. When we managed to do that, the shields didn't have time to regenerate and the machine was overwhelmed and destroyed.

It seemed to me, looking at the raw data, that these crawling machines had tougher shields than the ones that had invaded Earth so long ago, but they were also slower-moving.

Captain Sarin sent us hourly reports. At first, our strategy was working. She picked a target, had every gunboat aim at it, and after a while it died. But the machines were still making headway.

They'd set up a few underwater domes and were beginning to churn out workers. I had to wonder what the hell their long-term plan was. Right now, they seemed content to colonize Yale while under continuous fire. Maybe they figured they could just ignore us and keep building. The idea was galling.

By the time we were a day out from planetfall at Yale, Sarin had given up on bombarding them in the shallow ocean near the ring. She waited until they surfaced and raced for rocky cover. Then, like a thousand BB guns popping away at sea turtles in unison, the gunboats began their relentless bombardment.

There were two problems with our strategy that I could see: One, the machines kept coming. They seemed to be limitless, while our salvos of railgun ammo were dwindling. Within a few days, our stocks would be depleted. Two, the Macros were clearly becoming harder to kill. They were redesigning themselves with thicker shields—it had to be that. Looking back through the vids and reports, I determined that it now took nearly ten hits to bring one down and had taken only three at the start of the invasion. I was alarmed, and so was Sarin. Our shooting-gallery battle had turning into a nightmarish grind.

Sarin requested permission to commit her fighters, and I denied that request. She then asked to employ her missiles—and I denied that too. The inhabitants of Yale had suffered badly enough. I couldn't in good conscious begin blasting and irradiating their wounded planet with thermonuclear blasts.

When we were less than six hours from joining her forces in orbit, Sarin called to make her final plea.

"Colonel," she said, "I can no longer hold them back. They've taken eleven islands near the underwater ring. They are setting up factories under heavy domes, two of them at the bottom of the ocean nearby. Railgun fire cannot possibly penetrate those domes. Already, smaller worker units are flowing from the domes to gather materials. According to my projections, Yale will be overrun within weeks."

I thought about her transmission carefully before replying.

"Captain Sarin," I said while gazing sternly into the vid pickup, "I understand your situation. Relief is on the way. I have reviewed your requests for tactical changes to our response operation, and again I'm rejecting them. All my prior decisions stand. You're not to use thermonuclear weapons, nor employ your fighters. We're holding those assets in reserve for now. The only thing I want you to send down into that atmosphere are conventional bombardment strikes: laser emissions and railgun salvos. Riggs out."

I paused with my hand hovering over the cut-off button. I'd frozen her image on the screen while I made my reply. I stared at her dark, olive-shaped eyes. I'd always had a soft-spot for Captain Sarin, everyone knew that. She had to be freaking out. This was her first Fleet task force, and it looked like she was failing in her mission. The planet she'd been assigned to protect was being overrun.

"Jasmine," I said, lowering my voice and putting some humanity into it. "I'll be there soon with heavy reinforcements. You've done well with what you had. You've slowed the enemy advance as much as you could. Don't worry, the Marines will handle this invasion when we get there. We've done it before."

With this addendum, I signed off and transmitted the message. She didn't send me a reply.

We arrived a few hours later and parked in orbit over Yale, joining Jasmine's forces. Altogether, we formed an impressive fleet.

I transferred my staff over to *Gatre*, and relieved Jasmine's command staff. Her people were competent, but slightly less experienced than mine. More importantly, they'd been sweating it out here for days and could use the break.

Jasmine didn't take these changes personally. She wasn't like most of my senior staff: she didn't have a big ego. She wanted to do her job as well as humanly possible. That was about it. I'd always found her quiet competence refreshing.

Within an hour after arriving, I was standing on the roomy but stark command deck of *Gatre*. The ship was equipped with a small holotank to display the local situation in three dimensions. There was also a large planning table. It was easier to manipulate, especially when discussing ground ops, which were pretty much two-dimensional affairs.

"How do you like your new ship, Captain Sarin?" I asked.

"Love it, sir," she said. "But I've yet to see my fighters do anything."

I nodded, twisting my lips. "You'll get the chance, don't worry. They're designed to operate under atmospheric operations as well as in space. We'll need air cover when we drop our marines. Let's plan that part of the operation now."

She worked the table's controls with deft strokes of her fingers. The image changed and blurred for a second, then came into focus. The islands around the ring at the bottom of the sea were stained red.

I frowned at the table. "They've taken them all? Every island in the archipelago?"

"Yes sir. I'm afraid so."

I looked up at Captain Sarin. Had there been a hint of bitterness in her voice? I couldn't quite tell. Unlike Sandra, you didn't always know what Jasmine was thinking. She kept staring at the map, making adjustments. She didn't look me in the eye. Finally, I turned my attention back to the islands.

"We have to get down there—right now," I said. "You'll operate as my exec. I want you to stay up here even after we've set up a beachhead. If things go badly on the ground, take over."

She finally looked up at me. "You're going down there? Personally?"

"Of course. You didn't think I'd dump ten thousand troops on a new world and hide in the sky, did you?"

107

Her lips twitched upward, a hint of a smile. She shook her head very slightly. "I suppose I shouldn't have thought that. Sandra won't be happy."

I frowned at her comment. "Fortunately, she's not in charge of this fleet."

Jasmine studied the table. She zoomed in on the largest of the eleven islands. She tapped on a mountaintop which instantly grew large and craggy. The table displayed an angled view, canted about thirty degrees to the north. The mountains were rugged and barren. Every rock was encrusted by coral-like growths and lime deposits.

"I've been examining possible drop-points," she said. "I'd recommend this one."

"That looks pretty rough," I said. "I'll have trouble setting up any kind of base there.

Jasmine nodded. "Exactly. That's why there are no machines at this location. At least, none of the big ones. There are a few workers tearing minerals from the cliffs."

I understood her reasoning immediately. When establishing a beachhead, it was best to land without being pelted by defensive fire. The mountain was steep and unfriendly-looking, but it would afford us higher firing positions and would allow us to land our initial deployment battalions with minimal losses. Still, I was unconvinced.

"What else have you got?"

She paged to a new spot. This one was underwater off a wide, rocky beach. There were no pretty sand beaches on these new islands. They hadn't had time to form yet.

"You could come down under the cover of water, here," she said. "This island is small and relatively undefended. There are no enemy factories here, so the machines seemed to have given it a lower priority."

I massaged my chin and stared. Really, neither of these drop sites appealed to me. But with only a few enemy-infested islands to choose from, we didn't have a lot of options. This wasn't like Earth, where you could always land farther away and advance on foot to your destination. There was very little land to fight over. And I didn't want to get into a deep undersea battle if I could help it. I'd done that before, and it had been a grim experience.

"All right," I said at last. "I'm going to take these two locations and hit them immediately."

Captain Sarin looked up at me with wide eyes. I could tell I'd surprised her. She looked pleased and alarmed at the same time.

"I imagine there are other locations to choose from, if you went over every island carefully."

I nodded. "Probably. But we don't have another day to screw around. The Macros are growing stronger every hour, sinking their teeth into this world. We're not gaining in strength, in fact we're losing in relative terms. So, I'm going to trust your judgment. As far as I'm concerned, these are the best spots to land."

She nodded and began working on the details of the plan. I saw battalions appear on the map as if they'd been dropped. Our Marine battalions had a fighting strength of about a thousand men each, broken into ten companies. She grouped them on both landing zones, placing three battalions underwater and the rest on the mountainous island. The three on the ocean floor were arranged in a crescent near the beach they were assigned to invade.

I tapped at the three battalions she'd placed in the water.

"These will have to wait," I said. "Prep the land drop first. I've got something planned for these oceans before we put a single boot into them."

"Something planned?"

"Yeah. Where's Marvin?"

The robot showed up a few minutes later, looking excited. "You requested my presence, Colonel Riggs?"

"Yes, I *ordered* you to come up here, Marvin. I want you to link up with that ring in the seabed again. I want you to reverse your prior command sequence."

Captain Sarin and Marvin both stared at me. When he'd first slithered up, most of his cameras had been trained on the tactical displays. Now there were too many cameras on me to easily count them.

"Let me verify that command," Marvin said. "You want me to reset the ring—to cause it to empty the oceans of Yale again? I was under the impression we'd taken great steps to stop that process."

"Yes," I said. "But now I want you to turn that ring into a giant sucking hole."

I looked down at the display, and zoomed in on the dark central circle of water the islands surrounded. "If we can, we're going to flush every machine that hasn't made it out of the water yet back to wherever they came from."

The glare coming up from the screen under-lit my face. I knew I was smiling broadly, and my teeth were probably shining with bluish light.

But I didn't care if I looked half-mad to my staff. I was really looking forward to this little surprise. The machines were going to regret crawling onto this world—if they were capable of regretting anything.

-15-

Our drop-troop technology had improved over the years. Our first efforts had been makeshift at best. I recalled loading up marines into steel boxes resembling railroad cars and carrying them with the cargo arm on my Nano ship. We'd later advanced to small one-man flying disks we called "skateboards".

Lately, I'd had a new set of problems. Not all my marines were human now. I found that the Centaur troops operated best on modified versions of our self-mobile disks. We'd changed the name from skateboard to surfboard, as they were longer and more powerful. These units could carry a marine with full kit across a star system if necessary, but we rarely went more than a few million miles on them.

The Centaur troops liked them a lot, because they could travel in space without having to be confined in a tight compartment. Even after the Microbial baths Marvin had worked out to change their brains slightly, the Centaurs still shied away from being crammed into a troop pod. Riding the surfboard gave them freedom of movement and more wide-open vistas than anyone could want.

The problem with surfboards came into play when dealing with a large planet that possessed an atmosphere. They simply couldn't drop fast enough to the target. As any old-fashioned paratroop will tell you, dropping from a high altitude into a battlefield is not a fun experience. You're completely exposed up there. In a modern combat environment with automated anti-air weaponry that could pinpoint a missile and fire in less than a second, floating down on the breezes was unacceptable. You had to get down to the ground in a

111

hot LZ as fast as technologically possible in order to survive the enemy AA.

I knew the machines would be gunning for us when I left Eden, so I'd left most of the Centaurs behind. I'd come out with human marines and our latest designs for encapsulated drops.

The men had a special term for these new contraptions. They called them "torpedoes"—or, if they were in a sour mood, "flying coffins". I'd decided to stick to the first term as it was more positive and slightly more accurate. The units actually looked like torpedoes or old dumb-bombs when they were dropped from space. They were about ten feet long with sleek ceramic exteriors made to absorb heat. That was their primary purpose: to allow our troops to drop from orbit at extreme speeds without burning up in the target planet's atmosphere. They were designed for single use and used simple materials, so they could be mass-manufactured by our Macro factories.

We had two kinds of alien production units: Macro systems and Nano systems. Our Macro units were big, dumb and amazingly powerful. They produced things like the hulls of our ships and our biggest generators. The smaller factories, courtesy of the Nanos, were much smaller and produced finer goods. Most of these were made up of nanites, which could be used to make almost anything from intelligent brainboxes to smart metal walls. Of the two, the Nano units were probably more valuable to Star Force, but I always wanted and needed both types of factories.

I decided to go down with the first wave. Sandra wasn't happy about this, and she let her feelings be known about ten minutes after I'd made my decision.

She found me in the main passageway less than a hundred yards from the sally port. I was wearing my heavy exoskeletal armor, and trotting happily for the exit when she appeared in front of me, hands on hips and eyes blazing.

I pulled up short, clanking and screeching to a stop. Around me, about five hundred other troops kept thundering by. They gave me smirks as they went by, no doubt knowing what I was in for before I did. My relationship with Sandra was well-known among the troops. Few of them talked about it in my presence, but I found it slightly embarrassing anyway.

"Where do you think you're going?" she demanded.

112

"To Yale," I said, "the hard way. Now, please step aside so I can invade this moon, Sandra."

"I would like to have a little talk with you first."

I hesitated. As always, probably since time immemorial, I weighed my options when confronting my girl. Sure, I could blow her off and soldier on. But sometimes putting up the pretense of listening carefully to her complaints could defuse a major blowup later on down the line.

Against my better judgment, I stepped into an alcove stuffed with emergency equipment. There were fire hoses, med-packs and nanite injection kits strapped to every surface. I had to place my foot-wide armored boots carefully to avoid smashing anything with them.

"These suits are getting more bulky every day," I complained. "I think the next generation should be lighter and more mobile."

"Whatever they look like, I don't want you wearing one," she said. "At least not without a very good reason."

It was about then another person wandered into the alcove with us. It was none other than Lieutenant Alexa Brighton. Her eyes were wider than ever. I wasn't sure if she'd ever seen a company of marines in full battle-kit before. She looked stunned. Unfortunately, she also provided the marching line of men something interesting to look at. They paused at the alcove, examining the scene. They looked at the two women in confusion for a second, then suddenly brightened. Several of them grinned and gave me the thumbs-up behind Sandra's back. It took me a second to realize what was going on: they thought Sandra had caught me with the girl. It had happened before, and the results were legendary.

I did my best to ignore them as they tramped steadily by. This was difficult, as the level of noise a line of power-armored marines made was near that of a passing freight train.

"This discussion will have to wait," I told her. "I've got a planet to save."

"*Why* do you have to go down there personally?" Sandra hissed at me.

I heaved a sigh. Lieutenant Brighton stared at the two of us with an expression of dazed curiosity, but didn't interrupt.

"I'm a marine, first and foremost," I said. "I'm going down with the troops to personally oversee the defense of Yale. I can't do that as well from space."

113

"Yes, but you're risking your life for a small benefit," Sandra argued.

My face twisted in annoyance. "I'll be fine," I said. "I always am."

"No you're not always fine. Sometimes you lose an arm, or something."

"We've got the best medical now," I chuckled. "I'll grow a new one."

The women studied me for a moment. I had to wonder what Alexa was thinking.

Two more passing marines paused and made a slightly obscene motion behind the women. Then they high-fived one another and trotted away. I frowned, but decided to pretend I hadn't noticed.

"You know what I think?" Sandra said. "I think you just can't keep out of the excitement. I think you love it too much, Kyle. It will kill you one day."

"What do you think, Lieutenant?" I asked, turning to her.

Alexa thought about it for a second. "I think I'd like to go down with you. It does look exciting."

This wasn't the response either Sandra or I had expected.

"No way," Sandra said, eyes blazing. "You're staying up here with me."

Alexa dropped her eyes and nodded. I felt a moment of compassion for the girl. Sandra had probably been a harsh woman to follow around. If Alexa wanted to drop with me, Sandra had to be giving her hell.

"That's right," I said, "it's out of the question. You have no armor training, no nanites, and no place in ground-based operation." I turned to Sandra. "Has she been giving you any good information about Earth?"

"Yes," Sandra said. "Her father is very highly ranked. She has a lot of stories to tell. Things aren't going well back home, Kyle. It's turned into some kind of crazy cult-of-personality dictatorship."

I nodded, unsurprised. Crow had always been big on himself and he'd wanted total power since day one. Now, except for the stellar frontier, he had it.

"When I get back in a few days, we'll go over it in detail," I said. "Thanks for your help, Lieutenant."

She nodded, and I turned to go.

114

A thin arm like a steel band blocked my way. I could have tossed Sandra aside, but I didn't. I turned back to her.

I had my visor open and she pushed her face into it. It wasn't easy to kiss a man in full power-armor, but she managed it. She practically had to climb onto my suit to do it.

Hooting broke out from the hallway full of streaming marines before we disengaged. A general cheer arose as I finally turned and trotted with the rest of them before she could think of another way to delay me.

I stepped onto a circular pad about twenty feet in diameter. Above me, a loud hissing sound erupted. I knew this was the hydraulics issuing a new pod. Just in time, I snapped down my visor and put my arms flat at my sides.

There was a crashing sound and everything went dark for second. If seemed as if someone had dropped a safe on my head. It was the drop-pod being lowered by powerful nanite-arms. The pod snapped into place and I felt as if I were being picked up—because I was.

Inside full power-armor it's easy to feel claustrophobic under the best of circumstances, but when they seal you in a flying coffin on top of it all and throw you out into space, the sensation is inescapable. The circular pad was really a smart metal door. Once the pod was in place, the pad had disintegrated and let me fall through it into the firing chamber.

Dropping us like bombs wasn't good enough for Star Force. Some underling of mine had determined more speed was needed. Under the launch pad was a long tube that essentially served as a cannon. I, inside my tight ceramic pod, was the cannonball.

There was spinning, rolling sensation for a moment as I was aimed downward, headfirst. Then the cannon fired.

A terrific shock of force struck my shoulders and skull as I was hurled out of the bottom of the ship. Accelerating at about thirty Gs for a brief period, I knew what it felt like to be a bullet. I shot downward, encased in darkness.

The acceleration was painful, but brief. The pod was carrying me downward with fantastic speed toward the planet's surface. As I dropped, the speed slowly increased.

It was a grim sensation, being locked inside this thing. There were no screens to look at, just a few readouts from my helmet's HUD. Except for numbers like altitude and speed printed in colored

115

digital numbers on the inside of my visor, I was cut off from the world.

When falling into a planet's atmosphere from space, there was always a few minutes of radio blackout. It was an empty, gnawing feeling. You were already alive or you were already dead, and there was absolutely nothing you could do about it.

Those few minutes passed, and I was still breathing. The pod tumbled until I was falling feet-first. The next question in my mind was easy: was I over the right target?

Finally, data began streaming into my helmet. A few details about the ground flashed up, displayed in 2D as elevations. Piled shapes spiked up toward my descending rear-end. The spikes grew and my feet hurt just looking at them. The protrusions were mountains, of course. Rugged mountains crusted in coral and lime deposits. They'd been at the bottom of a black ocean a few weeks ago. Now, I was about to walk on them.

The retros fired next, and slammed up into my feet. I wasn't really ready for the shock, even though I should have been. I made a mental note to add a warning buzzer when this transition was five seconds from hitting the men riding in these tin cans. If my knees had been locked at that moment—well, it would have hurt.

Massive G forces slammed up into my boots, shocking my entire body. I'd been relatively comfortable and weightless a second before, freefalling at about ten thousand miles per hour. Now, that velocity had to be reduced. I gritted my teeth and strained my muscles. Everything hurt. The burn seemed to go on longer that the initial firing had, primarily because I'd been building up some velocity on the long fall into Yale's gravity-well.

I almost had a heart attack when the final stage began. The pod around me blew apart. It flashed open and fell in eight twirling, burning pieces.

I was freefalling now, and since I hadn't really been ready for it, I inverted, then rolled right side up, then found myself inverted again. I was in a tumble.

I fought the suit's controls and cursed myself for not having done practice jumps with this new drop-pod system. The ground was alarmingly close.

About a second after I got my feet under me and the automatic stabilizers kicked in, I hit the ground. I landed on an ancient seabed, which was now dry for the first time in probably a billion years. My boots hit the surface and kept on going, punching through the crust and into the slimy mud beneath. When I was about three feet down, my boots found solid rock.

That stopped me.

I could move my arms, but not my legs. They were buried like a spearhead from space in the mountainside. There was something all around me, something that looked like drifting snow.

It took me a dazed second to realize it was salt and sand and dried-out crap from the ocean floor. I'd hit with such force I'd fired up a plume of debris.

I was on the surface of Yale.

I wondered hazily how many alien worlds I'd walked on in total—I'd lost count by now.

-16-

"You okay, sir?"

To me, in my slightly dazed state of mind, the question seemed to come from inside my helmet. I didn't immediately associate it with anyone in my surroundings. The voice was familiar, but my brains were addled—it took me a second to think about who it was... After a moment, I had it.

"Kwon?"

"Of course, sir," he said.

A big shadow fell over me. Something grabbed my gloves and pulled.

"Just let me get you out of there, Colonel," he said. "You're gonna be fine."

I realized that Kwon was standing over me, tugging at me as if I were a nail sunk halfway into a chunk of wood. It was an embarrassing situation, and I forced myself to get going. I knew that if Kwon was there, others were close by. I didn't want to look as bad off as I felt.

I had to appear to know what the hell I was doing, at least. Half of leadership, in my opinion, entails appearing to be strong and confident—even if you aren't. If you're feeling weak and you let the men know it, they get nervous.

I began churning my power-suited knees. White dust plumed up. Brownish-green slime from under the crusty surface layer came up next, fountaining out of the growing hole around my legs.

"You must of hit pretty hard, sir," Kwon said when he had me out and standing on the mountainside.

118

All around us, Marines were busy helping one another, securing equipment and looking for targets. Nothing threatened us immediately, but I was sure the machines knew we were here and would be taking action against us soon.

"Did we lose anybody?" I asked.

"No sir. Not in this unit."

"Excellent!" I said, trying not to sound too surprised. "Let's form up the company and head downslope. I want us dug in around the waist of the mountain, then we'll call in the next battalions."

"They already coming down, sir," Kwon said, pointing upward.

I tilted back my helmet to the limit. The neck region on these power-suits only rotated so far. The sky was full of burning, falling objects. They moved too fast to be flares, but too slow to be meteors. They were drop-pods, hundreds of them.

"All right, everyone move downslope!" I roared. "Get them moving, Kwon. Those drop-capsules will make quite a dent in the helmet of any marine left in this LZ."

Kwon gazed up at the falling stars overhead. His big mouth gaped open. "You think they might hit us?"

"The chances of a direct collision are small, but I want everyone moving downslope just in case. We can setup firing positions in case the enemy is deploying to contain us."

Kwon began roaring and clapping his metal gauntlets together. The sound was teeth-jarring, even through the thick helmet I was wearing. I couldn't argue with his results, however. The marines responded as if kicked, trotting down the salt and brine crusted mountainside. They created a small avalanche of dead seabed materials which was kicked ahead by their pounding metal boots.

I joined the herd and trotted downslope, using my suit's grav-power now and then. In these new, heavier suits it wasn't a good idea to fly unless it was really necessary. The armor was thicker and therefore the mass to be moved was greater. Power consumption during flight was an issue and I didn't know how long it would be before I was able to get a fresh charge.

The atmosphere became steadily thicker as we descended and was so full of dust and steam by the time I reached the rocky spur we were planning to call home, I couldn't see more than a hundred yards in any direction. It was as if I'd been immersed in a massive, clinging fog.

"This is good enough," I told Kwon. "We're about four thousand feet above the new sea-level. That'll give the enemy a hard climb to get up to our positions. I want everyone digging in right here. Once he has a trench large enough to cover himself, each man is to keep right on digging. Every marine is to dig enough trench-space to shield three men. We're expecting more companies from above soon, and they might not have time to dig their own foxholes."

There was some grumbling as Kwon relayed these orders. The officers of the company we were embedded with were doing most of the grousing. They felt I was taking direct command of their unit— which I was. But I didn't lose my temper with them as they didn't offer any direct objections. I could understand how they felt. Having brass in the middle of your team taking your decisions away wasn't fun.

Digging the holes themselves was nothing like the grim chore of yesteryear. We had powerful, whining suits of armor on that did most of the work. Every movement was accentuated and exaggerated. We bent, we lifted and we moved massive mouthfuls of loose earth with every scoop. Even if we'd been doing the job without power-suits, our nanotized bodies would have found the work acceptable. Wearing what amounted to a forklift folded around your arms and legs made it positively easy.

Joining the fun, I deployed two scoops, which fanned out from my gauntlets. Each of these was smart metal and about a foot across. I felt like I was pantomiming the motions as I shoved the blades into the ground and heaped up an earthen wall in no time.

As we dug, we kicked up more earth until a dust cloud formed, but a breeze came up the mountain and began to blow the dust away. I could see the water shining far below us for the first time, about two miles away. It was strange to think that seawater had covered this world just weeks ago.

After the first hundred scoops or so, the work began to get a little more taxing. I welcomed the prickling of sweat I felt as I kept going.

"Sir?" asked Kwon, coming to stand over my growing trench.

I looked up at him, feeling a trickle of sweat run down from my face. "Trouble, Kwon?"

"No sir. But I don't know why you're digging your own trench."

"It's good exercise, First Sergeant. I highly recommend it."

120

Around me, the men made quiet, appreciative comments as they worked to connect their trenches to mine. I knew they liked seeing an officer dig a hole, and it was a rare sight. But I wasn't really doing it to generate good will or to raise morale. I'd been in space and eating air-swimmers for weeks. It felt good to get in a solid workout.

After staring down into my dust-filled trench for a full minute, Kwon finally joined me. I guess he felt guilty, or else it looked like fun to him. He spread his hand-shovels and laughed, then dug in. When we hit hard rock, we burned it, and our visors darkened so much we could hardly see.

I imagined that from the bottom of the slope, our activities must look like we were tearing the mountain apart. The enemy would be barely able to see us, if they were looking. We'd be buried in a plume of billowing gray dust.

When I was tired of digging, I contacted Fleet. This time I was looking for Marvin, not Captain Sarin.

"Marvin? What is the story with the ring? Have you managed to gain control of it yet?"

"All my attempts to do so have failed, Colonel Riggs," he said. "The enemy might be jamming my efforts by sending in a flood of conflicting command signals. I'm getting resonance readings from the ring that seem like static, but I suspect someone is transmitting signals to it."

I shook my head in disappointment. "That blows my easy victory," I said.

I'd hoped to land, then hit the machines by surprise by reversing the flow of the ring. If I could have gotten the ocean currents to suck a few trillion gallons of seawater out into another star system somewhere, the Macros in the vicinity would have been destroyed or at least seriously inconvenienced.

"Well," I said, "keep trying. If we can get the ring to suck them back where they came from, we'll pretty much win right there."

"Will do, Colonel," Marvin said, "but I calculate the odds of success as rather low."

I glared up into the sky, wondering about Marvin and his true motivations. Too often, that robot was a mystery to me.

"Just keep trying," I snapped, and disconnected. I turned to Kwon and told him the bad news.

"We're going to have to do this the hard way," I said.

Kwon was overjoyed. "No problem, sir! We'll gut every machine personally. Ha!"

I nodded unhappily. Kwon loved nothing more than a good fight, but sometimes he didn't seem to see the big picture. The machines weren't going to go down easily.

Our first surprise came when we were about half-way done with digging. It came in the form of a series of blazing lights and ripping sounds from above us. I looked up the mountainside to see what was going on. It was hard to make out due to the visibility issues, but there was something happening up there.

I connected to the command channel and tried to make sense of the chatter. The various tactical channels were buzzing. Something was happening, and it seemed to be centered on our original LZ. I didn't like the sound of that.

"Kwon!" I shouted over my local chat—then I remembered the chain of command, "Kwon, Captain Marcos, report!"

They quickly responded. "Captain, get your men into firing positions. We're done digging for now. Kwon, assist the Captain, please."

They began relaying the instructions and the marines around me started to hustle. They tromped and even flew past, stowing their smart metal hand scoops and unlimbering heavier equipment. Within a minute, they were all sitting in an assigned trench with weapons pointed watchfully in every direction.

In the meantime, I'd received my first reports about what was happening upslope. The machines had broken through the crust of the mountain and attacked the second wave of freshly-dropped troops as they were landing.

Any invasion force is at its weakest when in the very act of making landfall. No one wants to drop directly into a fight. The Macros had never been known for giving us a lot of breathing room.

"Kwon!" I roared again. "I mean, Captain Marcos...dammit...assign a squad to distribute barrels of constructive nanites. I want every trench we have layered with a network of nanite strands. Then, have half your men continue with the digging while the rest stand ready to engage anything that hits us."

"But sir," objected the Captain. She was another lump of metal to me in her suit, but the pitch of her voice was higher than most.

"Those nanites are on reserve for a permanent base structure. Our supply is—"

"The supply is more than adequate to comply with my orders as given, Marcos. Get moving."

She didn't say anything more to me, but a lot of shouting began on the company channel. I muted that one and tried to raise someone up at the LZ. Finally, a Captain Ling answered my questions.

"We're in action, sir. Not many of the machines here, but they are hard to kill. We've only encountered the small ones that dig. They're coming at us from inside the mountain. Repeat, they're burrowing, sir."

"Just as I thought. I want you to conduct a fighting withdrawal downslope, Captain Ling."

"I can't see a thing, sir."

"I know, but you can tell which way is down, can't you? The machines can't be hitting you very hard up there yet. I'm sure you can get out and move. I've established a makeshift firebase down here. We're waiting for you on that mountain spur below you on your maps, at an altitude of four thousand feet. Get down here, we'll cover your retreat."

"Yes sir."

Every instinct urged me to call in support: fighters, heavy beams from above, or even to advance with Captain Marcos' company to meet them. But I resisted the temptation. In the chaos of a general landing which had been hastily planned and executed at best, we all had to make due. I wanted to keep major assets like the fighters in reserve until I knew where they could best be deployed.

I didn't want to abandon the fortifications I was building, either. I knew this firebase we were in the middle of constructing would form a much needed strongpoint as the invasion progressed. The troops were going to keep falling from the sky for the next day or so. As the battalions kept coming down, Captain Ling and a dozen men like him had to fight their own battles independently until we established a coherent front and could set up lines with the enemy to push against.

One of the problems with fighting the Macros was their reactions in combat. Human troops were predictable, they would typically break when a certain level of losses were taken, for example. In a situation like this one, humans usually wouldn't react quickly. When the Allied forces invaded France on D-day, for example, the German troops were slow to react. They held back and allowed the Allies to get a critical stronghold before counterattacking. Experiencing a short state of shock was pretty normal for a human army when attacked suddenly.

The Macros, however, were machines. They weren't experiencing any kind of shock. They weren't going to fall back and try to figure out a safe course of action. They were going to throw themselves at us and bleed us wherever they could. They didn't really care about dying, other than seeing it as a form of mission failure. If they could win a battle by dying, through self-sacrifice, they were very happy to do so. It was like fighting a nest full of gigantic, intelligent insects with bad attitudes.

Looking over my maps, I contacted Captain Sarin next. She was overseeing the entire drop from space. "Fleet, this is Colonel Riggs. Respond, please."

It took a second, but I had the Captain on the line very quickly.

"What is it, Colonel?" Sarin asked. She sounded harried.

"I know you have a lot going on, Captain, but I want you to change the targeted LZ. Don't send the next battalion down at the same location."

There was a moment of quiet, during which I heard rasping sounds. Possibly, she'd taken up a microphone and switched the channel to a private line.

"Are you sure you want to second guess the plan now, Colonel?"

"Yes," I said firmly. "The Macros are already digging under the initial LZ. I want you to drop each remaining battalion in a random pattern at about the eight thousand foot level. Find a good shelf of rock and drop them on it. We'll establish firebases wherever we can lower down for the men to assemble."

"A random pattern?" she asked. "That is not good procedure, Colonel. I can't condone it."

"Yeah, well, you're up there with the Fleet. Things look a little different down here."

I quickly filled her in on the lightning-fast enemy reactions to our landings.

"We're going to have to keep shifting our LZs," I said. "They're harassing us much faster than we suspected they would."

Jasmine was a stickler for details and didn't like changing plans in mid-motion. As a commander, I considered this to be a strength

124

and a weakness at the same time—depending on whether she was right or not. But in this case, I overruled her objections and ordered her to move the LZs.

"What about the fighters, sir?" Kwon asked from behind me. "I thought we were supposed to have air cover."

He was standing in my trench. I wondered what he'd overheard. I had him on the command channel feed because he operated as my personal aide. Figuring he'd heard it all, I shook my head.

"I'm not calling down any fire support until I have something big enough for them to shoot at. So far, the enemy are just digging up out of the ground under our feet and trying to slice them off."

Kwon chuckled at that idea and made stomping motions with his amazingly large boots. "They're going to have a hard time taking the feet off of these suits, Colonel!"

I had to agree with him.

Shortly after I disconnected from the command channel, I saw a shower of loose white dust rising up directly above us. It was clear after a few moments of observation that whoever was making that dust cloud was coming directly toward us.

I zoomed in and saw the dark shapes of marines racing down the mountain ahead of the billowing cloud.

"Captain Marcos!" I boomed. "Get a few long-ranged turrets set up. I want them on overwatch in case anything is chasing those men!"

The company surged into action around me. They'd been busy laying out nanites in the fresh trenches. The nanites themselves were lacing together the soil, hardening it and forming polymer filaments in the dirt that were as strong as steel.

Now, the troops switched to pulling out and deploying our heavy-weapons pods. Every drop company had three of them: automated laser turrets with beam projectors that were about six feet long from tip to base. These were placed on tripods and attached to three critical elements: a generator, a brainbox and a small sensor array. Set on automatic, these units operated primarily as air cover.

But they could also be switched to manual control. With a marine as a gunner, they'd been designed to serve as a heavy gun against ground targets.

Three corporals with specialized training stepped into the gunner's slot when the pods had been put together and powered.

Today, if we were going to be hit, it was going to be by ground forces.

The first clue came when I saw a marine get sucked into the dust cloud. He'd been running along steadily, kicking up a huge plume of dust behind him one second. The next second, he was gone.

I attempted to connect with Captain Ling again. "Ling? Are you there? Report your status. You are less than one mile from my position, in my estimation."

"Big ones, Colonel!" came Ling's response. It was almost a scream. "They are coming up out of the mountain, under our feet."

"Well then, fly man!" I shouted. "Fly! Gunners, if you see anything unusual, you have my permission to take a shot at it."

"Negative, Colonel," Captain Marcos said. "We can't do that. We'll be hitting marines if we fire blindly into that dust cloud."

I shook my head in frustration. I didn't argue with the captain, because she was right. But it was disturbing.

What could be chasing those men? It couldn't be just a few worker Macros. They were no match for drop-troops in power-armor.

It had to be something else.

-17-

I saw flying power-suits now, rising up above the dust cloud itself. Looking like tiny black and silver dolls riding a hurricane, they came at us as if they'd been thrown in our direction.

Reaching the upper limits of the cloud and cruising there above it, the men were burning their power supplies at an alarming rate. These suits were highly protective and had many functional advantages over lighter gear, but long operating life wasn't one of them.

I frowned and zoomed in tighter. I thought I'd seen…yes, I was sure of it. A silvery rope-like tentacle had reached out and grabbed a marine. One second he'd been there, riding over the cloud. The next he'd been sucked back down into the dust, yanked out of sight.

"Ling?" I called. "You still there? Report."

There was no response.

"Whoever is in command of Bravo Company, Sixth Battalion, please—"

I didn't get any farther, because suddenly the dust cloud settled. What was revealed beneath it made the words die in my throat.

The fleeing company had hit a stretch of exposed flat rock. With nothing much to kick up, they left the cloud behind and I finally saw what was chasing them: a nightmare of burnished metal.

The machine coming at us was unlike anything I'd ever encountered. It was big, with more bulk to it than the largest robots. It wasn't shaped like a typical Macro, either. Instead of having eight legs like a steel spider, it had the shape of a horseshoe crab.

Underneath was a churning mass of small legs, which I realized as it got closer were really whipping, snake-like arms.

The moment I saw it, I could only think of one thing. Kwon thought of it too, and he put the thought into words first: "It looks like a giant, crazy version of Marvin, sir," he said.

"Yeah, it kind of does."

From the armored back of the monster sprouted longer arms. These could stretch a hundred feet into the air. As we watched, it used these thick tentacles to deadly effect, reaching out and snatching flying marines as they tried to escape it. The unlucky troops were dragged down to the front of the machine, where they were unceremoniously shoved into the monster's maw. The opening was more of doorway than a mouth, as there didn't seem to be any teeth or jaws. I could see inside now, and it was filled with a livid red heat that reminded me of a lava flow. I figured it had some kind of melting furnace inside, probably built to digest ores it found in the mountain.

"What the bloody hell is it, sir?" Kwon asked.

"Some kind of mining bot, I'd assume," I said. "What matters now is that Ling's company is bringing it right to us. Get those heavy beamers firing on the carapace! It has to have a weak point!"

He relayed my orders, but orders weren't really necessary. The gunners could see the monster now, and they didn't need any encouragement. They knew what to do. My visor dimmed as streaks burned the air and punched through the roiling dust clouds. Two of the gunners focused on burning off whipping arms, while the third tried for a lucky hit on the thing's mouth. None of these beams seemed overly effective.

"Why didn't Ling just blow it up?" Kwon asked wonderingly.

I knew he was referring to the tactical nuclear grenades many marines had as part of their kits. Each company had been equipped with ten of them.

"It probably got in too close," I said. "They couldn't get away to that quarter-mile safe zone around it before lighting a grenade."

"I might of done it anyway," Kwon remarked, still staring at the approaching monstrosity."

"I bet you would have."

Kwon had been officially forbidden to touch heavy explosives. I'd been personally injured more than once by his negligent use of tactical grenades.

"All right," I shouted, engaging the company override. Every helmet in the immediate vicinity buzzed with my voice. "This is Riggs. Get into your holes and flatten yourselves out. We'll burn this thing from underneath if it overruns our position. If it has a thousand legs, it probably can't operate with only five hundred left."

Kwon looked at me in surprise, but then quickly jumped down into a foxhole. A hundred other marines did the same. They'd been expecting a battle, but this was more like surviving a stampede. We couldn't stop the thing, it was too close now and going too fast. Momentum alone was going to carry it downslope and directly overtop of us even if it died in the next second.

What had looked bizarre and alien at a distance was absolutely terrifying up close. The sound it made—it was almost indescribable. Like ten freight trains bearing down on me at once and running me over while I shivered in a hole. I'd heard descriptions of tornadoes tearing at homes while the owners huddle in the basement—this was louder than that.

A moment later, the sun went out and I knew I was under it. I felt as if a battleship with legs had walked over me. I learned then that the small feet underneath weren't all that small. They were each a foot thick and twenty feet long. The entire monstrosity had to be five hundred feet across.

We laid on our backs down there in our holes while dirt sifted down onto our visors and we fired our beams up into the belly. My plans of fighting the thing from underneath quickly disintegrated. I'd thought maybe we could chop off those legs and disable it—but instead it was the legs that disabled us.

There were so many of them. Hundreds of thick, steel, squirming legs. They were tube-shaped and moved with rippling segments. The worst part was that they came right down into our holes with us.

The monster robot *stepped on* us with its hundreds of legs. The fantastic weight of the machine was distributed over all those supports, but it was spread unevenly. Some men were hit with a thousand pounds of downward pressure or less, which only left bright scratches on their metal casings.

Others were not so lucky. Some must have been treated to ten or even a hundred tons of weight. Legs, chests and most certainly visors were crushed. Men shrieked or died in silence, depending on the nature of their injuries.

Still, my marines were firing their weapons as best they could. They howled in pain, fright and fury. They burned at the legs and the black wall of metal that loomed over them, cutting out the light of the white sun.

Dirt sifted down over me, and I couldn't see much. I felt as if I'd buried myself in a grave of my own design. Lying there, I had time to think about how considerate I'd been to the Macros. I'd ordered my entire company to dig their own graves and plant themselves at the bottom of them. My foresight would save the enemy a lot of time disposing of us later on.

After an eternity that was probably less than thirty seconds in real time, the shadow lifted. Sunlight glared in my face again. I sat up, but had to struggle to turn around. My right leg had been damaged. It didn't hurt, and it was still attached to my hip, but it wasn't bending. Clearly, the machine had stepped on me and damaged my power-suit's leg. I checked the read-outs: liquid flows indicated bleeding down around the knee.

Grunting and heaving with my arms, I levered myself around to face the retreating monster, which had overrun our position and kept going downslope. I didn't have time for injuries. I had to get back into the fight.

My marines were in the same frame of mind. The survivors popped up like gophers all around me and we sent a hail of burning fire after the creature. Within less than a minute, there was a shocking result: the machine exploded.

The booming report and brilliant flash caused all of us to take cover. Seconds later, dust, shrapnel and chunks of rock came twirling down to rain on us.

"Someone finally nuked it," Kwon said from beside me. "About time. I would have done it right off."

"Yeah," I said. "And this time, I think you would have been doing the right thing."

"Yeah," Kwon said. He climbed up to the rim of the foxhole we were in. It had turned into something that more closely resembled a smoking crater. He extended a big hand down in my direction.

I took it, and he helped me climb out of the hole. My right leg still wasn't operating. After going over the data, I determined it was lacerated and pinched inside the crushed armor. My power-suit's right leg was about an inch thinner than it was supposed to be, but it was still attached and the nanites were working to repair the damage.

All around us, the men tended to the wounded. Some marines had to dig themselves out of their own foxholes, which had been filled in by the passing monster.

Captain Ling showed up a few minutes later, coming from the north. I greeted him without enthusiasm.

"You could have warned us what kind of company you were bringing with you," I said.

"Sorry sir, but we didn't really know what we were dealing with. We crossed a wide gash in the mountain which looked artificial. We paused to investigate, but a shower of dust plumed up, obscuring everything. Before I knew what was happening, my men were running, saying some kind of monster was in the hole."

"It was a monster, all right. How many did you lose?"

"I just did a headcount. I've got thirty-three effectives left."

I stared at him. "Including the losses of in my company, we're down about a hundred marines. Captain Marcos was also killed, her visor crushed by that machine. That's unacceptable. You're reduced in rank to second Lieutenant. Go get your most senior platoon leader and change places with him."

Ling looked shocked. He dropped his eyes and stared at my boots.

"Yes sir…but, sir? My senior lieutenant is dead."

"Do you have *any* lieutenants left?"

He finally located one, a short African-America man with a gravelly voice and a cocky look on his face. He had narrowed, squinting eyes and a bad attitude. I liked him immediately.

"Lieutenant Gaines," I said upon meeting him. "Congratulations. I'm promoting you to captain. You're in charge of this new, melded company. I've chosen you because Captain Marcos is dead, and I've lost confidence in Ling. I'm folding both units into one as of now."

He looked at me with quick eyes. He didn't appear eager, but he didn't look worried, either. "What about the other lieutenants in Ling's company?" he asked.

I shook my head. "They'll serve under you. They're fine men, but they didn't just ride down this mountain on the back of a battleship-sized machine and survive. You did. I like survival traits. If you keep staying alive you'll get promoted again."

He nodded and flashed me a hint of a smile. "I'm going to hold you to that deal, sir."

I chuckled and turned back to rebuilding the firebase. The survivors were almost all injured in some way, but they were still game.

I sat down with my newly-minted captain and had a little talk with him while a medical bot worked on my leg. Mostly, it ripped off my power-suit's leg and hammered it back into shape.

Exposed, my flesh felt odd and prickly. I knew the nanites were at work in my bloodstream, having a race with the microbials that also called my body home to see who could repair my flesh the fastest. It was strange, having two colonies of microscopic creatures working to heal you at once. It was also itchy.

Fortunately, the atmosphere of Yale was breathable for humans. The nitrogen was a bit high, but not toxic. I could smell the air that drifted up from the opening at the suit's hip-socket to my helmet.

Every planet has a smell, and I had to say this one wasn't a good smell. It reminded me of a beach covered in dead fish. I guess that was to be expected. The oceans had been drained and heated. Lots of things had died here lately and they hadn't finished decaying yet.

"Colonel?" Gaines asked me, looking around with his helmet off. "Are we going to stay on this shithole for long?"

I looked him in the eye. "I don't think that's the question you really want to ask. What you want to know is what every marine in this unit wants to know: why are we here?"

Captain Gaines nodded.

"Well, we're here because there were about a trillion intelligent biotic beings on this world a month ago, and the Macros have already killed half of them. The rest were about to die when we arrived. I think we've done pretty well already. Looking over the casualties so far, we've lost about one human for every million Crustaceans we saved by coming here."

"Sounds like a good deal," Gaines said. "But the Crustaceans are still technically the enemy."

I shook my head. "I don't think so. They could have hit us when we landed, but they didn't. They're cooperating with us by staying out of it. By the end of this battle, I expect to see human and Crustacean marines fighting side-by-side. That's why we're really here. To gain another powerful ally against the machines."

Captain Gaines appeared to think about it. I could tell he wasn't fully convinced, but at least he had listened.

The truth was that few humans liked the Lobsters. If they all died, not too many of us would cry about it. They were irritating when you talked to them, and even worse when you fought with them. They were tricky, arrogant, and very difficult to convince of anything that wasn't their idea to begin with. But I hadn't given up on them yet. I couldn't afford to. There were just too damned many of the bastards. I needed their numbers to swell my ranks against the machines.

"There's something else I'd like to talk to you about," Gaines said. "It's about that machine—it wasn't a normal Macro design. You noticed that, didn't you?"

"How could I not?"

"It wasn't a pure Macro, as I understand these things. It had those arms—that's nano-tech, isn't it?"

"Yeah," I said. "I know what you're getting at, and I've been thinking about it too. I don't like the implications. If the Macros have begun to weave the Nano technology into their systems designs...well, that removes one of our key strategic advantages."

"That thing was some kind of hybrid. It reminded me of that robot friend of yours. What's his name?"

"Marvin," I said, "yes, there was a resemblance."

Gaines gave me a hard stare. "He hasn't been in touch with the Macros, has he sir?" he asked. "This Marvin bot of yours? You don't think he's been giving them ideas?"

"Do you have any evidence on which to base that accusation, Captain?"

"Sorry if you don't want to hear that, Colonel."

I thought about it, and his question made too much sense. He had to ask it. The thing had looked like a gigantic version of Marvin, after all.

Where had the Macros gotten the idea to build such a thing? Had they examined Marvin from afar and copied him? I shook my head slowly.

133

"Don't be sorry, Captain," I said. "I want you to keep giving me ideas like that, whenever you have one."

"Sure thing."

We had some coffee and talked about less disturbing things for a few minutes, such as gun emplacements, patrol schedules and enemy sightings.

All the while we spoke, however, my mind was in a different place. How *had* the Macros gotten the idea to use Nano tech? Where had they found the factories to make the nanites in the first place? The Macro factories couldn't do such fine work.

Distracted, I went over recent events in my mind carefully. Marvin had been in contact with the Macros as a translator on many occasions. He'd also transmitted codes through the ring in an attempt to shut it off—but he had ended up reversing it, which had allowed the Macros to invade. Had that been an actual accident? I couldn't be a hundred percent sure.

It would be easy enough to assume that the Macros had observed us and adapted to our behavior patterns. We were now using both Nano and Macro factories and producing equipment that combined both technologies. But the Macros in my experience had never been so adaptable that they could begin using tech they were unfamiliar with. They almost had to be reprogrammed to go in an entirely new directly. But how had the idea originated? Who had given it to them?

I just didn't know, and not knowing disturbed me.

Over the next hour, our base swelled as four more companies arrived. Upslope, more and more troops kept dropping in. There were eight firebases like mine now, scattered over the mountainous island. The enemy had yet to put in a major appearance, but I expected a counterpunch at any moment.

When the strike came, it wasn't a surprise. Often the Macros behaved in a predictable fashion. But they did hurt us.

"Missiles sir!" Captain Gaines shouted in my headset.

I didn't bother to ask for confirmation, range or numbers. The enemy concentrations were only twenty miles distant, and their missiles flew like ICBMs. We didn't have much time to react.

I tapped into the general override for the entire mission. "Marines, this is Colonel Riggs. We have incoming enemy missiles. Activate all defensive systems. Take immediate cover anywhere you can."

134

I switched over to operational command and contacted Captain Sarin.

"Jasmine? This is it. They're making their first play. Send down your fighter wing on CAP to give us air cover."

"Already done, Colonel," she responded crisply. "They're on the way down. They'll reach effective range in ninety-five seconds. I've scrambled my second wing as well. Will you require more coverage?"

I didn't know enough yet to answer her. I didn't even know if two minutes would be quick enough. Part of me wanted to second-guess myself, to chide myself for not having brought the fighter cover down earlier.

I hadn't done it because we couldn't be sure how this attack was going to play out. The machines might have come at us with a massive ground attack. In that case, the fighters were not going to be as effective as ground troops. Because these Macros had shields, they were hard targets for low-wattage lasers on a fighter ship. The tiny craft couldn't penetrate the shields and they couldn't fly into them either, as the shields would turn rigid and destroy something moving as fast as a fighter.

I hadn't wanted to waste my fighters, so I'd held them in reserve. Now it was turning out that I needed them. Each tiny ship possessed a gun that could be fired manually or in an automatic mode when slaved to a brainbox. When full-auto was selected, each fighter became a small, flying point-defense laser turret. It was harder to hit something when both the platform and the target were moving, so they usually sat at altitude and hovered.

That's the mission I had in mind for them today. The pilots wouldn't like it much, as there wasn't much glory in sitting at a hundred thousand feet watching your ship shoot at missiles, but that was just too bad.

"Jasmine," I said, "you've got better data up there and a more stable situation. You make the call. What are we facing?"

"I've got about four hundred incoming birds, sir. They've just left the sea and are inbound for your beachhead. ETA: four minutes."

"Four hundred?" I asked, disheartened. "Are they nuclear or conventional?"

"Unknown."

I grimaced and thought hard for a second. This didn't look good. Our fighter wings contained four squadrons of twelve fighters each— we hadn't bothered with dividing them into groups. The carrier I'd brought with us was capable of transporting two fighter wings— about a hundred ships in all.

Right now, I was pretty sure that wasn't going to be enough guns. Only forty-eight fighters would be in range to provide us defensive fire. Even combined with the small turrets our companies were carrying with them…there just wasn't enough guns to stop all those missiles. Some were going to make it through.

"Are you there, Colonel?" Sarin asked.

"I'm here. I'm just regretting coming to save the Crustaceans about now."

"I understand, sir."

More alarming thoughts piled on top of my first ones. I realized that if the enemy hit us hard enough right now, they could break our invasion before it really got started. In fact, the more I thought about it, the more I believed that was exactly what they were attempting to do.

"Captain Sarin, contact your fighters. Move them to a higher elevation. Place them at maximum range to hit those missiles effectively."

"They can't possibly shoot them all down from that high, sir."

"I know that, but I believe these weapons are nukes. Or at least, a large number of them are. That's why the Macros have more or less sat quietly while we unloaded all our troops. They wanted us all down and set up as sitting ducks. Now, they'll unload on us in one hard, smashing blow."

Sarin was quiet for a long second. When she spoke again, there was dread in her voice. I knew she could see my logic and agreed with me. "What are your orders, Colonel?"

"Let's try what we did in the past. Intercept their missiles with a volley of our own."

"Should I use nuclear warheads?"

"Of course," I said.

"How many should I launch?"

"All of them."

"Plotting…the mission is in the computer, sir. The birds will fly shortly. Flight time to intercept range…forty seconds. Launching— now."

There were a million things either of us could have said in this horrible moment, but we both knew there just wasn't time to talk things over. I'd half-expected her to point out, for example, that I'd made it our policy not to use nukes on Yale for environmental concerns. But that just didn't matter anymore. This had become a matter of survival.

We had to operate on the worst-case basis. We had to assume the incoming missiles were nuclear, not conventional. To do otherwise might be committing suicide.

I knew that if we were wrong, the enemy would have scored a coup. We were expending all of our nuclear missiles blowing up the Macro barrage. Quite possibly, we were doing nothing more than creating a very large radioactive cloud for nothing.

But there wasn't time to debate. There wasn't even time to second-guess. We had to assume this was doomsday, because if it was and we didn't play it right, my little invasion force wasn't going to exist five minutes from now.

"The birds are reaching their target altitudes," Jasmine said in my helmet. "Darken your visors, sir."

"We're ready."

"Good luck, Kyle," she said quietly.

This was a big breach of protocol for Captain Sarin. When under battle conditions, she rarely used my first name. I figured she believed my situation could well be terminal. I had to agree with her.

"Thank you, Jasmine," I said. "If this goes badly, you'll be in command of the task force. Miklos will be in overall command of Star Force. Riggs out."

I felt like I'd just written my own epitaph. Jasmine knew what I meant: if I die in the next few minutes, take over. It had been a hard thing to say. But what followed over the next two minutes was worse.

Around me, the men had all taken cover. The signal to darken visors had gone out, and every faceplate was jet-black. We all hunkered down, waiting for doom. Most of the men didn't know what was about to hit us. A few did. All of them stayed low and quiet.

137

It's a hard thing, waiting in an alien hole for hundreds of missiles to land on top of you. I knew every breath was quite possibly my last. It was frustrating not being able to do anything about my own fate. I'd much preferred facing down that bizarre mining Macro, for example, to this. At least then, I'd had something to shoot at. Taking action makes a man fear death less.

Sitting in a hole as the seconds ticked by…it was one of the hardest things I'd ever had to do. Fortunately, I didn't have to wait long.

The flashes began out over the eastern horizon. They were pretty at first, flaring greenish-white through our blacked-out visors. Fantastic power was being released out there. I didn't have a tactical table handy to figure out how many we'd stopped, or how many were still coming.

I couldn't see the fighters, they were too high up. Hanging in the upper atmosphere, I knew they were stabbing down at the surviving missiles with hot invisible beams of light, but I couldn't see any of that, either.

In the last seconds, I did see contrails. I knew that was a very bad sign. Incoming trails could only mean one thing: some of the enemy missiles had made it through.

A moment later, the impacts began. They were nuclear. There were no mushroom clouds yet, those would rise up later. In the first moments after a nuclear explosion, there's nothing but a blooming sphere of heat, light and a sound that's beyond all sounds.

These effects combined into what we call a shockwave, one of which rolled over my unnamed firebase.

Because my visor was the weakest part of my armor, I'd rolled over and hugged the dirt facedown. When the shockwave hit, it felt as if something huge had jumped on my back, and I lost consciousness.

-18-

I was still breathing. At first, I wasn't entirely sure about that, but after a few hitching gasps, I knew it was true. I was still alive—for now.

Groaning, I tried to roll over. It didn't happen. My suit seemed to be dead. I wasn't sure what was wrong, but it felt like about two thousand pounds of dead weight.

I realized I was having trouble breathing. The air mix in my suit—I looked for the readouts, but of course there was nothing. The HUD was dark.

My first thought was that the generator on my back had gone out. Possibly, it had been damaged by whatever had landed on my back. I struggled to get up.

I'm a powerful man. Quite possibly, I'm the most powerful man physically that's ever lived. I've undergone treatments that the rest of my men hadn't. Microbial baths had been piled atop of the changes the nanites had made, and had scarred my guts and muscles until they couldn't be toughened or improved any further.

My conclusion was that I should have been able to move in my power-suit, even if it had gone dead. Like power steering in a car, a man could still wrestle with the wheel even if the hydraulics failed.

I strained and grunted, and I felt myself shift, but not by much. I couldn't get a breath—that was the problem. I was suffocating, and the suit that was supposed to protect me was now killing me.

I fought to think clearly. Everything hurt, my head was buzzing, and thinking was harder than it should be. Oxygen deprivation, that had to be a factor.

A growing certainty came over me: I was going to die right here, face down in this dusty hole. I wondered if I'd rate a tombstone on this spot someday. I thought about what the inscription might say: *Here lies Colonel Kyle Riggs of the infamous Riggs' Pigs. He dug his own grave, laid down in it, and buried himself for the convenience of the machines.*

Angrily, I thrashed about, trying to move my limbs in any possible direction. There did seem to be some lateral range of movement to my left arm. I could swing my gauntlet back and forth, working the elbow joint.

I found also that I was able to turn my head. Getting an idea, I turned my head to the left, pushed away my fist as far as it would go, then smashed it into my faceplate.

I did it with a little too much force, as it turned out. My nose was pulped. But the visor did break, and dusty, smoke-laden air rolled in. It wasn't good air, but there was some oxygen in it. I coughed and wheezed. After a few seconds, I felt better.

Star Force marines are tougher than normal humans. We'd been toughened further over the years. I recalled reading that the aboriginal peoples of the past were much hardier folk than soft, modern humans who sat all day at their computer stations. We marines had changed all that. We were the ones in the record books now.

I breathed in dusty, radioactive soot and I did so greedily. My lungs burned, as the air was hot. I had to guess the ambient temperature was around one hundred fifty degrees Fahrenheit. It was hot enough to kill a normal man, but for someone who'd once rebuilt himself to go down into the atmosphere of a gas giant, it wasn't all that bad.

Feeling stronger, I heaved. The thing on my back shifted and swayed. I knew now that it wasn't a ton of earth or a huge rock. I couldn't be buried if I was getting air in through my visor.

Roaring and straining, I managed to get to my knees. Finally, the fantastic weight on my back rolled away. Then I saw what had pinned me down: it was Kwon.

I checked his suit, and it was dead as well. I punched out his visor and reached inside. Blood trickled from his face.

For a few long seconds, I figured he was gone. I've known Kwon for years, and there'd never been a more faithful, loyal person in my life. I didn't want to lose him.

I should have gotten up and called for a corpsman, but I didn't. I knew I had better things to do. I had an army to look after, and a war to fight. But instead, I spent the next few precious minutes trying to save Kwon.

He'd been without oxygen for a considerable length of time. Normally, four minutes resulted in brain-death for a human being. But in the case of a Star Force marine, that could be extended considerably.

Even after our bodies shut down, the nanites in us didn't. They had programs to maintain, and could even keep blood trickling when the heart stopped pumping. In emergencies, they could go to the lungs, gather oxygen and distribute it to critical centers of the body. These extreme measures wouldn't keep you alive forever, but they might double the time a man had before suffocating.

After working on him with a first aid kit and a fresh nanite medical injection over the heart, I was able to get a pulse. He didn't wake up, but he was alive.

I slumped back in my incredibly heavy suit, gasping for air myself. A figure appeared at the top of my dusty hole and looked down at me.

"You're alive, Colonel?" asked Captain Gaines.

"It would appear so," I mumbled.

"Here's some water."

He handed down a bottle and I sucked on it, spat out a gray mass, and sucked on it some more.

"You survived again, Gaines," I said when some of the dust had been cleared from my throat.

"Yes sir."

"If you get off this rock in one piece, I'm going to make you a Major."

"I'm going to remember that, sir."

Just about then, Kwon sneezed. It was a big sneeze, the kind only a big man can make. A fine wet mist rose up from his smashed visor. The mist was part blood and part snot. I grimaced. He reminded me of a whale, clearing its blowhole.

"You awake, Kwon?"

141

"No sir," he said. "I'm still dreaming."

I nodded. I knew exactly how he felt.

"Colonel," Gaines said, "with your permission, I'm going to check on the rest of my company."

"Do it. I'll join you soon. Are communications up with Fleet?"

"Negative sir, the blast that hit us was laced with an EMP. I think that's what killed our suit functions."

I nodded. "Bastard machines. They know how to hurt us. Let me know when you have communications up again."

"Will do, sir," he said, then he trudged away.

"I can feel the radiation," Kwon complained. He had yet to move. He just laid there on his back like a beached whale. "I hate that feeling. It makes my teeth ache."

"Yeah," I said. "I recall reading about the Russian troops who were tasked with cleaning up the mess after the nuclear reactor at Chernobyl exploded. They called them human robots."

Kwon's face stirred and his eyes looked at me. He hadn't bothered to sit up yet.

"Didn't they have real robots?" he asked.

"Yeah, they had some. But it was 1986, and they didn't have good ones. Strangely, delicate electronics are more vulnerable to radiation than biological systems—such as humans. The real robots all broke down."

"What happened to the men?" Kwon asked. I could see the whites of his eyes in his helmet. He stared up at me, looking at me from an odd angle. I figured this was easier for him than turning his head.

"Most of them lived, surprisingly. They had lots of problems, of course. And they tasted metal in their mouths for the rest of their lives."

"Yeah, I think I've got that right now."

I nodded. "Can you get up yet?"

"No sir. That's going to take a while."

I knelt and frowned down at him. "What's wrong?"

"I'm pretty sure my neck is broken. I'm paralyzed. Sorry about that, Colonel."

"It's all right."

Over the next half-hour, we were in emergency recovery-mode. No follow-up assaults came from the seas or the Macros that we knew were crawling all over the other islands in the region. I prepared to inject Kwon with a pasty mixture of nanites and microbial "sauce", a medical concoction we used for serious injuries. The package said "bone injury" on the side, so I hoped it could handle cracked vertebrae. I was more worried about his spinal cord damage, but couldn't find anything that referenced that.

The needle on the syringe was about six inches long and as thick around as a ballpoint pen. Kwon looked at it, his eyes rolling in concern.

"I'm not going to feel that, right?" he said hopefully. "I mean, I can't feel my arms or legs."

"Sure," I lied, and jabbed him in the neck with the needle. The bulb at the end of the syringe was smart metal. It sensed it was go-time and started pumping beige fluids into his flesh.

Kwon squinched up his eyes and made a hissing sound. "I hate needles."

I patted his helmet and pulled the dripping needle out of his neck. "You'll be fine in an hour."

I left him there, flat on his back in the foxhole. I figured it was the safest spot available at the moment.

Next, I sought Captain Gaines. He'd been taking in reports and we went over some numbers together, which we reported back up to Captain Sarin. She was in a better position to see the entire battlefield situation, so I put her in charge of ops—with guiding suggestions from me.

"We lost about eleven hundred men due to missile strikes," she said. "Added to those lost in the initial drop and various mishaps, such as the mining machine, that totals up to about fifteen percent of your total force, Colonel."

"Not bad," I announced, "not bad at all."

I looked around and was mildly surprised when I realized my command staff didn't share my enthusiasm. They weren't wreathed in smiles. They obviously didn't agree with my assessment. I tried not to notice their sour moods, but after a few seconds, I grew angry with them.

"Did you people come here not expecting to take serious losses?" I demanded. "We just hot-dropped on an uncharted planet. That takes huge balls, and so far, I figure we've been lucky."

Captain Gaines lifted his hand. "I didn't expect heavy losses so early, sir."

I glared around at the rest. Majors and captains shifted uncomfortably. Some appeared about to speak up, but thought the better of it and remained silent.

"Some of you might be under the impression we dropped too close to the enemy lines. But we had no choice. We're less than ten miles from the enemy concentrations because we *couldn't* drop at a safer distance. These islands are the only scraps of available land."

"But so many lost…" Captain Gaines began.

"Back in World War Two," I said, interrupting him, "the Americans lost twenty four hundred marines on Omaha Beach in a few hours. During the invasion of Okinawa, over a hundred and fifty thousand died on both sides. The lesson here is that beachheads are often hard to establish. Quit whining."

No one was actually whining, but they still managed to look glum. I turned away from them and continued planning the next stage of the assault. I gathered a few nearby officers and connected the rest up via their HUDs. Captain Sarin was there in a virtual sense, as were a number of others.

"Now, it's time to bring down the second wave. I want those three battalions water-dropped off the beach, here," I said, working a thin, flexible computer screen that looked pretty much like a piece of shelving paper. The sheet was impregnated with photo-reactive nanites that knew their jobs well. Activated by my touch, they collected data from networks that reached all the way up to the ships in orbit.

"So soon, sir?" Captain Gaines asked.

I glanced at him in surprise. He was a junior officer in the extreme, having been a lieutenant earlier in the day. I was somewhat taken aback to be second-guessed by a man who barely deserved to be this meeting.

"Yes. Why not?"

"They just hit us hard. They're probably preparing their follow-up. If we land in the middle of a second missile barrage, we'll take high losses again."

"Presumption, Captain," I said. "Incorrect assessment. The enemy is well-known to me. In their mechanical brains, they marked that last attack down as a failure. They expended a great deal of missiles hoping to take us out early. They lost a lot of ordnance and only killed fifteen percent of our overall ground force. To them, that's a failure."

Gaines shrugged. "So why not do it again?"

"Because they don't like to repeat the same mistake twice in a row. They'll adjust their plans and do something else. That's pretty typical for the machines. They like to hit hard, but they don't hit hard the same way unless it worked the first time."

Gaines nodded. "If you say so, sir."

I stared at him flatly for a second. "I just *did* say it. What we need to do now is get all our forces down out of space onto the ground, where they can do some good."

Gaines raised his hand again. I felt a surge of irritation, but suppressed it. Due to the virtual conference setup, most of the staffers were listening in. They were staying quiet, while this man was interrupting my presentation of the plan with regularity. I could tell he was green and had been fooled by the fact only a few of us were standing here in the dirt together. He was behaving as if it was just he and I on a hill, having a chat.

Reluctantly, I recognized Gaines with a nod.

"I'm assuming we'll now focus on digging in and preparing for their next assault, right Colonel?" he asked.

"Absolutely not," I said. "We're going to attack. That's how we'll cover the water-drop and make sure they make it up onto the beaches, by giving the Macros something else to think about."

Gaines's mouth was open, but there wasn't any sound coming out. I kind of liked him that way. For the first time, I saw a new look in his eyes. It wasn't fear exactly…I would describe it as extreme alarm.

"Are we ready for that, sir?" he asked finally.

"No, of course not. Most military commanders never feel they're entirely ready to attack. But we're going to do it anyway. It will throw the enemy off, and grab the initiative. If they're worried about us coming at them, they can't plot our deaths so easily."

"I don't think that's a good idea, sir."

I'd had enough by now. "Look, Gaines, I've cut you some slack because you're new to operational command. Let me put it to you this way: should I be losing confidence in you? Do you feel unfit for the duties assigned?"

"No sir," he said quickly.

"All right, then shut the hell up. We're all Star Force Marines, and you have the particular misfortune of being directly associated with Riggs' Pigs, meaning whatever unit I'm marching with. My Pigs, whoever they are, aren't known for crouching in holes on mountaintops waiting for enemy assaults. You can read the wiki on that one."

Gaines just nodded. I figured he was going to keep quiet for a while, so I turned my attention to the rest. "I want to hear any other objections the rest of you are bottling up. I want to hear them right now."

Perhaps it was my tone of voice, which was gruff and angry, but no one spoke up.

I showed them their positions, gave them an hour to get their men back on their feet, and broke up the meeting.

A minute or two later my com light was blinking. It was Jasmine Sarin.

"Yes, Captain. What is it?"

"Sir, I wanted to discuss the battle plans with you."

"I just finished rolling up the damned map. Did you think of something else?"

"Well, no sir...I wanted to give you my input concerning the morale of the staff. It's low, sir."

"Yeah. People are always deflated when their team loses one. I'm trying to give them a win now, so they can feel good about themselves again. That's what I am, you know, a glorified grief counselor."

She was quiet for a moment. I could tell she didn't like my sarcasm. Suddenly, I felt a touch of remorse. I liked Jasmine, and I didn't want her to doubt me.

"Is something wrong, sir?" she asked.

"I don't know," I said, sighing. I checked to make sure the channel was a private one. I didn't want to accidentally broadcast even a single second of self-doubt.

"Just between you and me," I began, "Every time I have dealings with the Thor system—with the Lobsters—I end up feeling like I've been duped somehow. I've felt like a puppet since we came out here. At this moment the Crustaceans are hiding in their underwater holes,

146

and by some voodoo they've gotten us to fight battles for them. They didn't even give us a guarantee of an alliance when this is all over."

"These people have suffered grievous losses," she said.

"Yeah. That's about the only thing that allows me to tolerate them."

"You've allowed them to get away with this, because you want them to join us so badly. Perhaps you could contact them and demand commitment."

"I've thought about that, but rejected the idea. I'll do it after I show them some victories. They won't respect anything less. That's a big part of my frustration. So far, we're not looking like big winners on Yale. That means we have no leverage with the Crustaceans."

After we broke off the conversation, I returned to the foxhole with Kwon. I sagged down into it and slumped back to rest. My helmet had repaired itself and was functioning normally, and I was able to set an alarm to wake me up ten minutes before go-time. Soon, Kwon and I were both snoring.

-19-

When my alarm went off, it was a gentle, beeping sound. This soon rose and rose to a shriek. I woke up, slapping at my helmet. This did nothing of course, as the controls were all inside the helmet.

The suit detected that my eyes were open, however, and canceled the alarm. Sourly, I struggled to my feet. I almost fell over Kwon as I checked on him. It was funny how tired a good bombing could make a man once you were used to them. When I got into battle-mode, I tended to shut down for sleep whenever there was a lull in the fighting.

Kwon's eyes snapped open as I regarded him.

"You're ugly," he said.

I snorted. "Same to you, big man. Are you okay? Can you move, First Sergeant?"

Experimentally, he rocked his head from side to side.

"Feels a little crunchy—in my neck area."

"Yeah. That's the dead microbials. They'll drain out of you over the next few days."

Kwon heaved, and managed to sit up. I reached out a hand, but he pushed me away. "No sir," he said, "let me do it."

He climbed to his feet and swayed.

"How old are you Kwon?" I asked him.

"I don't know sir," he said. "I mean—I'm not sure right now. I guess I'm about thirty. Haven't thought about that in a long time. Dates don't mean much when the sun is crazy in the sky. Sometimes, there's no sun at all."

"Yeah, I know what you mean. We've been on so many worlds, I don't think about little stuff like birthdays anymore. But I think I'm forty."

"We should throw you a birthday party. I'll find some black candles somewhere."

I laughed. I clapped him on the back and he winced.

"Sorry," I said. "Still tender back there?"

"I'll be fine."

I knew Kwon was worried he'd be left out of the action to come if I thought he was too injured to fight. He obviously was, but I knew he hated to miss a fight against the machines. I figured it would probably be another hour or two before we made contact with the enemy. That was plenty of time for a nanotized marine with a fresh batch of juice in his blood to recover. Hell, an hour ago he'd been crippled.

"Okay then," I said. "Let's march."

Kwon put on his best show, beating his gauntlets together and bellowing for people to move. I could hear a twinge of pain and weakness in his voice, but I doubted anyone else caught it. Even while half-dead, Kwon was more of a marine than most of them.

Our battalion gathered itself and moved in loosely grouped companies downslope. The machines were concentrated around the beaches in most cases. There were no domed factories on this big island, but then there weren't as many machines per square mile as there were on the other scraps of land. That was one of the reasons I'd landed here.

"Okay," I said over command chat, "you all know the plan. Move in battalion-strength groups down from the mountains to the nearest beach and begin to sweep. Destroy every gathering machine you find. We'll clear this island quickly, then identify our next objective."

I hadn't let my staff in on it yet, but if this mop-up patrol went well, I planned to cross the sea to the nearest island with a macro factory on it. With luck, we'd capture it. In that case we could subjugate the factory and command it to output the supplies we needed. Without luck, it would be destroyed by our assault or self-destruct. Whatever happened, the invaders would be significantly weakened. At least, that was the plan.

Lightning attacks. Shock the enemy lines and dig deeply into them before they could react fully. No matter what, keep moving. That was my plan and I was sticking to it.

Within an hour my battalion, under-strength as it was, had destroyed hundreds of gathering machines. These resembled metal grasshoppers about the size of a luxury sedan. They were easy to kill as long as they didn't mass up or arm themselves. The ones we found went down fast to laser fire and we continued on.

On the beach, we met up with a dredger. It was my first, and it was big. It rolled up out of the water to greet us. I was reminded of old, Japanese monster movies I'd seen as a kid. The thing was impossibly large.

Flashing metal cylinders with grinding teeth rose up, dripping seawater. These resembled the blades of lawnmowers. It came toward us and I knew a moment of concern. Those blades could slice through rock and sand with ease. Surely, they could sever a man in half, power-suit or no.

Fortunately, the giant was slow and relatively easy to disable. The control cables were exposed and we burned them away at every opportunity. About when it reached the sandy beach, it collapsed with a tremendous howl of twisting metal. It thrashed for a while until it gave up and died.

Some of my men cheered and stood on the big blades. I didn't join them.

"Good job, marines. Let's keep marching."

Darkness finally fell over the world about an hour later. It was what we would soon come to call "second night" on Yale. The moon had two kinds of night: the first type occurred when the spinning planet turned away from the sun. That was a natural enough pattern. The rotation period of the world was about ninety hours long, so it took quite a while for a full day-night cycle to occur.

Rotation didn't cause the only kind of nightfall, however. What we experienced was the other kind of night, which happened when Yale passed into the shadow of the gas giant it orbited. These "second nights" were shorter and occurred more abruptly. Really, it wasn't night at all, it was an extended eclipse. From the surface of Yale, however, it was hard to tell the difference. Other than the fact that darkness came within a ten-minute span, once you were in the gas giant's shadow the sky was as black as it had ever been back on Earth.

I'm not sure if the machines had waited for second night to hit us or not. Maybe, they'd calculated that we would be disoriented by the sudden shift from light to dark, or that we'd have trouble seeing in the starlight. Fully equipped, a Star Force marine had no such difficulties. Our visors compensated for any level of light, whether it was bright or dark.

Whatever their reasons were, they hit us about eighteen minutes after darkness had enclosed my men in its chilling shroud. I'd almost realized my goal of securing this entire island. In about an hour, I'd planned to announce the island was clear and that it was time to glide our power-suited butts a few miles over the waves to the next one in the chain. They didn't let me have that much time.

We were marching on the shoreline, making good time, when the attack began. It started with a rush of missiles. It was a light barrage, really, and localized on my battalion. Fortunately, we had eyes in the sky. Sarin's ships were able to give us nearly three minutes warning.

"Colonel," Captain Sarin said, "I'm registering a large concentration of machines off the coast, coming in your direction."

"Big or small?" I demanded, halting my march.

Kwon stopped beside me. A dozen marines streamed past, weapons in hand. They were chatting and oblivious.

"Big ones," she said. "Big enough to have shields, anyway."

"Thank you Captain," I said, switching to the battalion-level channel. "Stop the chatter, please. This is Colonel Riggs. I want everyone in this unit to take cover and—"

That was as far as I got. When the first machine rolled up out of the sea, I thought to myself that Sarin had cut it rather finely. We barely had time to react before it charged us.

Fortunately, the water slowed the machine just as it would a charging man. The dome of force that covered its back shimmered where it touched the waves, releasing little bright flashes of discharged power.

The command channel became a cacophony of sound as people sounded the alarm. I switched to company level and heard the newly-minted Captain Gaines giving his unit orders. They were good ones, so I kept my mouth shut.

"We have to get under that shield as fast as possible," he said. "Hold your fire until you get inside that dome, you'll just be wasting energy. Ignore Riggs' order to take cover. Fly out there and attack it."

I nodded inside my helmet. He was making the right move. I'd thought we were going to have more time, but they were on us already. I'd have to ask Jasmine about that later. Maybe Fleet's sensors needed some calibration.

Behind the first machine, another dozen of monsters were surfacing now. Gaines's company took flight as a group and charged out over the water. Kwon and I went with them, in the middle of the pack. Our foot-wide steel boots skimmed the waves.

Maybe the machine deduced our intentions, or maybe not. In any case, it slowed and backpedaled, bringing its big beams down to bear. Twin lasers lanced out. Independently targeted, the heavy beams cut down two charging marines in about a second. Then the projectors swiveled, locked, and fired again.

I was flying with the rest of the company. We were charging at full speed until the last moment, then slowing to allow entry. We had to slip under the shields at a walking pace.

We had to get in close, under that machine, under its dome. Once inside, the shield dome would protect us, not the Macro itself. Being cut down by one machine was bad enough, but if all of them could fire at us at once, we'd be shredded in minutes. The dome would prevent the Macro's fellows from helping out.

We pressed close and no one else died before we pressed into the shield dome and forced our way inside. Macro shields were triggered by energy emissions and by any physical mass moving at high velocity. A laser beam or a bullet couldn't push through, but a marching man could. This weakness in their design was precisely why we'd invented the marine force in the first place.

Once inside the Macro's dome, of course, it wasn't any kind of picnic. There were thrashing legs a hundred feet high, moving with violent speed and unstoppable power. It was like dodging massive, sweeping tree trunks made of steel. These Macros, like their brothers I'd fought so long ago, had anti-personnel turrets underneath. They were independently operated by the machine and stitched us with laser fire.

152

Fortunately, our armor came into play here. The enemy showered us with glittering sparks of light, but every hit wasn't deadly. The power-armor was gouged and scored when struck, but didn't rupture unless a single target was hit with a steady pounding for several seconds. Similarly, our weaponry was superior to what it had been in the old days. A single marine was able to destroy an anti-personnel turret with less than a focused second of beam-time.

The turrets popped like light bulbs. In less than a minute, we'd destroyed them all and only lost three more men, two of them having been knocked flat by the thrashing legs. I figured we could probably revive them—if we had time.

Next, we cut down its legs and burned our way into the CPU. Ten seconds later the machine sagged down in death, and the company cheered.

I wasn't happy, however.

"Gaines," I said, "you still here?"

"Yes sir!" he shouted back, obviously overjoyed to have survived in my presence for nearly a full day in a warzone.

"Congratulations," I said. "Good work on the Macro, too. But I want to change-up our tactics for the next one."

Already, we were coasting toward the next Macro in line. This one was behaving the way the last one did, backing up like an elephant being charged by metal mice.

"Why?" Gaines asked. "That was a textbook kill, sir."

I rolled my eyes briefly, and urged myself to be patient.

"I know," I said. "I wrote the textbook. Check your power gauge, Gaines."

"Ah, sixty-four percent."

"Yeah," I said. "We just expended about ten percent of our charge killing a single machine. Have you counted how many machines we have to kill?"

Gaines paused. "We're going to run out of power before we get through them all. Power or manpower."

"Exactly. The trouble is, our method works, but it takes too long. We're forced to use the grav-lifters to keep these heavy suits above the water surface, and the whole maneuver is taking too much power."

"Point squad has reached the next hostile. What are you orders, Colonel?"

"Tell them to ignore the anti-personnel turrets and the legs. Just burn through to the CPUs and kill it as fast as you can."

"It will go crazy, sir. We're supposed to just take all the incoming fire?"

"Relay the order or I'm hitting the override."

Gaines did as I told him. The marines were stunned. They'd all practiced our classic-kill approach to this kind of enemy before, and they'd just seen it work as advertised. Changing it up didn't make much sense to them. But they were marines, and marines followed orders and got the job done.

The next machine went down in half the time it took to knock out the first one, and we only lost a single man. His power-suit sank to the bottom of the sea and laid there, inert and spread-eagle.

"Kwon, I'm getting life readings from that fallen marine. Go get him and drag him back to the beach. Stay on the bottom so that the enemy machines can't target you."

"Aw, sir...I'm fine to fight."

"You have your orders First Sergeant!"

"Yes, Colonel!"

Kwon dove away from me toward the sandy bottom. I felt better now that he was out of the battle. He'd been reacting slowly for the last several minutes. It was only a matter of time until one of the machines caught him, and then it would take more than an injection of nanites to put him together again.

By this time, my company had destroyed three of the machines. We only had three full platoons left, so I made another refinement to our tactics.

"We're going to spilt up on these next targets. We're running into each other as it is, and the machines are going to get smart soon and change their own tactics or retreat. I want to take them all out. One platoon each will attack the three closest machines."

Not even Gaines objected. The next kills went faster than before. We were down to thirty percent power, but we were getting the moves down. As far as I knew, Kwon and I were the only ones out of the entire company who'd ever had the pleasure of fighting under the legs of a steel behemoth. I knew the improvement wasn't due only to my improved tactics, it was also the men themselves. They were learning fast.

154

The next machine went down, and then another. I was breathing hard and sweat poured down my back. Seawater had gotten into my left boot somehow, and was sloshing all the way up to my hip joint. I suspected I had a burn-through there as my left thigh was numb. I was trying to ignore it, even though the added weight was making my entire left side sag and list as I cruised over the waves.

I checked my gauge as the Macro did its death-roll. We hadn't lost a single man. Seventeen percent left in the juice-box.

"Marines," I said over company chat, "I want you to know I'm proud of you all this day. None I've served with could do better. After these next few fights, we're going to start running out of power. If you get down to five percent, I want you to let yourself sink to the bottom, then escape by walking in any direction you can. You're generators will recharge your armor in time, if you don't push it—"

"Sir?" Gaines spoke up, interrupting me.

"What is it now, Captain?"

"Sir? All the machines appear to have been knocked out."

I looked around, swiveling my helmet and scanning the night. The inky black ocean was empty. A few steaming wrecks bubbled here and there, emitting internal light as they arced and sizzled. But there were no Macros left standing.

"Oh," I said, and then laughed. "I guess I'm surprised we're still alive. Hah! Well done, marines!"

They cheered tiredly. I cheered too, and kept laughing. A few of them had the energy and the spirit left to laugh with me.

20

We charged up, then swept the big island clean over the following five hours. The machines were still out there, I knew, making their plans. But they didn't have any ships to cover them. Their forces were made up purely of walking units and missiles. We had the high ground of space, and I kept the gunships firing down into the atmosphere, working to pin down their roaming concentrations of big machines.

During the night hours, the railgun salvos showering Yale were more visible. The white streaks rolled down, taking several seconds to go from a tiny pinpoint of light to a brilliant flash as they struck home. It looked as if the world were being hammered by an endless series of slow-motion meteors.

I knew the Macros would come again if we didn't hit them first. They'd never be content to let us share ground so close to them. But that could wait until another day because I had my beachhead, and I was happy.

The next island target was one of the smallest in the archipelago that surrounded the undersea ring. Shortly after my group had cleared the seas near the big island of attacking machines, three battalions splashed down in the shallow seas off the smaller island, which I'd named "Tango". It was shaped like a "T" and my battalions had landed just above the top crossbar on the map. Following their orders, they assembled underwater then advanced on the shoreline.

The first reports I received concerning the assault weren't positive.

"Colonel Riggs?" Captain Sarin asked, hitting my helmet with a private channel.

I stopped going over casualty reports and vids of our assaults on the big machines to take the call.

"Go ahead, Captain."

"The beach assault is meeting stiff resistance. The machines were forewarned by your attack, I believe."

"What kind of resistance?"

"Gun emplacements and a series of ridges lined with smaller machines. I've ordered the marines to retreat into the water where the laser turrets can't hit them."

"Can we use our fighters to support them?"

"Yes, but I calculate a high loss rate."

I gnashed my teeth. I didn't want to lose the fighters, nor any more marines. The fighters were primarily designed to fight in space, not for ground support. My marines should be able to do what they were destined to do.

"If three battalions of marines can't take a beach, we're going to lose this anyway."

"I believe they *can* take it, sir. But I wanted to ask you for support. If some element of your force on the big island could cross the water and hit the enemies flank, I think we could lower our losses by seventy percent."

"On what basis did you arrive at that calculation?"

She showed me her numbers via my computer scroll. I flattened the screen, which wanted to roll up at the corners. Even smart screens tended to curl.

"I see your point," I said after reviewing the data. "If we come in on the eastern peninsula, they don't have much there. We'll be able to get our boots on the ground and advance under cover. While the enemy is busy with us, the three invading battalions can charge the front line and take the turrets out. We can even bring the fighters in when the enemy is engaged and hit them with combined arms."

"Exactly, Colonel."

I chewed it over unhappily. "We'll still suffer harsh casualties," I said, "but short of retreating I can't see what else we can do. Those men can't sit there at the bottom of the sea forever."

"How long do you think it will take you to get a full battalion to the peninsula?"

I thought it over, and while I did, it occurred to me that Sarin really *was* running this op. It wasn't the sort of situation I was accustomed to. Normally, my officers didn't call the shots—not on something as big as this. But she was doing a good job, and she was in the better position to do the job. It wasn't her fault I'd insisted on coming down here and doing the dirty work personally.

"All right," I said at last, going over timing and readiness issues with her. "We'll be there in about twenty hours. It will be a long night, crossing the water and all. I'll take only our freshest troops along with a sprinkling of veterans who have experience with our newest tactics."

Captain Sarin inquired about the tactics I was talking about, and I explained how we'd brought down so many of the machines so quickly. If she was impressed, it was hard to tell. It usually was with her. Unlike most of my troops, she didn't express herself with vigor.

"You're results are impressive, sir. I'll relay these tactical refinements to the rest of the officers."

"Fine. But I still want an experienced crew with me. I'll take Captain Gaines's company, for starters."

Captain Gaines heard his name and wandered closer. "What's up, Colonel?"

I held up my hand, shushing him.

"Very well, sir," Captain Sarin said in my ear. "I've placed his company on the roster. Please move west as quickly as possible and merge with Fourth Battalion. They are full strength and positioned close to the crossing point."

"Got it, let them know I'm coming, Riggs out."

"Anything I should know about, sir?" Captain Gaines asked.

I grinned at him. "Yeah. You're going to love it."

Over the next ten minutes, I briefed the Captain, who didn't voice any objections for once. I thought he might be in shock.

"I know your men have been through a lot, Captain," I said. "But that's how most marines feel the day after an invasion. Our work here isn't through, not by any measure. Less than ten percent of the machines have been taken out—and that's only counting the ones we can see from space."

Nodding numbly, Captain Gaines followed me to brief the men. There were a few groans, but they gathered their kits quickly enough and we set out. We had about sixty effectives in all. I frowned at that.

Hadn't we started out with two full companies? These men had indeed gone through the ringer. I decided to split them up when we merged with Fourth Battalion. If I put a fireteam of about four men in every company in the fresh battalion, they could disseminate the tactics and lead by example—they'd also be less likely to be taken out entirely.

"We're going to merge up with the Fourth and serve as reinforcements for them, bringing the battalion up to full strength."

"Oh," said Gaines, sounding disappointed but resigned. "I guess my company is finished then. I'm sorry to see my first command disintegrate."

"What?" I asked, giving him a frown. "No, no," I said. "They've taken a few losses. It just so happens they lost a Captain. I'm giving you a new company. Choose a fireteam to take with you from the old one."

Gaines perked up. "Yes, sir!"

He trotted away, and I looked after him, smiling. Then I had to get back on the radio with Sarin. I checked, and found out Fourth Battalion hadn't lost anyone. I ordered her to transfer a junior captain to another outfit we were leaving behind on the big island.

"I don't care what you assign him to," I told her. "Put him in charge of digging latrines. Think of something."

I signed off again, muttering that I had to do everything around here. When Gaines came back, he had a hard-eyed group of killers at his back. They didn't look like the cleanest cut team, but they looked like they could shoot.

"These men will do fine," I told him.

By the time we reached Fourth Battalion, another hour had passed. I let the men rest while I went to talk to the Major in charge. I was surprised to see a familiar face. The commanding officer of the Fourth was none other than Major Randal Sloan. I laughed when I shook his hand.

"I get it now," I said.

"Sir?"

"I mean I now understand why this battalion is almost entirely intact."

Sloan's face fell. I guess I shouldn't have said it. Major Sloan had a reputation for self-preservation on the battlefield and in space. Somehow, he was always the first man to reach the airlock or the

159

lifeboat when the ship was breaking up. He was a soldier, just like all my marines, but he had the survival instincts of a junkyard dog.

"Quit pouting, Sloan," I said. "I didn't mean anything by it. Remember, I appreciate men who can stay alive. You've got a knack for it, and it's something I need today. In fact, that's exactly why Captain Gaines is here at my side."

I briefly explained Gaines's rapid advancement. Gaines tried to look tough while I spoke. When I finished the introduction, Sloan shook Gaines's hand and welcomed him aboard.

"You've got Alpha Company," Sloan said, gesturing toward the beach. "They've recently lost their commander."

"It will be an honor serving under you, Major," Gaines said.

After another round of salutes, he trotted toward the beach. Behind him, his handpicked fireteam followed closely. They'd almost never spoken since we'd broken up their original company.

Sloan looked after Gaines's crew wonderingly. "You sure can pick'em, sir."

"Never mind that," I said. "Are you ready to cross the water or not?"

"Negative, sir. We stopped mop-up operations as soon as we got your call, but our suits haven't fully recharged. I would imagine that your people's suits need an hour or two to top off as well. We can't make the crossing with people sinking into the waves on the way."

"Yeah," I said, looking at my gauge. It read forty-seven percent. I hadn't fully charged before I left, but that was still an alarming number. "We flew here to save time," I said, "but possibly that was a mistake. These new power-suits take some getting used to."

"The men love them—as long as they have power left in them."

Our suits had generators, of course. All our marines carried generators and laser projectors. But the generators could not, by themselves, generate enough power to keep the suit fully operational under battle conditions. Our big, hard-hitting laser projectors sucked too much power. So we'd designed the suits to operate on batteries most of the time, and they automatically recharge themselves back up to full when idle. Unfortunately, that recharge period often took too long.

I called Sarin again and demanded that a power source be dropped from orbit. Ten of them, in fact, one for every company in the battalion. We had to get recharged and moving soon. The longer we delayed the assault on the target island the longer the machines had to dig in and set up an ambush.

Captain Sarin was nothing if not efficient. Within twenty minutes, she had the big generators ferried down from orbit by destroyers with black-nanite arms. They were placed in a neat row on the beach and the men rushed them the moment they were down and humming.

"They must really need a charge," I said, watching. "You would think we'd laid out a buffet and rang the dinner bell."

"Their suits mean life to them, sir," Sloan said. "And power keeps the suits operating."

A few minutes later I walked up to the nearest hulking generator. It detected me and sent a tendril of nanites threading their way across the sand to my suit. It looked as if someone had poured out a bottle of mercury—except that the liquid ran uphill.

The line of nanites met my left boot and the tickling sensation of heavy power passed through me. There was always some detectable level of bleed when you dealt with this kind of amperage.

We relaxed, ate and talked while our suits charged up. I reflected that, although it was strategic downtime, maybe it wasn't all that bad to have suits that needed a charge. Sometimes, marines needed to recharge, too.

In less than an hour after I'd merged my company into Fourth Battalion, we were on our way across the waves. To me, this was the most fun you could have in power armor. I'd always enjoyed Jet Skis back home, and this was a close equivalent.

The huge metal toes of my boots touched a cresting wave now and again, but otherwise I stayed fairly dry. Hundreds of other marines zoomed along in loose formation all around me. Beneath us, our grav-lifters pushed at the water making it dish-outward and form small wakes. Behind us, we left a thousand white trails in the black seawater that rippled and bounced until the sea smoothed out again.

Soon, I could see Tango with my helmet set to infrared. It was a greenish zone of warmth on the near horizon. We were still in the middle of 'second night' on Yale, and we were using our infrared systems to see. The land was much cooler than the hot seawater, so it registered green while the ocean below my feet was a glaring white.

Beach invasions are always problematic, but natural conditions on Yale made this particular invasion worse than the norm. We would have to come in at night, flying over the water. This made us perfect targets for enemy emplacements on the target island.

Yale's climate didn't help. One of the biggest concerns was the behavior of the tides here. On Earth, our relatively small moon gave our oceans pretty impressive tides for its size. The difference in ocean depths on a given beach was often four feet between high and low tide.

But Yale was much more dramatic when it came to moving water around the surface than what we were accustomed to on the relatively placid oceans of old Earth. Here, there was the gas giant itself, a massive gravitation force of crushing proportions. There were a number of local moons in the planetary system as well, each exerting their own significant forces on the oceans of this world. As a result, tides were rather chaotic and could vary by as much as thirty feet in an hour. It was almost like witnessing a continuous series of rolling tidal waves.

Our power-armor would keep us from drowning, but we had to take the tidal movements into account. The islands literally lost or gained ten percent of their surface area depending on the time of day. It was safe to say that humans would never be able to swim on these dangerous beaches.

We hit the shores of Tango at low tide. The last thousand yards were a muddy slog, but I ordered my men to turn off their grav-lifters and hump it to cover. We needed to save power.

The dark beach was soon full of clanking marines. We made it about a quarter of the way to cover when something spotted us and opened fire. Streaks of incoming fire spat out, and to my surprise they weren't lasers—they were pellets. Hard-hitting rounds of ballistic ammunition flashed out to greet us from a dozen machinegun nests on the ridge ahead.

I shouted over the command channel, giving the go-ahead to fly again. The men barely needed to hear the order. They were already lifting off in droves and zooming forward. The longer we were on this open beach, the worse it was going to be.

The streams of bullets were different than normal automatic weapon fire back on Earth. First of all, there were no tracers. I supposed the machines didn't need to light up every fourth round with an incendiary just to see what they were aiming at. Due to my sensory gear, I could still see the incoming streaks of hot lead.

162

The bullets were different in other ways as well, I soon realized. They were bigger, being about the size of felt pens. About four inches long and more than half an inch thick, these rounds struck with real force.

Ten rounds hit my armor in a burst as a hosing spray swept near at chest-level. A normal man would have been cut in two.

Fortunately, my armor didn't even rupture. But the kinetic force was such that I was tossed back and thrown onto my can. I couldn't believe it. Nothing less than a Macro's leg should have knocked me down in this power-suit.

"Major Sloan? Are you reading me?" I asked over the unit channel.

"Here sir."

"We've got to get to those nests and take them out, now!"

"I'm well aware, Colonel. We've got casualties."

I jumped up and rushed forward. I was very conscious of the fact that my chest-armor had been seriously damaged. Another hard hit like that might punch through. Even with all my modifications, I didn't think I would survive it.

"Should we use grenade-launchers, sir?" Sloan asked.

The grenade launchers Sloan was talking about weren't old-fashioned, under-barrel units like the American M203. When we fired a grenade, we fired a small tactical nuke at the enemy.

"The ridge is too close," I said, "and I don't want to expend that kind of ammo on this position. Permission denied."

"I'm putting a sharpshooter squad on every pillbox then," Sloan said. "Maybe we can get a lucky hit."

"Good idea. Right now, I'm wishing we had brought along some heavy weaponry."

"We could call for air support, sir."

"Forget it. By the time they got down here, this will be over with and I don't want them exposed to enemy AA until we know what we're up against."

"Roger that."

Now, from our advancing lines, counter-fire was being thrown back at the enemy. As far as I could tell, this had little or no effect.

We charged onward. It seemed to take forever, but really it was probably less than a minute before the first elements of the Fourth reached the ridge. That's when the enemy really let us have it.

Up until we got close, the enemy guns had been spraying at all of us, like someone with a broom trying to push away dust. When that didn't work and we got in dangerously close, the automated guns changed tactics. They chose an unlucky marine at the front of the charge and hammered him until he went down. Then they kept hammering him.

I wasn't at the very front wave, but I was within a hundred yards of the brave men who were. I watched as a dozen of them went down, being shot to death by a thousand orange sparking rounds. The men fell, struggled, fell again. There was nothing we could do for them, and their suits kept them alive for several ghastly seconds.

Even after they'd stopped moving, the streams of bullets poured into dead marines. The beach ran red and flesh flew after the shell-like armor was finally breached. When the guns were satisfied, they traversed their turrets to the next victim.

Then, at last, we reached the ridgeline. It's hard to describe how you feel at a moment like this, when you finally get to sate your urge for revenge on your tormentors. I guess attackers who've suffered losses and abuse during a long charge have felt the emotion since time immemorial.

We roared and strained, grappling the machines, burning them. They weren't easy to take out. Guns operated by humans were relatively simple to destroy—the key was that the human soldiers firing the guns were softer than the guns themselves. But in this case, there were no soldiers. Just the heartless guns, chattering away relentlessly. We had to destroy them in detail, ripping barrels from tripods, stripping away snaking belts of ammo and burning smoking holes into their CPUs.

Finally, it was over. While the Fourth spread out on the ridge, seeking cover and checking on the wounded, I went to find Major Sloan.

He was just coming up from the beach when I met him on the ridge. I gave him a single raised eyebrow. He was practically the last man to reach the ridgeline.

"I was with one of the sharpshooter teams, sir," he reported. "Negligible effects."

"I noticed. How many casualties?"

"Fourteen dead, six wounded."

164

An alarming statistic. Normally, my men were very hard to kill. It wasn't uncommon for us to have two hundred wounded and no deaths after a hard fight, due to our individual survivability.

I frowned. "I guess the enemy tactics of overkill worked for them in this instance. The machines didn't stop us, but they made us bleed."

"Agreed," Sloan said. "Your orders, sir?"

"Request rescue for the wounded. The rest will pack up and advance."

Sloan looked westward at the dark hills. Ahead of us a series of ridges loomed, separated by flat, rocky terrain.

"There could be a large number of ambushes ahead, sir," Sloan said. "Maybe we should scout first."

"Excellent idea, Major!" I said.

I walked forward and clamped my arm around his shoulders. His helmet swiveled to regard me. I couldn't see his expression through the dark plexiglass, but I could bet it wasn't a happy one.

"I've got just the man for the job," I said, giving him a little shake.

"Are you sending me on point, sir? I'm a major."

I laughed. "No. I'm just screwing with you, Sloan. I can't afford to lose my unit commander. I'm sending Captain Gaines and his team of toughs."

"An excellent suggestion, Colonel," Sloan said, brightening. He trotted away to relay the order.

A few minutes later, Captain Gaines showed up and asked to speak with me. I waved him to sit down. I was crouching with my back rubbing against a ferro-crete pillbox wall. I had a nanite sprayer out, which was working on repairing my armor with repeated light coats. I'd found that if you sprayed a thin coat several times on the damaged area, they seemed to work faster.

"Colonel, have you got a problem with me?" Captain Gaines asked.

I looked up at him.

"I do now," I said.

"What do you mean, sir?"

"I like you Gaines. I have you down in my private book as an up-and-comer. But this is a bad moment in your personnel records as far as I'm concerned."

Gaines shuffled uncertainly in his armor. Finally, he threw up his hands. "I just don't get it, sir. First, you praise me and put me in charge of a company. Then you give me a series of hazardous duties, the latest of which seems to be tailor-made to get me killed."

I shook my head and stood up. On my chest, a mass of nanites bubbled and worked to patch up my suit. It was sort of like watching acid eat at something—but in reverse.

"Captain, I'm going to give you a pass on this one, because you and I haven't been in close contact before. Here's the deal: I need officers who can do anything and everything I ask them to. I'm asking you to do one of a nasty mission right now. Are you requesting another assignment?"

"So, this is all some kind of test?"

"Not exactly. It is a test, but it's also an opportunity. You can't prove what you're capable of if I don't give you the chance to do so. Right here, right now, I'm giving you that chance."

"I see."

"I'll ask again, do you want another assignment?"

Captain Gaines hesitated. Then he straightened his spine.

"No sir," he said. "I'm taking this mission, and I'm going to complete it successfully."

"Excellent! I knew I could count on you."

He turned and trotted away to gather his hand-picked group of hard-eyed vets. I'd done a little checking up on Captain Gaines during my brief downtime before we'd crossed the sea from Big Island to Tango. He had a checkered past. He was one of those Star Force types that had joined us to get away from troubles back home. He'd been a gangster and had a rap sheet as long as my arm. But Star Force had given him a second chance, and the structure he seemed to need. I felt he'd excelled under my command. Now, it was time to see what he was really made of.

As he led his group of scouts off into the darkness, I sincerely hoped I'd see him again.

21

The first report back from Captain Gaines and his recon group came in less than an hour after we'd reached the beach. I'd decided not to sit around and was making headway up to Tango's ridges. We were moving slowly, expecting an ambush at every twist in the land.

I felt we could afford the time. The three battalions at the bottom of the sea offshore weren't drowning yet; they had another forty hours of air and supplies. Major Sloan and I decided they would do best by staying in position. If they could hit the island defenders from the front, while we were rolling up their flanks, we could destroy them in detail. Their trap would become our trap.

All these fancy ideas faded when Gaines called in and made his report.

"Colonel Riggs, we have problems," he said.

"I can see by your locator you're pretty far up the ridge, Gaines. Are you under fire?"

"No, sir. That's the problem. I'm going from gun nest to gun nest. They're all empty. The enemy has clearly been repositioning."

I cursed quietly. "Where the hell are they?"

"Unknown, sir. They have plenty of those automated gun turrets, wherever they are. We've counted twenty-two empty gun sites."

I was stunned. "You ran into twenty-two gun emplacements just while climbing the next ridge of the island? How many do they have at their stronghold?"

"I'm not sure they have a stronghold, sir."

"Trust me, they do. Their tactics are clear. They saw us hitting their flank and reacted by sending out worker machines to withdraw their defensive systems from this side of the island. That means they're building up a concentration, probably at the center of the T."

"That makes sense, Colonel, but I can't confirm any of it. I haven't met up with a single active defensive system yet."

"All right, keep going until you do. Riggs out."

I turned to the mass of men trudging up the hillside all around me. "Sloan!" I roared. "Get them moving. There's nothing to stop us for the next few miles. Let's pick up the pace."

Shouted orders rippled through the units. Soon, every knee joint was whining and rasping as armored legs moved faster. We stopped crawling over the land looking for an ambush at every turn and began trotting.

The power-suit batteries were in pretty good shape at this point. We'd designed the generators to be able to keep up with a light drain and still retain a full charge. A man could trot along for hours in them and never move the needle on his battery levels. But firing his weapon or flying would begin the inevitable drain.

Along the way uphill, I contacted the commanders of the battalions that were still sitting off the coast. I ordered them to ready themselves to advance onto the shores. Sloan trotted up next to me as I made these arrangements.

"I've done a little math, sir," he said. "The Macros are very predictable, even for machines."

"Tell me what you've figured out, Major," I said encouragingly. Sloan was naturally laid-back—some may even say a lazy officer. But when he felt his safety and the safety of his unit was in question, he suddenly turned on the steam. He became a much more efficient officer in dangerous situations, which was partly why I kept placing him in harm's way.

"They like to use predictable patterns for the spread of their resources, especially when they don't have any critical basis on which to make their placement decisions. Basically, if they had ten square miles to cover and ten guns, they would place one on each square mile."

I nodded. "So, you're saying they probably covered the island with defensive systems evenly, up until now. When they realized they were under threat from two fronts, and their systems as placed weren't enough to stop us, they rewrote their algorithm."

"Exactly, sir. They'll cluster them up on the top of the highest point, making it harder to take the entire island."

"We pretty much knew that, Sloan."

"Yes sir, but I've figured out how many weapons they have, based on the number found and the number of square miles covered."

"Ah, okay," I said, getting where he was going with this. "That's good thinking, and might even be accurate. What did you come up with?"

"Two hundred and ninety guns, sir. That's only if they withdrew all the guns from all three legs of the island."

"Two hundred and ninety," I said, thinking about it. I didn't like the image that number conjured in my mind. It was grim, in fact. They would tear up my men.

"The number of guns a force faces does not cause a precisely incremental number of casualties to the attacking side," I said. "You know that, don't you?"

"Yes, sir. There are plenty of factors, like the shock of the strikes on the men. They'll tend to advance more slowly while their comrades are falling. Also, they'll be able to concentrate fire and take people down much faster with so many guns."

"Ten guns would be nothing. We'd take them easily. But two or three hundred—that kind of force could stop our attack cold."

"The enemy will rip us a new one. That's my conclusion."

I glanced at him suspiciously. Sloan was not known for his self-sacrificing nature. "I guess you're about to request we drop a nuke on the center of the island."

"I thought about that, but I think it would fail. The enemy is sure to have enough AA to stop a small barrage of missiles. We'd have to abandon the island and pound the place from orbit, expending a large amount of our stockpiles."

"What is your recommendation in this case?" I asked, honestly curious about what he'd come up with.

"We should call in the fighters, sir. We haven't seen any systems with good AA capability yet. These ballistic guns are good against troops at close range, but they should be easy to take out with fast-moving aircraft."

I thought about it, and I agreed with the Major. I contacted Captain Sarin and asked her to throw a wing of fighters into the attack. Striking just as we came into range of these guns and made

169

contact, we could sit back and let them make a pass. The air strikes should soften up the target.

"I'll get her to put the gunships on it, too. We'll bomb them into the stone age, then mop up with ground troops."

"I'd like to show you something else, sir," Sloan said. He handed me a pod of some kind. It was crusty and black.

"What's this?"

"I think it's an egg, sir. A Crustacean egg."

I looked around in alarm. I'd noticed the bulbous objects in the gun nests of the enemy. I examined the object for a second. It did indeed look like a sea creature's egg—a big one. It was a little bigger than a chicken egg.

"I thought Lobster eggs were carried around by the parents or something," I said.

Sloan threw up his hands. "We don't know much about their physiology. They do lay eggs, and those are eggs. They're all over the island. The nests form nice circular depressions, like little craters."

I nodded thoughtfully. "And the Macros have been using the nests to set up their guns. They're perfect for the purpose."

"For what it's worth, sir," Sloan said.

"Thank you, Major. It might be worth quite a bit."

Sloan dismissed himself as I pondered the black egg and hustled up the slope after my troops. I knew the Crustaceans were in the area. They had troops here, sitting in the shallow areas of the ocean. So far, they hadn't been willing to commit their forces to aid us. I knew they weren't sure we would win, and the risks were high if we failed and they had to deal with the Macros on their own after we lost the battle.

But now we were facing a tough fight. This single island had already cost me a number of casualties. There were nine more islands to go, and the machines were building replacements out there under the sea as fast as they could. From the moment I'd landed, I knew I was in a race against time. The basic problem with fighting the machines had always been attrition. They could build a new soldier and load a program into its brain in hours. Human troops took about twenty years to mature and train. We just couldn't keep up.

I looked upslope. I could see the peak now, the crown of the island. It was about five thousand feet high and it was a rocky, ugly crag. Climbing that under fire, just to take an alien island…

"Marvin?" I said, calling him directly. "Marvin, are you there?"

"Yes, Colonel Riggs."

"Marvin, I need you to translate while I talk to the Crustaceans. Can you do a video link to my helmet camera?"

"Yes—but the quality will be poor in low light, and there will be a transmission delay."

"That's all right," I said. "They don't have to get a perfect picture. They probably won't want one, anyway."

"Opening   connection…"   Marvin   said.   "Testing connection…Link made."

"Now, connect me with the Crustacean command council."

"Connection request denied."

"What?"

"Connection request denied."

I rolled my eyes. "I got that. Why are they rejecting the request?"

"No reasons were given, sir. It's a protocol element. A hand-shaking process is established between the initiating transmission device and the—"

"Yeah, yeah," I said, growing impatient. "Okay, just send them the video feed. Send it to them as a series of still images, if you have to. No words, no two-way channels. Just images."

"Transmitting."

I stopped marching and dipped my head down to aim the camera at the broken egg in my hand. The camera on my helmet activated, causing a red light to glow inside my visor. An external floodlight snapped on.

Kwon came near and stepped from foot-to-foot. I knew he wanted to say something, but I was determined to get the attention of these responsibility-ducking Lobsters. They knew why I was calling. They had to know I wanted help, and they didn't want to hear about it.

After a few seconds of staring at the damaged egg, I wandered over to the dished out nest where a gun had been. It was littered with broken shells.

"What are you doing, sir?" Kwon asked at last, unable to contain his curiosity.

I waved for him to hush and walked to another nest. This one was bigger, and I found it had scars where the tripod had been set. I examined these square holes which had been punched down into the walls of the nest.

"Are you still transmitting images, Marvin?"

"I've sent approximately six thousand stills, sir."

"All right, turn off the feed. That should be enough to get them interested."

Kwon picked up a broken egg shell and crushed it in his gauntlet before I could stop him. About a second after he did so, the camera light went out.

"Dammit, Kwon, quit fooling with that. It's a Crustacean nest. They raised their young right here."

"Their kids?" he asked, dropping the egg. "Did you take a picture of that?"

I thought about it. "Yeah, I think I did."

"Bad idea," he said, then stomped away after the rest of the battalion.

I hurried after him, frowning fiercely. I hoped Kwon hadn't blown it. I hoped against hope that Marvin had stopped transmitting when I told him too, not when my helmet shut down. But I couldn't be sure. I thought about asking Marvin, but it wasn't worth the effort. The Crustaceans had either gotten the images or they hadn't.

Marvin called me back about ten minutes later.

"Colonel Riggs? I have an incoming channel request from the Crustaceans. The request is flagged as urgent."

"I bet it is," I mumbled. "Okay, open the channel and translate for me, Marvin."

"To the being known as Colonel Kyle Riggs," said the aquatic voice. "We have received your images of violence and desecration. You're barbarism quotient has reached new, unprecedented levels."

"Please excuse any accidental damaging of your nests," I said quickly, before they could call me any more names. "The purpose of the images was to inform and educate, nothing else."

"You have achieved your goals. Never have we viewed such gruesome behavior on the part of a thinking biotic being. We've already commissioned a task force to rewrite our thesis on the topic of brutality among lower species. Up until this point, we'd believed

172

the machines were heartless monsters, but you have reeducated us. We now know that biotic beings are worse."

"Worse?" I asked. "How so?"

"Because you have young, and you therefore understand the protective instincts of a fellow biotic species. Had a machine crushed our young so callously, just to make a threat clear, it would been a lesser crime, as they are incapable of experiencing the agony they are causing. They would have the excuse of the ignorant."

"Okay, look," I said. "Let me stop you right there. I didn't send you those images to threaten you. I sent them to show you what the machines are doing. They're using the beds of your young—your nests—to place weapons systems. Check the images that study the Macro tripods and the imprints they leave."

"Always, when the cheater attempts to explain his crimes, the discussion goes in this fashion. He vacillates from one lie to the next, hoping against hope one of them will hold sway. We have examined the evidence, and it is damning. Do you think we are mental incompetents?"

"Hold on a second—Marvin? Could you dig through the files on my helmet? I took video of the original gun emplacements about an hour ago, when we first encountered them on the beach. Transmit those. Transmit the battle we had to win to knock out those guns."

"Searching...transmitting."

The Crustaceans complained further while Marvin worked on complying with my orders. I had to hear all about how dumb I was, how cheaters were always caught and harshly punished, and how Crustaceans were not fools to be duped by the lowliest student. I endured this invective, trying to understand how they felt. They'd been horrified, and they needed to unload on somebody. Still, I was gritting my teeth by the time they stopped and switched directions.

"How were these images fabricated?" the Crustaceans asked suddenly.

"With my helmet camera," I said.

"The Macros have a treaty with our people. They would not violate it in such a direct fashion."

"Does that treaty take into account the treatment of your dead? Those sites were exposed and inactive when the Macros decided to make them into machinegun nests."

The Crustaceans fell silent for several seconds. I was about to ask if the connection had been broken, when the voice came back on the line. "The desecration of grave sites is not specifically mentioned in the agreement," the voice said, sounding defeated and sad.

"I'm sorry," I said. "The machines have no consideration for others. Nothing like what we call 'common decency'. We humans, on the other hand, are fighting to aid you against these monsters. We're not the heartless ones, we're your liberators. And yet, you will not help us."

The connection was silent for a time. I sensed they were talking it out amongst themselves. I let them make their decision. I figured I'd made my point, and it was time for them to man-up. I'd stopped short of threatening to abandon the campaign, but that thought was in the back of my mind.

I trotted after Fourth Battalion to catch up. Several minutes later, the Crustaceans finally responded.

"We have reconsidered," they said. "We've been monitoring your advance toward the machines. We will march out of the water on the western side of the island to join you when the attack begins."

"Thank you," I said. "I'll give new orders to my men. They will avoid damaging any more of your nests if possible. Let's hope this combined assault will begin a new era of cooperation between our two peoples."

"Possibly, it will," the Crustaceans said. "Pain is instructive. Let the learning begin."

I frowned after the connection was broken. I wasn't entirely sure what they'd meant by their final statement.

-22-

Major Sloan was pleased to hear I'd gotten a commitment from the Crustaceans. In his mind, they'd been entirely too complacent during this campaign.

"Those Lobsters have been lying back and milking it all along," he said. "It's about time you got them on board, sir."

I nodded disinterestedly. Everyone I'd spoken with felt that way. But what seemed like a no-brainer to most of my officers was a big move for the Crustaceans. I understood that they'd already suffered significantly in this war, and if Star Force failed to push back the machines, they'd suffer a great deal more. They were taking a big risk. The change of heart on their part was a very serious decision.

"What made them do it?" asked Sloan.

I looked at him vaguely. I'd been thinking about how to take down the fortifications we were about to walk into.

"What was that, Major?" I asked him.

"How did you get these water-chickens to join us? How did you talk them into it?"

I thought about Kwon and his starring role in the egg-crushing vid I'd sent them. What a brutal image that must have been for them. I decided to leave that detail out of my explanation.

"I just put out the facts as I saw them," I said. "They've been watching us, and they know the score. They know we're pushing their enemy back for them. The machines have mistreated them horribly, and there was a tipping point that made them decide to act."

I went on to briefly explain the desecration of their nests. I showed him a few stills of the crushed eggs and told him how the

175

nests were being used by the machines to emplace automated weaponry.

"Ah," Sloan said, eyeing the pictures. "They finally got mad."

"Yeah, I guess so. A lot of wars are declared that way."

About a mile ahead of us, I heard the ripping sound of heavy automatic weapons firing. I zoomed in with my visor, but could only see a few plumes of smoke.

"Looks like the recon team has made contact," Sloan said.

I attempted to contact Gaines, but with no success. While I was doing that, the sounds of combat became louder and more widely dispersed. I still couldn't see anything as the action was occurring higher up on the mountain out of my line of sight.

I felt an urge to fly up and have a look around, but resisted it. There was no sense in making a more visible target of myself.

Finally, Captain Gaines responded to my queries.

"Pinned down, sir. We've lost one man, another injured. Three of the gun nests woke up at once. We've taken cover for now. Requesting assistance."

"Gaines, light up the nests for me," I said. "I'll call in air support."

"Will do."

I worked my HUD system to contact Fleet. In the meantime, Major Sloan tried to get my attention.

"What is it, Major?" I asked.

"I just wanted to remind you that you told the Lobsters we'd leave their nests alone. Since we recently reached a new level of relations with them…"

"That's just too bad," I snapped. "We can't take out those weapons without breaking a few fossilized eggs, I'm afraid. I'm calling in the strike."

Sloan threw up his hands in defeat and got out of my face. I called Sarin, and learned she was one step ahead of me.

"We've tracked the enemy positions and a squadron of fighters is dropping. They're sub-orbital now, and will be there in about fifty seconds. Tell your men to duck, Colonel."

"Will do, Riggs out."

I relayed the information, got every marine to take cover and we watched the show. It happened so fast, it was hard to track with the eye. The fighters fell like curving meteors, they were fireballs in the

176

sky. There was no mistaking where they were, as they left contrails of burning vapor.

"The whole mountain is lighting up," Major Sloan said in awe.

It was true. In response to the airborne threat, streams of enemy fire rose up into the sky.

"Good," I said. "They're giving away their positions."

The enemy guns send a storm of bullets upward to greet the fighters. But they were shooting where the fighters had already been. They couldn't track fast enough to hit our ships.

Making an extremely fast, low run over our heads, the squadron performed a hit and run strike that lasted about two seconds. Before we really knew what was happening, they were past the central mountain range in two groups of twelve, one veering north and other south. As they passed, they fired a stabbing series of laser pulses down at the enemy targets, both those lit up by Gaines and others that were showing themselves now. As far as I could tell from the ground, not a single fighter had been shot down.

"That's it!" I shouted over the general channel. "Fleet did their part, now it's our turn. All companies advance, double-time. Let's finish the job!"

A roar went up in my headset as men gave their battle-cries and got their metal-encased legs churning. We charged forward on a wide front. At the same time, reports flooded in from the other battalions offshore. They'd been crawling up to a point where they were just under the surface of the sea. Since it was mid-tide now, that let them in considerably closer than they'd managed to get before.

Unfortunately, not all the gun nests had been knocked out. We quickly discovered this as we rushed into range of one defensive fortification after another. There was no clean way to slow down or break off at this point, so I ordered the companies to get in there and take the nests apart with their gauntlets if they had to.

The fighting became intense when the enemy troops finally made an appearance. I'd known all along that someone had to be moving these gun emplacements and servicing them. I realized as the Macro marines had been hiding up here all along when they surged forward out of burrows in the limestone crags. They'd been letting their automated weaponry do the defensive work, but something had changed Macro Command's mind about that. I suspected it was the hard-hitting strike by Sarin's fighter squadron.

177

Even as we charged, they boiled out of the ground to meet us. I hadn't fought a Macro marine in close combat for nearly a year, and I'd forgotten how big they were when compared to the workers and technicians.

Like termite soldiers, they were twice the size and weight of the workers. They were outfitted with ballistic weaponry as well as lasers this time. I immediately theorized the design was meant to make them operational in the varied environments of Yale.

The head-sections had heavy beam weapons mounted alongside most of the optical inputs. The thorax sported dual heavy guns to back up the swiveling head section. These were fixed-directional fire, and the machines had to move themselves around to get a bead on a target.

Once they did, however, the results were impressive. The output of high-velocity lead hammered a marine in power armor, pushing him back physically. The swiveling head-mounted beams burned and slashed, scoring our suits and leaving inch-deep gouges in our chest plates.

That was about all I had the chance to observe before I was in the middle of my own private firefight. I'd been working my way around a spur of rock out of the enemy line of sight. When I was in position, I sprang up, using my suits grav-lifters to propel me forty feet into the air. When I came down, I was standing almost on top of an enemy automated gun.

Taking two crunching steps forward allowed me to lay my gauntlets on the steaming barrel. I had surprised it, and it was busy showering my men farther downslope with thousands of rounds.

The machine's reaction was almost human. It began to struggle and twist in my grasp. I held on and heaved. The strength of my exoskeleton, combined with my own physical power, was shocking. I ripped the gun loose from its moorings despite the fact it had to weigh more than a ton and hurled it down to crash on the nearest set of spiky rocks. There, it squirmed and malfunctioned.

I experienced a surge of triumph, but it was short-lived. Now that I was up high on a nesting site, the rest of the battlefield participants took notice of me. Passing marines struggling up the cliffs waved and gave me a ragged cheer.

The machines, however, were not so accommodating. They unleashed a barrage of bullets and laser fire. I dropped to the ground and rolled off the steepest side of the hillock I was on and crashed onto a pile of fallen boulders. A single crack had appeared in my visor, making a jagged line of bright white that obscured my vision.

I laid there for a full second, stunned. A huge figure loomed over me, and I struggled to get up. For a moment, I thought it was a Macro marine moving in for the kill.

"You're armor is smoking," Kwon said over proximity chat.

I groaned and let him help me up. I wondered how many times he'd helped me to my feet. I didn't want to know the answer, really. I was sure it was depressing.

"I'm getting too old for this shit," I said.

"You say that all the time," Kwon said. "I'll be old when I fall over dead. Until then, I fight."

I nodded and stood beside him. The world was no longer spinning, and the cracks in my armor had been sealed over by the industrious nanites. Internal injuries were also being repaired with similar steady efficiency.

"You're a philosopher, Kwon."

"Thank you, sir."

We marched back up the hill I'd just been blown off of. By the time we reached the peak, this section of the fight was over. My marines had done well. I counted no more than a dozen men on their backs, and most of them were probably going to make it. They only had to be left alone long enough to heal up.

I wasn't sure they were going to get that chance, unfortunately. The enemy marines had dug in on the next ridge. I could see them up there now, hundreds of flashing metal bodies moving around. They were obscured by the ridge they were hiding behind, but showed enough of themselves to tip their big lasers down and take pot-shots at my struggling marines.

In turn, we were firing back. We'd taken out all the gun nests at our elevation, but there were plenty more above and plenty more enemy marines supporting them.

"All right," I said, contacting Major Sloan, "We've advanced as far as we can with this rush. If we push up that next ridge without support, we'll be cut to pieces. Tell every company to seek shelter and find a rock to hide behind. Put half the men on digging, half the men on pinning down those Macro snipers and the rest on clearing the tunnels."

"That's three halves, sir," Sloan complained.

"Are you telling me a Star Force marine isn't worth an extra half-man?"

"Wouldn't dare sir. I'm on it."

While he relayed orders and assigned specific companies to specific tasks, I made some calls to find out how the beach assault was going. The short answer was: "not good."

"Colonel Riggs, sir? This is Captain Grass, Second Battalion."

I squinted my eyes, trying to recall having put a Centaur in charge of a battalion. I failed. I was pretty sure I'd put a Major in charge of every battalion.

"What happened to Major Dansk?"

"Her blood waters the grass, sir."

"I see. You're the most senior officer in the battalion, right? I'm placing you in acting command of the Second, do you read that?"

"Yes, Colonel."

"Now, report your status."

"We've taken the beach sir, but we can't get any farther uphill. The dishonorable enemy had hidden a portion of their forces. They're fighting with marines now sir, not just automated turrets."

I frowned. "I know that. They can be taken out."

"We're pinned down and waiting for support from the heavens."

My frown deepened. "You're not getting another pass from the fighters, if that's what you mean. Not right away. The fighters are back up in orbit, and the Macros know we have them now. They might have set up AA in response to shoot them down if they make another pass."

"I understand, Colonel. The machines feel no wind in their fur, because they have none. What are my orders?"

"You're orders are to take the frigging ridge. If you can get up there, you'll be able to link up with the Ninth. It's only about a mile, I don't think that's too much to ask."

"What are our rules of engagement, sir?"

I was getting angry. For a moment, I forgot I was talking to a Centaur. They had good hearts, and they'd learned to interact with us more naturally, but they still weren't human. I thought back and relived the conversation later. If I'd made a mistake, it was in believing the little mountain goat's brain operated the way a human's brain did. But they didn't, and they were about to reeducate me on this point.

"Stop hiding on the beach. Charge up there and take the next ridge, by any means necessary. Do you understand, Captain?"

"Your words are like cold spring waters, Colonel."

I broke the connection, shaking my head. I walked over to Kwon and went over a computer scroll with him for about a minute. The scroll depicted the battle situation in detail. I frowned as I went over the fresh data, transmitted from Fleet by Sarin.

There were an alarming number of red blocks lined up against the beach the Second was on. I looked at that, and suddenly understood: they were never going to take that ridge. If they tried, it might turn into a slaughter.

Cursing myself and the Centaur who hadn't clearly told me what he was up against, I tried to raise Captain Grass again, but couldn't.

As I tapped on my helmet, my visor went pitch-black. A tiny fraction of a second later, the blackness brightened as the filters were overwhelmed by the intensity of the light.

I staggered back and threw myself on my chest. "Everyone down!" I shouted over my headset to every marine in the force. I don't think anyone heard me, as a tremendous roar had swept over us by now.

I was lifted up and slammed down again. It felt as if the rocky mountainside under my body had bucked me into the air. I rolled and loosened rocks rolled with me.

When I could stand up, I fought my visor controls, forcing them to let my eyes see what was happening to the north. In my heart, I already knew what I'd see.

There was a rolling cloud there, less than a mile off. It was just beginning to take the traditional mushroom shape as I watched. The core of it still glowed with fire.

"They say one of those crazy goats ran up the ridge and blew himself up!" Kwon said, coming to stand next to me.

"Yeah?" I asked, feeling a little sick inside.

"Yeah. He blew up his troops with him, too. Must have gone nuts."

"Maybe," I said, "or maybe he just thought he was following orders."

Kwon looked at me strangely and shook his head.

181

I watched the mushroom cloud until it dissipated. I decided then and there that Centaurs weren't going to be rising in ranks above the level of Captain again anytime soon.

-23-

In the end, the sacrifice of Captain Grass helped our assault. First of all, it blew a hole in the enemy line. Secondly, it made me realize the enemy wasn't going to give this island up without a hard fight, and that I didn't want to suffer those kinds of losses. I decided it was time to call upon Fleet again.

I ordered a heavy bombardment by every gunship I had, followed up with another series of air strikes by the fighters.

I knew I might weaken my ships for a later battle in space, where the fighters would be far more decisive, but I couldn't take this mountain without help. Besides, if we didn't use them when we needed them, they might as well be knocked out already.

I gritted my teeth and squinted as a squadron made another pass. This time, the machines were ready. Beams stabbed up into the murky sky to meet my fighters. Three were lost before they reached attack range. Three more were lost as they passed by and vanished into the sky again.

"Dammit!" I roared.

Twisted, flaming wreckage showered the island. Glowing flares of red light sprang up all over the island at the same time, showing where the fighters had made their strikes.

I quickly contacted Sarin. "Did you get those AA positions zeroed?"

"Yes sir," she said, "the gunships are already bombarding them. Do you want another pass by the fighters?"

I took two hissing breaths before answering.

"Yes, one more pass," I said at last. "Don't send them until the gunships have suppressed all known AA sites. After that, have the gunships soften them up for ten full minutes, then I'll order another ground assault."

After I broke the connection with Sarin, I turned to Sloan. I wasn't in a happy mood. "We're about to lose more fighters," I said.

"I heard."

"Where are those troops the lobsters promised us?"

Major Sloan tapped at the roll-up screen we had spread over a rock between us. "We've got contacts here," he said.

Four blue rectangles had appeared on the shoreline at the foot of the central mountain we were assaulting.

"They're still on the beach?" I demanded.

"Not really sir, it's still high tide. So…they're underwater."

"Those bastards. What did you call them, water-chickens? They're worse than that. Chickens have no choice, they're born cowards. No one expects a chicken to help you. I'm relying on these foot-draggers."

I contacted the Crustacean High Command through Marvin. There were some gurgling sounds before the translation kicked in.

"You told us there would be no nuclear strikes," complained the High Lobster, or whatever it was he called himself.

"Listen," I said, "we're having a tough time retaking your planet for you. I'm sorry if a few things are being broken on the battlefield, but you're not helping out, and we have to do what we must."

"False logic. Attempts to shift blame always fail to move us. Many nests have been destroyed, we're monitoring you closely."

I closed my eyes in frustration. "If you can see what we're up against, you can see that we need help. You have four large troop formations offshore on the opposite side of the island. We're going to hit them again from the air in a few minutes. If you want us to kick the machines off your homeworld, you'll assault your front after the bombardment stops. If you don't it will be the last assault Star Force makes on this world. We'll pull out and leave you behind to face the machines on your own."

Kwon had shown up to listen to this speech. He clapped his big hands together slowly, making loud popping noises. "Tell 'em how it is, Colonel!"

"Sir," Sloan whispered, "can we really afford to make that threat now?"

I ignored them both and listened closely for the Crustacean response. It took a few seconds, but they finally replied.

"Message understood," they said. Then they broke the channel.

"What does that mean?" Kwon asked.

I looked at him sourly. "Quite possibly, it means we're screwed," I said. "Maybe they figure they'll sit out another round and see how we do before they make their decision. Who knows?"

"I bet they're milking us for one more attack," Kwon said. "Before we dump them."

I nodded, admitting he could be right. "There's no way to tell. But I am certain the fighters are about thirty seconds out. Time to duck."

The third screaming pass by the squadron wasn't as devastating to either side as the last one was. The enemy AA was thin, but there were fewer fighters hitting them, too. We lost two more fighters, and the rest went back up to the safety of space. Above us, the mountain was a haze of smoke and bright flames.

The gunships sent down a steady drumbeat of railgun salvos. They streaked down, looking like white balls of lighting. When they hit, I could feel my steel boots shiver under my feet.

After the ten minutes had passed, we called the all-clear and began the ground assault. We'd been repelled before, but this time the enemy resistance was ragged. The Macro defenders that managed to aim down at us and fire were slow-moving and obviously damaged. They looked like bugs that had been accidentally stepped-on but were still struggling to fight.

An uphill battle is never fun. The enemy was hidden by the contours of the land, while our bodies were fully exposed. Often, we could only see the muzzle of the enemy weapons and their optical pickups staring down at us. They showered us with bullets, laser bolts and heavy ripping fire from their last operating gun nests.

It was a grim fight. Battles like this were worse for me than for the average marine, in my estimation. A trooper on the hill only had to worry about his own skin, his rifle, and what was in his sights. But I had to worry about all those things plus what was happening across the planet.

We took the next ridge, and the one after that. I took a chance to tip my visor out from behind cover long enough to see the last peak—the mountain's crown. A splatter of fire greeted me, and I ducked back before they could blow my helmet off.

"All right," I said, breathing hard. "Snake power up from the support units below. My suit is down to twenty-nine percent and some of us have to be about empty. We'll keep pressing to the top after we take a breather."

Kwon slumped his form down next to me. We both leaned against a rock and sipped the water the suit recycled to our lips in a slimy straw.

"My neck hurts," Kwon complained, pushing a gauntlet at his shoulders pointlessly.

"You're wearing about a foot of armor," I said, "you can't possibly feel that."

"No, I can't. But my hand wants to rub up there where my neck broke."

"It will feel better in the morning."

"I don't know, second day after bones break—sometimes that's the worst. Nanites start coming out of the bone. They always leave those tiny little holes, you know?"

I did know. It wasn't good when they did that. The holes were pin-pricks, but somehow they caused pain. The nanites had to get out of the bone somehow, and they knew our bodies natural healing process would fill in those tiny holes with fresh bone cells soon enough. Still, knowing why they did it didn't make it feel better. It wasn't any marine's favorite experience.

"We'll take a break after we take the crown," I promised.

"I don't believe you," he said. "But that's okay…I don't want a break. I get bored."

I clapped his back and then pulled my hand away quickly when I saw him wince. "Sloan? Major Sloan? Where are you?"

"I'm coordinating the transfer of the wounded to the rear lines, sir," he said over my radio.

I made a face. "Get up here."

It took a few minutes, and there were splattering moments of enemy fire that came showering down the mountain when he was exposed, but Sloan worked his way up the mountain to me. When he finally made it, he didn't look happy.

"Take a good look around," I told him. "This is what's called the front line."

"Yes, sir."

"You should see more of it."

"Yes, sir."

"You ready for the final assault? In ten minutes, we go right over the top."

I could see through his dusty visor an expression of grim determination. This man was the polar opposite of Kwon. He preferred to fight with his brain—preferably at a great distance. But he was game, and he didn't object.

"Fourth Battalion is ready, Colonel," he said.

"Don't worry soldier. The machines are down to ten percent effectives and nearly broken, in my estimation."

"I'm not worried, sir," he said.

I knew he was lying, but I didn't call him on it. It was all right to be afraid in combat. Just as long as you did your part, you were still a solid marine in my opinion.

The ten minutes passed quickly. We had just long enough to tap into a silver thread of nanites worming their way uphill with fresh power. We didn't get a full charge—nothing like it. But we all had enough for one hard fight by the time we moved again.

I didn't bother to tip the machines off with another bombardment this time, figuring it wasn't really needed. There were limits to my count of fighters and the number of salvos my gunships could launch. I decided to save the firepower for another day. There were plenty of islands left, after all.

We ordered the attack, and when marines were streaming past us upslope, we joined the second wave. Kwon was in the lead, with Sloan and me in his bulky shadow.

It was going to be daylight soon, but for now, second night still shrouded Yale. We were thousands of feet up and surrounded by inky black seas. A yellowish moon loomed close to the northern horizon, providing some light. It was bigger than Earth's moon, but looked just as barren. As far as I knew, it didn't even have a name. The moon's reflection on the inky black seas below us shimmered and cast a ghostly light over the battle scene.

The machines waited for us. When we reached the last open stretch of ground below their rocky peak, they finally scrabbled forward and blazed at us with everything they had left. Fortunately, it wasn't much. I saw two marines on the front line go down, but they both bounced up again.

We returned fire and kept marching upward. My steel boots were grinding on loose stones.

"Everyone has permission to fly for the final assault. Don't save your suit power any longer, men. This is it!"

I barely got the words out over tactical chat before dozens of figures leapt into the air. They'd been waiting to do this all along.

Flying isn't always a good thing in combat. It's cool, and it rattles biotic enemies, but it also makes you a target without cover. More significantly, these machines didn't get flustered, they just kept fighting until you dismantled them completely.

What flying did do is move an army quickly, especially if the ground is rough. I followed my leaping horde of marines a few seconds later, seeing that Kwon was airborne. Even Sloan got into the spirit of it and came after us, roaring and firing his beamer almost continuously. If we'd had much more fighting to do, I would have admonished him to conserve his charge—but I knew we didn't.

We reached the crown in a rush. There was surprisingly little there. The space was crowded with damaged machines. I grappled with the first one that grabbed me by the waist and pulled me down. The machine was a marine, equipped with pinchers, two bullet-dispensing carbines and a laser projector mounted on the head section. Unfortunately for the Macro, none of this gear was operating at full capacity. The pinchers squeezed, but the carbines rattled drily. They were either out of ammo or jammed, I couldn't tell which.

The laser projector did work, however. It stitched a line across my armor at pointblank range. I couldn't get my own projector into the fight, as it was pinned to my side by the pinchers. Instead, I grabbed the laser projector with a gauntlet and levered it away from my body.

The tube ground and whined as gears tried to force it back on target. My arms were vastly more powerful, however, and it was an uneven contest. I tried to crush the tube itself, but couldn't manage to exert that much pressure with my gauntlets. My next move was to wrench the laser from side to side, heaving it back and forth. While I did this, the Macro fired a rippling series of laser bolts into the night sky over my head.

I finally managed to wedge my head and shoulder under the base of the projector, then used a free arm to lever it down. That did the trick. My shoulder served as fulcrum, and the machine's construction couldn't take the stresses exerted on it. There was a ripping sound, and the projector came off like a loose tooth. Cords and metal strips hung from the projector, which I tossed to the ground.

By that time, a team of marines had come to help. They pushed their lasers against the thorax and let loose. My visor darkened, and so did the optical pickups of the Macro.

The pinchers relaxed and I was back on my feet. I looked around and saw that the battle was about over. As I'd predicted, they didn't have much fight left in them.

"I told you!" I shouted to Sloan when I found him gazing down over the far side of the cliff. "An easy win. I doubt they killed a single man. That's what happens when you do it right, Major."

"You might want to hold up on the celebration, sir," he said, pointing down into the darkness.

I peered over the edge, hunkering down beside him. I quickly saw what he was talking about. The side of the far mountain was crawling with metallic shapes.

"What the hell?" I asked aloud.

"I think it's their reinforcements," Sloan said. "Smaller machines they must have called up from burrows that go back out to the sea."

I studied the approaching troops. There must have been thousands of them.

"I think you might be right," I said.

-24-

The following few minutes were tense. The Fourth had reached the crown and taken it solo, as it turned out. The other battalions had been slowed by heavier resistance on the lower ridgelines.

What that meant in practical terms was that we were the only ones up here to face this new arrival on the battlefield.

"Let's get those damned Lobsters on the line," I said. "They should be coming from that direction. I don't see any kind of fire down there."

"Neither do I, sir," Major Sloan said.

He was flat on his belly beside me. We were both peeking over the cliff wall down toward the horde of metallic shapes that moved up the mountain toward us.

Kwon walked up munching on something. He stood on the edge of the cliff and gazed downward.

"What are you doing, Kwon?" I asked. "You've got your visor open!"

"I was hungry."

"Well, get down here in the dirt before you get your nose shot off."

"By who? I thought those Lobsters were our allies."

I stared at him for a second or two, then looked back down at the metallic humps below. I fiddled with my visor, trying to get the infrared contrast up. The night vision on these things was far from perfect. The visors were more concerned with protecting our eyes from laser fire than they were with enhancing our sight in darkness.

The shapes below *were* rather lobster-like. But their suits were different than the ones I'd met up with in the past. They were bulky and armored, rather than bag-like survival suits full of liquids.

I stood up slowly, exchanging glances with Major Sloan.

"Right you are, Kwon," I said.

Kwon flipped his visor open again and pushed a snack bar into it. He chewed for a few seconds before he finally caught on.

"You guys thought they were machines, didn't you?" he asked.

Major Sloan looked embarrassed. "My fault. Those suits—they didn't look like anything in the briefing."

"That's true, Major," I said. "They must have built a new armor prototype. In fact, they look rather like us. It wouldn't be the first time the Crustacean's copied our technology."

Kwon produced his huffing laugh and wandered off. I looked after him in annoyance. There was a definite discipline problem in my outfit. I guessed it was due to working on the front for so long together. In our case, the lines between officer and non-com had been blurred.

I soon forgot about it and went back to working with Major Sloan. We had to consolidate our position. After going through so much effort to take these islands, it would be unacceptable to lose them again.

I spent the following hours reorganizing troops, distributing supplies and talking to Fleet. I also talked to the Crustacean High Command and thanked them for their help. After reviewing the data Captain Sarin had gathered, I saw that the native troops had indeed contributed. They'd marched up the hill against only light resistance, but had served to cut off any route of retreat for the trapped enemy. They'd performed as an anvil against the Fourth's hammer, and that was good enough for me today. They were in the fight now, one way or the other.

In typical fashion, the machines had fought down to the last kicking, grasshopper-shaped metal marine without asking for quarter. That was fine with me, as I hadn't been in a merciful mood anyway.

By the end of second night, I was feeling pretty good about the whole thing. Sure, we'd lost a thousand marines and a few fighters. But we'd given the enemy a bloody nose. If we kept up the pressure, we would eradicate them all in time.

But, as I soon learned, that wasn't how this war was going to play out.

It was about an hour after dawn that the enemy made the next move. Captain Sarin alerted me, as she was in the sky, ever vigilant and on the lookout for new threats.

"Colonel Riggs?" she said into my ear. "We have a serious problem, sir."

I threw my hand up in the face of the Lieutenant that was reporting to me about our supply situation, and turned away. I listened to the feminine voice in my helmet, and to gain privacy, I flipped my visor back down.

"Go ahead, Jasmine," I said.

"The machines—they're coming to take the island back."

"Which one?"

"Tango—the island you're on now, sir."

"Okay…" I said, stepping out of the command tent and looking around. I didn't see anything. I took a moment to examine my computer screens, but they were empty as well.

"I'm not sensing anything," I said.

"They're in the water, sir. They've been building up under their domes. They're marching—big machines, about two hundred of them so far."

"So far?" I asked in surprise. "Two hundred, and they're still being deployed? Am I reading you right, Captain?"

"I'm afraid so, sir. I'll transmit the latest data down to your command post. The readings are new."

I felt a wave of—something. I almost felt sick. We'd fought so hard, and it had looked as if the enemy had been beaten back. But now that I'd taken this mountain, now that I sat upon its lofty crown—I was going to have to defend it.

Captain Sarin was still talking, but I was no longer listening. While she did so, the computer scroll spread out on a makeshift table in my command tent began to update. It now showed dozens—no, *hundreds* of large red contacts. They were in the sea, and they were coming up toward us slowly, marching on the bottom. They were going to surface all around the island and assault it, just as we'd done ten hours earlier.

"I'm sorry," I said, tuning back into Captain Sarin's report. "Could you give me that updated count again?"

192

I was shocked when I got the final numbers. Somewhere between three hundred and five hundred of the big ones were coming. We had the high ground now, and we had the Crustaceans backing us up—but that was a whole lot of giant robots. With a veteran crew, it took a platoon a minute or two to take down one of the big ones. Theoretically, we could beat them all, given time.

But it wasn't going to happen that way. When they had numbers, when they had the crushing weight of massed machines, they would break my lines. It would be the machines that were ganging up on platoons of men, not the other way around. I'd seen them do it before, most vividly during the South American Campaign. It would be a feeding frenzy, with each machine competing to see how many of my troops it could kill.

"I'm not sure we can hold against those numbers, Captain," I said.

She hesitated. "I know. What are your orders, sir?"

Instantly, I knew what she was thinking. It was time to pull out. That made me angry. I didn't want to give up this island. Why had we fought all the way to the highest peak and lost so many good marines if we were going to run away back into space a few hours later? I didn't want those earlier sacrifices to have been made in vain.

At the same time, I wasn't sure that I had any choice. The machines weren't going to just wait around until I made my decision. They weren't charging up the beaches yet, but when they had their entire force positioned, they would.

"Prepare for evacuation, Captain Sarin."

"I took the liberty of drawing up a plan for our withdrawal, Colonel. Do you want to see it?"

I compressed my lips tightly. Had she predicted this? Maybe up there, safe in space with Fleet, she would pass her hat around to collect on her bets.

But no, I knew that wasn't how we'd gotten to this point. Sarin was a good officer. It was her job to anticipate contingencies. There was always a chance we would fail, and she was the type who thought of everything.

"How long ago did you draw up these plans?" I asked her.

"Before you dropped, sir. I've been updating them steadily as the campaign has progressed."

"Of course you have," I said with a hint of bitterness.

193

"I didn't develop the plans because I had no faith in you, Colonel," she said. "I felt it was my duty."

"I know, I know. I'm just sorry things turned out this way. We don't seem to have the strength to battle the machines this time. We didn't have time to build armor or enough specialized equipment."

I'd forgotten just what kind of a sidekick Captain Sarin was. She wasn't a masterful strategist who looked for enemy weaknesses, but she was a logistical wizard. As was the case with most wizardry, she achieved her results through hard work and discipline.

"I'm glad you drew up plans," I told her, "but I'm changing them. We aren't withdrawing from Yale. We're withdrawing from Tango. We'll shift our force over to the Big Island and set up heavy defenses there. With all our troops in one place—"

"Sir, Sandra is requesting to join the channel."

I sighed.

"She's insisting, sir."

"I bet she is. Okay, switch me over and get to work on prepping the escape. We don't have much time."

"Kyle?" Sandra asked a moment later.

"What is it, hon?"

"I hear you're coming back up here. I want to see you the moment you arrive."

I hesitated for a second, wondering if I should tell her about the change of plans. I had no intention of withdrawing from Yale just yet. At the end of my one second's pause, I decided *not* to tell her. Now was not the time to start a domestic argument.

"Yes," I said enthusiastically, "we're wrapping this up. It'll be good to see you again. Anything else? I've got to—"

"There is something else," she said. "There are a couple of things, in fact. One is Alexa."

My voice grew cautious. "Is she still alive?"

"Of course she is, Kyle! What a terrible thing to say. We're getting along quite well now. She seems sweet, in a military way. She's told me a lot about life under the Empire."

I smiled. That was just like Sandra, to be jealous of another woman, then make friends with her later on. She got along well with other women, but she had trouble when they paid too much attention to me.

"That's good," I said, making my second play to disconnect, "but I've got to—"

"There's something else. It's about Marvin. He's been acting weird—even for Marvin. I think you should have a talk with him."

"What's he doing?"

"He's roaming around outside the ship. He's been out there crawling on the hull all day. It sounds like we have giant metal rats. I'm sure he's scarred up the ship. The nanites are worked up about it, and the ceiling in our quarters never stops shimmering now."

I frowned. "What's he doing crawling on the hull of the ship?"

"He says he can get a better signal out there, whatever that means."

"A better signal?" I asked, my frown deepening.

When Marvin began behaving oddly and went off on his own, that sometimes signaled a dramatic shift in the tactical situation. The robot was often sneaky, especially when he was doing something he wasn't supposed to.

"Connect me over to Marvin, immediately," I said, my irritation growing. First it looked like we were going to be kicked off this island, and now Marvin was up to something nefarious. I couldn't believe my misfortune.

"Aren't you forgetting something?" Sandra asked.

"What? Oh yeah—I love you."

"Good. I do too. Here's that crazy robot."

There were a few odd sounds, then Marvin's voice came in. He sounded distracted.

"Hello...Colonel Riggs."

"What are you up to, Marvin?" I demanded. "Have you been talking to the Macros? I'm seeing a lot of evidence down here that they're building equipment that reminds me of your designs."

I'd finally said it. I'd been thinking about it for a long time, but I'd finally gotten around to telling Marvin about my suspicions. I reminded myself that they weren't just my suspicions, several people had noticed the similarities between new Macro equipment designs and Marvin himself.

"I'm taken aback, Colonel," Marvin said. "If I did contact Macros directly and independently, I'm sure they wouldn't trust me enough to take my advice on self-design."

It was a pretty good argument, but I pressed ahead. "You haven't directly answered the question. Have you been engaging in independent communications with the Macros?"

"Not lately, sir."

I ground my molars together. "Not lately? That's another dodge, Marvin."

"I did have contact with them some months ago. It is possible they misconstrued my efforts to transmit data through the rings as a communications exchange."

I frowned. "What?"

"Recall that I pioneered the technology we all now use for instant, interstellar communications—"

"Not exactly," I said, "you pioneered the effort to steal the technology from the Blues."

"A minor, but noteworthy detail. In any case, when I transmitted data to test the system, I did so at that time using an unprotected data format."

"Ah," I said, catching on. "So the Macros were listening to you? Is that it? What did you tell them by accident? Did you happen to send along a roster of our ships, or our personnel records?"

"Nothing like that. I transmitted design documents I'd been working on. Random data, I thought at the time."

I nodded. "And these design documents were of equipment you thought we might want to build? Something the Macros might pick up and find useful?"

"No. The design documents were all optional configurations for my own body. Ideas I'd worked on while my backup-brainboxes were relatively under-utilized."

I chuckled. "You're telling me you sent them imaginary configurations of yourself?"

"Is that amusing, Colonel?"

I thought about the mining robot I'd met up with that had a thousand twenty-foot long tentacles for legs. That had essentially been one of Marvin's doodles. The Macros must have believed they were getting classified information and had attempted to build some of the things Marvin had designed.

"Yeah," I said, "it is funny. All right. Just don't do it anymore. What are you up to now? Why are you out on the hull, sending messages again?"

196

"I'm following your orders, sir. In fact, this is excellent timing. I wanted your permission."

"Permission for what?"

"Permission to transmit the final sequence."

I rolled my eyes. "I have no idea what you're talking about, Marvin."

"Have you sustained an injury, sir?"

"Several of them. But I haven't lost my memory, if that's what you're implying. Just tell me what you think you're supposed to be doing."

"I'm breaking the Yale ring's code, sir. You told me to turn it on again and flush the Macros back out into the system they came from."

"Oh yeah," I said. "I did tell you that. How's that coming along?"

"I'm ready, sir."

"When?"

"Right now."

I froze for perhaps two heartbeats. I looked over my shoulder, and then turned around fully to see the ocean. North of Tango the ring lay at the bottom of a thousand foot deep bowl of seawater. I couldn't see it, but I knew that the Macros had placed their factories under domes down there.

"Do it Marvin," I said in a hushed, excited voice. "Flush them all to Hell."

"Transmitting, sir. Message sent. Is there anything else?"

"Yeah," I said, frowning with an immediate afterthought. "Can you turn it back off again? I mean, after the Macros are sucked down?"

"My orders did not include an imperative to research a third reversal of the ring's state. The enemy is jamming my transmissions in any case. Just getting this command to the receiver—"

"Marvin," I said, interrupting him. "I need you to turn off the effect again. You did it before!"

I'd been watching the ocean to the north while we spoke. As I stood there on the mountaintop, witnessing the event, the water miles out to sea suddenly blackened. A white ring grew around the dark region. I knew a vast whirlpool had formed, like a giant drain sucking the ocean down an endlessly deep throat.

"You have to turn it off again, Marvin. You've got five minutes."

"It took me several days to figure out how to reverse the flow on each occasion. The ring does not have a simplistic interface, I'm afraid. It's not 'user-friendly'. Let me explain: the encoding system seems to alter itself on the basis of the last command successfully executed. When an operation is performed, part of the artifact's system rewrites the code. I suspect this is some kind of internal security precaution against tampering—"

"For God's sake, Marvin!" I shouted.

Everyone had stopped what they were doing and was now staring out to sea. It was impossible not to. The sky had even shifted, and the winds were picking up. The mass being transported off -planet must have been tremendous. A singing, roaring sound rose up and up in volume as I listened to Marvin. I realized a hurricane was forming out there, a few miles from shore.

"Can you stop it? I'm sure the flood you've created so far is enough. The machines must have been sucked down by now."

"We're having trouble with confirmation on that point," Marvin said. "Are you sure you want to stop the procedure without confirmation?"

"YES! Dammit, Marvin! *Turn it off!*"

I felt sick inside. All around me, the men were moving again, getting over their initial shock. Major Sloan came close, shouting at me. I couldn't hear him and I didn't care what he was saying anyway. I pushed him aside with a single shove and stepped to the edge of the cliff. The wind was so strong now, I could feel it through my bulky suit. It was like having a hand pushing on my back, pushing me toward the drain in front of me.

Marvin was talking to me about dry technical details while he attempted code sequences to turn off the growing whirlpool. He was hacking, and talking, and I was barely listening. My men stopped asking me what was happening, as it was becoming painfully clear by now.

I staggered away when the water level all the way to the coastline of Tango was affected. Even this far out, the water turned white, like one endless series of breakers going down into nothingness. I knew the entire planet was draining away, the way it had been before we'd come out here and interfered.

I knew the Crustaceans were watching this turn of events with horror. I wondered if they knew that we had been the ones to turn the ring on again. I wondered, too, if they'd ever figure out I'd failed to ask if it could be turned off a second time before I'd ordered Marvin to pull the plug.

If they did figure it out, they'd know the truth: that I had killed them all.

For the next seven long hours, the oceans continued to drain. Marvin had made no progress at all.

I hooked up my maps to Fleet's sensors and watched as the Macros were indeed swept away into the hole at the bottom of the ocean. The power of moving water could carve rock, and even with their shields and vast weight, the machines couldn't hold onto the seabed.

The armies they had offshore sat quietly at first, but when they realized they were being exposed and many had been dragged away into the unquenchable maw behind them, they charged the beach. It was a vicious battle, but one where we had the upper hand. Most of their forces were swept away to sea and down the hole in its black depths before they managed to struggle up onto the rocky beaches. When the last of them did reach the beach and make their ragged assault, there were less than a hundred of them left.

As any accountant can tell you, numbers matter. We met them as they rushed out of the water and destroyed them before they could press up to the heights. Even the Crustaceans joined in. I gathered from some of their messages they were under the impression the machines had opened the great drain in the sea again with the intention of killing all life on Yale. I didn't enlighten them on this point.

Three races of biotics fought side by side, and when the last machine was brought down and the last Star Force marine raised his fist with a shout of victory, the beach was wider than it once had been.

No low tide in the history of Yale could compare. The water was leaving this world, and I knew the rest of it would soon heat up and begin killing those who'd survived the first great bleeding. I imagined in the Crustacean archives, this would go down as a bittersweet day. At a terrific cost, we'd swept the machines from the planet with a single hard push. We'd cut out the cancer, but killed the patient in the process.

Marvin kept working at his hacking effort. I checked in with him twice an hour, but his answer was always the same: he was working on it.

I knew there was no speeding up something like this. I'd worked with software myself. Technical projects tended to get done when they got done. Beating on the workers didn't always yield the results anticipated.

But I beat on him anyway. I complained, raved, and almost frothed at the mouth in our discussions. Seeing the ocean drain away and knowing it was all our fault was just too much to take. I paced atop Tango's highest peak and growled at anyone who came near.

First Night came and lasted a long, long time. When we were in our thirtieth straight hour of unrelenting darkness, the miracle came at last.

"It's stopped, sir!" Kwon said, shaking me awake.

I'd been dreaming of running water, faucets left on and flooding bathrooms. I came awake with a lurch, and grabbed his hand. He was one of the few people in the world that didn't flinch when my hand closed on his. He pulled me to my feet.

"What are you talking about, Kwon?"

"The water—I think that crazy robot has done it."

I walked out onto the cliffs and stared down. It was storming lightly outside. It was hard to see through the night rains, but using my visor with the light enhancers and zooming optics engaged, I determined that the waters had indeed settled. They were still sloshing and disturbed. Tidal waves would race around the planet for months. But the draining had stopped.

I contacted Marvin immediately. "Well done!" I told him.

"It wasn't me, Colonel. As much as I'd like to have solved the problem, I didn't do so."

After a few more questions, I realized he didn't have a clue who had closed the ring or how. I disconnected and stood in the wind and rain, wondering what to make of it. If the Macros had done it, could they reverse the ring yet again? Could this entire thing start over again? Or was it a trap, baiting my Marines to go down to the seabed and investigate?

A few hours later, I contacted the Crustaceans. I knew almost right away what was going on. They were insufferably proud of themselves.

"We have stopped the machines," they said. "We've been studying your primitive algorithms, watching as the ring is vibrated day and night. Is this truly all the sophistication Earth creatures have when dealing with a quantitative problem? To simply install a random answer into the equation and check to see if it works? Such wasteful iteration."

"Congratulations!" I said, so relieved they weren't all going to die and blame me that I didn't care if they made a speech about it or not.

And speech they did. I was forced to politely listen to every technical detail of their achievement. Like all nerds with wounded pride, when they finally got one right, they crowed about it for hours.

I gave them ten minutes, then five more, before giving them something to get off the subject.

"High Command?" I asked. "I'm sorry, but I must get back to my duties. The crisis here seems to have come to an end. Perhaps we can discuss the matter further at the next Council meeting."

I waited one second, then two. I knew their translators were generating question marks. It made me smile just to think about it.

At last, they spoke up again. "What is this 'Council meeting'?"

"Haven't you been informed? Now that you've joined Star Force officially, we can proceed to place your representatives on the council."

"Joined Star Force? I'm afraid you're under a series of misconceptions. Possibly, the translation equipment has failed us. It is highly inadequate. We've been working on designing our own superior model."

"I'm sure you have been," I said. I'd given them brainboxes that knew English and their language to ease our conversations. But they'd never quite accepted any of the technology. It wasn't good enough for them.

"Perhaps I'm presuming too much," I said. "But after you ended your state of neutrality and declared open war on the machines, I thought it was clear that you would have to become part of the local alliance of biotic species. The Macros are our shared enemy now, and that simple fact keeps us together."

"We do not object to occasional cooperative acts. We are not ungrateful for your aid in this recent misunderstanding. But we do not consider ourselves to be at war with the machines, nor do we accept a state of alliance with Star Force."

I heaved a sigh. I thought it might go this way. The Lobsters were 'takers', people who wanted whatever you could give them and always begged for more. They did precious little in return, however.

"All right then," I snapped. "We'll be lifting off and shipping out within—ten hours. Glad we could be of service."

Another hesitation, then, "your service was appreciated. A continued presence on Yale might benefit both of us, in fact. May we propose—"

"Sorry," I said loudly and with perhaps a touch of relish, "no, we can't spare these forces any longer. We'll be moving back to our own borders. As non-alliance members, your neutrality must be respected. It's in our charter."

The conversation soon ended after that. I could tell they weren't going to budge and they'd wasted my time. I was glad to have saved billions of lives, but it had cost me time, resources and manpower for very little gain.

Ten hours later I was back on my command ship. I headed immediately to the observation chamber, which had real windows that let out on the profundity that we call space. Yale hung there under my feet, and I examined it moodily in my shipboard uniform. Simple smart clothes were more comfortable than armor, but they felt flimsy after clanking on Yale for the last several days. I felt like I was walking around in pajamas.

The storms hadn't subsided yet on the moon below. There were white swirls dotting the atmosphere over slate-gray waters. The islands were still there, but rarely visible through the cloud layer. To me, they seemed like floating bones in the flood. It could have been my imagination, but they looked a little larger than they had a week earlier.

Sandra came into the observatory to join me. I was surprised to see Alexa in her wake.

"Hello, ladies," I said. "I'm sure you've seen this view before. Quite fascinating to look down upon a world you were standing upon only hours ago."

"Especially when you helped tear it up," Sandra said.

"Oh no," Alexa said, speaking up. She no longer seemed timid to me. I guess hanging around Sandra for days had given her some self-confidence. "You did the best you could, under the circumstances."

We all looked down at Yale for a quiet moment. I couldn't see the tidal waves and the rains that I knew were lashing the planet along with sheets of lightning. Most worlds looked peaceful from the sky.

"The techs told me the storms would go on for years," I said. "This world will take time to heal, but there are still hundreds of billions of live lobsters in that ocean and they aren't going to boil or go down a giant drain today. Star Force has accomplished its mission."

"I'd love to hear the details," Alexa said. "We've watched the vids, but you only get so much from those. What was it really like down there, Colonel?"

I looked at her and saw her eyes were bright with interest. I smiled.

"You're right," I said. "Vids aren't like being there."

"Alexa," Sandra said with a new, cold note in her voice. "I think it's time we left the Colonel to his strategic planning. He has to figure out his next move, and he prefers to be alone on such occasions."

I looked at her for a second in surprise, then I caught on. Sandra didn't want me getting too close to this young lady. Not even for a conversation. I nodded, thinking perhaps she was right.

"I'll catch up with you two at dinner," I said.

Alexa looked disappointed, but Sandra ushered her out of the chamber successfully. I looked after them both, hoping Sandra wouldn't get angry and take it out on Lieutenant Brighton. I couldn't help but notice both ladies were attractive from every angle. In fact, it was something of a contest as to who had the best curves.

That bothered me, for just a moment. It did seem that Alexa Brighton was uncommonly attractive. What were the odds that one of

204

Earth's best-looking female officers had suddenly become determined to defect to Star Force? Could she be a spy after all?

I decided to pursue the matter with Sandra later. She knew the young lady better than I did, and she was in a much better position to judge the veracity of her story at this point than I was. Besides, I had the feeling I wasn't going to be allowed close enough to the girl to ask her any probing questions.

As all seemed quiet now in the Thor system, I decided to pull out. The Crustaceans weren't joining up, so I figured they needed to feel left out. Maybe when they didn't have our fleets protecting them, they might be in a more cooperative mood.

We flew back to the Eden system at a stately pace. I debriefed Marvin and Sarin on the tactical details of the operation. We'd done fairly well, when all things were considered.

"I want to thank you two for your expertise on this mission," I told them. "Marvin, you were flying by the seat of your pants—uh, tentacles. I know conducting scientific experimentation and research under fire isn't easy. There were a few screw-ups, but at the endpoint, we came out alive and so did the biotics we came to assist. That's what counts in my book."

"I'm disturbed, however, Colonel," Captain Sarin said. "The Crustaceans still aren't fully accepting our help."

"I know, but I think they'll come around eventually."

"At this point, they're at war with the Macros. Don't they know that?"

"I think they do, but I also think they've managed to maintain a semi-neutral stance throughout this war. They assaulted us, but only with a few ships full of troops. They were attacked by the Macros, but only indirectly, by the draining of their oceans. I think they believe they can keep pulling tricks like this. And, they think it's in their best interests to maintain a balance, because they are in a precarious position."

Jasmine shook her head. "I don't agree with them. They must commit. They'd be safer firmly on one side. This way, they could suffer great consequences."

"Arguably, they already have. History isn't without precedence in this regard. Nations have been stuck between two military powers before and worked hard to maintain neutrality. Turkey in World War Two is an excellent example. Hitler wanted to invade, but could

205

never find a good pretext for doing so. Russia was kept at bay as well on Turkey's eastern front through careful diplomacy. A similar example would be Switzerland in the same time period."

"What about Poland?" Jasmine asked.

I cleared my throat. "Yes, well, I didn't say that *every* nation manages to maintain their neutrality when circled by wolves. Most fall. But maybe Crustacean history is different in this regard."

"It sounds like you approve of their position."

"I don't. But I understand it. Maybe it's an exercise in self-denial. In any case, I want to withdraw to put pressure on them."

"And if the Macros attack again while we're out of reach?"

I shrugged. "They probably won't. And we're watching. We'll maintain the fleet at Welter Station. If the machines put a new fleet in the Thor system, we'll fly out to meet them again."

Marvin, who'd been quiet throughout this exchange, ruffled his metal tentacles. Knowing he did this when he wanted attention, I turned to him.

"Colonel Riggs," he said. "The Crustaceans have made a critical error."

"I agree with you," I said. "But how can we convince them of that?"

"I don't believe we'll have to. They will figure it out on their own."

I frowned at him for a second, not quite sure what he meant.

"I hope you're right about them figuring out the situation," I said. "We could use them as allies. I don't think they'll join us until they have no choice, however."

Another day and night passed. The following dawn my ships reached the ring and slipped through to the far side, where the battle station stood vigilantly at the border.

It was there that my life would take a turn for the worst.

* * *

The next day we awoke on Welter Station, and I started my usual morning routine. Sandra and I got reacquainted in the shower capsule, and I came out refreshed and ready for work.

There was plenty to do. Miklos had left a raft of reports for me. The first news item on the list surprised me: General Kerr had left Eden-8. He'd said he couldn't wait any longer, and couldn't accept my proposals as stated. He was going to have to consult with the Emperor personally and get back to me.

I wasn't happy about it, but I figured I could understand it. I'd left him sitting around Shadowguard eating air-swimmers for a full week. Probably, he'd just gotten antsy.

But I knew he didn't have to fly all the way back to Earth to get word from Crow. He could have transmitted a message to communicate. It would have taken quite a while, but it would have been faster than flying back home.

I shrugged, throwing the hard copy on my desk. I couldn't expect to go from a state of war to a productive peace in a few days. Such talks always seemed to drag on, even if peace was in the interest of both parties.

I downed a mug of real coffee and headed for the battle station's bridge. We'd finally found lands where we could grow actual coffee beans on Eden-7, and the first crops had been harvested. The brew tasted a trifle bitter to me, but I was glad to leave the fake stuff behind forever.

It was just before I reached the bridge that I got an unusual call. It was from Sandra, or at least that's what the channel indicated.

The unusual thing was that the red "urgent" flag was blinking beside the call on my com link. Sandra didn't mark things down as urgent unless she meant business. I halted in the passageway and tapped at it, frowning.

"What's up, hon?" I asked.

There was a moment of rustling. I frowned, and was about to repeat my words, when a voice spoke. It wasn't Sandra's voice.

"There's been an accident," said the voice.

It took me a second to recognize who it was. "Alexa? Is that you? What's wrong?"

"Could you come quickly? It's Sandra, I'm using her com-link. She's not responding. I don't know what's wrong."

"Where are you?"

"We're in the pool room, on Deck Nine."

I was already running. I was close to the lift, and I rode it impatiently down. Just in case something serious had happened, I

207

contacted our medical people and ordered them to send a team down to the pool room.

The pool room was possibly the only sport that the members of Star Force had invented among themselves. It wasn't a game that normal humans could play, and even if they tried, it had to be played in low gravity. Our kind of "pool" did involve hard, colored balls, just like the traditional game. But the pool sticks were essentially baseball bats and the "pockets" were the other players. The goal of the game was to nail your fellow nanotized marine with a pool ball by bouncing it off the walls.

The game often became dangerous. I could easily believe Sandra had been showing off and knocked herself out by firing pool balls on wild banking shots to impress Alexa. She was good at pool, possibly the best I'd ever seen, but everyone made mistakes sometimes.

I was worried, but nothing could have prepared me for the scene that met me when I reached the pool room. Since it was the start of a new shift and technically "morning" aboard the battle station, no one else was around. People normally played our favorite violent sport in the evening after dinner.

I pushed on the sealed door, and it swished open. I felt a little resistance, and I knew instantly what it was. I'd felt the dead weight of a body against a door before. I slipped inside and looked down at Sandra.

She was a mess. A puddle of foam tinged with pinkish blood matted her hair and face. I knelt beside her, putting out a gentle hand onto her shoulder.

"Sandra honey? What did you do?"

I heard a sob. I turned, and saw Alexa. She stood behind the door, trembling. She had a hand to her face, and the other at her side.

"What the hell happened?" I demanded.

She shook her head, and didn't answer. I could see she was in a highly emotional state. I turned back to Sandra, and reached down to caress her hair. She was a fallen flower to me. I felt my own emotions surging.

I saw Sandra's eyes then. That was when I felt cold fear hit me. They were open, staring…blank. Up until that point, it hadn't occurred to me that she was actually dead.

My hand left her cheek and went up to my com link. I planned to open a channel to medical and order them to get their butts up there, pronto. We could cure practically anything, even death, but she could be out of commission for months if they didn't get her under emergency care right now.

I felt for her pulse, but there wasn't any. I looked for other vital signs and found nothing.

My mind was filling with memories. It was impossible to stop the flood. When I'd first met Sandra, she'd died soon after. She'd fallen into the cold, cold ocean. I'd gotten my ship, *Alamo*, to fish her out and repair her body that fateful day. Later, when battling with Macros, she'd been seriously injured again. In a coma for a long time, she'd been called a "turnip" by my charming medical staff. But she'd come out of that one too. It was such a twisted joke if she could have been taken out in a pool room accident now—

Alexa said something behind me at that moment, while I stared down at my dying lady love. She whispered: "Sorry."

That was all I needed. I didn't have to see her, and I couldn't really, because I didn't have time to turn my head and see what she was up to. Instead, I threw my arm back behind myself and made a sweeping motion, as if hurling something.

My body is unlike any human known to me. My bone and muscle density is, in fact, *inhuman*. My flailing arm had unspeakable power in it, even when I wasn't in armor, and even when I wasn't in a good stance to deliver a blow.

I struck her. I heard a cracking sound, and felt her lift from the floor and go flying. Alexa sailed a good twenty feet to the far wall and smashed into it. Something reflective fell from her hand and tinkled on the floor.

I rose up on the balls of my feet and advanced. My fists were at my side. I was breathing hard, ready to fight.

But the fight was already over. She was unconscious—and possibly dead. At her side was a silvery needle attached to a rubber bulb. Liquid dribbled out from the tip onto the floor.

Paranoid, I felt my back with my hands. Had she managed to scratch me with that thing—whatever it was? I'd been poisoned before and it wasn't fun.

As far as I could tell, she hadn't managed to jab me with the needle. When the medics arrived, I explained the situation as quickly as I could and screamed for Marvin to get down here and perform an analysis on the liquid in the rubber bulb.

When I was certain both women were getting the best of care, I headed up to the bridge. I wanted to get to the bottom of this assassination attempt.

I reminded myself as I sat in my command chair that this time it had been more than an attempt, as Sandra was technically dead. Normally, I would have stayed at her side in the infirmary, but I knew that every second lost might be critical.

I also knew who my prime suspect was in this case: the amazing, vanishing, General Kerr.

-26-

I seethed with emotions and was barely able to sit on my command chair. Both armrests were seriously damaged, due to my hammering and cursing.

The staff was staying quiet. Word had gotten out about the attack and no one wanted to approach me right now. I shouted for Miklos until someone went and got him. He stepped up, standing at attention.

"Are you aware an imperial assassin was in our midst for over a week, undetected?" I demanded. "This is your command territory, Commodore. Security is part of your duties. I'm holding you responsible."

"I'm sorry, sir. I hope Sandra will recover."

"You have some explaining to do," I told him. "When I left, I put you and your carrier on duty at Helios ring. If you were there now, you could chase down Kerr. He's running and has reached the Helios system by this time."

Miklos looked concerned. "The carrier itself is still there, sir," he said. "But I don't think that ship could catch the General in any case. Recall your removal of several of the ship's engines…"

"Don't try to put this off on me!" I shouted.

I shook my head and took a deep breath. All around me, everyone else had frozen again. I suspected they were waiting to see if I had another violent outburst. I tried to calm down, but didn't entirely succeed.

"I was suckered," I said. "This entire thing from Earth—this sham about peace talks...Kerr just wanted to come out here and kill us."

Bravely, Captain Sarin approached me. I was surprised to see her aboard the battle station.

"You are away from your post, Captain," I growled at her. "Why have you left your carrier?"

"I heard about what happened," she said quietly. "I wanted to see if I could help."

I barely listened to her. I wasn't looking at any of them.

"Last time Crow sent some newsy to sucker us with her charms," I said. "This time he sent an old acquaintance and worked the knife again. This time, he drew blood. Why am I such a fool?"

"What do you mean, sir?" Miklos asked.

I focused my eyes on him. "Isn't it obvious?" I asked. "Crow is clearly behind these last two attempts on my life. But there have been many in the past. Remember the first, the young Asian girl he'd just hired? Or the Dutch commandos after that? I blamed Major Barrera for those plays, but now I think it went higher up. Barrera and the rest of them were all working for Crow."

Miklos and Jasmine exchanged glances. I noticed, but I didn't react. Let them think I was crazy. I could see everything now. It was all so very clear. Crow hadn't been able to arrest me and remove me from power directly, so he'd made a half-dozen underhanded attempts to end my life. Now, he'd managed to strike down my closest confidant, my best bodyguard. If nothing else, I would be an easier target for the next blade that came out of the dark without Sandra watching my back.

"Get Kwon up here," I said suddenly.

Startled, Miklos and Jasmine both relayed the request. Less than thirty seconds later, Kwon walked onto the bridge. I felt my face smile, even though it was only a grim twitching of the lips.

Kwon was in full battle-gear. His visor was shut, and his laser projector was cradled in his arms.

"I see you came well-prepared, First Sergeant," I said.

"Actually, sir, I thought you might call," Kwon said, placing himself beside my command chair. "I was standing in the passageway outside."

"Of course you were. Well, I have need of you now. I don't know who's going to poison or shoot me next. Since Sandra's out of the picture for the moment, I want you on hand to do her job."

"Very good, sir."

I noticed that the command staff looked intimidated. I often wore armor on the bridge, but somehow seeing Kwon there, staring at each of them in turn as if he suspected them of treachery, unnerved people.

I turned to Miklos. "What assets do we have in play to catch General Kerr? I assume he's crossing the Helios system on full burn by now?"

"That's correct, Colonel. We don't have much in range, actually. The task force at that end of the Eden system is small and slow. If you recall, you placed a squadron of gunboats and a single carrier there as a defensive force. None of these ships can catch General Kerr's battleship, as it is now too far ahead on the acceleration curve."

I asked for the data and got it immediately. I walked to the planning tables and did some calculations. We couldn't catch him with a ship, but...

"What about a missile?" I asked. "Or better, a *lot* of missiles? What do we have on *Defiant*?"

Miklos squirmed. "You didn't authorize missiles to be placed on the new carriers," he said.

"Yes...?"

"But, it just so happens that the ship in question has some aboard."

I snorted. I knew Miklos loved those ships and loved to improve their designs. I knew I'd ripped his heart out when I'd torn up his plans and deleted so much optional equipment. At this point, I was unsurprised that he'd continued outfitting them to match his original plans.

"Under the circumstances," I said, "I'm glad you made certain...*improvements* upon the agreed carrier blueprints. Captain Sarin, please check my numbers, if you would."

She eyed them closely. "I think they're correct, sir," she said, "but there isn't enough time. The missiles could reach Kerr's ship if they were fired right now, but the command to fire must cross the

213

Eden system. That's nearly twenty light-hours. By the time the command reaches the carrier, it will be too late."

"Maybe," I said. I turned back to Miklos. "I recall that your original design placed a ring-to-ring communications unit aboard these carriers. Did that deleted item somehow make it back onto the roster?"

"Uh," said Miklos, his eyes sliding around between the two of us. He seemed flustered and mildly embarrassed. "Yes it did, sir. I thought that since the carriers were natural taskforce command ships—"

"Enough of that crap. Call them up and order them to fire everything they have."

Miklos nodded and hurried to the communications consoles.

Jasmine stepped closer to my chair. Kwon twitched at her approach, but she ignored him. "How did you know he would disobey orders and build that equipment onto the carrier?"

"I didn't," I said, "but I probably would have done the same thing. His design was superior, and he knew it. I changed it because his plans would have taken too long to build at the time. Since I've been off campaigning in the Thor system, he made some worthwhile edits, that's all."

"Kyle," she said quietly, her voice almost a whisper. "I know you're upset, but are you sure you want to kill Kerr this way? We don't know everything yet. There hasn't been any kind of investigation."

"If I wait for an investigation, Kerr will be safely home on Earth by the time he's been declared guilty. There might not be enough evidence to be certain, anyway, without capturing and questioning him."

"But you might be making a serious mistake, and a major diplomatic error."

I stared at her coldly. I liked Captain Sarin, but she didn't always know what she was talking about.

"I play the odds," I said. "I always do. Instinct must be part of any commander's arsenal of tricks. I trust mine in this instance. Kerr was behind the assassination, and Crow was behind him."

I stood up and towered over her. She looked up at me, clearly unconvinced. I brushed past.

214

"Which reminds me, I need to check up on Sandra and her would-be murderer."

I headed down to medical, and Kwon stayed firmly in my shadow. We didn't talk, which was just fine with me. I wasn't in the mood to explain anything to anyone. I left Kwon on guard in the main passage as I inspected the facilities.

Marvin's body filled a good portion of medical. He was bigger than the last time I'd seen him. Today, I would estimate he was the size of a pickup truck, and twice as heavy. The medical staff wasn't too happy about his presence, but they were tolerating it. They had little choice.

Marvin's tentacles seemed to have been elongated. Maybe he'd made some special changes just for this occasion. In any case, the tentacles flowed over the floor and up to the ceiling like black, metallic ropes. They then dangled down directly over the patients or snaked up from the floor like self-mobile cables. Occasionally, the doctors and nurses stepped on one of the appendages and muttered a curse.

In a modern Star Force facility, the doctors and nurses didn't do much. They were mostly there to monitor the process, make executive decisions and fill out reports which I normally read later on casualty update screens. This time, I was more emotionally tied up with the process than usual.

"Do you have a moment, Doctor?" I asked, grabbing the arm of a passing woman with a Fleet medical insignia on her shoulder.

She turned to me, startled. "Colonel? I wasn't expecting to see you so soon. We're not done yet. Nothing's been determined."

I frowned. She seemed nervous. I checked her nametag, it read: Kate Swanson, M. D.

"What do you know so far?" I demanded.

She looked down at her computer tablet and shook her head before she replied. I could see she was building up to give me some bad news. Even before she spoke, I felt butterflies in my stomach. It had been a long time since I'd experienced that sensation.

"It was a neural toxin, sir," Dr. Swanson said. "Something we've never seen before. It was tailor-made for this purpose."

"Designed to kill a Star Force marine who is otherwise unkillable?"

She looked me in the eye for a second, then dropped her gaze again. She nodded. "Yes, that's a good way to describe it. Fast-acting, too fast for the nanites or the microbials to adjust. Tissues were damaged so quickly the body didn't have time to respond."

"But the nanites and microbes should clear toxins. They flush them before they can do much harm."

"Normally, yes. By the time we got to Sandra, they *were* flushed out of her system. But they'd already done their work."

"Where did you get your data?"

"From the empty syringe. There was a residue—enough to run tests."

I nodded, thinking hard. "You mentioned tissue damage, but you said it was a neural toxin, right?"

She nodded, eyeing me, then looking down at my hand. I realized at that moment I still had a grip on her arm. I forced myself to release her. She seemed to breathe more easily after that.

"You're talking about brain damage, aren't you?" I asked.

She compressed her lips together into a tight line and nodded.

"But we can rebuild her," I said. "Any cell that's been damaged can be reconstructed if there's something left."

She gave me a wan, flickering smile. "That's true sir."

"So, why are you looking at me like someone killed your cat?"

"It's too early to tell what we're dealing with," she said.

Her voice was soothing, but I didn't feel like being soothed just now. I stared at her with hard, narrowed eyes.

"You're telling me Sandra's mind has been damaged," I said.

She shook her head. "It's been less than half an hour. We don't know everything. Give us some time, Colonel."

I tried to think. I felt as if I'd been given a dose of neural toxins myself. "Can she breathe? Is her heart pumping?"

"Yes sir—with help."

"What about the other one? The assassin."

"Lieutenant Brighton was severely injured," the doctor said. "Apparently, you struck her very hard."

I looked at her sharply. Was that a reproachful tone in the good doctor's voice?

"Don't be taken in by her youth and attractiveness," I said. "I was fooled, and she almost got both of us. She's an accomplished

216

actress—an assassin who succeeded where a half-dozen others have failed."

"Well, I don't know about that," Swanson said, refusing to meet my eye again. She was reading a chart from a computer tablet. "She has a fractured clavicle, two broken ribs and a broken wrist. There's also a hairline fracture at the base of her skull. She had a blood clot in her left lung due to a complication from the broken ribs, but we managed to dissolve that with a nanite injection."

I put a hand out again and touched the doctor's wrist. "Don't give her nanite injections. She doesn't deserve that. I'd rather see her die of her injuries."

Doctor Swanson looked horrified, but she made a note on her tablet. I left her and went to talk to Marvin.

"Hey Marvin, can you fix Sandra up?"

"Unknown, Colonel," Marvin said. He didn't sound sorrowful, but then, he never did.

I looked around for cameras. They seemed to be split between me and Sandra, who was lying on her back on a table. A few more cameras followed Kwon and the assassin.

"What do you mean 'unknown'?" I demanded.

"Unknown as in 'not yet determined' or 'dependent on input not yet gathered' or—"

"Yeah, yeah, I get it. Listen, I want you to do whatever you have to, within reason. I need her up and around again within a week."

"There are some options…" Marvin said. More cameras had swung to regard me now. I knew he was interested in my reaction. "But they will take longer than a week to accomplish. And I'm not sure if they fit within the category you described."

"You mean they might not be 'within reason'?"

"That point of judgment is very subjective. I would find the treatments reasonable, but I'm also aware that some human beings might not agree with me."

I frowned at him. When Marvin got into the business of healing people, funny things tended to happen. I was also concerned to hear that Sandra's condition was so grave.

I lightly touched Sandra's cheek. It was warm, and she was breathing, but I could see she was being aided by apparatus that had been cemented to her face by a silvery ring of nanites. My eyes ran down the length of her body. There were electrodes and veins made

217

of nanites which formed themselves into mercury-like tubes. There were other devices attached to her as well, most of which I couldn't even identify. They were all over her.

"Can she breathe on her own?" I asked.

"No, those motor centers have suffered damage," Marvin said. He had a lot of cameras watching me now.

I took in the part about damaged motor centers slowly. I'd never heard of a poison so strong it could kill such basic functionality for a prolonged period. But when I thought about it, and I realized something as simple as botulinum, commonly known as *Botox*, could do that.

"Nerve damage? Brain damage? How serious is this? Will there be long term effects?"

"Undoubtedly."

I didn't like where this was going. Usually, any marine that wasn't killed outright could be repaired from drastic battle injuries. The medical people had gotten to her pretty fast, but her condition wasn't as simple as a severed limb or a blast-hole. This was a specially designed poison. I was about to question Marvin further when a call came in from the command center. It was Miklos.

"The missiles are away, Colonel," he said. "They should catch the imperial ship about two hours before they reach the ring to Alpha Centauri."

"Are we at war with Earth again, Colonel Riggs?" Marvin asked me.

I threw him a displeased glance and turned to walk away. Marvin had excellent hearing and vision, but he didn't seem to know when it would be considered impolite to use them. He always eavesdropped whenever he could.

"Good, Miklos," I said. "That should give the General a little going-home present. If they take him out, will he have the opportunity to contact Earth?"

"Unlikely, sir. But Earth will require an accounting in any case."

I considered that point. Technically, the General was under diplomatic immunity.

"We haven't declared war," Miklos pointed out. "And we haven't finished an inquiry that *proves* he is guilty."

"I wouldn't have given the order to fire the missiles if I wasn't very sure Kerr was guilty," I snapped.

"I know that sir. I just wanted to point out that there are larger issues at stake. We are starting a new conflict by doing this, and we might not have all the facts as yet."

"I'm willing to take the diplomatic risk. An independent political group can't stand as a nation for long if it allows its leaders to be assassinated by another power and does nothing about it."

"That is your call, sir."

I disconnected and turned back to Dr. Kate Swanson. She didn't look happy, and I surmised she'd listened in to at least half of my conversation. Fleet doctors were rarely pleased when a conflict started. I had to question their rationality on this point, as there would be no point to having them in Star Force if we never fought anyone. In fact, there would have been no point to Star Force, period.

"How long until I can question the prisoner?" I asked the doctor.

She made a face that indicated she thought I might do something barbaric to the girl during this "questioning".

"She can't even be moved. She's in an induced coma while the nanites do their work."

I opened my mouth to say that I'd ordered her not to use nanites, but I closed it again. If I wanted information, I needed her strong enough to talk. I nodded my head.

"All right," I said. "Use everything you've got to heal her. But stop with the pain-killers. Let her feel what the nanites are doing. I want her awake and talking as soon as possible. I also want both these patients moved to my personal ship."

The doctor shook her head. "That wouldn't be wise," she said. "We have the best staff and facilities right here on Welter Station."

"I know," I said, "that's why you're coming with me."

I didn't bother looking at the questioners as I marched toward the door.

"Doctor Swanson is in charge," I loudly told the rest of the staff. "She'll fill you in on what you need to do. You are all Fleet medical personnel, and key members will be going for a little voyage."

I ignored them all after that announcement and headed for the Command Center. Swanson's sputtering exclamations didn't interest me. Swanson had her job to do, and I had mine. Kwon stumped after me. He had to hustle, because I was moving fast.

Before I hit the doors and left, the word had already spread. Every staffer followed our march with stares that were disapproving and stunned.

"Where we going, sir?" Kwon asked.

"The CC."

"And after that?"

"We're going to fly to the Helios system and have a little talk with General Kerr."

"Uh," Kwon said, frowning, "I thought he was running away."

"He'll turn around," I said. "You can count on it."

-27-

When I reached the Command Center, I headed right for the tactical board. Kwon stood around in the background. Everyone tried to ignore his battle-ready stance.

Miklos was there, and he tapped at something as I arrived. I looked around, and Captain Sarin showed up a minute or so later. She'd probably been getting some well-deserved rest. If I'd been in a better mood, I would have smiled. The Commodore had called in reinforcements.

"You're right in your assessment," I told him.

"Pardon me, Colonel?"

"You've judged that I'm not in a reasonable mood. You're correct in that regard."

Miklos looked at me seriously. He didn't ask what I was talking about, because we both knew the score. "What are your intentions, Colonel?"

"Here are my orders: I'm leaving you in command of the system defense here at the battle station—not that I expect anything serious will happen. I'm taking Sarin and the fastest cruiser we have on hand to fly after Kerr."

"There is no mathematical possibility that you will reach him, sir," Miklos said patiently.

"I was always bad at math," I said, "but I passed the classes anyway."

"And how did you do that, sir?"

"I took shortcuts, did heuristic reasoning to derive answers—and I cheated a little."

"I see."

"Now's the time to cheat. Sarin, since you're here, I need you to connect me to the sentry ships we have at the Helios ring—the one that connects the system to Alpha Centauri."

She tapped at her screens for several seconds. While she followed her orders, Miklos looked increasingly concerned.

"Sir," he said, leaning over the command planning table. "What are your intentions? We only have a few escort-class ships out there. They can't possibly stop General Kerr's battleship."

"I know that."

"Then what are you doing, sir?"

I gave him a dark look, but he didn't wilt. I took a deep breath.

"All right," I said. "I suppose as my exec you deserve to know what I'm planning. I would have brought you into this earlier, but there hasn't been much time to have a staff meeting about it."

Miklos waited patiently.

"Our scouts out there have systems capable of communicating with us instantly via the rings. I'm going to give them a message to relay to the Worms. It is the Worms who will stop General Kerr, along with your missile barrage."

Miklos' face registered alarm. "This is another breach of the peace!" he said. "Sir, I understand you want revenge. I agree with you that General Kerr was probably involved in the assassination attempt. But I feel this is taking our response too far. If the Worms destroy Kerr's ship, it will get back to Earth. They are our allies, but are outside our protective reach at this time. Earth would be well within its rights to reach out and destroy the Worms."

I nodded. "You're quite correct. Under the circumstances you describe, Emperor Crow would be well within his rights to snuff out the Worms. In fact, I believe he's been looking forward to just such an opportunity."

Miklos stared at me with wide eyes. "You see this? You agree? But still, you persist in these orders? Very well. I can tell by the look on your face that you will not listen to reason."

"I'm going to let that slide, Commodore," I said severely. "But you should control yourself in the future. I did not say I was going to have the Worms attack Kerr's ship."

"What are we doing then, sir?"

222

Just then, Sarin signaled me. "The scout ship commander is on the line, sir."

"Hello, Commander Becker?"

"Yes sir," she said.

"I recall your name. Didn't you serve as a scout when the Macros attacked the battle station last year?"

"Yes sir, that was me."

"Still on scout duty, huh? Well, you did well last time, so I'm glad I'm talking to someone with experience. What you're going to do is ask the Worms to fly to the ring and stand guard. A hundred ships ought to do the trick."

"What are their orders going to be, sir?"

"No orders. Just to stand there at the ready. Tell them it's an exercise, or that we wish to test our targeting and navigational systems with our forces in close proximity."

Commander Becker was quiet for a few seconds. "Do you think they'll believe that, sir? I'm sure they can see the Imperial battleship racing away from our missiles across their system."

I smiled tightly. "I think the Worms will understand. They're smarter than people think."

"All right sir, I'll relay the message. Can I get help from Marvin with the translation into pictographs?"

"Of course, I'll transfer you right over," I said, then nodded to Captain Sarin, who passed the connection to Marvin.

Miklos was smiling thinly and had his arms crossed when I looked up at him again. "You had me worried, sir," he said.

"I'm sorry about that."

"No you're not, but it's okay. You think that General Kerr will stop? He might just crash your little simulated barricade."

"He's seen the Worms in action before. We'll give him a few hours, long enough for him to see the ships waiting for him and detect the missiles on his trail. Then we'll transmit an ultimatum to him."

"You'll demand that he turn around and come back?"

"Yes. He'll have to surrender his ship."

"Will he do that, Captain?"

I nodded confidently. "I've known General Kerr a long time," I said. "One thing that stands out from his resume is the ability to know when he's beaten. He'll turn around, don't worry."

I walked off the bridge then and boarded a small transport, which took me out to the cruiser *Lazaro* which I'd commandeered for this special mission. Several hours later, I was joined by Marvin, a stunned-looking Dr. Kate Swanson, and two critical-care units. They were coffin-like affairs full of nanite arms and gurgling liquids. Long glass windows allowed me to see inside. One of them held Sandra, and the other held Alexa Brighton.

We converted the ship's hold into a large medical center for these two patients. Alexa was aware now, and twitching in her coffin. Her eyes were squinched shut. She looked scared and her mouth was twisted in pain. I forced myself to remember what she'd done, and not to feel sorry for her. It was hard on me, as a male, to watch her suffer. My kind naturally wanted to protect her kind. I steeled myself. She'd used these same instincts, and Sandra's, against us.

As it turned out, I never had to make the call to Kerr. He called me just after we'd cast off and begun accelerating across the Eden system. I was down in the hold, helping to adjust the gravitational dampeners to prevent the acceleration Gs from affecting the two injured women when the call came in. As it turned out, it was good timing. Being in the presence of Sandra put me in just the right mood to talk to Kerr.

"Riggs? This is General Robert Kerr of the Imperial—"

"I know who it is, General," I said, interrupting him.

The communications system, using the rings, was amazing. They operated on the basis of entanglement theory, and used a sympathetic resonance between our phonic system and the giant rings in space that interconnected our star systems. The actual device that interacted with the rings was a miniature model of the ring in question, which, when altered physically, caused tiny vibrations in the structure of the titanic rings in space. This effect altered the state of the transmitting device, the ring, and the receiving device simultaneously, no matter where the three objects were. After that, it was a simple thing to detect the vibrations and transmit them to my personal com-link. The system was so fast and efficient we were able to talk as if we were on the phone. It seemed like we were only a few miles apart.

"I bet you know why I'm calling too, Riggs. Is this how you start a peace talk? By firing on the diplomat if they decide to leave before you want them to? I'm not usually in the diplomacy business, but to me, this is a capital 'F' for failure on your part."

"Are you done with the bluster yet?" I asked. "You know why I'm stopping you. Your little care-package went off."

"What the hell are you talking about? Is this another of your fantasies about bombs and women, Riggs? 'Cause if it is, I think you need to see an entirely different kind of doctor."

Growing tired of the General's tirade, real or acted, I made a spinning gesture to Captain Sarin, who had a vid queued. She transmitted it to Kerr's ship now. It detailed the attack by Lieutenant Brighton upon Sandra and myself.

For several long seconds after it had ended, Kerr was quiet.

"I can see how this looks bad," he said at last.

"Yes sir, it does."

"Is Sandra okay?"

"No sir, she's technically dead."

"I'm sorry about that, Kyle, I never suspected Brighton was a fanatic. Some people are just really into Crow. It's odd, I know—probably downright unbelievable to you. But he has a cult of personality going now back on Earth. Young Alexa must have fallen under his—"

"Cut the shit, General, please. We're adults, here. Now, let me tell you how this is going to happen. You're going to pull the emergency brake on that battleship of yours, and you're going to turn it around. When it reaches a full stop, I'll transmit the order to the missiles to self-destruct. I'll also tell the Worm ships to hold their position. They won't fire upon you unless you try to run their blockade."

"This is a huge breach—" Kerr began.

I was happy to hear the nervousness in his voice.

"Not as big a breach as coming to my system and sitting down at my dinner table to place a mole in my headquarters. You used my hospitality to violate the peace, General."

"If you'll allow me to give you a few words of advice," Kerr said, "You'd best be careful, Riggs. We're playing with interstellar relations, and it appears to me that you're doing it on an emotional basis. Everything you've told me is conjecture—"

"I'll tell you what's *not* conjecture," I snapped. "I'm pissed off. If you don't turn around, I'm blowing up your ship. The next move is yours, General. Riggs out."

I closed the connection before he could utter another word. I was tired of his lies and excuses. I didn't even care if there was a grain of truth in any of them. I wanted him to sweat for a change. I wanted him to agonize.

Nothing changed for the next hour. Every ten minutes or so, Jasmine informed me Kerr was requesting to talk again. I ignored every call. I hoped he was raving, walking around his battleship, kicking asses and ripping out hair. The very image brought a glimmer of amusement to my deadened face.

At last, he stopped trying to engage me in pointless talk and took action instead. I'd half-expected him to wheel and fire on my ships. If he turned to fight now, he'd avoid tangling with the Worms. My force outclassed his, but with a well-fought battle he could hope to take a few of my vessels down with him. If he wanted to play it that way, I was ready.

"They're braking, Colonel," Captain Sarin said. "Commander Becker is able to see the exhaust plume visually now. They've stopped their burn and they're braking with what looks like full power. From my calculations, I'd say they started doing it right away, after you got off the phone, as they are over a light hour out from Becker's position."

I nodded, unsurprised. "Have they fired anything? Any missiles on the loose?"

"Nothing like that, sir."

"Too bad," I said to myself.

"There's another message coming in," Jasmine said. "It's General Kerr again. Do you want to talk to him now?"

I shook my head. I stared out a viewport into the blackness of space.

"No," I said. "Let him twist in the wind for a while longer."

-28-

As we flew across the Eden system, I became more and more concerned about the state of Sandra's health. They had her on full life-support. She couldn't breathe by herself, and her heart didn't beat without constant stimulation. After living in a world where tiny nanites and microbial creatures could repair any sort of damage to tissue, I was accustomed to people getting better, and doing it quickly. This was not happening in Sandra's case.

I went down to the medical center frequently to check on both the women. Kwon was no longer following me around, as we were pretty sure by this time the assassin had been working solo.

The assassin herself was doing much better. Alexa had sweated a lot due to the pain of nanites healing her without anesthetic, but she was past that stage now. I hadn't felt sorry for her during the ordeal. It was nothing every Star Force marine hadn't gone through.

I'd noticed that the staffers were avoiding me when I went down to check on Sandra's status. It was about when we reached the ring that transported us to the Helios system that I decided I'd had enough of dodging nurses and evasive answers from Dr. Swanson.

I grabbed the good doctor's arm again, firmly. She was just about to slip by, saying something about being "very busy". I looked at her, and she looked at me.

"Doctor," I said…then I caught the look in her eye. It was undeniable, she was afraid of me.

Among my subordinates, my physical strength had become the stuff of legend. I'd never intended to be a superman; it had just turned out that way. Part of being able to withstand the gravitational

227

field and atmospheric pressures of a gas giant was the necessity of possessing an extreme physique.

I'd often performed tricks on vids for the staff. That sort of thing built morale for fighting men, especially marines. No doubt, Kate Swanson had seen me bend girders and work trees from the ground with my bare hands. She was Fleet, and had been nanotized like everyone aboard any Star Force ship, but she couldn't hope to face me if I lost my temper. I could rip the arms off a normal marine, and she knew it.

Not wanting to be a bully, I let her go. She looked relieved, but no longer attempted to slip by, or to give me weak excuses.

"Kate," I said, forcing my voice to soften, "I need to know what Sandra's real prognosis is. She's not getting any better, I can tell that. What's wrong?"

Dr. Swanson licked her lips, then squared her shoulders. Around me, I noticed the room had quieted. I looked left, then right. The orderlies had vanished. I saw that the place was pretty much empty except for Marvin, who was panning his cameras like mad, and Sandra in her box. I caught sight of Alexa's box, and frowned as it was empty.

Dr. Swanson finally began talking, "As you must know, Colonel," she said, "Sandra's situation is far from ideal, she—"

"Wait a minute," I said, my frown deepening. "Where the hell is that woman, Lieutenant Brighton?"

"She's been transferred to the brig, sir."

"So, she's fine, but her victim is still in a box? Tell me why."

"Sandra's body has fully recovered, sir," she said. "There are a few spots of scarring, but really she would normally be fit to return to duty in another day or so—normally."

"Right, just tell me," I said, trying not to become angry.

In the back of my mind, I figured I was going to hear something about a coma state, something that had triggered in Sandra's mind that they couldn't reverse as yet. I honestly thought Kate would tell me Sandra was going to sleep for a long time, maybe a month or a year, but when she finally did wake up this would all be over. Sometimes, the human mind can ignore the evidence set before it. Possibly, that trait was one of the things that kept us going in times of great strife.

"She's never going to recover, Colonel Riggs," Dr. Swanson said finally.

I looked at her. I saw her turn her face to one side, then the other. She glanced up at me briefly each time, before finding some reason to look away again. She was about my age, but was still an attractive, vivacious woman. I could see that in her youth, she'd been a rare beauty. I saw all that in her face in a single moment. But mostly, what I saw was pity—pity for me. It was not an expression I encountered often.

"I don't—I don't understand," I said. "I mean, I know there was brain damage, but a brain is just a mass of cells like any other organ. It can be repaired, can't it?"

"Yes," she said. "But it's not her brain that's damaged, really. It's her mind. There's nothing there, Colonel Riggs. She's been erased."

"Erased?"

I felt funny then, it was an old sensation—one that I'd almost forgotten. Then, in a flash, I remembered when and where I'd felt it before.

Years ago, my wife had died in a car accident. Sometimes, I still dreamt of her. And my two children had died years later, the night the machines came to Earth. This felt like those times. It was a sinking feeling, as if my guts were falling out of my body onto the floor, as if I weighed a million pounds suddenly, and couldn't move.

Dr. Kate Swanson kept on talking, but I no longer heard her. My mind was racing; I wanted to fix whatever had happened to my girl. I didn't need any more input, I needed to act.

I threw up my hands suddenly, and she flinched away. She'd finally stopped talking, and now watched me with big, round eyes.

I took several deep breaths, staring at the floor. I didn't know what to do. That was a shock all in itself. As a man of action and decision-making, I rarely was met with a moment like this, a moment that required drastic thought and action, when I had absolutely no idea what to do next.

I was a problem-solver. An engineer. Someone who lived by his wits and *made* things work, no matter how difficult or impossible-seeming the task was.

But this time, my mind was blank. Almost as blank as my lady-love, who lay in a glorified coffin full of feeding tubes and gently pumping bladders of oxygen.

"Alexa Brighton," I said aloud. I wasn't sure if I'd whispered it or shouted it, but I knew I'd spoken the name.

I turned and walked out of medical with a determined stride. I knew where I was going and what I was going to do.

Behind me, I heard Kate talking again. "He's going to kill her. Marvin, you have to do something."

"What would you like me to do, Dr. Swanson?"

"Stop him. He's going to kill the prisoner."

"Colonel Riggs is in command," Marvin said. His voice possessed none of her alarm or concern. He sounded calm and curious instead.

"That doesn't give him the right to kill a prisoner!"

"That is debatable," Marvin said. "But in my honest opinion, I don't think any of us are capable of stopping him."

I could no longer hear them behind me, and I no longer cared what they were saying. I headed back to the very farthest aft portion of the ship. There, between the main hold and the engines, was a closet-like chamber that served us as a brig.

It was rarely used, but sometimes one of our marines got too drunk and beat a couple other marines unconscious. Our version of military justice had somewhat less strict rules in these situations. Our people could recover so quickly, it wasn't a court-martialing offense to strike one another. However, there were exceptions that required discipline. If the disagreement was between men of the same rank, that was all well and good. But if it involved a superior officer, or if the aggressor just wouldn't settle down and apologize, we had to lock him up until he came to his senses. Usually, this resulted in a loss of rank for the drunk.

Today, there was a single occupant in the narrow, steel cage. I saw they hadn't even bothered to post a guard. If a nanotized, drunken, raging marine couldn't get out, this young woman was staying put.

I stepped up to the bars. Alexa jumped up and stood at attention. She stared straight ahead at the forward bulkhead, which was only about three feet from her face.

I felt sure she knew why I was there. How could she not? She'd known what the poison would do. She'd known how I would respond to her treachery, if she knew anything about me at all.

I reached out my hands and placed them on the steel bars. I gripped them, and squeezed. A strange sound erupted from the bars in my hands. It was like the sound of heavy old springs being pulled apart.

"Lieutenant Alexa Brighton," I said loudly. "I hereby charge you with treason, murder and assassination. How do you plead?"

"Guilty, sir," she said softly.

This surprised me somewhat, but not enough to take me off the track I was on. I summoned the strength that Marvin's baths and a million tiny alien robots had built into me. I summoned physical power I barely knew I possessed.

The bars were like wire in my hands. I pulled them apart and snapped them in places. The hinges gave me trouble for a moment, but not the lock itself. The bolt had nothing to latch with after I'd pulled the door off and held it over my head. Twisted, groaning and wrecked, I hurled the door up the passageway. It clattered and rang, making a horrible din.

Up that way, I knew, marines were watching. It wasn't that big of a ship, after all. They could hardly have missed this strange business.

I felt their eyes on me from the dark passage, but I didn't turn to look. I sensed that Jasmine was among them. She was the only one who might have been able to stop me, I thought vaguely, but she didn't say a word. None of them did.

That threw me into a greater rage, because I knew what it meant. They all knew Sandra was dead. They all knew that she had no mind left, that somehow this Imperial Assassin had finally struck the blow that so many like her had tried to land before. She'd brought down one of our best, and truly hurt me, personally.

I took a step forward. Alexa stiffened, but she still stood at attention, facing the wall.

"I have witnessed your crime personally," I said. "I have heard your plea. I will now pronounce the sentence: death. Do you understand, Lieutenant?"

"Yes, sir," she said very quietly.

I was impressed with her resolve. There were no tears. There was no begging, or lies. She didn't even tell me what a tin-plated bastard I was. She just stood there at attention, staring at the wall…waiting for death.

231

I took another step closer. I now stood in the cell with her. It was cramped, and stank lightly of urine.

How was I going to do this? I thought about it. I'd never executed anyone before, at least not a human.

I felt a surge of anger. Not about her crimes, but about the conflicting feelings she was causing within me. I stepped closer, and stood between her and the wall. Her eyes finally met mine for a moment.

"Why?" I asked her.

She opened her mouth, then closed it again. "Please sir," she said. "Carry out the execution."

I blinked. "You don't even have the common decency to tell me why you tried to kill me? Did I kill your family in South America, or Florida, or Italy, or—somewhere else?"

"No, Colonel."

"Why, then?" I demanded.

She did not answer.

I narrowed my eyes, suspecting a rat. Was I being recorded? Was this a propaganda vid I was making this moment? A million bizarre scenarios played out in my mind. I didn't want Crow to win this one somehow. I didn't want him to gain anything through my actions.

"I think there will be a stay of execution," I said. "I think we'll question you. We'll get every detail from you."

She shook her head and drew her lips tight. It was a determined, but sad expression. There was a weariness in it that I didn't quite understand.

"No, you won't, sir. I'm sorry to disappoint."

My mind was racing. I decided to try to a lay a trap for her. "All right," I said. "I'll tell you what I'm going to do. I'm going to ship you back to Crow. I'm going to tell him you tried to cause some harm, but you failed. Utterly. I'll tell him Sandra and I are both fine."

Finally, at long last, her demeanor changed. She looked up at me, and stared into my eyes. I saw fear there.

"No, you can't do that. Sandra is dead. I killed her. I almost killed you, whether you know it or not."

I nodded slowly. "Yes, you and I know that. But Earth doesn't. The Ministry of Truth will be fed doctored vids of Sandra and I, alive and well. We can do that, you know. Hell, I'll make a fake Sandra, if

I have to. She'll walk and talk for the cameras. You won't win. Not this one."

"Please don't do that. It serves no purpose."

"I'm not going to serve your purpose, whatever it is, nor am I going to let Earth get whatever it wants out of this."

"It will only hurt me, not Earth," she said. "My father—my entire family."

"Explain."

She finally told me why she'd become an assassin. Her father was indeed a marshal in the forces of Earth. But he'd gone against Crow and tried to remove him from power. The entire family had been arrested, and imprisoned in the ruins of Sao Palo.

I frowned. "South America?" I said. "There's nothing there. I've seen it. I was there when the city died."

"There are spots of life on the continent, but Sao Palo isn't one of them. In the middle of a blast zone, hot with rads, it's a massive prison now. The Committee for Public Safety sentences people like my father to be imprisoned there. It's where the unwanted go to be forgotten forever."

I suddenly began to understand Lieutenant Brighton. If what she said was true, she was here to keep the rest of her family alive.

"So, that whole thing with General Kerr was an act, a stunt designed to gain our confidence?"

"Yes, sir. That's all I can tell you. What else do you need to know, really? The Emperor wants you dead. Everyone on Earth must obey the Emperor, or everyone they love will be horribly mistreated."

I felt sick at the idea that Earth had fallen under the spell of such a monster. I knew Crow—or I thought I did. Was it possible that great power warped weak men? I'd always heard that, but I'd never witnessed it firsthand.

"If you think this confession will gain you forgiveness for your crimes, you are sadly mistaken."

There was a tiny popping sound in Lieutenant Brighton's mouth. I stepped back away from her. She kept her mouth shut, but she looked at me, she turned her head and exhaled, away from me. A strange gas rolled out of her mouth. It was bluish-white, like cigarette smoke. I took another step back, staring at her.

"I'm dead now," she said, "and I could have killed you. But I didn't. Remember that, and have mercy, Colonel. I—"

She slumped onto the floor. I walked out of the chamber, and called for a bucket of constructive nanites. No one moved for a second, and I repeated the order much more loudly. Then, Captain Sarin ran up to me. She handed me the container, and stared into the cell.

Lieutenant Brighton lay on the steel floor, twitching. Liquids bubbled from her mouth. I'd seen the effects before. She'd erased her own mind.

I threw the bucket over the entrance, sealing it. The nanites knew what to do. They covered the open space, forming an airtight door.

"Captain Sarin," I said, "jettison the brig into space, with all its contents."

"You really did it, Kyle. I didn't think you would."

I looked at her, not quite knowing what she was talking about for a second.

"But I understand," she said, staring up at me. I could see sympathy in her dark, pretty eyes. "Your grief overcame you. It could happen to anyone."

I got what she was saying now. She thought I'd struck Alexa dead. Another woman would have called me a murderer, and possibly never seen me the same way again. But not Jasmine. She was already making excuses for me.

"That's not exactly how it happened," I said. "Follow me to the bridge, I'll fill you in."

-29-

Some people have called me a hothead. Other people say the opposite is true, that I'm as cold and unfeeling as a glacier. There is truth in both these accusations. I have a temper. I act rashly at times, especially when under great stress. But I also get over things faster than most people. I can take stress in stride, and keep functioning. For me, life always went on.

I think it is this quality, above all others, that has contributed to my success as a commander. The Imperial British believed that one of the greatest attributes an officer could have was the capacity to remain calm under fire. To take death, blood, danger and pain all in stride. To think clearly, and act the gentleman, even when others might run, fall to their knees, or cry their eyes out.

I truly believe, at this point in my career, that a natural capacity to take emotional punishment has placed me where I am today. I'm not sure if I'm happy about it, but that's how it is. That was the kind of man I am.

I'd presided over a thousand tragedies, and millions—no, *billions* of deaths. What kind of man, I asked myself, would not be broken by these events? Could anyone hold up under the weight of it forever?

So far, I'd never cracked under the strain. I'd made countless mistakes, but I'd never been broken. I'd done the incredible often, and the impossible occasionally, but frequently failed when it came to the mundane.

With all that said, the death of Sandra's mind struck me hard. I think it might have been easier if she'd died in battle against the Macros. This lingering nonsense, with her body kept alive in a truly

235

vegetative state…it was painful for me. How could you say goodbye and move on when she was still lying there, breathing through a tube of gleaming nanites?

When under serious stress, I had a sure-fire short-term cure: beer. I know it might sound childish, but I'd never been in a truly bad state of mind that could not be improved by six or twelve brews.

That was where I found myself after Lieutenant Brighton's suicide. I sat in my office, downing beers. I'd laid down a stash from Eden-8, the only planet cool enough to grow good barley and hops. The farmers among us had found an excellent business almost immediately growing and selling crops we'd transplanted from Earth. Right now, I was very glad someone had had the wisdom and foresight to bring along the essentials for brewing one of man's greatest creations.

There was a tapping at my office door. I took no notice of it. Instead, I popped open another brew. It was number nine, I think—or maybe eleven. For some reason, those numbers sounded extremely similar to me at the moment.

I didn't worry about who was at the door. There had been a number of lost souls tapping out there since I'd placed myself inside, and as the ship was still in one piece, I'd decided they could all just wait until I felt like opening the hatch. Right now, I didn't feel like doing that at all.

Tapping, again. Soft tapping. I could tell, even with my hazy, alcohol-soaked mind, that the tapping was feminine. There was something about it... Kwon would have hammered, that was just a reality when you had fists like ham hocks. Marvin's knocking always sounded like someone was working a ballpeen hammer on a piece of sheet metal. Metal on metal had a distinctive clink to it that couldn't be imitated.

But this sounded like a small hand tapping on a hard door. It was a woman, I was sure of it.

For some reason—possibly it was the beer, I'll admit—coming to this conclusion made me grow curious. I wanted to know *who* was there, and if I was right about the persistent knocker being a female. I stood up, walked to the door and caused it to dilate open.

It was Jasmine. I didn't smile at her, however. I just stared, wondering what she wanted, what was so damned important she had to invade my worst hour.

"Excuse me, Colonel," she said. "I'm so sorry…I know you're not in a good state of mind, but General Kerr's ship is nearly at the rendezvous point."

"So what?"

"Don't you think you ought to sober up before you meet the General and accept his surrender? This is a matter of state. The stakes are high. You have to pull yourself together, Kyle."

I stood straight, and tried not to sway on my feet. I stared at her flatly.

"You knew, didn't you?" I asked. "Just like all the rest of them."

Jasmine looked worried and slightly hurt. "I knew she wasn't responding to treatment, but that's all."

"Nope," I said, sucking in air through my nostrils. "I don't buy it." I stepped out into the passageway and looked right and left, expecting to see others out there, lurking. But the passage was empty.

As there wasn't anyone else handy, I turned my anger toward Jasmine. "You knew Sandra was a turnip, and you didn't have the guts to tell me. No one did."

I noticed I had a fresh beer in my hand. I wasn't quite sure how it had gotten there, but I was glad to see it. Very glad. I took a big hit on it and walked back into my office.

"Kyle," she said urgently. "You only have a few hours before you have to meet with Kerr and talk to him."

"Maybe you should do it," I said. "I'm busy."

She followed me into the office and sat across my desk from me. Behind her, the nanites hastily rebuilt the metal skin that served as my office door.

"Let's talk about Sandra, if you want to," she said. "I was worried about you and her and all of us. But I actually didn't know it was hopeless. I thought she might recover. I've been as busy with matters of command as you have been."

I handed her a beer. She looked at in surprise. A cool vapor of frost wound up from the squeeze-bottle.

"How'd you get it so cold?" she asked.

I smiled. I showed her a compartment in the floor. "There's a tube from this box that leads right out to space. A few seconds in there, and it's just right. Marvin taught me the trick."

She shook her head and put the beer down on the desk. "I'm very sorry for your loss, Kyle," she said. "I haven't had a chance to tell you that."

"No one has. I've been holed up in this office since I figured it out."

We were both quiet for a moment, and my mind wandered. I thought of Lieutenant Alexa Brighton.

"I have to admit," I said, "she was dedicated to her cause."

"Who?"

"Alexa. She stood there, you know, ramrod straight and eyes ahead. Just standing at attention up until the very moment she dropped dead."

"Awful and strange," Jasmine said.

I shrugged. "I don't know. How do you want to go out? That was her way. Not on her knees, begging and sniveling. She maintained her dignity until the moment her mind was gone."

Jasmine fidgeted, looking uncomfortable.

"What is it now?" I asked her. With an effort of will, I set aside my beer. I decided it would be my last. It was a painful decision, but one that every drunk has to make at some point, unless they utterly fail nature's test and pass out.

"We did what you said. We sealed her in that cell. Then we jettisoned the entire chamber."

"Yeah, so?"

"Well, we could have possibly revived her, put her on life support."

I laughed. It was probably one of the least appropriate moments of my life for a laugh, but I was in an odd state of mind.

"What?" I asked. "Did you want two turnips in medical? She wanted to die, and I'd just pronounced a death sentence for her. In my opinion, an officer deserves to choose to take their own life in such a situation. I can only hope that in the future, someone will give me the same privilege."

Jasmine shifted in her chair as if uncomfortable.

"I hadn't thought about it that way," she said.

"There's another reason I wanted that cell sealed permanently. She released the toxin in a new way, via gas from her mouth. Probably, she cracked a false tooth and exhaled it. That worried me. I knew that the poison had been delivered as a liquid injection before.

238

We have no idea how long it might linger in the cell, erasing the mind of anyone who came near."

"Yes," she said, nodding. "I think you did the right thing then. You couldn't take the chance."

I almost yelled at her that this wasn't about *chances*. That girl had deserved to die right then and there, and the best way for her to go out was the way she'd taken down Sandra. It was a fitting end to an assassin. I was happy, actually, that she'd been erased the way Sandra had been.

But I didn't say it. I had that much self-control left. I realized I was already sobering up, unfortunately. It was the nanites and the microbes. They were metabolizing the alcohol in my blood nearly as fast as I could drink more. They knew a toxin when they saw one, and they worked pitilessly to eradicate such substances from my body.

In my mind, though, I kept seeing Alexa standing there, begging me to tell the Imperials that she'd been a success. That, more than anything, made me believe her story about being coerced into the attack. In my experience, people were pretty truthful in their dying moments.

"What are you going to do about Kerr?" Jasmine asked me.

I looked at her sharply, then nodded. "That's why you're really here. You're worried I'll do something crazy, right? Well, don't be."

I stood up, and she stood up with me. I took two steps toward the door.

"How long do I have?" I asked.

"About twenty minutes. I can delay them, if you want."

"No...no. I'll meet him at the airlock. He must come alone to this office. You already self-destructed the missiles that were headed to destroy his ship, didn't you?"

"I turned off their engines and blanked their targets. We'll retrieve them later."

That made me smile. "Always the efficient, frugal one, aren't you?"

I didn't mean it in a negative way, but her face fell. She didn't say anything.

I frowned, and then shrugged. As usual, I had no idea what was wrong with what I'd said. I didn't get most women. Hell, I hadn't even known what Sandra was thinking half the time.

I stood near the door, straightening my kit. Jasmine stepped forward to help. Her small hands felt like the fluttering touch of a bird to me. She arranged my epaulets and smoothed my smart cloth uniform where it had bunched up. Then she reached up and combed my hair with her fingers.

"Have you got a mint?" I asked.

She handed me three without saying a thing. I crunched them and enjoyed the biting flavor.

She did something then that took me totally by surprise. She gave me a tiny kiss on the cheek.

I shied away immediately. I glared at her. I knew my eyes were red and bloodshot. I still felt the burn of alcohol in my blood. A gush of words came out of me, and I regretted them all almost as fast as I said them.

"You'd jump in Sandra's grave so fast? She's still alive you know, technically. She's not even cold yet."

Jasmine looked as if I'd slapped her. She cast her eyes down, and reached out to touch the door. I could tell she was about to run off.

"I—I'm sorry," I said. "I'm not feeling well."

"No, I'm sorry," she said quietly, looking at the floor. "I shouldn't have done that. It was wrong."

Jasmine left then, and I stared after her. There were more than a few crewmen in the hallway. They took in the scene and tried not to gape.

She moved quickly, not quite trotting, but almost.

Good God, I thought. *I hope she's not crying.* Then I saw her hand go up to wipe at her face. Yep, she was crying. I let out a long sigh.

I retreated back into my office. The door melted shut. Already, I could hear and feel the ship making adjustments to it attitude with shivering jets. We were decelerating, coming in to dock. General Kerr was probably already boarding a tiny pinnace to fly over to my ship from his.

I moved to the tiny mirror in my tiny lavatory. I splashed some water and tried to sober up faster. I looked at myself, and frowned. Those red eyes were going to give me away.

"You could have handled that one better, Riggs," I said to my reflection.

So far, it was looking like a stellar day. I'd lost one girl, sentenced another to death, and sent a third running down the hall, crying.

-30-

We met Kerr and his four guards at the docking bay. The door melted away, and there was a hissing sound as the two pressurized chambers evened out.

General Kerr looked extremely unhappy. He wore what I thought might be the glummest expression I'd ever seen on his face. He knew the score. He'd helped deliver an assassin into my inner circle. I wasn't going to be wining and dining him this time around.

What he didn't yet know was what had happened to the assassin. We'd told the Imperials nothing about Alexa. It was obvious I'd survived, but how had she fared? I wondered if he would have the balls to ask the question. It must be burning on his mind.

"Just you, General," I said. "Leave your guards in the boat."

Kerr hesitated. The hard-eyed Imperial crewmen at his side looked resolute, but fearful. Looking at them, I figured they were probably nanotized. After all, Crow had Nano factories back on Earth. He was probably busy churning out troops faster than I could hope to do out on the frontier.

The Imperials wore fancy uniforms, dark blue, with gold braid at their wrists, shoulders and caps. They were all noncoms. As space veterans, I respected them. They'd probably seen their share of combat against the machines when they'd fought the Macros we'd let slip by Eden on their way to Earth.

I wasn't contemptuous of the men, I was confident in Star Force superiority. My men were marines, after all. Out here, that meant more than it ever had.

242

But right now, I didn't care about any of that. I made a shooing gesture toward the men surrounding Kerr.

He opened his mouth, closed it again, then nodded. "Go on back to the *Carrington*, Chief," he said. "I'll be fine. Riggs and I go way back."

"Indeed we do," I said.

The crewmen retreated reluctantly. My own guards relaxed somewhat behind me.

Kerr stepped forward with the air of a man walking into a viper's den.

"Do you intend to kill me, Riggs?" he asked. "I think I ought to know. I think you owe me that."

I shook my head. I wore a grim smile. "You don't want to know what I owe you, General. Right this way, sir."

I ushered him down toward the aft of the ship. He looked concerned. "This isn't the way to the bridge. Not unless you changed your designs all around recently. Wait, you're heading for the brig, aren't you? One old man has you worried? Gonna put me in chains, are you boys?"

None of us answered him. I stopped at the door that led to medical. The nanite door melted and Marvin loomed close.

"What in the nine hells—is that your crazy robot? What did you do, give him steroids?"

"I wanted to show you something, General," I said.

I led the way to the coffin that held Sandra. Kerr eyed the coffin in alarm. I saw understanding dawn at last on his face.

"Your assassin wasn't entirely unsuccessful," I said. "As you see here, your dinner hostess has been terminated. Her body still functions due to external impulses. We breathe for her, we pump her blood, we feed her glucose through needles. But she's quite dead. Her mind, as you know, has been erased."

"What the hell?" he said. "Erased? Is that what the plan was? I can see how that might work against your kind." He turned to me. "I knew something was going to happen. But I thought it might just be a spying mission."

I slammed my fist into his skull then. I didn't think it over, I just moved. It happened so quickly, I don't think I even knew what I was doing before I'd lifted my hand.

Kerr recoiled and flew several feet into the waiting arms of a startled marine who'd been marching behind him.

I felt an instant surge of regret. I figured I'd probably killed him. A blow like that—an older, normal earthman could never take it. His skull would be fractured at the very least. Internal bleeding, possibly a stroke.

It was the beer, I thought bitterly. I still had half of it in my blood, and even though the nanites were working their microscopically small tails off, I knew it was affecting my judgment.

I took two steps and stood over Kerr, who was still in the arms of the marine who'd caught him.

"General?" I asked aloud.

His right eye snapped open. It was wide, and there was blood in it. His left eye had already swollen shut.

"Heh," he said, struggling to his feet. He shoved away the man who'd caught him. "So that's how you treat prisoners of war in Star Force, is it? I'd thought all those vids by the Ministry of Truth were doctored up until this very moment. If I hadn't experienced it, I wouldn't have believed it."

I stared at him in amazement, then nodded. "You *are* full of nanites, aren't you sir?" I asked. "You should be down and out, permanently."

"But you didn't know that I'd been nanotized," Kerr said. He looked at me with his one good eye. "So, you meant to kill me?"

I shook my head. "No. That was just an emotional reaction. I've grown tired of Imperial lies. They've cost me quite a bit lately. I lost my temper, that's all."

"You shouldn't have been able to one-shot me like that," he said. "You've got more than nanites in you."

"That's classified."

Kerr nodded. His one operating eye drifted back to Sandra again, lying inert in her case.

"I didn't want it to go down this way, Riggs," he said. "I'm tired of all the bullshit, too. Whatever happens, I want you to know that. Sometimes, we do things because we've made a choice between two evils. Not because we wanted either of them. Do you understand me?"

"Yes, General, I believe I do."

"Your girlfriend wasn't supposed to be injured. I imagine she got in the way."

"She did. She wouldn't let Alexa get close to me."

"All right," he said. "I've come here, been clobbered, and I've apologized. I hereby respectfully request that I be allowed to return to my ship and leave your territory."

I laid a heavy hand on his shoulder. I closed my hand with crushing force, grabbing up a handful of his smart cloth uniform. It was a testament to the strength of the material that it didn't rip, not even as I lifted him up and marched with him held at arm's length.

His fingers clawed at my hand with surprising strength. His musculature was nothing compared to my own, however. The collar of his shirt cut into his neck, making him wheeze. I walked with him suspended above the deck, kicking and coughing.

I saw his one working eye roll around in fear in its socket. Mercury-like metallic liquids were already shining in his wounds.

"What are you doing, Riggs?"

"I'm granting your request, General," I said.

I marched him across the central passageway to a circular door, which I tapped open. General Kerr had a weapon out, I noticed. It looked like a pen, but I saw the dark glass projector at the end, which he was trying to point in my direction. With my free hand, I slapped it away. His wrist snapped at my touch. He didn't scream, but he did hiss, sucking in his breath between clenched, bloody teeth.

"That's the second time you've broken that arm," he complained.

I stepped into the sally port chamber. I waved for my marines to stay out in the passageway. Reluctantly, they obeyed. The door closed behind us and Kerr and I were all alone in the steel chamber. I hit a big button on the wall, and Kerr's bulging eye followed me. The indicator light on the wall went from green to yellow, and the air began being pumped out of the chamber.

"Out of this very room," I told him, "platoons of brave Star Force marines have made death-defying leaps into the void. In a way, it's an insult to those brave men that I'm allowing you to use the same portal. I should be tossing you out of the garbage chute."

The light shifted from yellow to orange and a warning buzzer sounded. The air was decidedly thin now.

"You can't do this, Riggs," Kerr rasped. "You'll be at war with Earth. There are only a few thousand of you out here. You're mad."

The light changed from orange to red, and I snapped my visor shut. Kerr wasn't wearing one. Then I reached out toward the portal release.

Kerr lurched in my grasp. Despite his injuries, he managed to wrap his legs and his one good hand around my arm. But it didn't do him any good. He strained and heaved, but I pushed the button anyway.

The gases still left in the room exited with a forceful gust. I shook the General loose from my arm and let him float outside. There, in the cold void of space, his eye stared back at me.

"You see that?" I shouted, pointing into the darkness. "That silver line out there? That's your ship. All you have to do is swim over to it. I'm doing as you asked, General. I'm sending you back to *Carrington*."

Kerr ignored my speech. I wasn't even sure he could hear it, as the air was gone.

He knew what to do, of course. He was a space veteran. It was pointless, but he exhaled, letting all his breath out. He had to depressurize his lungs as quickly as possible, or they would rupture. He could last a few seconds longer in total vacuum that way.

Unlike common misconceptions, humans do not instantly freeze in space. They *do* depressurize. The body is too hot, and too tightly compressed for space. Our blood begins to boil and the lack of oxygen quickly does its inevitable work.

But nanotized marines are a thing apart from normal humans. They're self-repairing and the little microscopic bastards just don't know when they're beaten. Kerr hung out there, in agony.

He's twisting all right, I thought to myself, *but there's no wind.*

A lot of things went through my mind as I watched Kerr die outside my ship in the heartless nothingness that is space. I thought of the moments we'd shared, both good and bad. We'd always found a way to live together, he and I. Others had died all around us, but we'd never struck the final blow against one another.

Maybe that was because we were alike in some ways. Determined men with iron resolve. Men unafraid to order others to die, or to die ourselves. It had always been difficult not to admire Kerr. I had to admit, in my heart of hearts, I blamed Crow for his recent turn to dark deeds.

Something about the way he was going out impinged on me. I'd just witnessed Lieutenant Alexa Brighton, standing at attention, accepting her death as calmly as she humanly could. Here was Kerr, fighting it hopelessly to the final second.

Alexa had died for her family. I believed that part of her story now. She was an honest young woman, and as Kerr himself had said, she'd chosen one devil over another, not because she loved either, but because she had no choice.

Crow would no doubt punish more innocents back on Earth, due to my actions today. Someone had to fall. Someone had to be proven disloyal. Wasn't that the way of every dictator, or at least, most of them? They ruled via terror, the terror of their subjects and of the dictator himself. Both were afraid of the other, and that fear kept everyone in line, forcing them to do horrible things.

And here I was, reacting. Killing Kerr for revenge, despite the fact he hadn't given the order in the first place.

I cursed under my breath, and said: "tether!"

A nanite line extended from my suit to the wall of the ship. I threw myself out into space, after Kerr. I reached out a hand, and grabbed him.

I tugged on the liquid steel tether and it drew me quickly back into the ship. I hit the button on the wall, and the lights went from red, to orange, to yellow, and in about thirty seconds, turned green.

I opened my visor and stared down at Kerr. There was frost on the walls, forming ice crystals in the cold chamber.

Kerr had stopped moving. In fact, he looked extremely dead. As I watched, frost formed on his eyelashes. His face was so cold, it was causing water vapor to condense and freeze upon it.

But nanites are cruel, heartless things. They don't quit. Dead bodies, charred and swollen, might look beatific the following day, after the tiny robots inside work their magic pointlessly on a corpse overnight.

I waited a minute, and I thought I saw something. A slight rise and fall. A redness replacing the bruised purple around the nostrils.

"Are you still in there, General?" I asked the corpse.

The right eye popped open. Although the eye rolled around, I knew it was too frozen to see. His breath wheezed and rattled in his throat. It sounded like the last gasp of a man on his deathbed, but he was breathing.

The blind eye kept moving, as if looking for me.

"I'm right here, Robert," I said. "It didn't look like you were going to survive your little journey to Carrington, so I had to reel you back in."

Finally, the one good hand the General had left rose up slowly. It curled, gesturing for me to come closer.

I bent my ear to his blue lips and listened.

"Fuck you," he wheezed.

-31-

I felt better after killing Kerr. Oh sure, I'd revived him, and I was now allowing him to recover in the very same coffin where Alexa had spent her final days.

But I *had* killed him. I took some perverse pleasure in that. He'd gone through the pain, the anguish and the fear. He'd experienced the hopelessness, the final black moments of succumbing. He'd died out in space, with the full and certain knowledge that he was well and truly screwed.

I'm not going to say that was good enough for me, because it wasn't. I'd kill a thousand General Kerrs to save my Sandra. But of course, she couldn't be saved.

The ordeal I'd put Kerr through didn't atone for his part in this evil scheme. I never would have reeled him back in, except for one thing: I didn't want to make Alexa's family suffer for nothing.

That woman had struck a hard blow against me and mine, but she'd done it to save her own people. I could understand that. If it had been my own family on the line, I probably would have done the same to her.

My family was all dead now, but her people back on Earth were presumably alive and possibly suffering under Crow's harsh rule. That's the part that had changed my mind, and had saved Kerr's life in the end.

"Sir?" Captain Sarin said, approaching me cautiously.

Everyone was treating me like I was a feral dog on the street these days, even Jasmine. No one liked to make a sudden move in my presence. Probably, that was wise on their parts.

"What is it, Captain?"

"It's the *Carrington* again, sir. The Captain is demanding that General Kerr be released."

"If I did hand him over, he'd probably die. They don't have medical equipment as good as ours."

Our medical systems included microbial baths, not just robotic arms, brainboxes and intravenous nanites. I knew Earth didn't possess our capacities to dispense life at will.

Jasmine paused after my last statement. She was probably hoping I was going to go on and say more. She was disappointed.

"Should I relay that to *Carrington*, sir?"

"No," I said.

Jasmine gnawed her lower lip. "They might fire on us, Kyle, if we don't even tell them what happened to the General."

I shrugged. "Let them attack, then. I'd like to take out one more Earth battleship."

"Sir, I don't understand your—"

I heaved a sigh and straightened. "I'm sorry, Jasmine," I said. "I'm being self-indulgent. I'll now give you orders that make sense: tell *Carrington* that we've got their General, and he's alive. But, he's had an unfortunate accident. We'll return him shortly."

After this, I honestly expected her to turn around and go. But she lingered in the passageway outside my quarters instead.

"Yes?" I asked. "What is it?"

"Why didn't you kill him?" she asked, her voice just above a whisper. "I know you wanted to. I know you almost did it."

I nodded, and looked at her. My quarters were dark except for a few LED lights that ran along the floor for emergency lighting. I liked it that way right now—dark. You couldn't pull the LEDs up without using a screwdriver, so I hadn't bothered.

Her face and body were silhouetted against the relative glare of the passage behind her. Eyeing her, I thought her hair was perhaps a trifle longer than it should be—certainly, it was past regulation length. But I didn't complain about it. She'd gotten away with that for months, and we both knew it was because I liked her to wear it long.

"Because if I kill him, Crow will abuse Alexa's relatives back home."

250

"The poisoner? Why would you care about her? And why should we worry about what the Imperials do to each other?"

I shifted uncomfortably in my chair. It felt constrictive to me, so I stood up and began pacing.

"They're our people, Jasmine," I reminded her. "Star Force is sworn to defend them against all enemies, foreign and domestic. But it's more than that. I feel partly responsible."

"What?" she said, raising her voice. "That's nonsense, Colonel. Everyone knows Crow is to blame."

"Exactly," I said. "And who do you think had the opportunity to take him out of the equation long ago? The kind of sin I've performed is one of omission—of inaction. I let Crow live and thrive like a spider in the dark, and now countless invisible people are suffering because of my oversight."

"Now you're blaming yourself for what Crow does? That's silly."

I took a few steps toward her. She backed away at my approach, out the doorway and into the hall. I wasn't surprised that she was physically afraid of me, but I was saddened. I guess that after you kill a few people with your bare hands, the rest get nervous.

"Burke once said: 'All that is necessary for the triumph of evil is that good men do nothing.'"

"But you didn't know he was evil, Kyle," she said. "Not back then."

"I didn't know exactly what Crow was going to do," I said, "but I always had a pretty good idea. I let it slide. That's why I'm taking part of the blame for this situation. The rest I lay at the feet of humanity. They could have stopped him; the men who follow him now could shoot him rather than serving under him. They must know what he is. In any case, I want you to relay my message to Carrington."

"Yes sir," she said, and left.

The door solidified behind her. A few minutes later, a light tapping began again. It was a feminine knock, and it sounded almost timid. With a grunt of frustration, I opened it.

"What is it now, Jasmine?" I demanded.

But when the door melted away, it wasn't Jasmine that stood in the hallway. It was Dr. Kate Swanson. She looked wary, just the way they all did lately.

251

I rumbled in my throat inarticulately. "What do you want?" I asked finally.

Then I caught sight of something. It was a camera on a stalk, peeping over her shoulder. I leaned forward and followed it back. About ten feet away, Marvin filled the passage with his bulk.

I nodded in sudden understanding. "You figured I would open the door for a female—is that it, Marvin? Profiling me again?"

"There's something we'd like to discuss, Colonel," Marvin said.

I glanced at Dr. Swanson. She looked pale and her eyes were big. She hadn't said a word yet.

"I take it the topic of discussion isn't going to make me happy," I said.

"On the contrary, Colonel Riggs," Marvin said with a touch of excitement in his voice. "It may well be the best news you've heard all day."

Marvin had me now, and we both knew it.

"Out with it, robot," I said.

"I've begun a series of experiments in necrological reconstruction. It's possible these efforts will bear untold benefits in the future."

I squinted at him. "Necro-what?"

"Necrological. It's a new term. Do you like it? I've just coined it, actually. As the inventor of this new science, I felt I'd earned the privilege."

Dr. Swanson cleared her throat at this point. I eyed her and thought she looked worried.

"Marvin," she said, "it's not actually a *science*. It's a *theory*. A research proposal, to be exact."

"This is about Sandra, isn't it?" I asked. I tried to keep my voice steady. "I don't want you cutting her up, or anything like that."

"No, no, certainly not," Marvin said.

I stared at Marvin's cameras and they stared back at me. They shifted and whirred. Neither of us said anything for a few seconds. We both knew he'd laid out the bait, and I was on the hook.

By this time, I'd pretty much figured out what was going on. Marvin had gotten a crazy idea about healing Sandra, and it was so awful that Dr. Swanson wasn't sure she wanted to be a part of it.

I knew right away I should just steer clear of the whole thing, that I should tell him "no" and march down to medical and pull the plug on Sandra's coffin myself. *Let her rest in peace*, some part of my mind told the rest.

But there was another voice there, too. A voice that whispered of hope and the powers of science. I recalled that voice from my distant past. Miracles of healing *had* happened. I'd witnessed them with my own eyes.

"Once bitten by hope, a man is forever its plaything," I said.

"Is that an idiom, Colonel?" asked Marvin. "I'm not familiar with it."

"Can't you just leave well enough alone?"

"Sandra's condition is hardly 'well enough'. I believe I can improve upon it dramatically. Do you want me to try, Colonel Riggs? Do I have your permission?"

By this time I was leaning against the wall. I felt the faint vibration of nanites against my skin. No wall in a Nano-ship is ever completely still.

"You know you do," I said, beaten.

Marvin didn't say another word. He knew enough not to blow it. He slithered away on a dozen rasping metal tentacles. There was excitement in his movement, and he held his cameras higher than before.

I turned to Dr. Swanson. She looked a little green, and a little frightened. Did everyone think I was a wild-eyed murderer today?

"Kate," I said. I shook my head, looking after Marvin. "Is this going to end badly?"

She was quiet for a second, then she sighed and shook her head.

"I honestly don't know, sir," she said. "But that's not the only reason I'm here. What are we supposed to do with General Kerr?"

"Can he survive outside his box yet?"

"Yes sir, but he looks like hell."

"Good," I said. "Release him. Put him back on his pinnace, and have him transported back to *Carrington*. I don't want him completely healed up before they get a good look at him."

"Don't worry, Colonel. It will take more than a few days for his nanites to clean up the damage you inflicted upon that man's body."

With that, she turned and walked away. I watched her disappear.

Had I just been scolded? I was pretty sure that I had been.

-32-

I was dubious in the extreme, but I couldn't deny that Marvin's injection of hope had brought me back to life. Even if he failed to do the same for Sandra herself, I reflected, he had done his work on me.

I knew it could be a sugar-high. A temporary state of mind that may come crashing down, forever weighing upon my spirit. That's how it had been with my kids.

But I also knew I was a tough-minded person. I didn't feel emotional damage the way others seemed to. When I suffered a loss, I was shaken, but I never went to pieces completely. At least, I hadn't been broken yet.

When I was sure General Kerr had made the transfer over to Carrington and the battleship had wheeled and blasted away without bothering with a farewell, I headed up to the bridge. I'd pretty well sobered up by now, and wanted to get back into the game.

I told myself along the way that Sandra's state was due to my choices as much as Crow's or Kerr's. I'd tempted fate on a regular basis. I'd taken my love into combat, for God's sake! How could one expect to live forever in a heartless universe like the one we inhabited when you continuously took grim chances? We'd rolled the dice enough times and we'd finally lost the game. It could have happened to anyone, but it had finally happened to my Sandra.

I arrived on the bridge and greeted no one. The conversation among the staffers, whatever it had been, immediately died. I sat in my command chair, brooding.

I glanced around, and noticed that everyone was evading my eye. Then I figured it out: The topic of conversation had been *me* or, possibly, Sandra and Marvin's crazy plans.

I didn't know what Marvin was doing down there in medical. I didn't *want* to know. I'd come back to the bridge because I knew I needed something to keep my mind off the topic. I was here to keep myself from going mad.

"Give me a sitrep, people," I barked suddenly.

A timid ensign brought me a tablet brimming with charts, written logs and numbers. I flicked my way through it until I found a few items of interest. I frowned as I read data coming in from Eden-12. Something was happening back home.

I snapped my fingers until the ensign came back. She was young, and had a scared look about her. I figured they'd sent her because she was junior among the group. The staffers were brave enough in battle, but a bunch of cowards when it came to talking to the titular leader of Riggs' Pigs.

I read her nametag. "Ensign Kestrel?" I asked. "What's this?" I pointed to a spike on the charts which indicated increased activity at both the Eden and Thor system rings.

"Emissions readings, sir," she said.

A single lock of her brown hair slipped down into her face, covering one eye. She didn't seem to notice, but I found it distracting.

"Is your hair regulation length, Ensign?"

She opened her mouth and closed it again. "I don't know sir," she said. "I'll check. I'm sorry."

I took in a deep breath and tried to relax. "Never mind," I said. "It looks okay, and lots of Fleet people cheat on the regs, anyway. Forget about it."

"Thank you sir."

I went back to poring over the charts. I touched the emissions spike, and a box came up on the screen, giving me more data.

"These numbers are out of bounds," I said. "I should have been alerted about this activity at the rings, not to mention these planetary anomalies on Eden-12."

"I'm sorry sir. I think we *did* try to contact you." She looked over her shoulder helplessly at the others. They were studiously involved with their screens.

"Ensign," I said, regaining her attention. "It's all right. I've been out of sorts lately. I guess it isn't staff's fault."

She looked so relieved she seemed to melt. "Thank you, sir."

I nodded, pondering the numbers. "These readings on Eden-12…they're spiking again. I want to know what they are. I want a scout ship sent to the gas giant. We've got to ask the Blues what they're doing down there."

"How do we do that, sir?"

I nodded thoughtfully. "How indeed?"

We hadn't had the best relationship with the Blues since the very beginning. They were an enigmatic cloud-race that seemed to be made up of structured aerogels. They lived in the soupy atmosphere of the Eden system's only gas giant, swimming in the thick air like it was an ocean thousands of miles deep.

The Blues had originally built the Macros and the Nanos, the machines that plagued us today. They'd let them loose upon the universe. They'd let them do their exploring and conquering by remote control.

As a victim species of the machines, humanity had taken offense to these actions. We'd attempted diplomacy, but rarely been successful. We'd only managed to force them to cooperate in a single instance, and that had only been after bombing their homeworld indiscriminately.

Now, there was something strange going on down there on their massive world. They were quietly doing something, without telling us what it was.

I looked up again, and saw that the Ensign was still lingering, uncertain what her orders were.

"We're going to go to Eden-12 ourselves," I told her. "We're going to scan the planet as best we can, and we're going to ask the Blues what the hell they think they're doing. Now, go relay that order to the navigators. Tell them to lay in a course and fire up the engines."

Ensign Kestrel nodded, taking the tablet from my hands as I offered it. I gave her a flickering half-smile. I didn't really feel like smiling, but I forced myself.

My fractionally softer expression worked on her like magic. She relaxed and smiled back. I watched as she returned to the others and reported to them how her little mission had gone. They seemed relieved. They talked in low voices and studiously avoided looking in my direction.

The next two days were tense. There were precious few reports, either from medical, or from Shadowguard. The strange energy surges on Eden-12 continued, as did the transmissions someone was attempting to send via the rings. I ordered that the transmissions be recorded and analyzed. Without Marvin's help, however, the analysis was going very slowly.

We were jamming the rings ourselves, by sending garbage signals to them. An infinite series of random, meaningless vibrations constantly buzzed and shivered the big artifacts. But as the transmissions continued, I became increasingly worried. I summoned Captain Sarin as my carrier taskforce approached the massive gas giant, Eden-12, and parked itself in orbit.

"Captain," I said, going over the data with a deepening frown. "Could they be overcoming our jamming somehow?"

"I don't see how that could be possible," she said.

"Yes, but…they must know we're jamming their signal. Why would they continue to transmit if it wasn't working?"

She looked concerned. "We could monitor the data at the far end to see if it's related. We don't need Marvin to do that."

I nodded. "Do it."

Jasmine spent the next few hours working the staff. She soon came back with a worried frown.

"I've sent something to your tablet, Colonel."

I paged through about a hundred reports. Sometimes, I found the modern age of information-overload to be frustrating. We had more data than ever, but the sheer volume of it was overwhelming. It was difficult to sort out valuable items from what amounted to a massive pile of spam. I considered assigning an underling to going over my reports, trying to find the proverbial needles in the binary haystacks.

My eyes left the tablet and drifted toward Ensign Kestrel. She'd been handling my input over the last few days, a job Sandra used to have. She had her back to me and her jumpsuit was alarmingly tight. I thought to myself that she might work out as a spam-detector. She might work out very well.

Captain Sarin cleared her throat. I took in a deep breath, then went back to the reports. Finally, I found something interesting.

"Right here," I said, touching a data point that proved my theory. "About seven hours ago, the ring on the far side of the Thor system shivered in a pattern that matched the activity at the Eden ring."

Sarin came close. She leaned near me and I smelled her faint perfume. She had a hot smell to her, underneath the perfume. I knew it came from long hours of work on the bridge without a break.

I began to feel a little warmed up myself with her leaning so close, but I knew that if I moved she'd realize we were in close contact and be embarrassed. So I just sat there and stared at the screen she was reading. Why did they have to make these tablets so damned small?

"I see it, sir," she said at last. "It's buried in the data, but the signature is there. I'll work on a filtering program. I'll take out the data that represents our jamming pattern, and I'll see if it becomes clearer."

"That's the problem," I said. "Our jamming isn't random enough. There is a high frequency signal buried in here. We're hitting the ring with our own random garbage, and that worked for a while. But now, they've become more sophisticated in order to bypass our crude techniques."

"I don't get what you mean, sir."

"Well, let's say we send a signal that shifts every millisecond. That means that in-between those time slices is a window to squeeze in some data. Maybe they can hit the rings ten times inside that millisecond, and then skip a beat for our pulse, then go right on sending. The receiver knows to ignore our signal, because it is too regular."

She narrowed her eyes and bit her lip. She turned back to the data. She nodded slowly.

"They're communicating," she said with certainty. "I mean, *someone* is. But who is talking, and what are they saying?"

"I think that's pretty clear. And that's why we're orbiting Eden-12 right now."

Her expression changed to one of alarm. "You're saying the Blues are talking to the Macros again?" she asked. She leaned close to me again, and spoke in a low, urgent tone meant only for my ears.

"You aren't going to bomb them again, are you, Kyle?" she asked. The last time—the Blues called it barbaric, and I think they were right."

"I don't know. Was the bombing of Dresden barbaric in World War Two?"

"Yes," she said seriously, "I think it was."

"Well, if they don't stop plotting with the machines, I won't have any other choice. I don't want to do it. I've done everything I can to convince them to ally with us. They don't even have an excuse not to be on our side. They aren't exposed like the Crustaceans. They're right here in Eden where we can protect them."

"Maybe they don't want to be part of our alliance, because they're too proud. I think they want to lead the alliance, or at least stay independent."

"That's not going to happen," I said, "the only logical thing for them to do is join us. Unfortunately, the Blues don't see it that way. I have to admit that in the end, the Crustaceans turned out to be the more trustworthy race. They were shooting at the machines during this last battle. So far as I can tell, the Blues have never helped us willingly."

"But," she persisted, "are you going to bomb them?"

"If I have to, yes."

Jasmine retreated from my command chair without another word. I could tell she wasn't happy. I reminded myself it wasn't my job to make the people under my command happy. It was my job to beat the machines.

Getting in touch with the Blues was never an easy task. We'd gotten better at it with time, but it was still a frustrating process. We spent the next three hours transmitting down into the stormy methane-soup they called home. There was no response. Not even an acknowledgement.

What we did notice was a cessation of the signal going through the rings. They'd stopped sneaking transmissions in between our ham-handed jamming techniques.

As hour four began, I became restless. We'd been patiently knocking on their door for long enough.

"Let's drop a few," I said, going over our stocks of thermonuclear weapons. "I'll set the depth at—"

"Sir," Captain Sarin said, "can I speak to you?"

I looked up in surprise. She and all the rest of the staffers were staring at me. Most of them looked pale. I frowned back, becoming annoyed.

"Do you have unexpected news?" I asked. "Let me guess, the Blues have announced they're ready to talk, right?"

"No sir, it isn't that."

"What did they say, then?"

"Why—nothing, Colonel. They've yet to respond."

"Captain," I said, leaning back in my chair. "You're from Calcutta, aren't you?"

"I fail to see what—"

"Indulge me."

She muttered something I didn't catch. A few of the staffers struggled not to grin. My frown deepened.

"What was that?" I asked.

"I said 'yes sir, I'm from Calcutta.'"

"Right. Now, imagine you're a suspect in a serious criminal case back home. When the cops come to your door in your hometown, and they hammer on it and yell for you to open it and talk to them, how long do they wait before they break it down?"

She hesitated. "Not long."

"Far less than four hours, I'll bet. Well, that's the situation we have here. We're the cops and the Blues are our prime suspects. I'm not waiting any longer. Load the missiles and set the warheads to explode at a depth of six thousand miles."

There was some confusion amongst the staffers.

"Excuse me," Ensign Kestrel said as they nudged her in my direction. "Sir?"

"What is it?"

"According to our intel, the Blues reside much deeper than that."

"Thanks for the trivia, Ensign. Now, drop those bombs. I want ten warheads going off in a descending pattern. Start at six thousand and work your way down to sixty-five hundred. Fire them off slowly, with a ten second interval between each of the launches."

They programmed it in and we all watched as the first burning spark went down, down, down, plunging into the coffee-mocha-cream atmosphere. The spark was swallowed up, like a match being dropped into liquid. I ordered more missiles to be launched. We'd fired three by the time the first one went off.

A brilliant light flared deep inside the sea of gases below us. A hydrogen bomb, twenty megatons of force, looked like a lightning strike seen through a raincloud from our perspective.

After the seventh warhead was launched, Jasmine waved at me frantically. I lifted my com-link to my ear, and listened.

"You're presence has not been requested," said a strange voice. I knew in an instant that I was talking to a Blue.

I signaled Jasmine, and the staffers worked to stop the bombing and disable the last warhead we'd dropped.

"Well," I said to the Blue, "I thought maybe nobody was home. What's your name, creature?"

"I am known as *Tolerance*."

"That's an encouraging name," I said. "Have I spoken to you before, in some previous iteration?"

"No," said the voice. "I would have remembered a dense-thing such as you. The being known as 'Colonel Kyle Riggs' is notorious on our world."

"I'm notorious in a lot of places. Now, let's talk business. As part of our previous agreement, it was stipulated that you would not attempt to contact the machines. We know you have breached—"

"There are limits even to my pity, and you have exceeded them. Do you understand that your weapons have brought this matter incredibly close to the end? Do you understand that annihilation is at hand?"

I frowned. Sometimes, the translator brainboxes didn't interpret idioms quite right. I figured that this might be one of those times.

"I sorry," I said. "I'm not sure I understand you. We dropped our weapons to force you to give us your undivided attention. We have no intention of destroying any of your people today, as long as you answer our questions to our satisfaction."

"Answer your questions? The conceit is amazing. I was informed of this unbridled arrogance, but I did not credit it. Now, however, the evidence is overwhelming. Your species must have a very low regard for life."

"On the contrary," I said, not quite sure again if I understood the Blue, but trying to go with the flow, "we regard life highly. We do not regard the machines highly, however. We plan to destroy the artificial race we call the Macros in any way we can. Toward that end, we'll promise not to drop any more bombs into your atmosphere if you will accede to our demands. You must not converse with the Macros in any way."

A strange sound came over the speakers. It took me a moment to identify it.

"Excuse me, Tolerance? Are you laughing?"

"I almost do not know where to begin. Your misunderstanding of the situation is almost total."

"All right then," I said. "Enlighten me. You spoke of annihilation, yet we don't intend to harm you."

"I was not speaking of the annihilation of Blues at the hands of dense-things such as yourself. I was speaking of the annihilation of humanity by my species."

I sat there in my chair for a second. Then I stood up and slowly walked toward the central console. The staffers made room for me in their midst. I muted the audio pickup on my collar.

"Jasmine," I said, "have they fired anything at us?"

"Nothing that I can see."

I relaxed a little, but not much. I unmuted the channel again. "Tolerance," I said. "Are you claiming your people have the power to damage us?"

"No," said the voice. "I'm informing you that we have the capacity to erase you from the cosmos. All of you."

-33-

How did that old saying go? That you should be careful what you wish for? Well, I'd wished for the Blues to talk, and now I was regretting it.

Our conversation continued for another half-hour after Tolerance had informed me that the Blues were considering the annihilation of all humanity. I got nothing else of use out of him. Rather than presenting any evidence of his claims, he discussed my shortcomings as a sentient being at great length.

"...we've encountered a number of creatures claiming to possess self-awareness, but your kind stands out as unique," he said.

"Yeah? How's that?"

"The details are too numerous to list, but in the interests of raising your collective consciousness, I will stipulate your worst traits."

"I'm looking forward to it."

"Without a doubt, the greatest flaw in your species is a refusal to recognize the wisdom of your elders."

"You want respect, is that it? You've been technologically advanced for more centuries, so—"

"Not centuries. Countless millennia."

I nodded, pushing out my lower lip thoughtfully. "Maybe you're right on that point," I conceded. "We might not have exhibited the proper respect for you, as an elderly species. You must understand that we've naturally interpreted your slow, deliberate actions as incapacitation. It's only natural when dealing with weakened beings."

"Weakened?" asked Tolerance, his voice rising.

I could tell I'd pissed him off. He was threatening me, and I'd told him he looked pathetic to me. Captain Sarin came close to my chair again. She was wearing a deep frown. I muted Tolerance, as he went into a huffy speech about how cool and powerful his cloud race really was.

"Why are you baiting them, Kyle?"

"To find out what they have. I want him to brag."

She nodded, but kept frowning. I could tell she didn't appreciate my diplomatic techniques.

"Insulting them is hardly the way to win a new ally," she said.

I shrugged, and unmuted the line.

"...it is the bitter destructiveness and lack of comprehension that astounds us the most," Tolerance said in my ear. "I don't recall any species we've encountered who were so utterly naïve and ignorant of their place in the universe."

"How many species have you encountered, exactly?"

Tolerance hesitated. "Many more than you have."

"What's happened to them? Where are they now?"

"Most of them have fallen to the machines."

I leaned forward, sensing I was about to reach some new tidbit of data, some kind of explanation as to the number of star systems that the ancient rings interconnected.

"Are we talking about twenty star systems?"

"An order of magnitude higher."

My heart pounded. *Two hundred systems?* Could it be true?

"We've seen nowhere near that number of systems in this chain of rings," I said. "How can that number be right? Are you saying the Macros have two hundred stars under their control beyond the six we know?"

"Possibly. It is unknown."

I narrowed my eyes. Was he pulling back? Becoming reluctant to share information again? My mind raced. I was trying to think of something to say that would get this Blue to spill some further hard data. At the same time, I was worried he'd clam up again if he knew what I was really interested in. I decided to steer the discussion closer to our original topic.

"Well," I said, "I have to admit, I'm impressed. I did not know there were so many stars in this chain of rings. You've shown a great depth of knowledge concerning this topic."

"Naturally, indisputably...undoubtedly."

Realizing how pleased he was with my snippet of praise, I decided to take it away again.

"But," I said, "you did use a term that undoes all the rest. I'm afraid I must withhold my opinion of your claims for the time being."

"What word?"

"A small word, but a critical one."

"Explain, frustrating creature."

"The word was *unknown*," I said. "It's a powerful word, because it unravels all the rest. If you control the machines, how can you not know the extent of their spread?"

"We do not control the machines. We created them, yes, but does any parent fully control its adult offspring?"

"Usually not," I admitted. "But you're at least in communication with them. Why not ask them to clear up this unknown value? Surely, they must know the extent of their own conquests."

"You do not understand," Tolerance said, "and it is not my task to enlighten you further. This interview has been taxing, and now draws to a close."

"All right," I said, "I'm tired of you, too. What I want to know is this: will you continue to use the rings to communicate with the Macros?"

"We will cease the transmissions for the time being. Will your species continue to damage us?"

"No," I said. "We will not."

"Then your annihilation will be postponed."

I frowned and asked him what he'd meant by that, but the channel had been closed. I tried several more times to strike up the conversation again, but they were ignoring me.

I put aside my com-link.

"They got what they wanted out of us, I guess," I said to Jasmine as she came near. "They wanted us to stop bombing, and I promised we would as long as they stop transmitting to the Macros."

"What do you think they meant about destroying all of us? Do you think they have some kind of special weapon?"

"They've been building *something* down there in the deep gas. That's obvious."

"Something so powerful it could wipe us out?"

I shrugged and leaned back in my chair. I yawned. "Probably not. If they'd had a real doomsday weapon that could get rid of us cleanly, they'd have used it when I dropped the first bomb last time around. I'd say they have something real, but they don't want to pay the price of fighting with us directly. That's why they've been trying to talk the Macros into doing it for them."

She watched me as I stretched in my chair.

"How can you sit there so calmly after all that, Kyle?"

"How can you walk around the bridge so tense, day after day?"

Jasmine shook her head and went back to the main console. I strolled over and joined the staffers circling the holotank and the primary display, which had the size and general configuration of a pool table.

"How long have you been on duty, Captain?" I asked her.

She avoided my eyes and shrugged. "I pulled a double-shift."

Ensign Kestrel caught my eye. She made a gesture, pointing upward, behind Jasmine's back. I figured it out after a moment. She meant the Captain had been on duty for longer than that.

Most command staffers don't really want their execs to be on the bridge all day. It makes them nervous and makes them feel they should do the same. I decided it was time that we all took a little break.

"How about we go get something to eat?" I asked Jasmine.

"All right," she said.

Together, we walked off the bridge. I could feel every eye in the place on our backs. I regretted the move almost immediately. I knew what they'd all be saying: *Sandra's still warm, and he's already chasing tail again.*

But I wasn't. I honestly had been thinking of Captain Sarin's well-being. Running a ship took more than dedication and iron resolve. You had to have good personal judgment concerning your state of readiness, too. In space there was no night and no day. Technically, every hour was the same as the last, and people had to pace themselves or they would burn out and make mistakes.

We made our way to the wardroom and I sat Jasmine down at the single table inside. There was no one on duty at this hour, so I fired up the grill and microwaved some fresh coffee. Sarin watched me quietly.

"Do you think this is a good idea, Kyle?" she asked.

"Don't worry," I said. "I know you don't like to eat anything heavy right before bed. Also, I'm pretty bad at cooking. How about a couple of frozen waffles?"

She laughed. "You know I don't mean that."

"Jasmine," I said, "I'm trying to get you to relax for a few minutes. You need to take a solid eight hour shift in your bunk."

She looked at me in mock alarm.

"I didn't mean it that way," I said.

"I know, I know," she said, and sighed. "How do you feel about Sandra, right now?"

"I love her, and I hope she's going to come back to life. But I doubt she will. I guess, I'm in a state of delayed grieving."

We stopped talking for several minutes. I cooked the waffles, then brought them over to the table and sat across from her.

"You certainly know how to lighten up a conversation," I said.

"Sorry. These are good."

I ate half my waffle and was surprised to realize she was right, they were good.

"I think we've got real grain in here somewhere," I said. "None of that reconstituted crap in this meal."

When we'd eaten most of our waffles, Jasmine drew herself up and squared her shoulders.

"I'll do it," she said.

I stopped chewing and stared at her in surprise. "Do what?"

She gave me a little bewildered shake of her head. I did the same, baffled. She leaned across the table and put her hand on mine.

"I'll come to your bunk tonight," she whispered. "If it will make you feel better."

I was more startled than ever. I swallowed and coughed. Suddenly the waffle was like cardboard in my mouth. I washed it down with coffee.

I realized I was on the spot, and I had a big decision to make. I'd wanted to spend a night with Jasmine for years. It wasn't a big secret that she and I had a thing for one another. But it seemed wrong to me—very wrong.

"I—I'm not ready for that," I said. "Sorry if I misled you. I honestly came down here to feed you some waffles."

Her hand leapt away from mine as if stung. I reached out and patted her hand, but she pulled it away farther and crossed her arms under her small breasts. She was staring down at her half-eaten waffle. I thought maybe she was going to cry again.

"Hey," I said, "I'm not telling you I don't like you. I'm telling you I'm not ready. You're a girl. You understand that, don't you?"

She heaved a sigh and uncrossed her arms.

"Okay," she said.

"Sorry."

"Fine. Drop it."

I knew that from her point of view, she'd made a fool of herself. She'd misinterpreted my actions, and I'm sure she was very upset that she now appeared to be the aggressor. I half-expected her to get up and leave, but she didn't. Sensing she had something else to say, I finished my waffles quietly. They really were good. The best I'd had since leaving Earth.

"What do you think of Ensign Kestrel?" she asked suddenly.

I didn't even look up. I knew a trap when one was laid at my feet in plain sight.

"Barely competent," I said in a professional-sounding, clipped tone. "She's too young to be on a bridge, in my opinion."

Jasmine glanced up at me in surprise. "Really?"

"Why? What do you think of her?"

"I think she wears her smart clothes too tight," she said. "She must stand in front of her mirror for ten minutes telling the nanites to cinch-up."

I snorted. Then I lost it and openly laughed. It was my first laugh since I'd seen Sandra drooling bubbles on the floor of the pool room. I couldn't help myself. Sadly, the laughter died as quickly as it had come.

"I think you're right about her clothes," I said.

"She's doing it for your benefit. You know that don't you?"

"Come on. I'm an old man to her."

"A very powerful old man. She's the kind that's attracted to that. I can tell."

I thought of a dozen rude things to say, such as "it takes one to know one." But I managed to say none of them. Usually, my mouth acts like a self-destruct system when around women. But today, I held on.

"She's part of your bridge staff," I said. "Transfer her if you want to."

Jasmine sat quietly. I could tell she was thinking seriously about doing it. I sipped my coffee as if I couldn't care less.

"No," she said at last. "That would be unprofessional of me. I'm sorry. I don't know what's gotten into me lately. I shouldn't be jealous of her. Why should I be jealous? You were never interested in me in the first place."

"I certainly was," I said, "but now is definitely not the time."

She stood up. "Good night, sir," she said. "Thanks for the waffles."

I nodded and watched her go. I wondered to myself, as I watched her posterior shift under that sheer layer of smart cloth, if the whole nanite-thing had changed our sexual behavior patterns. I'd have to say that Star Force marines, both male and female, were a randy bunch. We had bodies that brimmed with energy and recovered quickly. We looked younger and fitter than normal people, and we were often placed in stressful, isolated situations. All of this promoted an active sex life. Affairs between troops were common, and we generally didn't frown upon them. We were all disease-free, after all, as the nanites cleaned out our bodies routinely from stem to stern.

There was some concern about the females becoming pregnant. The topic had rarely come up in staff meetings, but when it had, the general consensus was that if pregnancies happened, they were good things. No human colonists had ever planted themselves on a new world before, and we'd just done so on three lovely planets. It was in our best interests to go forth and multiply vigorously.

There were bound to be other social implications dictated by our situation. I guess it was all part of our new way of life. It was totally unplanned. We were feeling our way, figuring out how our culture would behave one step at a time.

A harmless, healthy relief of stress. That's what my old college-teaching colleagues would have said. And they were the ones who ought to know...

269

-34-

I went down to visit Sandra in medical before turning in for the night. There was no significant change in her status reported by either Dr. Swanson or Marvin.

Marvin had, however, made progress after a fashion. He'd built something big, strange, and vile.

I recognized it the minute I saw it. A bulbous tank from which thick vapors arose. The numerous PVC pipe connections leaked, creating a steady patter of droplets hitting the floor. The entire medical chamber was dank now, with condensation dribbling from the roof and trickling down the walls. Something was going on inside that bubbling tank, and I thought I knew what it was.

"Microbes, Marvin?" I asked, inspecting his work.

He'd been watching me since I came into the chamber, but he hadn't said a word.

"Hello, Colonel Riggs," he said. "I'm glad you stopped by. As you can see, I'm completing my first developmental step. The colony is alive and well. I'm teaching them to work with neurological synapses now—dead ones."

"Where the hell did you even get a colony to start with?"

"Microbes are everywhere in our environment. Human bodies typically encompass more than a trillion single-celled organisms."

"Of course," I said. "We have them inside us. All you had to do was steal a sample from Sandra and build the environment…"

Marvin didn't confirm nor deny. He didn't have to.

I approached the tank, which was made of layered smart cloth and pipe-fittings. It pulsed and gurgled. I wrinkled my nose in

270

disgust. I performed a brief inspection and I noticed two things that were especially upsetting. First, there were what appeared to be *brains* floating in the tank. I wasn't sure if they were human or bovine—or what. Second, there were electrodes hooked up to the tank. I knew what that meant. When we'd first run into the Microbe race on a Macro cruiser, the machines had been shocking them to force them to cooperate.

"I seemed to recall having forbidden this kind of work," I said sternly. I ran a hand down a nanite wire that led to an electrode. Nanite wires tended to be like shaped-mercury, almost liquid in nature. They were rarely shielded. I could feel the current in it, like a buzzing sensation on my fingertips.

Marvin lifted a black tentacle. He snaked it under the tank and touched a large valve at the bottom. He studied me with his countless cameras.

"This is the release valve," he said matter-of-factly. "If I open it, the contents of the tank will spill into the drain you see below the tank."

"Drain? Where did that come from?"

"I had the nanites form it. The pipe leads down through the main hold and out into space."

I pursed my lips. "What are you saying, Marvin? You're willing to abort this abomination right now? No arguments?"

"If you say so, Colonel."

We stared at each other for several seconds. I looked away first. I walked to Sandra's coffin and gazed into it. She was as lovely in her deathly state as she'd ever been in life. Tan skin, dark luxurious hair and body sculpted with the muscles of an Olympian. She'd had a mole on her cheek when we'd first met, but somewhere along the line the nanites or the microbes had decided to delete it from her face.

I sighed, and my shoulders fell. I realized I still had hope. While there was hope, I couldn't let her go.

"You've got me, and you know it," I told my scheming robot. "But I want you to stop shocking them. Find some other more humane way to get them to cooperate."

Marvin's tentacle slipped away from the tank's release valve. He considered.

271

"All right," he said. "I'm sure something can be worked out. May I proceed with my work?"

"For now," I said. "Report when you have something tangible to show me. Carry on."

I turned around and left. Dr. Swanson's eyes followed me, but she didn't say a word. I couldn't imagine what she thought of the situation.

I felt emotionally drained, but I kept my face impassive in the passageway. I hid my state of mind until I reached my cabin. There, I sat on my bunk. It was the very same bed I'd shared many times with Sandra. I put my face in my hands.

I had no idea if I was doing the right thing or not. How many Microbes should die so that one human *might* live? Were a quadrillion of their lives worth one of ours? How much did it matter that the Microbes were intelligent, or that we humans were bigger and had vastly longer lives?

I felt overwhelmed by the weight of such ethical decisions. I figured that no one was really qualified to make the call. I searched my instincts for right and wrong. You had to go with your gut on stuff like this.

My gut was churning—but I let Marvin keep doing his dark work, anyway.

I spent the next two hours in my bunk, tossing and turning. Sleep didn't come. The bed felt cold and empty without Sandra. Painful thoughts of her, mixed in with Jasmine, Dr. Swanson and even Ensign Kestrel haunted me. Worst of all was Marvin and his vat of gurgling biomass, an image which seemed to pop into my mind whenever I was finally falling to sleep.

"Colonel?" asked Jasmine's soft, disembodied voice.

I had been dozing, but upon hearing her voice I startled awake and sat up in bed. Twenty-four hour instant communications systems weren't always a good thing. As the commander of Star Force, I'd been forced to give up a lot of my private time.

I cleared my throat and tapped the wall twice, unmuting the channel.

"Yes, what is it?" I asked, trying to sound alert.

"I'm sorry, sir, but an emergency call has come in from Commodore Miklos at Welter Station."

"Patch him through."

Miklos' voice came to my ears moments later. He sounded frazzled.

"Sir? Colonel Riggs?"

"Yes, go ahead, Commodore. This had better be good."

"It isn't good, sir. It's bad. We've got a new Macro fleet coming through at the far ring of the Thor system."

"How many ships? How did they fare against our mines?"

"We've counted about fifty cruisers so far. But about the mines—no hits sir."

I paused, blinked and frowned. I rubbed my face. "Did I hear that correctly, Commodore? No hits at all?"

"Nothing, Colonel. They have some kind of new approach. A ship led the way into the system, moving slowly and eating up our mines. They appear to have a mine sweeper."

"How does it work?"

"We have theories, but no data. It's complex—I'll explain when you arrive at Welter Station. I can assume you're coming, yes?"

I realized at that moment that the ship was accelerating under me. It wasn't the full-press roar that one felt on a destroyer or a cruiser, but we were definitely underway. The big carrier *Gatre* was somewhat underpowered, but there was at least an extra G weighing me down, despite the inertial dampeners.

"Looks like Captain Sarin has made that decision for me," I said. "We're underway, and leaving the Blue's homeworld behind. We'll be out there in about twenty hours."

"Make that thirty hours," Miklos said. "As you must recall, you removed several engines from the design, sir."

I could tell by his voice he was still hurting about that. I rolled my eyes.

"Right," I said. "We're taking the scenic route. Keep an eye on the Macros, and give me a count every hour."

"I could advance into the system, Colonel. The Crustacean homeworlds are undefended."

I considered pointing out that the Crustaceans were technically allied with the machines, not us, but I didn't bother. In some ways, Miklos was right. We had a responsibility to the Crustaceans. They'd helped me militarily when I called upon them to do so. They might well have permanently broken their alliance with the Macros by firing on them. Sometimes, it was hard to know for sure how the

273

machines had judged an event. I'm sure the Crustaceans were trying to deal with them, but that didn't always go as planned.

"A good idea," I said, "but I don't think they're after the Crustaceans. They're probably coming here, as the Blues have been calling for them. If I had to bet, I'd say they were planning to take another shot at your battle station."

"Let's hope the third time is not the charm in this instance, sir."

"It won't be. We'll gather our entire fleet into a single fist this time. I don't want to split up my ships in the face of the enemy again. Wait for me. An hour after I reach Welter Station we'll set sail for Thor-6 if we think we can take their fleet without the station backing us up."

"Very good, sir."

We signed off and I lay back down. Strangely, I found it easier to go to sleep this time around. Instead of worrying about Sandra or any other females, I had a war to fight. Battles were things I felt comfortable with. They were problems that could be solved.

-35-

I managed to get a good, long night's sleep. Knowing I had thirty hours before the carrier task force reached Welter Station helped me to rest. If bad news came in now, I wouldn't be able to do much about it. Every veteran knows that in wartime they should sleep whenever they can. I wished I could store up sleep now for the long slog I knew was ahead of me. Unfortunately, I hadn't figured out a way to do that yet.

About ten hours out from Welter Station we began decelerating at a stately, deliberate pace—the only pace *Gatre* was capable of. I was awake by this time and well-fed. I'd even begun a workout in the ship's cavernous gym. It was really an extra hold we were using right now, but with some well-designed ergonomic equipment I was able to feel some strain on my muscles.

A few of the cadet fly-boys were watching me with interest. Under two Gs of centrifugal gravity, I could curl about two tons of weight and bench-press more than three. I guess this impressed them. When I got up from the bench and mopped my brow with a towel, two of them applauded. One of these two ventured forward to talk to me.

"I bet you don't remember me, do you sir?" she asked.

It was a common enough greeting from Star Force personnel. Usually, they were right. But in her case, I *did* remember her. Not her face, but her name.

"Fleet Commander Becker? I'm surprised you're here."

She smiled, pleased that I remembered who she was. The first thing I noticed about her was her reddish-blonde hair, which was cut

275

short into what I would call a modified page-boy look. Her body was lanky. She seemed to be all arms and legs, but with the sharply-defined muscle tone that tended to identify everyone in Riggs' Pigs. Judging by her attractive but lined face and piercing eyes, I guessed her to be in her mid-thirties.

"Aren't you supposed to be out scouting around in the Helios system?" I asked. "As I recall you took part in the effort to run down General Kerr in his battleship."

"Freshly transferred, sir," she said.

"By who?"

"Captain Sarin and Commodore Miklos. I tested out weeks ago on the new fighters, and I received a top rating. They ordered me to switch from the scouts into the fighter wings."

"I thought we'd replaced all our lost fighters from the Thor action."

Commander Becker shifted uncomfortably. The lines in her face became deeper. She put her long thumbs into the pockets of her flight suit. I could tell she didn't quite know what to say.

"We built new *birds*, sir," she said at last after an awkward pause. "But not new pilots."

"Oh, of course," I said. I wanted to kick myself. Of all people, I should know that we could stamp out a new flying machine every hour, but pilots took twenty years or more to grow up and train. They were not so easily replaced.

"Well," I continued, "I hope you're commanding a wing of them!"

"Just a squadron, Colonel."

I lifted a finger and pointed it at her, squinting. I remembered where I'd worked with her in the past.

"You were at the first battle at Welter Station, weren't you?" I asked. "Back before we even called it Welter Station."

"Yeah, that's right. I was scouting both sides of the Thor ring back then."

"You did a damned good job in the face of an advancing horde of enemy ships. I'm honestly surprised you survived that mess."

"Everyone who got out of that alive was surprised. My scout partner wasn't so lucky, however. He was taken out by the Macros before they invaded the station."

I nodded, vaguely recalling the reports. "I'm glad to see you in this new position. A fighter jock's got to be a survivor."

"Yes, sir," she said, and turned to go.

I frowned, then said: "Hey, would you mind showing me around your fighter? I haven't had a chance to check out the new model."

She brightened immediately, and I could tell she'd forgotten about my slip-up concerning why new pilots were needed. I was still kicking myself about that one.

I followed Becker to the hangar. I knew that if there was one thing all fighter jocks like to do, it was show off their bird. I looked over the sleek craft with interest.

The fighters had never been very big, and this new model wasn't any exception. If anything, they'd managed to make it more compact. It was built like a plane, but with very short, stubby wings. The wings could extend or retract to provide more lift if needed when gliding down into an atmosphere. The tiny ship reminded me of the old, extinct NASA shuttlecraft, but on a smaller scale.

The wings weren't the only part of the ship that could be reconfigured. The canopy was designed to coat itself with metal and turn opaque, or it could be left transparent like traditional aircraft.

I knelt beside the ship and put my hand on the wing. The nanites inside shivered slightly at my touch. Looking at the undercarriage, I saw the ship didn't have wheels, but used skids instead. With grav-lifters for basic propulsion, I guessed the fighter would tend to land perfectly if you could get your airspeed down far enough.

I ran my hand over the wings, and the nanites again buckled at my touch.

"Jumpy, aren't they?" I asked.

"Yeah," she said. "This is a brand new bird. They tell me the constructives will settle down and stop squirming soon. They still think they're in programming mode, or something."

I chuckled and stuck my head into the cockpit. There was only a single seat inside, but it was roomy enough. In space, a pilot had to carry more gear than aircraft usually did. You never knew where you might end up when you were flying around an uncharted star system.

"Big backseat," I said. "What do you usually put back here?"

"A bladder full of nanites, or small explosives, maybe. Sometimes, it's just for ferrying food or even a passenger."

I nodded, and realized I was looking at another of Miklos' elaborate designs. He had a different set of tendencies than I did. He liked to build craft that were capable of multiple mission types. I tended to build craft that were specifically shaped for a single purpose. His ships definitely provided more utility, while mine were slightly more deadly.

"I guess that can come in handy," I said.

"Do you want to take a ride?"

I looked at her, startled. I realized she must have thought I was hinting around, hoping she'd offer. In truth, I'd been thinking about Miklos and his overly-robust designs. I didn't feel like telling Commander Becker that, so I smiled instead.

"Uh, yeah. I guess so. We can circle the carrier a few times."

She reached out, slapped the canopy, and it yawned open. She climbed in and ordered the ship to build a second seat. Less than a minute later, we were requesting permission from control to launch.

Captain Sarin gave us the okay personally. I winced when I heard her voice. She knew I was taking a joyride. What was she thinking now? That I was out playing around or maybe even hitting on Commander Becker?

Once we fired out of the launching tubes, however, such idle worries melted away. The fighter was much too exhilarating to allow me to think about anything else. I whooped when we hit mach I, and we hadn't even come out of the tube yet.

Friction and heat roiled around the craft, making it vibrate. The roar was deafening. The launch tube was really a railgun system. If I'd ever wondered what it would be like to be fired out of a cannon, I was in suspense no longer.

The launching bay was designed to get the fighters up to as great a speed as possible before releasing them into space. Accordingly, the tubes ran the length of the mothership, from stern to bow. We fired out of *Gatre's* nose as if we'd been spat into space.

"You can take the helm, sir," Becker's voice shouted in my helmet. "Careful though, the controls are—"

There was a sickening lurch and I was thrown against the left wall of the craft. We flipped over and went into a two-axis tumble. Becker was barely able to speak, and I wasn't doing much better.

"Sorry," I grunted through gritted teeth. Outside the canopy, the big carrier, the sun, and about a million stars flashed in a repeating loop. The speed by which they did so was sickening.

"I swear, I barely touched the controls!"

"Let go," she hissed out.

I did as she asked, taking my hands off the stick. The craft automatically righted itself after a few seconds.

I laughed. "That was great," I said.

Becker craned her head around, but couldn't quite look at me. "Are you serious?" she asked.

"Yeah, sure," I said. "There's nothing to run into out here."

"No sir…but a spin like that would cause many pilots to lose consciousness. You're not even a little sick?"

"Nah," I said. I decided not to tell her I was cheating. Marvin had engineered plenty of fixes into the body of good old Kyle Riggs. My many physical edits had originally been planted there to allow me to survive extreme environments, but they also did well in keeping my brain functioning during a teeth-rattling brush with centrifugal force.

Becker shook her head. "You should be a pilot sir. You'd be a natural once you got the hang of it. In fact, you're flying it again now, aren't you? Very smooth. Almost feels like auto pilot."

I nudged the controls very gently. I thought about doing some hard banking rolls, but I thought I should wait a few minutes and give the girl's stomach a chance to settle down. Instead of violent turns, I did a long, even bank and pulled around to face *Gatre* again. Then, I figured I'd gently cruised around long enough; I put the hammer down.

The ship responded like the very best of sports cars—only infinitely better. Even I felt compressed into my nanite-formed seat as the Gs built up.

"*Gatre* is dead ahead, sir," Becker reminded me.

"I've got it now, Commander. I want to see what an attack-run feels like."

She stayed quiet, but I knew I had her worried. I didn't mind. I worried a lot of people.

We buzzed *Gatre* at about thirty thousand miles an hour. At that speed, you really couldn't see the target against the black of space. You had to rely on your instruments. I twitched the stick up, and then down again a tiny fraction of a second later. That was the only thing that kept us from smashing into the big ship and splattering ourselves like a big bug on *Gatre's* windshield.

I could hear Becker's breathing over the intercom. It was labored. But to her credit, she hadn't taken the helm from me in a panic. I knew she could, as the ship's pilot. But she'd held on and trusted me with her ship and both our lives.

A few minutes later, we parked the fighter on the flight deck and a half-dozen crewmen rushed out to service her. Apparently, an alarm had gone out.

"Jasmine," I muttered.

"What's that, Colonel?" Becker asked.

"Nothing Commander. Thanks for the wild ride!"

"I think I should be thanking you."

I laughed and clapped her lightly on the back. Unfortunately, it was difficult for me to measure such contacts. Nanites and all, she was staggered. I was used to Sandra, who could take more punishment than anyone I knew—with the exception of myself and possibly First Sergeant Kwon.

"Damn," I said. "Sorry!"

"Didn't hurt, sir," she lied, rubbing at her shoulder.

In a great mood, I headed down the winding passages toward medical. I could feel the stares of everyone on the flight deck behind me, but wasn't bothered. When you're in high-level command you have to get used to things like that. The troops naturally stare. I'd long since stopped worrying about it.

I headed back to my quarters and took a shower, as I'd just worked out and then followed up with a thrilling ride in the fighter. Not even nanites could take the stink off a man; we still needed soap and water.

After my shower, I felt good. I headed for medical to check on Marvin, Dr. Swanson, and whatever it was they were doing to Sandra.

I didn't make it all the way to medical. A series of unexpected events began when a klaxon sounded, signaling all hands to report to battle stations. I did an about-face and I headed for the bridge. Marvin and Sandra would have to wait.

I could tell *Gatre* was already changing course and speed. First, I felt the engines cut out entirely. This threw me and everyone else onto the floor of the passage. We'd been leaning without thinking about it, and now that the G forces were gone, we were disoriented. I sprang up again and brushed myself off, muttering curses.

Then the ship began a slow spin, and I knew Sarin was bringing the engines around to the rear. We had been decelerating, preparing to dock with Welter Station. When decelerating, our ships had the main engines pointing forward in order to apply thrust in the direction of travel.

This new move confused me. Could we be there already? I didn't think that much time had passed. After another ten paces down the central passage, a new application of force assaulted me. This was a lateral motion that made me walk at a slant.

All around me crewmen were walking on the starboard corner of the ship's passages. Everyone had been caught by surprise by the all-hands klaxon, and they were scrambling in their haste to reach their stations. To get past one another, we had to run up the walls. We looked as if we were playing some kind of bizarre game of leapfrog.

I reached the command center wearing a deep frown. The ship had to be making a hard, prolonged turn to cause such a shift in our center of gravity. We had stabilizing systems to prevent that sort of thing, but they were clearly overwhelmed. I knew that if Miklos could see me now, he'd laugh and remind me yet again that stripping components out of his designs had consequences.

"What the hell is going on?" I demanded as I reached the bridge and found myself crawling on my hands and knees to my command chair.

All around the bridge staffers wore harnesses. They were rooted to the deck by the ship's safety tentacles, which the nanites grew up from the floor on these occasions. None of them looked happy; some were white-faced and ready to barf.

"I've plotted a new course," Jasmine told me unhelpfully.

"I can see that," I snapped, sitting at an uncomfortable angle in my chair. "Are we in some kind of spin? What's the deal with the centrifugal Gs?"

"This is a high-speed course correction, not a spin," she informed me. Her hands were clamped onto the navigational table. Her legs were wound up with supportive black tentacles, and she looked as if she was standing in a nest of rigid snakes.

"Commodore Miklos informed me before I took command that this may happen under heavy maneuvering thrust—" she began.

281

I sensed a lecture, so I cut her off.

"Yes, yes," I said, "I know all about the stabilizers. We removed them for good reasons. Maybe when we get to the station, we can throw in a new generator and wire additional stabilizers into the lower hold."

"Negative, sir," she said, still not looking at me. Her eyes were glued to her navigational screens. "We're not going to dock at Welter Station."

"Where are we going, then?" I asked. "Give me a sitrep."

"One moment, sir," Jasmine said.

Anyone else who tried to shush me when I was in the kind of mood I was currently in would have gotten an earful of invective. But I knew Captain Sarin very well, and I trusted her judgment more than most of my commanders. I waited quietly for her to brief me.

While I waited, I became increasingly concerned. Something big was going on, and I was only in on half of it. I worked a tablet, paging through reports and incoming streams of data. Apparently, the Macros were on the move, and they were not behaving in an expected pattern.

"Can you talk to me yet, Captain?" I asked when she'd stopped spouting orders to her task force.

"I think so. We're coming about now. We've made the course correction."

I could feel the G forces fade. It was a relief, even to me. I got up and approached her table. Excited nanite snakes reared up to clamp onto me. I cursed and slapped them away. I'd taught them to accept such admonishment and to back off unless it was an emergency.

"Sorry," said Jasmine. "We can turn those off now. Ensign? Lower the alert level to double-yellow."

I glanced over the table. There was Ensign Kestrel, looking disheveled and worried. She worked her part of the shared command console and the nanite tentacles and smart harnesses retreated reluctantly.

Jasmine turned to me. Her eyes met mine, and they were deadly serious. "The Macros have gathered their fleet and gone to flank speed. We can't beat them."

"Beat them? Beat them where?"

"They're headed for Thor-6, the Crustacean homeworlds."

282

I frowned, looking at the big picture of the Thor system. I examined the screen carefully. A large cluster of red contacts were indeed heading from the far side of the Thor system toward the Crustacean gas giant and its three, life-giving moons.

"So, they're not coming to smash their heads into our battle station again," I said.

"No, sir."

"What's Miklos doing?" I asked, paging back to the Eden system. I almost coughed when I saw the entire fleet had launched from the station and was advancing on the ring to the Thor system.

"He's heading out there."

I almost demanded to know why she thought she should make this kind of command decision without orders from me. But I held back, deciding I would have done the same thing. After all, they hadn't engaged in hostilities yet. They were simply gathering their forces together in the Thor system as quickly as possible. I could see by the dashed lines that predicted the path of every ship in both systems that Sarin's taskforce was going to blow right past Welter Station and shoot through the ring. Miklos' force was under hard acceleration, and would beat us into the Thor System. But, since they were moving slower than we were now, we would catch up to them and both fleets would merge about half the way to the Crustacean homeworlds.

"You two made the right play," I said.

Jasmine's face is usually difficult to read, but I knew she felt relief when I spoke these words. She had been worried about giving a number of high-level orders without consulting me.

"There wasn't time for a meeting and a strategic decision," she said carefully. "What are your orders now?"

"From your actions, I gather that you and Miklos believe the Macros intend to attack the Crustacean homeworlds?"

"What else could their intentions be, sir?"

I nodded. "I agree. They've decided to go for the Crustaceans, rather than us. I guess I should have considered this possibility. The lobsters are weak, and the machines already made an attempt to drain their oceans. Just because we stopped them, they haven't given up on their original prey. They've moved on to Plan B: direct assault."

"There is one more critical detail that hastened our decision to act. Miklos found it first, and insisted on flying out there as quickly as possible."

"Give it to me."

She brought up the Thor system again, and zoomed in on the enemy ships. "Notice the enemy fleet composition, sir."

I did as she suggested, and the anomaly was immediately apparent to me. I took a deep breath and let it out again in a sigh. I felt a new weight on my shoulders.

"They aren't escorting any invasion ships," I said.

"Exactly, Colonel," she said. "The Macros do not intend to invade the watermoons."

I met her stare with one of my own. "That can only mean...they intend to bomb them, don't they? To attack the Crustaceans from space, where they can't be reached."

"That was our assessment. When we realized what they were going to do, Miklos and I decided that we had to move all our ships toward them. Possibly, they will be distracted by our threatened attack and will attempt to deal with us first."

I nodded. "A good move, probably the best you could make. But the Macros aren't easily swayed from a path, once they have decided on a course of action."

"I know that sir, but we have to try, don't we?"

I didn't meet her eyes. I had a hard decision to make. The Macro fleet was equal to our own. We might well beat them, but that wasn't a certainty.

"I don't know yet," I said. "We have to weigh our options."

Her eyes followed me closely. She was looking at me, but I didn't return her gaze. Instead, I stared at the command map depicting the Thor System.

She took two steps around the table toward me and kept staring at me. I fiddled with the controls, recounting the Macro cruisers. I reached the same frightening number every time.

Jasmine was close to me now. She spoke in a quiet voice. "The Crustaceans attacked the Macros because we insisted they do so. We owe them, sir. Are we going to try to save them?"

I didn't answer her question. Instead, I asked one of my own.

"What's our ETA?"

"Twenty-one hours," she said. "If we arrive as a single force."

"That's the only way I'd consider it."

"I know."

Now, I had to ask *the* question: "What's the enemy ETA?"

"Seventeen hours, at current rates of acceleration."

I massaged my jaw. "It's the carriers, isn't it? They're slow."

"Yes sir."

I finally met her pretty eyes. They were big, brown and troubled.

"We're going in," I said. "We have to. They'll get four long hours to work over the lobsters before we get there, but it's the best we can do."

"I'll inform the Commodore, sir."

"Very good. And tell him that if we have any carriers left after this, they're getting more engines, more generators, and more damned stabilizers."

Jasmine gave me a weary smile. "That will make him happy, sir."

-36-

Charging across space toward an enemy fleet was an exhausting experience. In some ways, it made me envy the commanders of armies past. In a land battle throughout most of human history, you had little to no knowledge of the exact enemy position. You went out marching, and it took a long time. Long enough for you to almost forget that you were walking to what might possibly be your death at the hands of the enemy.

Sailing across the open sea wasn't all that bad, either. A ship's captain in the times of the Romans thru the Colonial Era didn't know where the enemy was or when he might run into him. He could relax and sip wine in his cabin until the lookout spotted something.

It was the capacity for long journeys without too much stress that I missed. In my era, war was often fought in space, with perfect clarity of vision for millions of miles. I could see the enemy with my optics. I was forced, in fact, to watch him grow and grow in perspective as he drew ever closer. I felt the thrill of a baron leading a charge of knights across an open field toward the shimmering line of the enemy—but this was a charge that would go on for hours and days, rather than minutes.

It was stressful for everyone aboard. People naturally tensed up when battle was near, especially when they could see the enemy coming right at them. All around me, crewmen were rubbing their necks, wiping away sweat and taking deep breaths. They were all under a great deal of pressure.

Deciding I'd had enough of it after we'd crossed half the system, I retired to my quarters—or at least I'd intended to. When I reached the door of my cabin, I found Dr. Kate Swanson waiting there for me.

For a few seconds, I misinterpreted the look on her face. She looked vulnerable, almost shy. I immediately jumped to the conclusion that she wanted to talk to me about personal issues. That part was right—but I was mistaken about the nature of these…issues.

"Colonel…" she said.

"Yes, doctor?"

She looked down and licked her lips. I took a moment to admire her. She was about my age, and I found that appealing. She was a mature, seasoned woman who'd grown up in the era I had. She was also a medical doctor on a ship that had seen plenty of battles. We had a lot in common.

Doctor Swanson straightened herself and looked completely in charge again. "Sir, I think you need to check up on Marvin."

We stared at each other for a few seconds. I realized then that Kate Swanson hadn't come to my cabin at night for reassurances about the coming battle. If she had, the meeting might well have turned into a glass of wine and a shared evening. Instead, she'd come because something had gone terribly wrong—in medical.

"What's he doing to her?" I asked.

She shrugged helplessly. "I really don't have any idea. But it's not going the way anyone had planned. I'm certain of that."

I nodded. "It never does with Marvin," I said. "It never does…thank you, Kate."

I walked with her toward medical. I didn't ask her any more questions. I didn't want to, and I didn't have to. I knew I would see for myself how bad things were very soon.

When I tapped on the door to medical, it didn't respond right away. The door wouldn't open. Frowning in immediate suspicion, I'm afraid I lost my temper.

I punched through the relatively thin sheen of nanites that formed the door. Really, it wasn't hard to do. The metal was less dense than steel, and only about a quarter of an inch thick. A bullet would have gone right through it. In this case my fist went through it so far that I fell against the door, and was left with my cheek pressing against the cool, trembling metal.

The nanites, which had been put into lock-down mode somehow, were forced to recognize me and react to my presence. They

287

remembered their programming, which was somewhat similar to that of an earthly elevator. When a human arm was detected protruding through the door from one chamber to another, they were compelled to relax and melt away. It was part of the safety protocol that kept them from accidentally slicing our bodies in half.

When I stumbled into the dimly lit chamber, I saw Marvin immediately. He was in a new configuration I didn't recognize. Then, staring, I slowly came to understand what I was seeing.

His central body structure was often cylindrical, but this time it was oblong and all in one piece, rather than segmented like a metal centipede. From this central box-like unit, all his tentacles and cameras extended in a halo of instrumentation.

"Oh…so nice of you to drop by, Colonel Riggs," he said.

I stepped forward three paces, squinting in the gloom. Behind me, Dr. Swanson lingered in the passageway. She showed no inclination to enter, and I didn't blame her. I'd seen horrors perpetrated by Marvin when he got really wrapped up in a biological project. They were never pretty to human eyes.

"Where's—" I began, but the word "Sandra" never left my lips.

Because I saw her then, or at least I saw part of her—her *feet*. They were visible through a small window that allowed one to look inside Marvin's body.

I finally came to fully understand what I was looking at. Marvin had subsumed the medical enclosure that was Sandra's life-support system. He had become one with the medical instrument, and was literally all over Sandra.

Oddly, this disturbing image eased my emotional state. Sure, it was frightening to look at. For someone not used to Marvin, and his self-designing behaviors, it might appear to be something out of a horror movie. But I knew Marvin, and I knew how he operated. He liked to reconfigure himself inventively.

"Marvin, that's Sandra inside your belly, isn't it?"

"An interesting metaphor," he said. "But as I'm not digesting her tissues, it's not really apt. I would rather say that I've reconfigured myself into a convenient formation to better address my patient."

"Right," I said. "Now, give me a progress report."

Marvin hesitated. That was always a bad sign.

"The subject is still alive—technically," he said.

288

My mouth opened, then closed again, twice. I took a few steps toward him. This earned me the attention of several more cameras. His tentacles, which often whipped about in a frenzied fashion when excited, slowed. Only a few of them still rustled quietly. These few retracted toward his body, like cords being dragged slowly across the floor.

"'The subject'," I repeated back to him. "'Is technically still alive…'"

"Exactly."

"Marvin, that doesn't sound encouraging. Have you managed to repair her mind? Is your new science of—what did you call it?"

"Necrological reconstruction."

"Right. Has any of that worked out?"

"No."

He stopped there, and so did I. For a long moment, neither of us spoke. I heard something behind me, and turned my head. Over my shoulder I heard Dr. Kate Swanson's retreating footsteps. She had left me here with Marvin and the thing in his gut which had once been my mate.

"What?" I asked him hazily. Just for a moment, I thought I must not have heard him correctly.

"The science is a failure in this instance. You see, she's not a valid subject."

"What are you talking about? Can't you revive her?"

"Technically, there is nothing to revive."

"What *are* you talking about?" I demanded again, louder this time.

"Her organs are generally functional, but her brain has been erased. Sandra is brain-dead. Worse than that, actually."

I felt like I was falling, but I locked my knees and stood ramrod straight. I also kept my voice even, despite every instinct within me, which wanted to scream and rave. I had to focus to speak calmly again.

"How can a person be worse than brain-dead?" I demanded. I wanted to scream at him. I began coming up with denials and rationalizations. I knew I was doing it, but I couldn't help myself. "She has some kind of amnesia," I said, "I understand that. People can usually work with that, they can recover. We have medical

289

powers no one in the history of humanity has ever had. Just get her breathing and pumping her own heart again."

"Those were my initial goals. Unfortunately, I failed. Neither the microbials nor the nanites are capable of creating new neural pathways, especially without knowing exactly which nerve-endings needed to be stimulated, or by how much, to cause the autonomic processes to continue."

"I'm not getting it, Marvin," I said. "People have lost their memories before. I understand she'd be a blank slate, but—"

"This level of brain damage goes far beyond simple amnesia. She has lost all her motor skills. Her brain doesn't even know how to control her muscles. A toxin has eaten away her neural connections. The synaptic interconnection points between the neurons are gone. Her memories, her instincts, even her motor functions in the reptilian region are gone. She can't breathe or make her heart beat without artificial aid because her brain has forgotten how to do these things. As an analogy, if she were a computer system, she would have a blank hard drive, blank memory and even blank ROM."

"What can we do to help her?"

Marvin shifted his bulky body. He seemed to lean closer to me, to loom over me, and all around me. His cameras panned and zoomed.

"I've identified possibilities," he said. "They all require that we start fresh. We could, in essence, use her cellular programming to create a new model."

"Cellular programming? Are you talking about her DNA?"

"Exactly. Her DNA hasn't been damaged. It contains everything we need to build new components. There would be several advantages to this approach."

"Advantages?" I asked, stunned.

"I've identified two distinct methods," Marvin continued. "The first would be to utilize a new brain, which could be transplanted into the existing unit's cranium."

I could tell he was becoming excited just by thinking about what he was saying. His tentacles were writhing with renewed vigor.

"A new brain?" I heard myself ask. "What, from a donor?"

"Not advisable. Rejection would be almost certain, and the mentality of the individual would be very dissimilar to the original Sandra—let us call her Sandra 1.0—even if we were able to manage the surgery."

290

I stared at him. I was in a haze. I'd only felt like this once before in my life, when my wife had died in a car accident. A calm, soft-spoken doctor had proceeded to lay out the grim facts to me then as well, and I'd felt like the earth had opened up and sucked my guts down into a black hole under my feet.

"How…how else would you get a new brain, if not from a donor?"

"That's where the project becomes interesting," Marvin said. Now that he was fairly certain I wasn't going to physically attack him, his tentacles had begun thrashing around with their normal vigor. "Within every human cell is the DNA required to build any element of the body, with the proper differentiation during development. Really, it's an ingenious system."

"Okay, so you want to grow a new brain for her?"

"Yes. That's option one. Still, I don't recommend it."

"Besides the obvious absurdity of the proposal, why not?"

"There's a time-factor. Even using chemical accelerants and hormone-therapy, an adult human brain that could operate her body would take years to grow. When we were finished, her body would be in an aged state, making the final surgery more difficult—"

"Okay, okay," I said, "What's option two?"

"Full replacement. I've gone over it many times, and really, it's the only option."

I took a few seconds to take this in. "You're talking about cloning, right?"

"Yes."

I looked at the feet in the tank. I couldn't even see her face. "She's already dead, isn't she? She's been dead for a week, and I've been fooling myself."

"Essentially," Marvin said, "but where there's a will, there's a way. And I'm fairly confident I can grow you a new Sandra. Let's call the new unit Sandra 2.0."

I shook my head. "But she would be a kid. The whole process would take years, wouldn't it? She'd have to be born, grow up, go to school… She wouldn't even be the same person."

"I disagree," Marvin said. "As a machine intellect, it's possible I'm more comfortable with the concept of self-duplication. It would be Sandra, and much of her personality would be recognizable. I've delved into the topic, and according to the articles I've read on the

291

internet, over seventy percent of human personality traits are due to innate neural structures. She wouldn't have the same memories, of course, but she would look and behave in a very similar fashion."

"But I would have to raise her as a little girl, right? That's weird, Marvin. I would be old when she grew up, I couldn't have the same kind of relationship with her that I have now."

"Do you mean a sexual relationship?"

"Well...yes."

"But you would have total control of her upbringing," Marvin said brightly. "Why not prepare her appropriately? Youth is preferred when human leaders pick mates, as I understand it. Even if you were to select a new mate now, she'd probably be much younger than you. Statistically, political leaders—"

"Just shut up, Marvin. It's not happening. Do you hear me? Forget about it. Come up with some other bizarre science experiment to sate your curiosity. Stop tormenting me in my grief. You're going to have to leave Sandra alone."

Marvin, I understood in that moment, was Frankenstein. He was a mad scientist fascinated by life and death. He wanted to create his own versions of both.

"But—Colonel Riggs, my intention was to *eliminate* your grief," he said. "Is that not an honorable goal?"

"Yeah, maybe it is," I said, "but not this time. Wanting to do something and having the power to do it doesn't mean you *should* do it."

"That's not entirely logical."

"I don't care."

"Could you explain it to me?" he asked.

I looked at him. I could tell that he really, honestly, wanted me to try to explain ethics to him. I knew I couldn't so I didn't bother to try.

"You're a robot, Marvin. There are some things about us you'll never fully understand."

It took several minutes for Marvin to extricate himself from Sandra's medical unit. After he'd finally managed it, I opened the hatch, kissed her forehead and said good-bye.

-37-

The next day I came to understand there was a curse upon my existence. The curse affected anything and anyone I came to love. These accursed individuals were doomed to die badly. All of them.

I've presided over more official Star Force funerals than I care to count. This one began no differently than a hundred others like it.

There was a somber crowd in perfectly creased smart uniforms. The medical unit, which had been designed to handily double as a coffin and disposal system, trundled down a preset path through the hold. We stood at attention as it passed us by. Kwon was at my side, as were Marvin and Dr. Swanson, but not Jasmine. She'd asked to come, but I'd ordered her to stay on the bridge. After all, we were only hours out from inevitable contact with the enemy.

I usually had uplifting words for my troops at these events, but I was an empty husk today. I fell back upon the classics, not knowing what else to do. I gave them our slightly edited version from the Book of Common Prayers:

"We commit her body to the stars; earth to earth; ashes to ashes, dust to dust. The Lord bless her and keep her, the Lord maketh his face to shine upon her and be gracious unto her and give her peace. Amen."

Sandra's coffin still had a long way to go. The nanites that were programmed to very gently propel it toward the launching tube weren't speeding up on my account. Not wanting to make everyone stand around uncomfortably for several more minutes, I decided to force myself to speak further.

293

"Typically," I began, saying the first words that came into my mind, "our Star Force members die their final deaths while fighting an alien machine. In this case, however, Sandra's death was not due to a clean wound delivered by an enemy on the field of honor. Instead, she was taken from us by the assassin's knife. A shot in the dark. Treachery."

Up until this moment, everyone had been gazing at the coffin. They hadn't been really listening to me, but were rather lost in their own thoughts. But I could tell that had changed. Heads swiveled to observe me.

I kept my eyes on Sandra's face. I could still see her through a small, triangular window in the medical unit.

"I pulled the plug on her only minutes before this ceremony. The simple act of disconnecting her life-support was probably the hardest thing I've ever done. But I felt I had to, as she has been taken from us, even if this vessel she's lived in so long still looks perfect to the eye. With help, perhaps I could keep it breathing and pumping blood forever. But I'm not going to do that."

I turned toward Marvin, who looked dejected. His cameras drooped and his tentacles were still.

"And I'm not going to clone a new Sandra, or a new Sandra-brain, either."

Only a single camera met my gaze. I turned back to the audience, who were looking at me with wide eyes now. They hadn't heard about Marvin's strange plans, apparently.

"For disconnecting you," I said to the coffin, "I apologize, beloved." She was passing me now, and the nearness of her form gave me an urge to save her, to push her from the tracks that bore her with relentless slowness toward the launch tubes. I stood firm, however, reminding myself she was well and truly dead.

"The third time was the charm, my love," I said to her. "Perhaps your soul has been wanting to go all along. Maybe your time really came back when Alamo dropped you into the cold, cold ocean. Or when we found you in a coma in space. I've brought you back to life several times, but no more. You must find your own way—"

"Sir? Colonel Riggs, sir?"

My earpiece was buzzing. I recognized the voice: it was Captain Sarin. I decided to try to ignore her. The coffin was only about a minute from the launch tubes.

I paused and cleared my throat. "You must find your own way back to the stars from which we all came. Stardust to life, then back again. It is the cycle of the universe, the—"

"Colonel Riggs, I'm sorry," Jasmine hissed into my earpiece. "There's no need to respond. I must report, however, that the Macros have fired a huge barrage of missiles."

I reached my hand up to my earpiece, and my face changed to a frown of concern. Everyone stared at me. I knew they suspected I was losing it. I straightened up and tried to pull together my thoughts. The damned machines wouldn't even let me bury my girlfriend in peace.

"Sandra," I said, "we're sending you back to the fires of this alien sun. The white star known as Thor will be your new home until such a time as your mass is transferred into space, and hopefully it will someday comprise a new living being. It is the immortality we know we all have: the immortality of the matter that forms our bodies. In the meantime, may God keep you."

Someone began crying behind me. I thought it was Ensign Kestrel, but didn't look back to find out. I watched the coffin enter the launch tube. There was a click, and a hiss. The tube was building pressure.

My final comment to her was made in a harsh whisper as the external door melted open and the light on the unit went from green to red.

"I'm going to find the man who ordered this, love," I whispered, "and I'm going to kill him. I promise you that."

I felt a darkness come over my heart and mind after the tube rumbled and released. With fantastic speed, the coffin shot sunward. I watched through the portal for a second or two, until she was lost from sight. I knew that Sandra herself could have probably tracked the projectile for a full minute, but my enhanced eyes had never been as good as hers.

A hand touched my shoulder. It was a soft touch. I turned and faced Dr. Kate Swanson.

"I'm so sorry, Kyle," she said.

Then she hugged me. The move caught me by surprise. I looked around, and saw several of the females were crying. A few of the males looked misty-eyed as well. Maybe my eulogy, as lame as I thought it was, had gotten through to them.

Kwon was stepping from foot-to-foot, not knowing what to do with himself. He was no good to anyone in a situation that didn't require shouting and shooting.

"That was a tough break, sir," he said, talking over Dr. Swanson's shoulder.

She was still clinging to me and squeezing me with grief. I didn't feel sadness—not exactly. I was pissed off and in some kind of shock. But mostly, pissed off.

I patted Dr. Swanson with an overly-cautious hand. I didn't want to damage the woman. She was being very supportive.

Then she surprised me again. She stood on her tiptoes and put her mouth up to my ear—the right one, which had no earpiece sticking out of it.

"If you want to feel better, come to my cabin," she whispered.

I pulled away slightly, and gave her a look of surprise and confusion. She must have read this as rejection—which I guess it was. She looked flustered and took her arms off me.

"I'm sorry for your loss, Colonel," she said, and moved away.

A dozen others who'd been waiting around for the woman to let go of me now surged forward. Unlike Kwon, they'd been waiting politely. Before they could tell me how sorry they all were, my earpiece crackled again.

"I'm so sorry, Kyle," Jasmine said. "But the situation is urgent. I know the funeral is breaking up. Did you get my last transmission?"

"Yes, I did Jasmine," I said. "Thanks for your condolences. How many missiles and where are they headed?"

"We've been calculating with optics, sir. At first we assumed the barrage was targeting us, but the band of space that could be targeted is narrowing every minute. This fleet no longer intersects with the projected path of the missiles."

I frowned. "What does lie in their path?"

"Thor-6 sir. The Crustacean homeworlds."

I froze with my hand pressed to my ear. I felt a chill.

"I'm on my way."

I pushed through the crowd and headed for the passageway. "I want everyone back to battle stations—now."

The murmuring crowd stopped murmuring and rushed for the exits after less than a second of hesitation. The passageway was empty when I reached it, but behind me came a crowd of crewmen.

296

When I reached the bridge, Jasmine surprised me with the hug. I returned her embrace with a tiny squeeze. It felt good to press her flesh against mine. Not just because I found her attractive, but because she was a real friend who'd shared a lot of pain with me over the years. When I released her, she coughed.

"Sorry," I said.

"It's all right. Take a look at the situation. I'm projecting two hours out."

I looked, and I didn't like what I saw. The missiles were going to crash into the Crustacean home moons hours before we could get there.

"Have you warned them?" I asked.

"Yes. I don't know what they can really do, however. Underwater strikes aren't like atmospheric bursts. The pressure wave will kill them. They don't have bomb shelters, and I don't think it would help if they did."

"Tell them to disperse," I said. "It's their only defense. They don't want to crouch in the sea, massed up at any one spot. If they just swim away from one another, spreading out over the seabed at different depths and latitudes, more will survive."

"Maybe," she said.

I looked at her sharply. "What do you mean, 'maybe'?"

She rubbed her face. "I've done some math. There are too many bombs. The radiation will spread everywhere within days. The tides of the singular sea will carry radioactive seawater all the way to both poles."

"Maybe they can stop a few of the missiles. Transmit our methods of killing missiles with concussion in mid-course. We know they have their own missiles, maybe they can stop the barrage."

"Already done, sir."

"Good. I'm sure the Crustaceans will do what they can to save themselves. The question is, what else can we do? Have you come up with any options?"

Jasmine looked at me. "Not much. But we do have six transports full of marines—a fair number of them are Centaur marines."

I looked at her sharply, and our eyes met. I shook my head. "You want me to ask the Centaurs to fly into the teeth of the enemy again? To sacrifice themselves on their tiny flying sleds?"

In an act of questionable ethics, I'd once sent the Centaurs charging into enemy ships and exploding themselves. That tactic had badly damaged the Imperial fleet when it had finally broken through into the Eden System. We'd used the tactic on the Macros too, upon occasion.

"It's a matter of numbers," Jasmine said. "There are billions upon billions of Crustaceans out there, defenseless. A few thousand Centaurs could do a lot of damage. We'd save a large net number of lives."

"Would you listen to yourself? 'A large net number of lives?' I'm not an accountant, Captain Sarin."

"You've told me yourself that this is a war to the death—to extinction. We want the living beings to win it, don't we?"

"Yes," I said, nodding. "All right, I'll look at the numbers."

We examined them, and determined the move would be unfeasible. Launched on their flying one-man sleds, the Centaurs wouldn't have enough acceleration to get to the enemy missiles before they reached Thor-6. Almost as important, by the time they'd gone so far ahead of our fleet, they would be moving very fast. It was unlikely they could target and intercept the missiles and explode themselves at the precisely right moment.

"It was too much to ask, anyway," I said. "I have another idea."

Jasmine cocked her head to one side. I could tell she didn't really believe there were any other viable options. This was proof to me that even my best officers liked to stay inside the box with their solutions.

"We could send our fighters," I said.

She frowned for a moment, unsure what I was suggesting, then her eyes widened.

"Oh no, sir."

I nodded my head, becoming more certain by the second that my idea was the right move. "We can send the fighters in now. They have plenty of range and a much greater rate of acceleration than this slow-moving fleet. If we launch quickly enough, they might even be able to shoot down some of the missiles that are going to rain down on the Crustaceans."

She shook her head rapidly, making her non-regulation length black hair fly. "You can't do that. They'll be wiped out without Fleet support. Worse, you'll be leaving the main fleet undefended. Never

298

split your forces in the face of the enemy. Isn't that what you're always telling your officers?"

"Yeah," I said. "But this is about more than winning a battle as cleanly as possible. This is about preventing an extinction event. The Crustaceans are an allied species, whether they want to admit it or not. And don't forget, I talked them into giving the Macros a good look at their middle claw, which is why they're being targeted now."

She crossed her arms and took a step back from the table.

"What are you orders, Colonel?" she asked.

"Have both carriers launch two of their fighter squadrons. Each ship will hold the other half of their wing in reserve."

The crew complements on our carriers were smaller than earthly carriers. *Gatre* only had a crew of about two hundred service people, plus the pilots and a platoon of shipboard marines. I'd kept the command structure streamlined as well, and we didn't have a CAG officer. We did have a Tactical Operations officer, and a Gunnery officer for ship defense. But Captain Sarin was in direct and overall command of everything that happened on her ship, including the actions of her fighters.

Jasmine relayed my launch order to Miklos, who commanded the second carrier. I could tell her conversation with Miklos was heated, but after a few terse comments, he apparently accepted it. Then she spoke to Tactical Operations, who gave orders to the crews in *Gatre's* launch bays.

Klaxons sounded all over the ship. Soon, the deck began to shiver under our boots as the fighters were shot from the four long tubes once every fifteen seconds or so. It looked and felt a lot like launching a barrage of missiles.

I wondered if Commander Decker was among the pilots, and if she would survive the day. I didn't bother to check the rosters. That sort of decision was up to the carrier captain and I didn't want to interfere.

I took a break once the fighters were away. I headed to my cabin and washed my face, which felt sticky from stress and sweat. Then I went to the wardroom and was served coffee that looked like a mug of crude oil.

The voyage had been a long one. The coming battle would be difficult, but we had long ago formulated our plan of attack. I had a little time to think.

Sitting there, sipping my coffee and wincing with each bitter swig, I went over my long relationship with Sandra in my mind. It had been turbulent and exciting. I wasn't yet able to comprehend how life would be without her.

At length, my mind came around to the subject of the unexpected offer I'd received from Kate Swanson. The doctor's cabin was quite near the wardroom, and I figured she was probably in it at the moment. Medical was empty now that our single critical patient had been given a one-way ticket to the hot, white star that irradiated *Gatre's* hull.

I had sensed earlier that Kate might be entertaining ideas about forming a relationship with me, but I hadn't been sure. After the proposal she'd delivered at the funeral, she'd left no doubt in my mind.

Her suggestion of companionship seemed a little crass in retrospect. After all, Sandra's body had barely cleared the funeral tube before the woman had made her play. She was a fine-looking lady, and the fact we were close to the same age held some appeal to me. She was sophisticated, educated and experienced. A person of substance.

But I told myself I didn't want any pity-sex, if that was what had been on her mind. At least, not on this terrible day...

-38-

Our fighters didn't make it there in time to intercept the enemy missiles. We considered firing missiles of our own to form a force-wall against the enemy barrage. But the physics of the situation were against us. In space, even a nuclear warhead does not form a large region of destruction. Firstly, because there was no air to push together into a moving shockwave, and secondly, because space was incredibly large. The enemy missiles were simply too far apart for us to kill more than a handful of them before they reached the water-moons. I made the hard call, deciding I would rather shoot at the enemy ships in close battle than waste the ordnance now.

When I returned to the bridge, everyone seemed more tense than when I'd left. I stepped up to the tactical consoles, and Ensigns melted away to make room for me. I was wearing battle armor now, and Kwon was still following me around. The staffers gave us sidelong stares.

"Can someone give me a sitrep?" I asked.

Captain Sarin turned to me. "Both fleets are converging on the gas giant and her flock of moons. We're decelerating hard, as are the Macros."

"How about turning off the engines, coming about and coasting in?" I asked.

She hesitated. "We thought of that, sir. But the idea has been rejected."

My eyebrows rose high. "Who did the rejecting?"

Miklos, who was on my viewscreen as a headshot, shook his head vigorously and leaned forward. His nose loomed into the camera alarmingly.

"I did sir," he said. "We could coast in and arrive earlier, but we'd have to fight the entire battle in one flyby if we did it that way. Due to our high velocity and inertia, we can't just do a U-turn. We'll have to zoom past the enemy and do a long turn-around to come back into range again."

"I know that," I said. "The question is what we can do to them in a single pass. Can you guarantee me we can visit enough destruction on the Macros to stop them from giving the Crustaceans a deathblow?"

"In short," Miklos replied, "the answer is no. We can't do it. Their ships are as tough as they've always been."

"What about the fighters?" I asked. "They can decelerate much faster than the bigger ships can. Let's get them in there and let them harass the enemy, up-close and personal."

"We can't do that Colonel," he said, then he hesitated. "Let me amend that. It would be an unwise use of a limited resource. In fact, I suggest we recall the squadrons we've sent already."

"Explain."

"They can't stop the missile barrage," he said. "We know that now. They—"

"I want to know why that happened, too. Give it to me, we have time."

Miklos' eyes traveled toward Jasmine, who met them. There was a tiny, unspoken communication. I could see it happening, despite the screens and the relative distance between them. I hated these moments when my officers tried to manipulate me. I had to fight to stay calm. I assured myself I'd get to the bottom of whatever scheme they had in mind and make my own decisions. I knew my staff, even at the highest levels, thought I was a loose cannon. Perhaps, they were even correct in some instances, I'll give them that. But as the overall commander of Star Force, I wanted to be in the loop at all times. It was my job, and it was their jobs to present the facts clearly and completely.

"Very well," I said loudly, "since you have no clear objections, I'm going to order—"

"Please sir," Miklos interrupted. "Let me explain."

I tried to cross my metal-encased arms. I was annoyed when I realized the movement was impossible. This new battle armor was too thick to permit it. Sparks flew from my gauntlets and bracers for a moment, then I gave up and let them drop back to my sides. This did nothing to improve my mood. I stared intently at Miklos' image on my screen.

"The situation has changed slightly. Our optical systems have now pinpointed the enemy target. It is Princeton."

I frowned. "Princeton? All the missiles are going there? They're all headed for one moon?"

"Yes sir," he said. "That is problematic for us. As you know, it is difficult to tell the exact flight path of a missile from this distance. They can retarget and shift. But now, due to their extreme velocity, they are past the point of no return. They can't shift their goal and hit anything else of value, not even if they want to. They're simply moving too fast to change course with the remaining time and fuel they have."

I nodded, studying the tactical layout. "Let me guess, Princeton is the farthest moon from our fleet. The easiest target for them to hit. But why just that world? This is a huge barrage—surely they could knock out whatever military capacity the single world has with far less."

Another glance was exchanged between Sarin and Miklos. Again, I tried to ignore it.

"We don't think that's their plan," Captain Sarin said. I turned to her and I saw a haunted look in her eyes.

I frowned. "Not their plan? What then—ah…"

I understood, suddenly. The implications were horrifying. The Macros had no intention of disabling the Crustacean military. They weren't planning to invade at all. They were here to kill the population.

I swallowed and stared at the screens. "We can't stop their missiles, and they're all targeting one planet. What are our damage estimates? How many civilian deaths?"

"All of them, sir," Captain Sarin said. "Nothing will survive. Much of the ocean will be blown to vapor. The crust might even crack open, if they strike with enough fusion warheads along a single fault line, here…"

303

She went on for another minute or so, detailing how billions upon billions were doomed to die. An entire world teeming with life was about to be extinguished and I couldn't do anything to stop it. I tuned Sarin's voice out, as the finer points didn't matter.

"Get the Crustacean High Command on the line, will you?" I asked when she had finished.

It took longer than it should have, but soon I had someone who identified themselves as a "Research Coordinator" on the line. It was a male this time, and as far as I could determine, his name was *Nagog*. Marvin did the translating, and I did the talking.

"Coordinator Nagog," I said, "it is a sad day, and I have grim news for your people."

"Please keep your comments terse and to the point, human," said Nagog. "I'm involved in a variety of projects at the moment."

"I can well imagine. Are you aware of the approaching fleet and its intentions?"

"Of course."

"Have you got a battle plan to meet the enemy?"

"We have plans to meet all our enemies. Your actions will be repaid a thousand fold. Your young will boil in their nests tomorrow, as surely as ours will today."

I frowned. "Perhaps there is some kind of misunderstanding. Our fleet is coming to help you against the Macros. We will fight a great battle in your space to defend you. Do you understand our intentions?"

There was a hesitation. "We will meet all our foes with equal ferocity."

"That's just my point. It may look like we are on an attack course against your worlds, but we aren't. Don't waste any resources shooting at us. The Macros have launched their missiles, and they are all headed for you, not for us. We will destroy the machines for you, but we're requesting your aid to do so. As far as I'm concerned, Star Force is allied with the Crustacean people."

"We can't accept an alliance on a permanent basis."

I rolled my eyes. These people were impossibly difficult to deal with. They were facing their own destruction as a people, and still wanted to maintain neutrality.

"All right then, how about we ally for the next twenty hours? After that, we'll break it off. Is that temporary enough for you?"

304

Another hesitation ensued, this one was longer than the first. At long last, the Crustacean returned to the phone.

"We would like to address the process. It is not being adhered to. Proper protocols have been established, and shall not be breached unless—"

"Unless what?" I demanded suddenly in exasperation. "Is this not enough of a circumstance for you to break your bureaucratic vows?"

"There are no such 'vows', as you term them," Nagog said huffily. "But we will accept your offer of a short term peace. Any violation of these terms will—"

"Yeah, right," I said, "good luck to you too. Just aim your guns at the machines, not us, and we'll do the same. Riggs out."

Captain Sarin turned to me reproachfully when the connection closed. "We should coordinate with them more closely than that."

I threw up two gauntleted hands. "What am I supposed to do? It took me ten minutes just to get them to agree not to shoot at us while we defend their worlds for them. I'm not going to waste another minute trying to tell them how to best use their own defenses, whatever they are. These people are impossible to deal with. It's all about procedure and protocol. I'm surprised some predator didn't eat them all a million years ago."

Jasmine looked at me with her lips pursed in disapproval. I turned my full attention back to the screens.

"All right," I said, "I'm trying to look at and get the sense of their grand strategy."

"Whose?" Captain Sarin asked.

"The Macros. I mean, let's look at this from their point of view. First, they tried to kill a planet full of lobsters by draining it."

"Half of them are still alive."

I nodded. "Only because we interfered. But in any case, their next move was to send in a fleet. They don't have any invasion ships, so their goals lean toward extermination, rather than subjugation. They fired a huge number of missiles, all targeting a single world. Those Crustaceans are pretty much cooked now. That leaves us Harvard and what's left of Yale."

"What are you getting at, sir?"

"Where are their ships headed? What do the optics say?"

She brought up the report, and I examined it. The data was clear and undeniable.

"The entire fleet is heading for Harvard," she said, glaring at the trajectory. "I suppose they could change it…"

"But they won't," I said. "They haven't changed a thing since they started. Their intentions are very clear. They've managed to kill one and a half worlds. The main body of the fleet will kill another. All that will be left is the half of Yale's population that we managed to keep alive."

Captain Sarin looked at me in pain. "They mean to kill them all."

"Yes," I said. "Exactly. The question is: can we stop them?"

"I don't see how," she said.

"Have you recalled the fighters yet?" I asked suddenly.

"Yes sir. They're still decelerating, but—"

"I've got new orders for them. We're flying out there at flank-speed. We've got to hit them as fast as we can, but only when they're over Harvard."

"What are you saying, sir?"

"You heard me, come about and stop decelerating. Prepare to launch more fighters."

"How many fighters?"

"All of them. We have to get to Harvard before the Macros do. They're going to erase the Crustaceans, Jasmine. They're going to remove them from their homeworlds. Every last lobster will die if we don't get out there and fight with them."

I began stripping off my heavy armor. Inside, I was wearing a smart flight suit. The cloth smoothed itself out like unfolding paper once it was free of the armor.

Jasmine watched me do this with eyes that were big and dark. Her face was lit-up from below with blue light from the screens.

"You're going with them, aren't you?" she asked quietly.

I gave her a thin smile. "You know me too well."

I left the bridge and marched down the central passageway. I took a lift to the launch bays. Before I got there, the klaxons were sounding. I wondered if I would ever hear the battle cry of a big ship like this again.

What I was doing was pretty crazy, and I knew it. But I was acting on a hunch. I'd done it before, and if this one panned out, I planned to do it again.

Jasmine caught up with me on the flight deck. I heard her feet running lightly after me. I turned around, knowing it would be her.

"This is unnecessary, Kyle," she said.

"I knew you guys had talked about something before I got to the bridge. I also knew you two had to make a concerted effort not to call me back up there when this data came in. It took me a few minutes to figure it out, but I finally did."

"You don't have to do this," she said.

"Yeah, I do. I screwed the Crustaceans. The Macros are going all out to kill them because I gave them the excuse they needed. I talked them into attacking the Macros. Their extinction is all because of me, and you and Miklos know it as well as I do. The sad thing is that we didn't even need their help down on Yale. We would have won without them."

She bit her lower lip and nodded. It was an unusual, vulnerable moment for her. I could see she was conflicted.

I sighed. "I've been doing a lot of thinking, you know? Since Sandra died again—for the last time. I've been thinking of all the people who've tried to take me out, and why they did it. Remember Barrera? He was a good, solid officer. But he turned on me. He did it because he thought it was the right thing to do for humanity. Maybe he was right."

"No, he wasn't," she said with sudden emotion. "He was full of himself. Crow was too. Always, these smaller, meaner men come to hate you. They don't understand that you might not do things by the book, but you *win*. In the end, that's what humanity needs out here in space. A winner."

"I'm still going."

She looked defeated, then took a deep breath. "I know."

I chuckled. She hugged me and we kissed lightly. I felt a dozen eyes on my back, but I didn't much care right then. Let them talk. Let them say Jasmine really poisoned Sandra, to get to this moment. I couldn't stop them, because they were going to say crap like that anyway about any woman I touched.

So I kissed her back, more firmly. Then I let her go and looked at her face.

"I thought I might have bruised you," I said.

"I'm fine," she said with a smile. "Go kill the machines."

I nodded, turned, and marched to a bird they had ready for me. I saw Commander Decker standing there beside it.

"Is this your fighter?" I asked in surprise.

307

"Yeah," she said. "I figured you already knew how to fly her, so…why make any of my other pilots miss out on the fun?"

"Thanks!" I said, climbing into the cockpit.

"Good luck, Colonel," she said seriously, looking up at me.

Across the hangar, Jasmine was still lingering at the elevators. Then I frowned down at Decker.

"You're a survivor," I said. "That's why you're staying here and I'm making this flight, right?"

Decker opened her mouth, then closed it again. She gave me a little shrug.

I laughed, put on my helmet, and began the launch sequence. I really liked the feel of the fighter under my butt. It felt like power, speed and trembling potential.

-39-

I have to admit, I was roaring almost as loudly as the engine itself by the time the tiny fighter fired out of the end of that tube. I felt like it had been too long since I'd flown a ship solo, and this one was the most vibrant piece of machinery I'd ever had the pleasure of piloting.

Now that Commander Decker wasn't around to temper my judgment, I felt free to fly the bird the way Miklos had intended— violently. I had little choice in the matter, as I was the last one launched. The rest of the squadron was already en route to rendezvous with the first squadrons we'd launched over an hour earlier.

Meeting up with the other fighters wasn't as hard to do as it may sound. The first wave of fighters only had to coast, while we kept accelerating all the way in. The tricky part would be the deceleration. We were going to have a rough time of it to get our speed down in time to make a single mass and meet the machines as an organized strike force.

Captain Sarin and Miklos had worked hard on the math. We were going to rendezvous only minutes before meeting the enemy. In fact, we'd be inside their gun range when we did mass up. That was cutting it closer than I would have liked, but we didn't have any choice at this point.

For their part, the machines had so far ignored our fleet entirely. They hadn't even bothered to ping us. We knew they could see us; we were making no effort at stealth. Moving at flank speed with blazing tails of flame behind every vessel as we accelerated and decelerated, we looked like a swarm of comets, visible with the

309

naked eye from just about anywhere in the star system. Despite all that, they hadn't targeted us with missiles or sent us so much as a warning message. It was almost disturbing, how focused and cold the enemy could be. It was when they behaved this way that they seemed entirely alien to me. Even the Blues would have said *something* as we charged to war.

The joyride of the fighter lost some of its thrill after the first hour of hard acceleration followed by hard deceleration. My teeth ached in my head, and I could taste blood. It rolled down the back of my throat in a steady trickle, and with every swallow I felt like gagging. I knew the other pilots had to be experiencing similar side effects, but none of them mentioned it. Perhaps it was my presence that kept them from complaining. Fighter jocks were a proud bunch. I could almost hear their thoughts: *If this old man who barely knows how to fly his bird can endure the Gs, then we can damned well do the same.*

I had time to think, unfortunately. Time to think about Sandra's dead face, Marvin's excited probing of her body and Kerr's expression as I'd let him die in space. I thought about Jasmine's kiss, Dr. Swanson's whispered proposal and a dozen other pleasant things as well. In a way, I was disappointed. I'd partly volunteered to go on this flight so I wouldn't have time to think about recent events. In that regard, I'd miscalculated.

But as with all things, the journey came to an end. The water-moon we'd dubbed Harvard came into view. It was blue, white and purple. The waters here weren't pure, I knew, but the beaches were. They'd told me to expect the purple, as there was a lot of manganese garnet particles in the water of this strange moon. The colorful parts were the shallow areas, or the regions dotted with islands. The spectrometer readings from Fleet had given me the heads up, but really, you couldn't understand what you were going to see until you saw it with your own eyes.

The purple went in curving streaks, covering the island areas with magenta stripes that extended into the sea until the blue of the water took over. What a lovely world it was. I thought it would be a grand shame to let it be destroyed before a single human had the pleasure of walking one of those warm beaches.

"Sir? Do you read me Colonel?"

I was Jasmine, and by the timing I knew it wasn't going to be good news.

"Go ahead, Captain," I said.

"The missile barrage just hit Princeton. The warheads were fusion, as expected. The yields appear to be high."

I closed my eyes for a second in silent prayer. I couldn't see the third moon, as it was far from our position on the other side of the gas giant. But I knew those bombs were killing millions.

"Any casualty estimates yet?"

"Not yet, sir."

"What about the Crustaceans? Are they showing any signs of having a viable defense?"

"Yes sir, that's partly why I'm calling. They launched a large number of missiles at the approaching Macro ships. They've also sent up a flotilla of their own ships."

"Good!" I said, slamming a hand down on the fighter's dashboard. A few instruments dimmed in protest, making me wince. The smart metal dash began unfolding itself.

"Unfortunately, the Macro mine-sweeper ship seems to have stopped most of the missiles. We think it operates with some kind of magnetic-pulsing field. In any case, the missiles managed to destroy that ship, but only a few of the cruisers were damaged."

"What about their own fleet?" I asked. "You said they have ships."

"We've got new data on those ships—they all appear to be transports."

I frowned, checking my instruments. There wasn't anything to see there yet on my screens. One weakness of these small, fast ships was their lack of long-range sensors. There just wasn't room for that kind of equipment aboard.

"We should be meeting up with the first fighter wave soon," I said. "Where are these Crustacean transports? Maybe we can combine our attack and cover them."

"I think it's possible, sir. The transports are all converging on your position—they're heading to Harvard. I think they're trying to save that last, untouched world."

"A brave move," I said seriously. "They don't have much, but they're going to make their play here. Well, we'll do what we can to help them."

"As a final point, the enemy ships are now in range—I mean *you* are in their range."

311

"Roger that," I said. "Any sign of incoming fire yet?"

"It might be there, but we can't see it yet. You're too far away, about five light-minutes. You'll know before we do if you're under fire."

"That's great," I said. "Thanks for the update, Riggs out."

We'd been communicating with a small ring-resonance unit, which allowed instant communications. It was strange, being able to talk directly to another ship, but having them be so distant their sensors could not yet have picked up what was going on around my position due to the limitations of the speed of light. I imagined that eventually I'd have to invent sensory equipment that could relay its findings instantly using the ring-resonance technology. But that improvement would have to wait for another day—if I should be so lucky as to live to see another dawn.

Now, the excitement of battle finally fell over my mind. This was what I'd been seeking all along by coming out here, I realized: A clear enemy, a clear goal, and a planet that needed saving. No ethical dilemmas were about to present themselves to me out here. Destroying machines was always good.

The first of our fighters was hit about three minutes later. Analysis by my ship-board brainboxes assured me one of my wing-mates had been nailed by incoming point-defense fire.

"Countermeasures!" I ordered. "Everyone spread out. Random pattern on the approach. We're too far out and too small for them to get a bead on. If we can keep their AI guessing, we can get in close enough for a pass with very few losses."

It felt like bullshit, but it was good bullshit. The squadrons broke up and began weaving around like drunks. The bolts of light coming at us were invisible until they reached us, but they could be measured as they passed. The machines had finally taken official notice of us.

Two fighters blew up over the next three minutes, and then one more. I looked at the numbers. We were still out of range.

"Let's put the hammer down, people," I said. "The enemy have no fighters. They are big, slow targets. Pair off, and make a high speed pass, aiming at their engines."

All around me, powerful little engines flared in the endless night of space. I followed suit, and we were all plunging forward toward ships we couldn't even see yet. I checked my instruments every few seconds, but the brainbox had no firing solutions for me yet.

I chose a wingman, and followed him on our first wild pass. We were going too fast, that was obvious to any observer. But we had engaged the enemy before they'd expected it, and I knew I was buying time for the Crustaceans to make whatever play they had up their sleeve. I hoped it would be a good one.

Less than a minute later, the Macro cruisers were in visual range. There were about two hundred of them. They had more cruisers than we had fighters. It was a daunting realization. The main body of my fleet was nearly an hour behind us. I was in this alone with the Crustaceans, about a hundred fighters against two hundred cruisers. For the first time, I felt as if we were doomed.

To their credit, every Star Force pilot followed me into that mess without a complaint, or a moment's hesitation. My marines often thought of themselves as the braver men, true warriors who fought the enemy as close as the sights of their rifles, but these Fleet pukes were impressing me.

Now that the cruisers were visible, I could see their weapons firing as well. Huge cannons blossomed with round after steady round. All of this pounding went down, down to Harvard itself. None of the big weapons were aimed at us. They were all blasting the helpless planet beneath them.

I bared my teeth, angry with the cold calculation of the enemy. They knew they weren't likely to hit a fighter with a heavy weapon. Instead, they were going to take out the civilian population below us.

The cruisers swelled in size in my canopy. We were already in the middle of the pass, and I felt all of my insane speed as we drew close. The cruisers looked like they were standing still in comparison.

When my ship finally started firing its primary weapon, it kind of shocked me. The fighters were armed differently than other ships I'd flown. The small hulls didn't have the size to operate a heavy laser— basically, there wasn't room for a large enough generator. The only laser aboard was about the size of a marine's rifle and was useful only for defensive purposes. It couldn't damage anything bigger than an incoming missile.

The ship had waited until we were in close to use it single primary armament. I'd laid in firing orders long ago. The fighters used kinetic weaponry, essentially a Gatling gun of six barrels, each of which accelerated a stream of depleted uranium pellets up to fantastic speeds. The result was a deafening ripping sound. The cockpit shivered with the recoil.

The canopy flared white, and for a second I thought I'd been hit. Then I realized it was just a gush of flame washing over my bird. There was no smoke, as we weren't in an atmosphere, but the released plasma by-product more than did the job of obscuring my vision. It was hard to see what was happening when the gun fired.

Fortunately, I was moving very fast. The moment the firing stopped, the canopy instantly cleared. I could then see for a few seconds and retarget if necessary, before the next burst began. To allow the ship's gun to cool down, the weapon fired in short bursts.

Our first pass was short and violent. Fighters took fire and exploded. Any hit was pretty much fatal in these thin craft. Our only defense at this range was our speed.

We made a fateful pass by the rear of the enemy column, spraying millions of rounds into the enemy engines. The results were dramatic. Seconds after the first fighters reached optimal range, the cruisers were hit with what looked like orange-white lines of flashing sparks. It was like watching a spray of incendiary tracers, but the streams traveled faster than that, and they were burning from their initial launch, not because of friction with any atmosphere.

More streams of bullets appeared. They grew in number and intensity. More and more of my fighters had reached effective range. The cruisers were no longer sedately sailing along, looking impervious to attack. They shook with internal explosions. Engines flickered and died. Blue exhaust choked off on several ships. Suddenly being stricken and thrown off-balance by uneven thrust, they went into spins. Two of the cruisers slammed into one another as we completed the pass, creating a very satisfactory explosion. Three more dropped down into the atmosphere of Harvard and began to burn. I personally counted six kills, and I was sure there were more outside of my range of vision.

Still, as we roared past the enemy fleet and shot to the far side of the planet, I knew that we hadn't done enough damage.

"Wing commander?" I called out. There was no response.

"Squad leaders, do I have anyone—"

"Here sir," said a voice. "I'm Commander Firebaugh. We've lost some people—I'm in charge now, sir."

"Congratulations," I said. "You're from *Defiant*, right? I'm taking tactical command of *Gatre's* squadrons."

"Um, okay sir…"

"Here's what we're going to do. We're out of range now, on the far side of Harvard. We're going to make a quick orbit and make another pass, but we're going to do it differently this time."

"How's that, Colonel?"

"We're going to slow down, and we're going to engage."

"Sir? We can't dogfight with cruisers, sir."

"I know that. Listen closely. We have less than six minutes before this orbit is over and we're back in range of the Macros again."

Commander Firebaugh was quiet for a second. I waited impatiently.

"Colonel, if we decelerate, their point defense lasers are going to shred us."

"I'm well aware. That's why on this pass we're going to feed our ships different target priorities. We're going to take out the enemy laser turrets. We're too small to hit with missiles or their primary guns. They won't be able to touch us if we take out their PD turrets."

There was another, longer hesitation. I felt a familiar red heat rising up my neck. I didn't like to be ignored or to be kept waiting in the midst of battle.

"Commander," I began, when I couldn't wait any longer, "I'm not accustomed to—"

"Sorry sir, I was just checking with Commodore Miklos, he suggests that—"

"I don't care to hear his suggestions, Commander," I said loudly. "Here are your orders: have your pilots retarget and decelerate for the next pass. We'll stay engaged, working from the top of the enemy fleet where most of their weaponry can't come to bear on us unless they turn upside down."

"They'll just invert and burn us out of the sky, sir."

"No, they won't. Trust me. Riggs out."

Reluctantly, the Commander relayed my orders. In my headset, I heard a number of bitter complaints from the pilots. They were brave, but they weren't stupid. I didn't go onto the general chat. It was enough that they knew what they were supposed to do.

About two hundred seconds later, we came screaming around the southern pole of Harvard and plowed right into the stern of all those bombing cruisers. I had to hand it to the Macros. They hadn't missed a beat. They were pounding the world below us with relentless firepower. The purple beaches were now speckled with black pits.

The fighter swarm was moving slower now, and we were much more vulnerable to incoming fire. I watched tensely as the big ships ahead stayed on course and continued their relentless bombardment. They were killing millions, but they were also giving us the time we needed to get into effective range.

By the time we caught up with them on that second pass, we'd lost only six more fighters. We had nearly seventy percent of our force left, and we were all over them like a swarm of angry hornets.

-40-

Within five long minutes, our fighters had taken grievous losses, but we'd managed to trim off nearly all of their defensive armament. They had nothing much left to hit us with, but I was down to less than two full squadrons.

Still, I was alive and determined. The world below was pockmarked with glowing craters, black burnt scorch marks and whitewater impact points. Tidal waves were sweeping around the planet in every direction. The surface of the single, endless ocean resembled a puddle in a rainstorm.

But I knew that although the Crustaceans were taking a beating, they would survive if I could disable the rest of the bombarding fleet. Without thermonuclear missiles, the Macros needed many hours to render the planet uninhabitable—possibly days. The tidal waves were bad, but the native species was aquatic and should survive if they spread out and crawled along the stirred up bottom. Barring a direct hit from above, they could not be easily taken out.

Suddenly, the battle shifted. The Macros rolled over, turning their belly-turrets up into space, rather than aiming down at the planet below. This move took me by surprise, but I ordered the pilots to stay on task, destroying every laser turret they could. When we finished that, we could work on their engines and bring them down one at a time.

"They've inverted and are going to blow us out of the sky, sir," said Commander Firebaugh.

I thought there was a hint of "I told you so" in his voice, but I let it slide.

"Dive below their formation," I ordered.

We shifted our attack, moving below the enemy. I waited for Firebaugh to tell me they would just turn over and bring their guns to bear on us again, but he didn't. The Macros, for their part, kept firing out into space.

"Sir," called Commander Firebaugh, "Those big turrets are firing up at great range. They must be shooting at something. Whatever it is, it's not us."

"Nothing on sensors?"

"Negative."

"Our main fleet isn't close enough yet to engage them, so it isn't our ships they're firing on. I'll talk to Sarin. Maybe she can see what's happening."

"Should be disengage, sir?" asked the Commander hopefully.

"No, dammit, keep on them."

I hailed *Gatre*, and Jasmine answered quickly with happy news.

"It's not us," she said, "it's the Crustacean transports. They're coming in and unloading boarders. They're clearly planning to storm the Macro cruisers."

"That is fantastic news!" I shouted back. "For once, I'm glad these lobsters are so good at copying our tactics."

I was beginning to think we were going to win this, then the Crustaceans finally arrived and I became certain of it. Another minute passed, during which we didn't lose a single fighter. Every gun the machines had was spamming fire at the approaching transports. I couldn't see the damage they were doing, but I was sure the Crustaceans were taking a beating.

Despite this, I was elated. I could taste victory now, and it was sweet. We'd all come so far and lost so much. Taking out these machines would make my day. Sandra's sacrifice seemed more valid to me, given the number of lives we were saving.

A moment later I could see the transports. There were at least a hundred of them. And much closer, I could make out dark, tiny shapes falling like a shower of sand. These shapes were individual Crustacean marines. They fell in a cloud over the Macro fleet. They crawled over the surface of every vessel like cockroaches. I'd never been so pleased to see a thousand little crawling monsters before.

Then, the Macros shifted their tactics again. Their missile ports opened.

My heart pounded as I fought the controls on my ship and the communication system in my helmet simultaneously.

"Jasmine?" I shouted. "Get through to the Crustacean High Command. They have to stop those missiles. They haven't got half their marines down yet, and I'm sure the Macros mean to take out the transports and any flying troops that haven't landed on their hulls yet. The cruisers might even scorch one another to burn the troops off like fleas."

"Relaying," she said.

I waited impatiently, looping around a cruiser, seeking a valid target. The enemy ships had very few laser turrets left. I would have fired on their engines, but my main gun was out of ammo. These small ships had drawbacks.

"Colonel?" Jasmine said, coming back on the line. "I'm sorry sir, they say their transports can't stop them."

I cursed and switched over to the tactical channel. "This is to all pilots," I said. "Break off and chase those missiles. We have to take them out."

Dozens of engines flared blue-white and drew streaking arcs on my canopy. The fighters disengaged and charged after the missiles. But we couldn't catch them. We took out one or two with our lasers, but the majority streaked away. Our ships were fast, but a missile was nothing but an engine and a warhead. It was designed for speed and little else. We couldn't catch up.

I cursed and gnashed my teeth until my gums bled, but it was all in vain. My fighter was no faster than any of the others.

A moment later, the flock of missiles intermixed with the incoming transports—then shot past them.

I stared, dumbfounded. I contacted Jasmine again.

"Captain Sarin, am I missing something?"

"No, sir," she said. "The missiles went right through the Crustacean line without detonating. They're still flying, and accelerating. There is no chance you can catch them, Colonel."

"The question is, where are they headed?"

"We're plotting that. But it is so early after launch, they have options."

"If they're coming at your fleet, I think the enemy has made a mistake."

"I would agree, sir. But we don't know that."

I ordered the fighters to turn around and go back to harassing the enemy cruisers. Almost immediately, Commander Firebaugh was back on the line. I looked at the beeping light for a second in annoyance before answering it.

"What is it, Commander?" I demanded.

"Sir, we need to return to the carriers. We're out of effective ammo."

"I know that. But we can still help the Crustaceans by distracting the Macros and taking out the last of the enemy point-defense systems."

"I disagree, sir," he said evenly. "We're as likely to burn a lobster in the back as kill another turret now. There are hardly any left in any case. I respectfully request that we return and let the native marine troops do their work. They can finish these cruisers on their own."

I gritted my teeth, but finally agreed. "All right, break off to the enemy stern. We'll return to base."

I heard a great deal of relief in the Commander's voice as he relayed the order to his pilots.

We fell back behind the fleet, letting them glide away from us. They had turned back over now, and were again bombing the helpless world below. It was galling, watching them fire so many deadly salvos without being able to stop them.

"Colonel?" Jasmine asked in my helmet.

"Go ahead."

"We've plotted the course of those missiles. They are all headed for Yale."

I froze, staring straight ahead. Suddenly, I got it. The Macros had never changed missions, never for one second. They had started this attack by draining the seas of Yale in a scheme to kill all life on the planet. When we'd stopped them, they'd moved on to Plan B, the direct invasion of Yale. Now, they were taking another shot at it with the last of their missiles.

I understood in a flash that they didn't care about my fleet or any fleet. They weren't here to win a fleet battle. They were here to annihilate a biotic species entirely, burning their three homeworlds to rubble.

"Can you get in the way of that barrage, Captain Sarin?"

"No, sir," she said. "We've already plotted it out. We're out of position. We'll arrive shortly, and probably destroy the last of the cruisers. But we won't be able to save Yale."

I did some quick math in my head. The Macros had already wiped out one world, Princeton, with the first missile attack. Yale was half-dead and they were going to finish it now. The last world was Harvard, stretched out below us with scarred purple beaches and churning seas.

"Contact the Crustacean High Command," I said. "Tell them what the machines are doing. Tell them they have to stop these cruisers, or they might be extinct within the hour."

"How, sir?"

"Just tell them."

As she relayed the message, the Macro cruisers made their next move. They broke up, splitting the fleet apart into a hundred and fifty separate units. The ships spread out in every direction. Then they began dropping, dipping down into the atmosphere of Harvard. Their hulls turned orange, then white.

"What are they doing, Colonel?" Commander Firebaugh asked me.

I stared at the scene before I answered. I was humbled by the magnificent purity of the enemy. They had the single-mindedness that only a machine could have. They didn't care if they lost a fleet, or a hundred fleets. They only cared about taking us out. I had the feeling they'd gotten tired of dealing with us, and changed their strategy to a new one: extermination. Biotics were to be destroyed wherever they could be found. The war had entered a new stage.

"They're killing a world, Commander," I said sadly. "The friction will burn off the attacking marines. But they won't stop falling. They know our fleet is bearing down on them and they can't stop us from destroying them. So they'll come down in a hundred separate locations and ignite their cores."

"Just to kill the lobsters?" the Commander asked incredulously. "They'll sacrifice their entire fleet?"

"Taking out an enemy species is worth more than any fleet. The machines are winning today."

I watched, as did we all. There was little else to do. Within a few minutes, I had my answer. I'd hoped I was wrong—but I wasn't. One by one, the big ships exposed their cores and detonated themselves.

The cruisers blew themselves up in a chain of explosions. Each blast was huge and devastated a new spot on the beautiful world below.

Soon, the purple sands were gone. I couldn't even see the great ocean a minute later. The entire planet was shrouded in vapor and airborne debris. Still, the explosions went on. Beneath the thick clouds, huge orange flashes continued to rock the world. From my lofty perch in space the impacts were silent, terrible, and unreal to behold.

-41-

The surviving fighters limped home to their respective motherships. The pilots inside were as drained physically and emotionally as were their ships' power systems and ammo magazines. Of the two, the ships were the easier to repair. The pilots were damaged goods. We'd sacrificed so much, and yet failed to defend the last Crustacean world. We'd all witnessed the death of a lovely planet, and we'd never be the same afterward.

I kept thinking of Sandra. That seemed selfish, in a way. What right did I have to lament the loss of a single woman after having presided over this failed attempt to save a trillion individuals? The human heart has no sense of scale and balance, however. I would have probably traded them all to have my woman back the way she'd been a week ago. But that was not an option.

I was haunted in particular by Sandra's scent. It had been a unique thing. What was the source of the memory that lingered in my mind? Her shampoo? Her perfume? Or even her sweat? Possibly, it was a mixture of all these things. I don't know, but I'll always remember the way she smelled when I drew her close in my arms, and I'll miss it forever.

Fortunately, there were a thousand things that desperately needed doing. It was, perhaps, the single blessing awarded by a war of desperation: a man didn't have enough time to dwell and grieve. I buried Sandra and all my thoughts of her deep in my mind. I carried on because there was no choice, other than to go completely mad.

"Sir?" Jasmine said, signaling me.

I looked up and forced my eyes to focus. I was standing on *Gatre's* bridge, eyeing the tactical display. The big ship had come through the battle without a scratch. The machines hadn't been gunning for our fleet this time. They'd wanted blood, and they'd gotten it.

"What is it?" I managed to say to her.

I could tell from the look of concern on her face, she must have been trying to tell me something. I searched my memory for some hint. My mind was a blank, I hadn't heard her words. Then my eyes strayed to my com-link, which was blinking urgently. I picked it up.

"Who is it?" I asked.

"The Crustaceans," Jasmine said.

Great, I thought. "You mean their High Command?"

She pursed her lips, then gave a slight shake of her head. "I don't think they have a High Command anymore, sir."

"Right. Well, whoever it is, I owe it to them to answer the phone. Patch them through the translation circuits."

"Done."

"Colonel Kyle Riggs here," I said into my com-link.

An oddly watery voice came to my ear a few moments later. To me, it sounded as if their own equipment had malfunctioned somewhat. It sounded as if their microphones weren't good at handling the transition of audio from their aquatic environment to mine. I couldn't fault them for that. Whatever tech they had left, I was sure it wasn't their best.

"Colonel," the voice said thoughtfully. "You have survived."

"Yes," I said.

The individual had not identified himself, but I didn't have the heart to demand that he do so. I wasn't quite sure what to say next.

There was a lull in the conversation. I thought of a million things to say. I could give him my heartfelt apologies. I could tell him to buck-up, tomorrow would be a better day. I could talk about humanity's losses against the machines, and commiserate.

But I didn't have the energy for any of these approaches. They all sounded like bullshit to me. So, we both fell silent for several seconds.

"You have gotten what you wanted," the voice said at last.

"No," I said. "I wanted to defeat the machines. I wanted to stop them from damaging your people and your worlds. I've failed to achieve my goals today. This was a great defeat for the side of the biotics, for our shared side."

"That's not what I meant," said the voice. "You've won our allegiance. Our unquestioning loyalty and effectively, our obedience. We are at your mercy. What is your will, my ruler?"

"What? I want to help you. Tell me what *you* need, and I will attempt to provide it."

"There is no need for further deceptions, Great One," the translator warbled. "The slave does not dictate to the master. We accept our role, and wish only that you will in turn allow the few remaining members of our species to survive this day. We will grovel, if we must. We will scrape our shells from our flesh, if that is your will."

I was alarmed and saddened. Not only did these people seem crushed, they were certain I had wanted it that way all along. They believed I had personally plotted their downfall.

After having dealt with the Crustaceans for years, I knew they were not like us. They did not understand actions taken out of benevolence. Such behavior did not cause them to reciprocate, it only made them suspect a trick. Perhaps this was because they were not mammals. Maybe they didn't have a layer to their brains that allowed for interspecies compassion.

My mind raced, unsure as to how to proceed. I fell back on my past experiences with alien species. Often, it was best to be adaptable, as they usually weren't. If my mind could flex, the two races could come to an understanding for the betterment of all.

When working with the Centaurs, who were hung-up on the concepts of honor and herd-values, I'd learned to talk to them in their own idiomatic way. This had allowed us to form a tight, valuable alliance.

This situation required more of the same adaptability on my part. Accordingly, I took a deep breath, and went for it.

"I've considered the matter," I said loudly. Around me, the staffers watched and listened intently without seeming to.

"I've decided to accept the capitulation of the Crustaceans to Star Force," I said matter-of-factly.

This elicited a series of gasps and twitters around the bridge. I ignored them all. I didn't care about them at the moment. I had to save the Crustaceans from extinction. If they wanted a strong leader who was so terrible that he must be obeyed, I'd give them one. At least they could understand that relationship.

"What are your terms, Colonel?"

"There are no terms," I said firmly, "other than total obedience and servitude."

"We accept your terms. We beg for our lives."

"They are granted. Now, you must answer a series of queries. No omission or deceit will be tolerated."

"None shall be offered. Ask us what you will, Master."

I stumbled upon hearing them call me "Master". My staffers seemed scandalized as well. The level of background whispering swelled dramatically on the bridge.

I glanced toward Jasmine, who was looking at me reproachfully with her arms crossed under her breasts. She appeared to be shocked by this turn of events.

I had to stay in character, so I turned away from her. It helped me to think clearly. "Are any of your worlds habitable?"

"No, Master."

"You will address me as 'Colonel', not 'Master', is that understood?"

"Absolutely. Our apologies are profuse, Colonel. We did not mean to offend."

"Can you use your transports to salvage your civilian survivors?"

"Very few of them can be reached. The radioactive tides are rolling around the worlds, killing everything they contact. The atmospheres are so turbulent they are leaking away into space."

I closed my eyes, then opened them again. The scale of this disaster was incalculable.

"You will gather every strong, fit individual that you can with your transports," I told them. "You will do this immediately, and keep in mind you must create a breeding population."

"Where are we going to go when we have saved all that we can?"

"You will come with us. We have a world in the Eden System that is warm and largely covered by one vast ocean. It will be your new home. We must abandon the Thor System for now. Once you reach Eden, you will be on the safe side of our battle station, and Star Force will protect you from further attacks by the machines as best we can."

"Your wish is our command," the voice said. "Your command is our prayer."

Jasmine touched my arm, and pointed to the screens. I could see their transports moving off in several directions, dropping down into the turbulent atmospheres of their dying worlds. They would gather as many as they could, and they would come to a new world with me. It was the least I could do for them.

"We'll talk more when you've gathered your people."

"May I say one thing, Colonel?" asked the voice.

"Yes."

"Let me offer my sincerest praise. You have played this game masterfully. We were fooled from the first by your feigned idiocy. Now, we see the true genius behind your actions. I have awarded your people eleven full points on the cognitive scale. No species has ever scored so highly."

I blinked, and almost smiled. But I couldn't quite do it. The whole situation was too horrible to be amusing.

A moment later I realized who this individual I was talking to must be. I'd spoken to him before and talked about humanity's cognitive score at that time.

"Is this Professor Hoon?" I asked.

"That is my designation, unless you want me to change it, Colonel."

"The title fits you, Hoon," I said. "Keep it."

"Thank you, Colonel. Thank you."

-42-

I was in my anteroom just after the dayshift ended when a visitor rapped at my door. Of all people, Captain Gaines had come to see me.

"Congratulations," I told him after inviting him in, "you survived the great failed campaign of Thor-6. Billions of others didn't, but you did."

"Yes, sir."

"May I ask why you're here?"

"I think you know, sir."

I frowned, but then nodded after thinking back. "I promised to make you a major, didn't I?" I said. "And now you're here to collect."

"That's right, sir."

I waggled a finger at him.

"All right," I said. "Zap! You're a major now. Next time you wade into combat on some rat hole, you'll command a battalion rather than a company. Are you happy now?"

He stared at me thoughtfully. "No, sir. I don't think 'happy' correctly describes my mood."

I snorted and shook my head. I figured he would leave once he had his promotion, but he didn't. He lingered, looking troubled.

I took in a deep breath. I wasn't really in the mood for having a heart-to-heart, but sometimes a commander needed to provide guidance to his officers. I realized this was going to be one of those times.

Accordingly, I reached down under my desk and opened a small hatch in the floor. A number of chilled squeeze-bottles of beer were stashed there. I scooped out two of them and pushed one across my desk to Gaines. The bottle left a streak of white ice crystals on my desk, and he caught it neatly.

"May I?" he asked, indicating an empty chair.

I nodded and opened my beer. He did the same. We quickly gulped down our beverages with greed. There was something about a perfectly chilled beer. It demanded to be consumed with gusto.

When he was done, he set down the bottle and nodded. "Thank you, sir."

Again, I waited for him to leave. He asked me a question instead. This man had asked me a hell of a lot of questions since I'd first met up with him on Yale. But this one surprised me.

"Colonel," he said, "why don't you just make yourself a general? I mean, come on, get real. You command big armies and fleets. You're at least a general."

"That's a good question," I said, pulling out fresh beers for both of us. I slid his to him, and saw that the trail of ice crystals the first beer had left hadn't even melted to droplets yet.

"You see," I said, "I just made you a Major. That process felt real, didn't it? It felt real, because I'm in authority over you. Everyone accepts that state of affairs. So, if I give you a rank, everyone accepts the rank. In my case, things are different. I don't have anyone above me at the moment to award me a higher position. I'd have to just declare it, without anyone having approved anything. That would make it feel wrong—as if I'd cheated somehow."

Gaines squinted at me while he worked on his beer. I did the same. He seemed to honestly understand the nature of my problem.

"How about we all get together and vote, or something?" he asked. "What if we all vote, and whatever we come up with, that will be your new rank."

"Not a bad idea, but I'd be a little concerned I'd end up as a dog-catcher if I did that."

We both laughed. It was possibly the first real laugh I'd had since the lobsters had gotten collectively boiled.

Gaines had made me realize I had a problem. A problem with my legitimacy. Upon what basis did my authority rest? I wasn't sure. I'd frozen my rank long ago because I didn't feel I had the right to give myself a higher rank. Someone else had to bless it, or it wasn't real.

Back when Crow had at least been nominally in charge, I'd felt that I'd earned the promotions he'd given me. I'd believed there was some validity to my rise in rank. Maybe I'd been fooling myself, but I'd felt it. The promotions had seemed right.

But now, Crow had gone and declared himself an emperor. What would separate me from him if I made myself a general, king or even a god? What right did I have to do that? What would separate me from Crow if I pulled a stunt like that?

And so I'd stuck with the rank of Colonel.

"These aliens…" I said when we'd reached beer number four—or was it five? "They came at night, they plucked us from our beds, and they made us what we are today. They made us organize to fight for them. But there's no nation behind us."

"I understand what you're saying, sir. You want to know what makes your power legitimate. I think I have an answer for you: The fact that people follow you."

"Maybe. Maybe that's the best answer of all."

"Damn straight it is," he said with feeling. "If you shout an order and people obey, who's to say that you didn't have the right to give the order in the first place?"

"I understand what you're saying," I told him, "but I'm seeking more legitimacy than that. Napoleon crowned himself emperor, you know. He took the crown from the pope who stepped up to his throne, and he placed it on his own head. He did that because he figured if the churchman crowned him, that meant the church had authority over him. I feel the opposite urge. I don't want to be the man who crowned himself ruler. I want a body, a group, a legitimate organization of some kind to decide who I am and what I deserve for my efforts."

He nodded in understanding. His fingers made a scratching motion on my desk, and I automatically fed them a fresh brew.

I looked at him suddenly at that point in our conversation.

"You didn't come here and hang around my office to ask for advice, did you Gaines?"

He shook his head. A wintery smile played on his lips.

"You thought I was the one that needed to talk?" I asked.

"That's right, Colonel."

"Well, let me ask you this, Major: Who has the right to rule, and why?"

"I don't know about that, sir," Gaines answered. "But I do know that someone has to be at the top. And right, now, that's you."

I couldn't argue with the man, so I handed him another beer from my stash. He smiled as he received it.

"I've got another story for you," I said. "Did you know that Genghis Khan had a rule concerning his officers and drunkenness?"

"What was it?"

"That no commander of his could be caught drunk more than once a month. If he was caught drinking hard more often than that, he would be reduced in rank."

Gaines appeared concerned. "Seems like a good rule," he said. "But is this your way of taking back my promotion?"

"Have you gotten drunk yet this month?"

"No, sir," he said, shaking his head with mock sadness. "Unfortunately, no."

"I've got an easy solution for that."

He grinned, and I rolled out more icy drinks.

Much later, I found myself slumped over my desk.

I dreamt of Sandra. She'd been carried off by a marching row of metal ants on a sunless world, and I couldn't find her in the darkness.

When morning arrived, Major Gaines and I were in a sorry state. Even the nanites had trouble cleaning up my office. Fortunately, my kind recover quickly from physical neglect. It is our minds and spirits that heal slowly.

The way I saw it, my enemies had given me a difficult choice: which one of them to destroy first. Both the Empire and the Macros had landed heavy blows that demanded retribution. Crow and his baloney empire had snuck into my territory under a flag of truce and killed my lady love. I thought of revenge against him constantly. The Macros had slaughtered three worlds full of biotics. They were impossibly dangerous and evil.

And in addition to these two sworn enemies, there was a third that was rising as a potential threat: the Blues.

We'd been observing strange phenomena from their gas giant, Eden-12, for months. The activity had increased, as had the level of energy releases. According to Marvin, they now regularly generated

331

more EM output than the entirety of Earth. What in the nine hells were they up to?

I'd begun to suspect in my heart that I'd misjudged them. I'd always thought of them as neutrals that could possibly become future allies. I'd believed them when they'd said they'd released the machines by accident.

But possibly, I'd been duped. Some I'd spoken with had expressed regrets, while others had been remorseless. They hadn't cared about the billions their creations had slaughtered. Perhaps they weren't all of one mind on this topic.

But again, maybe that was by design. How do you conquer the universe without loss? Well, you get someone else to do it for you, and you back them in secret, and you play dumb when questions are asked. That way, the dirty job gets done while you maintain your ivory tower innocence.

My mind was finally eased the day after Gaines and I had gotten piss-drunk together. Relief came from an unexpected source.

Miklos came into my office with a large file on a tiny portable data-chip. The chip was about the size of a nickel and glossy black.

He flipped the coin-sized chip onto my desk. Immediately, the desk sensed it, linked with it, and began dragging files out to display. He paged through them with his fingers expertly, searching for something.

I watched him with raised eyebrows. I'd been sipping a fresh beer, my second of the afternoon. I quietly dropped the bottle on the floor between my feet and the ship's deck swallowed it. I knew the squeeze-bottle of delicious liquid would be released into space, where it would freeze and drift away with the rest of the debris our ships dumped every day. I didn't like wasting beer like that, but I didn't like letting my officers know I'd been drinking before dinnertime lately.

"To what do I owe this visit, Commodore?" I asked him.

"I have it right here, sir. One moment...ah, here it is."

He flicked a particularly large diagram out onto the desktop. It dwarfed the rest, and I realized in an instant it was a ship design document. The ship was big—very big.

"Another carrier design?"

"Exactly, sir," he said.

332

"We already have a pretty functional model," I said. "Let me guess, you want permission to upgrade?"

"No, sir," he said. "I want to leave the two ships we have as they are. It would not be cost effective to upgrade them, other than possibly adding a few components. These new ships will form an entirely new class of carrier."

I examined the diagram, expanding it with my fingers to fill my desk. "This thing is huge," I chuckled. "Why should I build such a monstrosity?"

Miklos smiled at me knowingly, and leaned on my desk. "This ship will allow us to extend our reach," he said. "This is an attacker's weapon. It can perform many tasks, but most importantly it is effectively a floating battle station, like this one—only mobile."

"What are you calling it?"

"A super-carrier."

"How many do you think we should build?"

"One, sir. To start with…then another, and another. As many as it takes."

"As many as it takes to do what?"

"To carry the attack to the enemy."

I stared at him thoughtfully. "And who do you think that enemy should be?"

Miklos raised his hands with his palms up. "I don't know. That's not my job. I fight the battles, you start the wars. But these ships will take out anyone you aim them at."

I sat back in my office chair thoughtfully. He had me there. I did want to attack.

"You're right, Miklos," I said. "For years, we've sat out here in the Eden System, far from home. We've built up an independent colony, but no one recognizes our right to exist. We've been on the defensive, while waves of enemies attempt to destroy us. They haven't managed to strike a fatal blow, but they are certainly wearing us down. We've faced battle after battle on two fronts for too long. I'd hoped the Macros could be stopped by my battle station. I'd hoped the Empire would come to its senses and normalize relations with Eden. These hopes have not borne fruit."

I stood up as I spoke and walked to a window I'd installed in the far wall. It was a real, honest window made of lead-impregnated glass. The nanites had to work overtime to keep it from fogging up, but I enjoyed gazing through it with my own eyes and seeing the universe outside as it really was. Viewscreens could only approximate reality.

"I'd hoped they'd come to accept us," I continued, "but our enemies have down nothing other than plot and work to bring us down. They've hurt me badly—not just my plans, but me personally. The Macros have slaughtered trillions of sentient beings and made me carry the weight of those deaths on my spirit. Crow and his Imperial Earth sycophants took away the woman I loved."

Miklos stepped up and gazed out of my window beside me. He spoke quietly: "That's right, Colonel. And no matter what you choose to do now, attack the Macros, the Empire or just sit here and hold on, you'll need a massive fleet."

I nodded in agreement. "All right," I said. "Build your carriers, Miklos. Improve the fighters too, and build thousands of them. I'm hereby ordering that ninety percent of Nano and Macro factory production be turned over to Fleet construction. Go crazy, but do it right."

"Thank you, sir! You will not regret it." He ran out of my office before I could change my mind. I didn't even turn to watch him go.

"It is they who will regret it, Miklos," I said quietly to the stars outside.

The way I saw it, both the Macros and the Empire owed me. The only question in my mind was who was going to pay the bill first.

The End

More Books by B. V. Larson:

STAR FORCE SERIES
Swarm
Extinction
Rebellion
Conquest
Battle Station
Empire
Annihilation

IMPERIUM SERIES
Mech Zero: The Dominant
Mech 1: The Parent
Mech 2: The Savant
Mech 3: The Empress
Five By Five (Mech Novella)

OTHER SF BOOKS
Technomancer
The Bone Triangle
Z-World
Velocity

Visit BVLarson.com for more information.

Made in the USA
Middletown, DE
11 October 2020